The Best
AMERICAN
SHORT
STORIES
2011

GUEST EDITORS OF
THE BEST AMERICAN SHORT STORIES

1978 TED SOLTAROFF
1979 JOYCE CAROL OATES
1980 STANLEY ELKIN
1981 HORTENSE CALISHER
1982 JOHN GARDNER
1983 ANNE TYLER
1984 JOHN UPDIKE
1985 GAIL GODWIN
1986 RAYMOND CARVER
1987 ANN BEATTIE
1988 MARK HALPERN
1989 MARGARET ATWOOD
1990 RICHARD FORD
1991 ALICE ADAMS
1992 ROBERT STONE
1993 LOUISE ERDRICH
1994 TOBIAS WOLFF
1995 JANE SMILEY
1996 JOHN EDGAR WIDEMAN
1997 E. ANNIE PROULX
1998 GARRISON KEILLOR
1999 AMY TAN
2000 E. L. DOCTOROW
2001 BARBARA KINGSOLVER
2002 SUE MILLER
2003 WALTER MOSLEY
2004 LORRIE MOORE
2005 MICHAEL CHABON
2006 ANN PATCHETT
2007 STEPHEN KING
2008 SALMAN RUSHDIE
2009 ALICE SEBOLD
2010 RICHARD RUSSO
2011 GERALDINE BROOKS

The Best AMERICAN SHORT STORIES® 2011

Selected from
U.S. and Canadian Magazines
by GERALDINE BROOKS
with HEIDI PITLOR

With an Introduction by Geraldine Brooks

HOUGHTON MIFFLIN HARCOURT
BOSTON • NEW YORK 2011

ISSN 0067-6233
ISBN 978-0-547-24208-8
ISBN 978-0-547-24216-3 (pbk.)

Printed in the United States of America

DOC 10 9 8 7 6 5 4 3 2 1

Contents

Foreword

A FEW YEARS AGO, as documented in a book titled *The Average American: The Extraordinary Search for the Nation's Most Ordinary Citizen,* Kevin O'Keefe, the author, set out to find the most "perfectly average" person in the nation. This person turned out to be Bob Burns. He was fifty-four years old. He was married, wore glasses. He worked forty hours a week as a maintenance supervisor at Windham Technical High School in Connecticut. This five-foot-eight, 190-pound man drank coffee each morning, read the newspaper each day, walked his dog each evening, and attended church most Sundays.

If I were to attempt to describe a perfectly average American short story, it might sound like this: disaffected child protagonist (I'll call him Wally), in the face of parents' recent divorce, finds solace as well as self-awareness in nonconformist flute teacher (I'll call her Ms. Note). The voice in the story would be quirky but not overly oddball, and the story might be told in the present tense, using a first-person point of view. The setting would be Wally's house and Ms. Note's living room—and maybe this living room would double as a dining room and bedroom, and maybe Ms. Note would have recently lost her job as a chef, and maybe Wally's father had several food allergies, which had always secretly irked Wally's mother. The ending would suggest resolution but hint at its opposite. I don't mean this description to sound belittling or quite as reductive as it might. I just mean to demonstrate some of the most common elements that I come across in the many short stories I read each year.

In my five years on this job, I have been lucky to work alongside guest editors with extraordinarily diverse backgrounds and tastes. Still, nearly all of them have been surprised at the enormous number of stories that share at least some facets of Wally's. Most taken aback, I would guess, have been the guest editors whose first home was not the United States. When I began working with the wonderful Geraldine Brooks, she promptly took note of the large number of naturalist stories set in the present time. I felt a bit like I had led her into a sprawling subdivision full of identical houses. "Welcome to American short fiction," I might have said with a slight grimace. "Please don't judge us." Although her task was of course *solely* to judge us.

I admit that I feel protective of all this domestic, realist fiction. The majority of my own life is spent tending to small children and folding laundry and emptying the dishwasher, that blessed dishwasher that seems to fill thrice daily as if only to spite me. I have grown accustomed to wandering down the streets of the abovementioned subdivision and knocking on the door of a putty-colored house and finding young Wally sprawled across his microfiber sectional texting a friend rather than practicing flute. And nothing is more welcome to me than a whopper sentence—maybe funny or deadpan, maybe horrifically dark—embedded in the first paragraph of such a story. *You know where you are—but hold on,* the good story promises. *I'll yank that plush Pottery Barn rug right out from under your feet.*

Young short story writers often start with familiar subject matter and manageable scope. I don't believe this is problematic. Familiar setting or characters or premise certainly does not necessitate familiar writing. Little makes me more uncomfortable than watching a new writer attempt a triple-triple lutz without sufficient control of language or grasp of form. That reading experience sometimes starts like this: second person (okay, that's fine, sort of) on a prewedding trip to Barcelona; florid or jerky language and vast generalizations about gender (now "I" secretly prefer the leggy barista in a café with luminous cleavage to my willowy and controlling grad student fiancée); excessive description of the rain in Spain that overtly reflects "my" inner state (ugh); sudden switch to first or third person (uh-oh); cut to barista naked on top of "me" (and I'm out).

To my mind, at least in terms of content, you've got an advantage if you choose less familiar settings or characters or premises. In some ways, it might be easier to write of a homophobic soldier in Afghanistan the day after Don't Ask, Don't Tell was repealed than to write Wally's story. The news is in the content itself. Welcome your reader to a prefab with central air, granite countertops, and walk-in closets and watch this reader slowly back away from the page. Your work is cut out for you. Of course, challenges do arise by setting a story in a war zone. Be careful with your form and language, which should ideally be indivisible from the subject matter. As always, try to avoid stereotypes or characters who exist only to dramatize your sociopolitical agenda. The homophobic soldier? Maybe she is a cabinetmaker from Vermont. Her effeminate battalion leader—he might have been raised in rural Texas by a gun salesman. Okay, I'm laying it on thick here, but I hope you see what I'm getting at. Dramatic content, diverse setting, and innovative form do not automatically entail good writing.

To be absolutely clear: I do not mean to say that I'm hungry to read thousands more stories about Wally or his warring parents or their neighborhood—or that I prefer this content, really, to any other. In fact I would love to read more stories about war (so terribly widespread these days) and the wide world outside the United States and our impact on the environment. I deeply respect writers who explore new territory and/or take risks with structure or form (see Jennifer Egan, Caitlin Horrocks, Steven Millhauser in the following pages, for starters). But to me, the quality of writing always takes precedence over the author's choice of content or form. I look for immediacy, freshness of language, and, perhaps more than anything, ease of language (see Bret Anthony Johnston, Rebecca Makkai, Ricardo Nuila—really all of the writers whose stories appear between these covers). Jonathan Franzen offers this wise bit of advice to writers: "The reader is a friend, not an adversary, not a spectator." I seek a certain intimacy when I read, a sense that the writer is someone knowable to me, someone I can trust—not a professor, not an acrobat. Certainly not a figure skater twirling like a tornado at the center of a cold, dark rink.

Ms. Brooks was a superb guest editor, eager to include different genres and confident in her excellent taste. As she writes in her introduction, plot has clearly become distasteful to many American short story writers. Interestingly, this series was in part developed to showcase stories that shunned a ubiquitous sort of plot that had "poisoned" much of the writing at the time, nearly one hundred years ago. But I fear that a new normal has evolved in its place, one conspicuously void of momentum and uninterested in maintaining the reader's attention. Happily, each story in this year's edition creates and sustains its own momentum, whether through premise or language, character or even perfectly placed silence. Each writer demonstrates an astonishing understanding of their characters and the worlds in which they live, wherever these worlds may be.

The stories chosen for this anthology were originally published between January 2010 and January 2011. The qualifications for selection are (1) original publication in nationally distributed American or Canadian periodicals; (2) publication in English by writers who are American or Canadian, or who have made the United States their home; (3) original publication as short stories (excerpts of novels are not knowingly considered). A list of magazines consulted for this volume appears at the back of the book. Editors who wish their short fiction to be considered for next year's edition should send their publication or hard copies of online publications to Heidi Pitlor, Houghton Mifflin Harcourt, 222 Berkeley St., Boston, Massachusetts 02116.

HEIDI PITLOR

Introduction

I WAS NINE YEARS OLD when a piece of fiction captured me utterly. It was a novel by the English children's writer Enid Blyton, and featured Nazi art looters, plucky kids, and a secret mountain hideout behind a waterfall. I couldn't put it down, and when someone advertised the other seven titles in the series for sale, I convinced my parents to buy the lot. They were used hardbacks with lavishly illustrated dust jackets, plastic-covered, meticulously kept. I lined them up in order, and I started to feel . . . odd. I was breathing fast. My neck was flushed. There was a taste, buttery and warm, in the back of my throat. It wasn't unpleasant, but it was unfamiliar and I didn't have a word for it. It would be six years before I felt that way again, in a very different context. And by then I knew the word.

Since that first encounter with lust, I have always thought of literature as a physical matter. A great piece of writing is the one you feel on your skin. It has to do something: Make the heart beat harder or the hairs stand up. Provoke laughter or tears. (The latter not hard, in my case. I once handed my sister a short story involving a tulip and a paper clip and said, "Read this—it made me cry." "So what?" she replied. "You cry over the weather report.")

There is some very good writing, of course, that does not stir the blood. It's cool, cerebral. Tricksy, clever. I admire it, in the same way I admire the technical proficiency of a Cirque de Soleil acrobat: "Look what she's doing up there. I didn't realize a rotator cuff had that range of motion." But I'm not moved by it. And by the end of the show, so many amazing things have been done that amazement becomes a kind of boredom.

Last fall, when the first fat pile of tidily copied stories arrived at my place, I felt like my nine-year-old self in distant suburban Sydney. I shook the stories from the envelope and laid them out on my dining table. They were crisp, dazzling, each with its own paper clip holding together pages of possibility. There were names I knew, and some I'd never heard of. It was like walking into the best kind of party, where you can hole up in a corner with old friends for a while, then launch out among interesting strangers. There would be two more piles, one arriving in the depth of winter and the last as the groundhog emerged blinking from his snowy burrow. One hundred and twenty preselected stories from a field of over four thousand. As the days shortened and the foghorn moaned, I sat beside the fire and read, and read.

It is spring now. The chickadees are back, and on the sunny side of the house the first hyacinth has poked a tight-furled green fist out of the soil. The stories sit on my desk, no longer clean and white but well thumbed and disheveled. Some are smudged with the charcoal residue of my fire-stoking fingers, others puckered from an accidental slide into the bathtub. Rumpled, lofted by handling, they take up more space now, in their nonvirgin state. This seems fitting to me: a page that has been read, pored over, should stake claim to more territory.

Another difference: on the front page of each is scrawled a single word:

Yes (or, in a few cases, Yes!!)

Maybe

And then a very large pile with the very small word, No.

It was not as hard as I thought it might be, to do this initial triage. Like the battlefield nurse dropping color-coded tags atop casualties, I moved with a kind of professional detachment from story to story. Triage is provisional, after all. It is a guess. It does not determine outcome. It was only when I went back, under deadline pressure, that the task became suddenly onerous, morally taxing. Now I was not the triage nurse but the euthanizer. No meant no. A story, often a very good story, would not be deemed among the best, because I said so. There are some I can barely look at as I go through the pile. They rebuke me, like a neglected friend, a jilted ex. "I still love you, but it just didn't work out . . ."

And who was I, anyway, to be making this call? I, who had never written a short story. (Okay, one. In the tenth grade. A dark sci-fi romance, destined for our school literary magazine, which we published on a hand-cranked Gestetner that reeked of wax and solvent.) In my adult writing life, I had leapt recklessly from journalism and narrative nonfiction to writing novels. I looked sideways at short stories, like a nervy horse at an unknown rider. I wasn't quite sure how they worked.

Not long after I started reading that first batch of stories, I found myself at a literary event in Dayton. After the dinner and the speeches, a few of the writers adjourned to a bar. During the first round of drinks, someone started telling jokes. We took it in turns then, dredging up ethnic jokes, light-bulb riddles, and shaggy dog stories from forgotten vaults of memory. Most of us ran out of material fairly quickly, but one had the recall of a Homeric bard, and kept us laughing at joke after joke until the bartender called time and kicked us out into the night. That jokester was Richard Bausch, master of the short story.

This was no coincidence. The best short stories and the most successful jokes have a lot in common. Each form relies on suggestion and economy. Characters have to be drawn in a few deft strokes. There's generally a setup, a reveal, a reversal, and a release. The structure is delicate. If one element fails, the edifice crumbles. In a novel you might get away with a loose line or two, a saggy paragraph, even a limp chapter. But in the joke and in the short story, the beginning and end are precisely anchored tent poles, and what lies between must pull so taut it twangs.

I'm not sure if there is any pattern to these selections. I did not spend a lot of time with those that seemed afraid to tell stories, that handled plot as if it were a hair in the soup, unwelcome and embarrassing. I also tended not to revisit stories that seemed bleak without having earned it, where the emotional notes were false, or where the writing was tricked out or primped up with fashionable devices stressing form over content.

I do know that the easiest and the first choices were the stories to which I had a physical response. I read Jennifer Egan's "Out of Body" clenched from head to toe by tension as her suicidal, drug-addled protagonist moves through the Manhattan night toward an unforgivable betrayal. I shed tears over two stories of childhood shadowed by unbearable memory: "The Hare's Mask," by Mark Slouka, with its piercing ending, and Claire Keegan's Irish-inflected tale of neglect and rescue, "Foster." Elizabeth McCracken's "Property" also moved me, with its sudden perception shift along the wavering sightlines of loss and grief. Nathan Englander's "Free Fruit for Young Widows" opened with a gasp-inducing act of unexpected violence and evolved into an ethical Rubik's cube.

A couple of stories made me laugh: Tom Bissell's "A Bridge Under Water," even as it foreshadows the dissolution of a marriage and probes what religion does for us, and to us; and Richard Powers's "To the Measures Fall," a deftly comic meditation on the uses of literature in the course of a life, and a lifetime.

Some stories didn't call forth such a strong immediate response but had instead a lingering resonance. Of these, many dealt with love and its costs, leaving behind indelible images. In Megan Mayhew Bergman's "Housewifely Arts," a bereaved daughter drives miles to visit her dead mother's parrot because she yearns to hear the bird mimic her mother's voice. In Allegra Goodman's "La Vita Nuova," a jilted fiancée lets her art class paint all over her wedding dress. In Ehud Havazelet's spare and tender story, "Gurov in Manhattan," an ailing man and his aging dog must confront life's necessary losses. A complicated, only partly welcome romance blossoms between a Korean woman and her demented mother's Jamaican night nurse in "The Call of Blood," by Jess Row. And in "Ceiling," Chimamanda Ngozi Adichie perfectly captures the yearning spirit of a man who has settled for the wrong wife, the wrong life, in the stultifying salons of Lagos's corrupt upper class.

Two stories in opposite settings got at large truths about friendships under stress. In "Soldier of Fortune," by Bret Anthony Johnston, the accidental scalding of a toddler severs and remakes bonds in a Texas military town. In "Peter Torrelli, Falling Apart," by Rebecca Makkai, a gay man tries to help his once dazzling best friend as he staggers through a public breakdown amid Chicago's artistic elite. Three beautifully crafted stories examined, with great originality, the parent-child bond. "ID," by Joyce Carol Oates, is a plangent tragedy with an unforgettable protagonist. The troubled savant of Ricardo Nuila's "Dog Bites" struggles to see his father through the overbright glare of his quirky vision. And in "The Dungeon Master," by Sam Lipsyte, a role-playing game bleeds into real life and seeps into the story's quirky prose.

In the end, the stories I fell upon with perhaps the greatest delight were the outliers, the handful or so that defied the overwhelming gravitational pull toward small-canvas contemporary realism. "Phantoms," by Steven Millhauser, takes the form of a dispassionate evaluation by one citizen of a town long visited by ghostlike apparitions. The assessor's cool tone plays beautifully against the eerie events he is describing. "The Sleep," by Caitlin Horrocks, is a suave, unexpectedly exhilarating satire about a beaten, blizzard-scoured prairie town that takes up hibernation as a way to manage the pain of ordinary living. And "Escape from Spiderhead," by George Saunders, was that rare example of full-bore speculative fiction to make it through the literary magazines' anti-sci-fi force field. Coming across this story elicited the same joyful surprise I once felt when offered a glass of wine after a dry week in Riyadh. In "Spiderhead," convict volunteers are the human test subjects for an array of psychoactive drugs that manipulate the deepest workings of the soul. The setting is fantastical and futuristic, but the heart is achingly familiar, and real human dilemmas are enacted against the highly imaginative backdrop. I would like to raise a small, vigorously waving hand in favor of releasing more such stories out of the genre ghetto and into the literary mainstream.

While I'm up here on the soapbox, I might as well set down a few more carps of the day:

1. Enuf adultery eds. Too many stories about the wrong cock in the wrong cunt/anus/armpit/Airedale.
2. Eros ≠ thanatos necessarily. Not all love stories have to have bleak outcomes.
3. Foreign countries exist.
4. There's a war on. The war in Afghanistan, in the year it became America's longest, appeared as a brief aside in only two of one hundred and twenty stories.
5. Consider the following: Caravaggio's *Conversion of Saint Paul*, Handel's *Messiah*, Martin Luther King. Female genital mutilation, military-funeral picketers, abortion-doctor assassins. So why, if religion turns up in a story, is it generally only there as a foil for humor?
6. Not that I want to discourage humor. There's so little. Why, writers, so haggard and so woebegone . . .
     La belle dame sans levity hath thee in thrall,
     And no mirth rings.

I should stipulate that the above carps refer to a hive mind that became apparent only because I read a mass of stories in a compressed time frame. There's nothing wrong with writing stories set in bedrooms, classrooms, kitchens. These are the places where we spend large slabs of our lives. But the air becomes stale there. And after a dozen — a hundred — such stories, I became claustrophobic.

When I was in journalism school I had a professor, Melvin Mencher, for whom the description "crusty" did scant justice. The man was a day-old baguette. When I tried to hide thin reporting under stylistic flourish, he would put a red line through my fine prose and scrawl: *You can't write writing.*

Later, reporting for the *Wall Street Journal,* I had an editor named Paul Ingrassia, whose pet hate was to catch someone in his newsroom looking up something online. He would creep up to the terminal and bark: "The story's not on Nexus. It's on the street. *Get out there!*"

So, for whatever it is worth, I'm passing on this advice to the next generation of short story writers, those *jeunesse dorée* who will come to the form at what might be the most perfect time in its history — a golden age to rival and perhaps surpass the era of the popular weeklies. The form is perfectly suited not only to the emerging platforms of our times but also to the users of those platforms, a new generation of young readers who love and demand good stories, their imaginations nourished by a decade-long boom in children's fiction. The right short stories, with their highly skilled writing, tough-minded, somber adult themes, but undaunting length, can be the perfect form for young readers still developing and experimenting with their fictional tastes. But here's the caveat: these kids have been raised on actual stories with plot, where x leads inexorably to y, with x being interesting and y being more interesting; on wizards and dragon riders, on Eoin Colfer's inspired *Die Hard*-with-fairies mashup and Philip Pullman's Milton meets string theory. I might be wrong, but I don't think affectless Carveresque minimalism, no matter how liminal or luminous, is going to cut it for them.

So, at the risk of calling down the wrath of the MFAfia, my advice to young writers is, read this book. Enjoy the stories, admire the craft. Then put it in your backpack and go. As far as you can, for as long as you can afford it. Preferably someplace where you have to think in one language and buy groceries in another. Get a job there. Rent a room. Stick around. Do something. If it doesn't work out, do something else. Whatever it is, you will be able to use it in the stories you will write later. And if that story turns out to be about grungy sex in an East Coast dorm room with an emotionally withholding semiotics major, that's okay. It will be a better story for the fact that you have been somewhere and carried part of it home with you in your soul.

GERALDINE BROOKS

CHIMAMANDA NGOZI ADICHIE

Ceiling

FROM *Granta*

WHEN OBINZE FIRST saw her e-mail, he was sitting in the back of his Land Rover in still Lagos traffic, his jacket slung over the front seat, a rusty-haired child beggar glued to his window, a hawker pressing colorful CDs against the other window, the radio turned on low to the pidgin English news on Wazobia FM, and the gray gloom of imminent rain all around. He stared at his BlackBerry, his body suddenly rigid. First he skimmed the e-mail, dampened that it was not longer. *Ceiling, kedu? I saw Amaka yesterday in New York and she said you were doing well with work, wife—and a child! Proud Papa. Congratulations. I'm still teaching and doing some research, but seriously thinking of moving back to Nigeria soon. Let's keep in touch? Ifemelu.*

He read it again slowly and felt the urge to smooth something, his trousers, his shaved-bald head. She had called him Ceiling. In the last e-mail from her, sent just before he got married four years ago, she had called him Obinze, wished him happiness in breezy sentences, and mentioned the black American she was living with. A gracious e-mail. He had hated it. He had hated it so much that he googled the black American, a lecturer at Yale, and found it infuriating that she lived with a man who referred on his blog to friends as "cats," but it was the photo of the black American, oozing intellectual cool in distressed jeans and black-framed eyeglasses, that had tipped Obinze over, made him send her a cold reply. *Thank you for the good wishes, I have never been happier in my life,* he'd written. It was complete bullshit, stupid posturing, and she had to recognize this; nobody knew him as well as she did. He hoped she would write something mocking back—so unlike her, not to have been even vaguely tart—but she did not write at all, and when he e-mailed her again, after his honeymoon in Morocco, to say he wanted to keep in touch and wanted to talk sometime, she did not reply.

The traffic was moving. A light rain was falling. The child beggar ran along, his doe-eyed expression more theatrical, his motions frantic: bringing his hand to his mouth, over and over, fingertips pursed together. Obinze rolled down the window and held out a hundred-naira note. His driver, Gabriel, watched with grave disapproval from the rearview mirror.

"God bless you, *oga!*" the child beggar said.

"Don't be giving money to these beggars, sir," Gabriel said. "They are all rich. They are using begging to make big money in this Lagos. I heard about one that built a block of six flats in Ikeja!"

"So why are you working as a driver instead of a beggar, Gabriel?" Obinze asked and laughed, a little too heartily. He wanted to tell Gabriel that his girlfriend from university had just e-mailed him, actually his girlfriend from university *and* secondary school. The first time she let him take off her bra, she lay on her back moaning softly, her hands on his head, and afterward she said, "My eyes were open but I did not see the ceiling. This never happened before." She was seventeen and he was eighteen and other girls would have pretended that they had never let another boy touch them, but not her, never her. There was a vivid honesty about her, which he had found so disconcerting and then so irresistible. *Longing for ceiling, can't wait for my period to end,* she once wrote on the back of his notebook during a lecture. Then, later, she began to call him Ceiling, in a playful way, in a suggestive way—but when they fought or when she retreated into moodiness, she called him Obinze. "Why do you call him Ceiling anyway?" his friend Chidi once asked her, on one of those languorous days after first-semester exams. She had joined a group of his classmates sitting around a filthy plastic table in a beer parlor outside campus. She drank from her bottle of Maltina, swallowed, glanced at him, and said, "Because he is so tall his head touches the ceiling, can't you see?" Her deliberate slowness, the small smile that stretched her lips, made it clear that she wanted them to know that this was not why she called him Ceiling. And he was not tall. She kicked him under the table and he kicked her back, watching his laughing friends; they were all a little afraid of her and a little in love with her. Did she see the ceiling when the black American touched her? Had she used ceiling with other men? It upset him now to think that she might have. His phone rang and for a hopeful, confused moment he thought it was Ifemelu calling from America.

"Darling, *kedu ebe I no?*" His wife, Kosi, always began her calls to him with those words: where are you? He never asked where she was when he called her, but she would tell him anyway: I'm just getting to the salon. I'm on Third Mainland Bridge. It was as if she needed the reassurance of their concrete physicality when they were not together. She had a high, girlish voice. They were supposed to be at Chief's house for the party at 7:30 P.M. and it was already past 6:00.

He told her he was in traffic. "But it's moving, and we've just turned into Ozumba Mbadiwe. I'm coming."

On Lekki Expressway the traffic moved swiftly in the waning rain, and soon Gabriel was sounding the horn in front of the high black gates of his home. Mohammed, the gateman, wiry in his dirty white kaftan, flung open the gates and raised a hand in greeting. Obinze looked at the yellow colonnaded house. Inside was his furniture, imported from Italy, his wife, his two-year-old daughter, Buchi, the nanny, Christiana, his wife's sister, Chioma, who was on a forced holiday because university lecturers were on strike yet again, and the new housegirl, Marie, who had been brought from Benin Republic after his wife decided that Nigerian housegirls were unsuitable. There would be the smell of cooking, the television downstairs would be showing a film on the Africa Magic channel, and pervading it all, the still air of well-being. He climbed out of the car. His gait was stiff, his legs difficult to lift. He had begun, in the past months, to feel bloated from all he had acquired—the family, the house, the other properties in Ikoyi and Abuja, the cars, the bank accounts in Dubai and London—and he would be overcome by the urge to prick everything with a pin, to deflate it all, to be free. He was no longer sure, he had in fact never been sure, whether he liked his life because he really did or whether he liked it because he was supposed to.

"Darling," Kosi said, opening the door before he got to it. Her dress was cinched at the waist and made her figure look very hourglassy.

"Daddy-daddy!" Buchi said.

He swung her up and then hugged his wife, carefully avoiding her lips, painted pink and lined in a darker pink. "You look beautiful, babe," he said. *"Asa! Ugo!"*

She laughed. The same way she laughed, with an open, accepting enjoyment, when people asked her, "Is your mother white? Are you a half-caste?" because she was so fair-skinned. It had always discomfited him, the pleasure she took in being mistaken for mixed-race.

"Will you bathe or just change? I brought out your new blue kaftan. I knew you'd want to wear traditional," she said, following him upstairs. "Do you want to eat before we go? You know Chief will have nice food."

"I'll just change and we can go," he said.

He was tired. It was not a physical fatigue — he used his treadmill regularly and felt better than he had in years — but a draining lassitude that numbed the margins of his mind. He went out every day, he made money, he came home, he played with his daughter, he watched television, he ate, he read books, he slept with his wife. He did things because he did them.

Chief's party would bore him, as usual, but he went because he went to all of Chief's parties and perhaps because Kosi liked going. She enjoyed being surrounded by glittery people, hugging women she barely knew, calling the older ones Ma with exaggerated respect, soaking up their compliments, dispensing hers, basking in being so beautiful but flattening her personality so that her beauty was nonthreatening. He had always been struck by this, how important it was to her to be a wholesomely agreeable person, to have no sharp angles sticking out. On Sundays, she would invite his relatives for pounded yam and *onugbu* soup and then watch over to make sure everyone was suitably overfed. *Uncle, you must eat oh! There is more meat in the kitchen! Let me bring you another Guinness!* When they visited his mother's house in Enugu, she always flew up to help with serving the food, and when his mother made to clean up afterward, she would get up, offended, and say, "Mummy, how can I be here and you will be cleaning?" She ended every sentence she spoke to his uncles with "sir." She put ribbons in the hair of his cousins' daughters. There was something immodest about her modesty: it announced itself.

At the party, he watched her, gold shimmer on her eyelids, as she greeted Mrs. Akin-Cole, curtsying and smiling, and he thought about the day their baby, slippery, curly-haired Buchi, was born at the Portland Hospital in London, how she had turned to him while he was still fiddling with his latex gloves and said, with something like apology, "We'll have a boy next time." He had recoiled. What he felt for her then was a gentle contempt, for not knowing that he was indifferent about the gender of their child, for assuming that he would want a boy since most men wanted a boy. Perhaps he should have talked more with her, about the baby they were expecting and about everything else, because although they exchanged pleasant sounds and were good friends and shared comfortable silences, they did not really talk. Her worldview was a set of conventional options that she mulled over while he did not even consider any of those options; the questions he asked of life were entirely different from hers. Of course he knew this from the beginning, had sensed it in their first conversation after his friend Chidi introduced them at a wedding. She was wearing a lime-green bridesmaid's dress in satin, cut low to show a cleavage he could not stop looking at, and somebody was making a speech, describing the bride as "a woman of virtue," and Kosi nodded eagerly and whispered to him, "She is a true woman of virtue." Even then he had felt gentle contempt that she could use the word *virtue* without the slightest irony, as was done in the badly written articles in the women's section of the weekend newspapers. Still, he had wanted her, chased her with a lavish single-mindedness. He had never seen a woman with such a perfect incline to her cheekbones, that made her entire face seem so alive in an architectural way, lifting when she smiled, and he was newly disoriented from his quick wealth: one week he was squatting in his cousin's flat and sleeping on a thin mattress on the floor and the next he owned a house and two cars. He felt as if his life were no longer his. It was Kosi who made it start to seem believable. She moved into his new house from her hostel at the University of Lagos and arranged her perfume bottles on his dresser, citrusy scents that he came to associate with home, and she sat in the BMW beside him as though it had always been his car, and when they showered together, she scrubbed him with a rough sponge, even between his toes, until he felt reborn. Until he owned his new life. A year passed before she told him her relatives were asking what his intentions were. "They just keep asking," she said and stressed the *they* to exclude herself from the marriage clamor. He recognized, and disliked, her manipulation. (The same way he felt when, after months of trying to get pregnant, she began to say with sulky righteousness, "All my friends who lived very rough lives are pregnant.") Still, he married her. Perhaps he was already on autopilot then. He felt an obligation to do so, he was not unhappy, and he imagined that she would, with time, gain a certain heft. She had not, after almost five years, except physically, in a way that he thought made her look even more beautiful, fresher, with fuller hips and breasts, like a well-watered houseplant.

Watching her now as she talked to Mrs. Akin-Cole, he felt guilty about his thoughts. She was such a devoted woman, such a well-meaning, devoted woman. He reached out and held her hand. She often told him that her friends envied her, and said he behaved like a foreign husband, the way he took her to all his social events, made her breakfast on Sundays, stayed home every night.

Mrs. Akin-Cole was talking about sending Buchi to the French school. "They are very good, very rigorous. Of course, they teach in French, but it can only be good for the child to learn another civilized language, since she already learns English at home."

"Okay, Auntie. I'll go there and talk to them," Kosi said. "I know I have to start early."

"The French school is not bad, but I prefer Meadowland. They teach the complete British curriculum," the other woman, whose name Obinze had forgotten but who had made a lot of money during General Abacha's military government, said. The story was that she had been a pimp of some sort, providing women for army officers and getting inflated supply contracts in exchange.

"Oh, yes. Meadowland. I'll look at that one too," Kosi said.

"Why?" Obinze asked. "Didn't we all go to primary schools that taught the Nigerian curriculum?"

The women looked at him.

Finally Mrs. Akin-Cole said, "But things have changed, my dear Obinze," and shook her head pitifully, as though he were an adolescent.

"I agree," Kosi said, and Obinze wanted to ask what the fuck it was she agreed with anyway.

"If you decide to disadvantage your child by sending her to one of these schools with half-baked Nigerian teachers . . ." Mrs. Akin-Cole shrugged. She spoke with that unplaceable foreign accent, British and American and something else all at once, of the wealthy Nigerian who did not want the world to forget how worldly she was, how her British Airways executive card was choking with miles.

"One of my friends sent her child to St. Mary's, and do you know, they have only five computers in the whole school. Only five!" the other woman said.

"We'll go to the British school and French school," Kosi said and looked at him with a plea. He shrugged. He would ordinarily not have said anything at all to Mrs. Akin-Cole, but today he wanted to pluck the sneer from her face and crumple it and hurl it back. But Chief was upon them.

"Princess!" Chief said to Kosi and hugged her, pressing her close; Obinze wondered if Chief had propositioned her in the past. It would not surprise him. He had once been at Chief's house when a man brought his girlfriend to visit, and when she left the room to go to the toilet, Obinze heard Chief tell the man, "I like that girl. Give her to me and I will give you a nice plot in Victoria Island."

"You look so well, Chief," Kosi said. "Ever young!"

"Ah, my dear, I try, I try." Chief jokingly tugged at the satin lapels of his black jacket. He did look well, spare and upright unlike many of his peers in their sixties. "My boy!" he said to Obinze.

"Good evening, Chief." Obinze shook him with both hands, bowing slightly. He watched the other men at the party bow too, crowding around Chief, jostling to outlaugh one another when Chief made a joke. They were all men who wore conspicuous watches, who had loud conversations about the things they owned, the sort of men that *City People* referred to as "Lagos Big Boys." They reminded Obinze of the three men he saw in Chief's house the first day his cousin took him there. They had been in the living room sipping cognac while Chief pontificated about politics. "Exactly! Correct! Thank you! You have just nailed the exact problem, Chief!" they crowed from time to time. Obinze had watched, fascinated. He was only a month in Lagos after being deported from England, but his cousin Amaka had started to grumble about how he could not just stay in her flat reading and moping, how he was not the first person to be deported, after all, and how he needed to hustle. Lagos was about hustling. His mates were hustling. She was

Chief's girlfriend—*he has many but I am one of the serious ones; he doesn't buy cars for everyone,* she said—and so she brought him to Chief's house to introduce them and see if Chief would help him. Chief was a difficult man, she told him, and it was important to catch him in a good mood when he was at his most expansive. They had, apparently, because after the three men left, Chief turned to Obinze and asked, "Do you know that song 'No One Knows Tomorrow'?" Then he proceeded to sing the song with childish gusto. *No one knows tomorrow! To-mo-rrow! No one knows tomorrow!* Another generous splash of cognac in his glass. "That is the principle on which the ambitious segment of the Nigerian society is based. No one knows tomorrow. Look at those big bankers with all their money and the next thing they knew, they were in prison. Look at that pauper who could not pay his rent yesterday and now because Babangida gave him an oil well, he has a private jet!" Chief always spoke with a triumphant tone, mundane observations delivered as grand discoveries. After Obinze had visited a few more times, drawn in part because Chief's steward always served fresh pepper soup, and because Amaka told him to just keep hanging around until Chief did something for him, Chief told him, "You are hungry and honest, that is very rare in this country. Is that not so?"

"Yes," Obinze said, even though he was not sure whether he was agreeing about his own quality or the rarity of it.

"Everybody is hungry, even the rich men are hungry, but nobody is honest. Twenty years ago I had nothing until somebody introduced me to General Babangida's brother. He saw that I was hungry and honest and he gave me some contacts. Look at me today. I have money. Even my great-grandchildren will not finish eating my money. But power? Yes, that one I work hard to have. I was Babangida's friend. I was Abacha's friend. Now that the military has gone, Obasanjo is my friend. The man has created opportunities in this country. Big opportunities for people like me. I know they are going to privatize the National Farm Support Corporation because they said it is bankrupt. Do you know this? No. By the time you know it, I would have taken a position and I would have benefited from the arbitrage. That is our free market!" Chief laughed. "The corporation was set up in the 1960s and it owns property everywhere. The houses are all rotten and termites are eating the roofs. But they are selling them. I'm going to buy seven properties

for five million each. You know what they are listed for in the
books? One million. You know what the real worth is? Fifty million." Chief stopped again to laugh and swallow some cognac. "So I
will put you in charge of that deal. They need somebody to do the
evaluation consulting, and I will put you there. Amaka said you are
sharp and I can see it in your face. Your first job will be to help me
make money, but your second job will be to make your own money.
You will make sure you undervalue the properties and make sure it
looks as if we are all following due process. It's not difficult. You
acquire the property, sell off half to pay your purchase price, and
you are in business! You'll build a house in Lekki and buy some
cars and ask your hometown to give you some titles and your
friends to put congratulatory messages in the newspapers for you
and before you know, any bank you walk into, they will want to
package a loan immediately and give you, because they think you
no longer need the money. Ah, Nigeria! No one knows tomorrow!"
Chief paused to stare at one of his ringing cell phones—four were
placed on the table next to him—and then ignored it and leaned
back on his leather sofa. "And after you register your own company, you must find a white man. You had friends in England before you were deported? Find one white man. Tell everybody he is
your general manager. It gives you immediate legitimacy with many
idiots in this country. This is how Nigeria works, I'm telling you."

And it was, indeed, how it worked and still worked for Obinze.
The ease of it had disoriented him. The first time he took his offer
letter to the bank, he had felt surreal saying "fifty" and "fifty-five"
and leaving out the "million" because there was no need to state
the obvious. That day he had written an e-mail to Ifemelu, which
was still in the drafts folder of his old Hotmail account, unsent after six years. She was the only person who would understand, and
yet he was afraid that she would feel contempt for the person he
had become. He still did not understand why Chief had decided
to help him; there was, after all, a trail of eager visitors to Chief's
house, people bringing relatives and friends, all of them with pleas
in their eyes. He sometimes wondered if Chief would one day ask
something of him, the hungry and honest boy he had groomed,
and in his more melodramatic moments, he imagined Chief asking him to organize an assassination.

The party was more crowded, suffocating. Chief was saying something to a group of men and Obinze heard the end: "But you know that as we speak, oil is flowing through illegal pipes and they sell it in bottles in Cotonou!" He was distracted. He reached into his pocket to touch his BlackBerry. Kosi was asking if he wanted more food. He didn't. He wanted to go home. A rash eagerness had overcome him, to go into his study and reply to Ifemelu's e-mail, something he had unconsciously been composing in his mind. If she was considering coming back to Nigeria, then it meant she was no longer with the black American. But she might be bringing him with her; she was, after all, the kind of woman who would make a man easily uproot his life, the kind who, because she did not expect certainty, made a certain kind of sureness somehow become possible. When she held his hand during those campus days, she would squeeze until both palms became slick with sweat, and each time she would say, "Just in case this is the last time we hold hands, let's really hold hands. Because a motorcycle or a car can kill us now, or I might see the real man of my dreams down the street and leave you, or you might see the real woman of your dreams and leave me."

Perhaps the black American would come back to Nigeria too, clinging on to her. Still, there was something about the e-mail that made him feel she was single. He brought out his BlackBerry to calculate the American time when it had been sent. In the car on the way home, Kosi asked what was wrong. He pretended not to have heard and asked Gabriel to turn off the radio and put in a Fela CD. He had introduced Ifemelu to Fela at university. She had, before then, thought of Fela as the mad weed-smoker who wore only underwear while performing, but she had come to love the Afro-beat sound, and they would lie on his mattress and listen to it and then she would leap up and make swift, slightly vulgar movements with her hips when the run-run-run chorus came on. He wondered if she remembered that. Kosi was asking again what was wrong.

"Nothing," he said.

"You didn't eat very much," she said.

"Too much pepper in the rice."

"Darling, you didn't even eat the rice. Was it Mrs. Akin-Cole?"

He shrugged and told her he was thinking about the new block of flats he had just completed in Parkview. He hoped Shell would rent it because the oil companies were always the best renters, never complaining about abrupt hikes, paying easily in American dollars so that nobody had to deal with the fluctuating naira.

"Don't worry. God will bring Shell. We will be okay, darling," she said and touched his shoulder.

The flats were in fact already rented by an oil company, but he sometimes told her senseless lies such as this, because a part of him hoped she would ask a question or challenge him about something, but he knew she would not, because all she wanted was to make sure the conditions of their life remained the same, and how he made that happen she left entirely to him. She had never asked him about his time in England either. Of course she knew that he was deported, but she had never asked him for details. He was no longer sure that he wanted her to, or even whether he would have told her about feeling invisible in that removal center, but it suddenly became a glaring failing of hers. Ifemelu would have asked. Ifemelu would not have been content to ignore the past as long as the present existed. He knew very well what he was doing, fashioning a perfect doll from ten-year-old memories of Ifemelu, but he could not help himself.

At home, the housegirl, Marie, opened the door and Kosi said, "Please make food for your *oga*."

"Yes, ma."

She was slight, and Obinze was not sure whether she was timid or whether her not speaking English well made her seem so. She had been with them only a month. The last housegirl, brought by a relative of Gabriel's, was stocky and had arrived clutching a duffel bag. He was not there when Kosi looked through it—she did that routinely with all domestic help because she wanted to know what was being brought into her home—but he came out when he heard Kosi shouting. He stood by the door and watched her, holding two packets of condoms by their very tips, swinging them in the air. "What is this for? Eh? You came to my house to be a prostitute?"

The girl looked down at first, silent, then she looked Kosi in the face and said quietly, "In my last job, my madam's husband was always harassing me, forcing me."

Kosi's eyes bulged. She moved forward for a moment, as though to attack the girl in some way, and then stopped.

"Please carry your bag and go now-now," she said.

The girl shifted, looking a little surprised, and then she picked up her bag and turned to the door. After she left, Kosi said, "Can you believe the nonsense? She brought condoms to my house and she opened her mouth to say that rubbish. Can you believe it?"

"Her former employer raped her so she decided to protect herself this time," Obinze said.

Kosi stared at him. "You feel sorry for her. You don't know these housegirls. How can you feel sorry for her?"

He wanted to ask, *"How can you not?"* But the tentative fear in her eyes silenced him. Her insecurity was so great and so ordinary. She was not worried about his lassitude, or about their not having real conversations, or indeed about their not truly knowing each other. Instead she was worried about a housegirl whom it would never even occur to him to seduce. It was not as if he did not know what living in Lagos could do to a woman married to a young and wealthy man, how easy it was to slip into paranoia about "Lagos girls," those sophisticated monsters of glamour who swallowed husbands whole, slithering them down their throats. But he wished she handled her fear a little differently, pushed back a little more. Once he had told her about the attractive banker who had come to his office to talk to him about opening an account. He had found it amusing and sad, how desperate the woman had been, in her tight pencil skirt and fitted shirt with one button that should not have been open, trying to pretend that she was in control of it all. Kosi had not been amused. "I know Lagos girls, she can do anything," she had said, and what had struck him was that Kosi seemed no longer to see him, Obinze, and instead she saw blurred figures who were types: a wealthy man, a female banker who had been given a target amount to bring in as deposits, an easy exchange.

She had, in the years since they got married, developed an inordinate dislike of single women and an inordinate love of God. Before they got married, she went to Sunday mass once a week at the Catholic church, but afterward she had thrown her rosary in the dustbin and told him she would now go to the House of David because it was a Bible-believing and spirit-filled church. Later, when he found out that House of David had a special prayer service for Keeping Your Husband, he had been flattered and revolted. Just as he was when he once asked why her best friend from university,

Elohor, hardly visited them, and Kosi said, "She's still single," as though that were a self-evident reason.

Marie knocked on his study door and came in with a tray of rice and fried plantains. He ate slowly. He thought of the day he was frying plantains for Ifemelu in the tiny room he rented on campus, how he had insisted on washing the plantain slices even though she had asked him not to, and how hot oil from the pan came flying out and left ovals of burned skin on his neck. Perhaps he should include this memory in the e-mail. *Remember the fried plantain accident?* He decided not to. It would be too odd, too much a specific memory. He wrote and rewrote the e-mail, deliberately not mentioning his wife or using the first-person plural, trying for a balance between earnest and funny. He did not want to alienate her. He wanted to make sure she would reply this time. It was alarming to him how happy that e-mail had made him, how his mind had become busy with her, possessed by her. He clicked Send and then minutes later checked to see if she had replied. What was this? Was he unhappy? It was not that he was unhappy, he told himself, it was simply that he had been long enough in his new life that he had begun to think of alternative lives, people he might have become, and doors he had not opened. He got up and went out to the veranda; the sudden hot air, the roar of his neighbor's generator, the smell of diesel exhaust fumes brought a lightness to his head. Frantic winged insects flitted around the electric bulb. He felt, looking out at the muggy darkness farther away, as if he could float, and all he needed was to let himself go.

MEGAN MAYHEW BERGMAN

Housewifely Arts

FROM *One Story*

I AM MY OWN HOUSEWIFE, my own breadwinner. I make
lunches and change light bulbs. I kiss bruises and kill copperheads
from the backyard creek with a steel hoe. I change sheets and the
oil in my car. I can make a pie crust and exterminate humpback
crickets in the crawlspace with a homemade glue board, though
not at the same time. I like to compliment myself on these things,
because there's no one else around to do it.

Turn left, Ike says, in a falsetto British accent.

There is no left—only a Carolina road that appears infinitely
flat, surrounded by pines and the occasional car dealership billboard. I lost my mother last spring and am driving nine hours
south on I-95 with a seven-year-old so that I might hear her voice
again.

Exit approaching, he says from the back seat. Bear right.

Who are you today? I ask.

The lady that lives in the GPS, Ike says. Mary Poppins.

My son is a forty-three-pound drama queen, a mercurial shrimp
of a boy who knows many of the words to Andrew Lloyd Webber's
oeuvre. He draws two eyes and a mouth on the fogged-up window.

Baby, don't do that unless you have Windex in your backpack, I
say.

Can you turn this song up? he says.

I watch him croon in the rearview mirror. He vogues like Ma-
donna in his booster seat. His white-blond shag swings with the
bass.

You should dress more like Gwen Stefani, he says.

I picture myself in lamé hot pants and thigh-highs.

Do you need to pee? I ask. We could stop for lunch.

Ike sighs and pushes my old Wayfarers into his hair.

Chicken nuggets? he asks.

If I were a better mother, I would say no. If I were a better mother, there would be a Ziploc baggie in a cooler with a crustless PB&J, a plastic bin of carrot wedges and seedless grapes. If I were a better daughter, Ike would have known his grandmother, spent more time in her arms, wowed her with his impersonation of Christopher Plummer's Captain von Trapp.

How many eggs could a pterodactyl lay at one time? Ike asks.

Probably no more than one, I say. One pterodactyl is enough for any mother.

How much longer? Ike asks.

Four hours.

Four hours till what?

You'll see, I say.

What I'm having trouble explaining to Ike is this: We're driving to a small roadside zoo outside of Myrtle Beach so that I can hear my mother's voice ring through the beak of a thirty-six-year-old African gray parrot, a bird I hated, a bird that could beep like a microwave, ring like a phone, and sneeze just like me.

In moments of profound starvation, the exterminator told me, humpback crickets may devour their own legs, though they cannot regenerate limbs.

Hell of a party trick, I said.

Our house has been for sale for a year and two months and a contract has finally come in, contingent on a home inspection. The firm I work for has offered to transfer me to Connecticut—a paralegal supervisory position in a state where Ike has a better chance of escaping childhood obesity, God, and conservative political leanings. I can't afford to leave until the house sells. My realtor has tried scented candles, toile valances, and apple pies in the oven, but no smokescreen will detract from the cricket infestation.

They jump, the realtor said before I left town with Ike. Whenever I open the door to the basement, they hurl themselves at me. You'll never pass a home inspection, he said. They're like spiders on steroids. Do something.

The exterminator already comes weekly, I said. And I've installed sodium vapor bulbs.

I'll see you Sunday, the realtor said, walking to his compact convertible, his shirt crisp and tucked neatly into his pressed pants. I'll come over for a walk-through before the inspection.

That night Ike and I covered scrap siding in glue and flypaper and scattered our torture devices throughout the basement, hoping to reduce the number of crickets.

You're coming down later to get the bodies, Ike said. Because I'm not.

He shivered and stuck out his tongue at the crickets, which flung themselves from wall to ledge to ceiling.

What if we live here *forever?* he asked.

People used to do that, I said. Live in one house their entire life. My mother, for instance.

I pictured her house, a two-bedroom white ranch with window boxes, brick chimney, and decorative screen door. The driveway was unpaved—an arc of sand, grass, and crushed oyster shells that led to a tin-covered carport. Growing up, there was no neighborhood—only adjoining farms and country lots with rambling cow pastures. People didn't landscape in fancy ways then. Mom had tended her azaleas and boxwoods with halfhearted practicality, in case the chickens or sheep broke loose. The house, recently bought by a corporate real estate firm, was empty now, a tiny exoskeleton on a tree-cleared lot next to a Super Walmart.

I thought about Mom then, and her parrot. If we moved, this might be my last time to hear her voice.

I pull into a rest stop, one of those suspicious gas station and fast-food combos. Ike kicks the back of the passenger seat. I scowl in the rearview.

I need to stretch, he says. I have a cramp.

Ike's legs are the size of my wrist, hairless and pale. He is sweet and unassuming. He does not yet know he will be picked on for being undersized, for growing facial hair ten years too late.

I want to wrap him in plastic and preserve him so that he can always be this way, this content. To my heart, Ike is still a neonate, a soft body I could gently fold and carry inside of me again. You can just see the innocence falling off a child's face—every day.

Ike and I lock the car and head into the gas station. A burly man with black hair curling across his shoulders hustles into the restroom. He breathes hard, scratches his ear, and checks his phone.

Next, a sickly-looking man whose pants are too big shuffles inside. He pauses to wipe his forehead with an elbow. I think, These people are someone's children.

I clench Ike's hand. I can feel his knuckles, the small bones beneath his flesh.

Inside, the toilets hiss. I hold Ike by the shoulders; I do not want him to go in alone.

Garlic burst, he reads from a cellophane bag. Big flavor!

I play with his cowlick. When he was born, I could see a whorl of hair on the crown of his head like a small, stagnant hurricane. Ike also had what the nurse called stork bites on the back of his neck and eyelids.

The things my body has done to him, I think. Cancer genes, hay fever, high blood pressure, perhaps a fear of math—these are my gifts.

I have to pee, he says.

I release him, let him skip into the fluorescent, germ-infested cave, a room slick with mistakes and full of the type of men I hope he'll never become.

The first time I met my mother's parrot, he clung to a wrought iron perch on the front porch as we ate breakfast outside. Claiming the house was too quiet, Mom adopted Carnie from a neighbor one month after Dad's funeral, and constructed an extensive cage for him both indoors and out.

Carnie could already imitate the sound of oncoming traffic, an ambulance siren, leaves rustling, the way Pete Sampras hit a tennis ball on TV. He could replicate my mother's voice completely, her contralto imitations of Judy Garland and Reba McEntire, the way she answered the phone. *What are you selling? I'm not interested.*

The bird moved from his perch to my shoulder without permission.

Mom, I said. Get this damn bird off of me.

Language! she warned. He's a sponge.

I was still grieving Dad, and it was strange to watch Mom find so much joy in this ebony-beaked wiseass.

What are you selling? he said. I already *have* car insurance. Carnie spoke with perfect inflection, but he addressed his words to the air—a song, not conversation.

You can't take anything personally, Mom warned.

The man of the house is *not* here, Carnie said. He's dead.

You really take it easy on those telemarketers, I said, looking at Mom.

Dead, dead, dead, Carnie said.

That night he shredded the newspaper in his enclosure, which smelled like a stable. Lights out, Mom said, and tossed a threadbare beach towel over his cage. Carnie belted out the first verse of Patsy Cline's "Walkin' After Midnight," then fell silent for the evening. His parlor tricks seemed cheap, and I hated the easy way he'd endeared himself to Mom.

Later that week, Carnie became violently protective of her. Wings clipped, he chased me on foot through the halls and hid behind door frames, not realizing his beak stuck out beyond the molding. As I tried to shoo him from the kitchen counter, he savagely bit my wrist and fingers. Then, days later, as if exchanged for a new bird, Carnie lightened up, and preened my hair while perched on the back of the couch.

I'll take him to a specialist, Mom said, mildly apologetic for her bird's bipolar antics. She was a perfectionist, and I knew she wanted a bird she could be proud of. But I think part of her was flattered by Carnie's aggressive loyalty.

Show me how you pet the bird, the behaviorist had said.

Carnie, inching left and right on Mom's wrist, cocked his head to one side and shot us the eye. Like a whale, he gave us one side of his face at a time, revealing a tiny yellow iris, one that looked out at the world with remarkable clarity, ensconced in a white mask the size of a thumbprint.

Mom ran her pointer finger down Carnie's chest.

I don't know how to tell you this, the behaviorist said, but you've been sexually stimulating your parrot.

Mom blushed.

Inadvertently, the behaviorist said. Of course.

He thinks I'm his mate? Mom asked.

Less cuddling, the specialist said, more cage time.

I called three places to find Carnie—the plumber who took him after Mom, the bird sanctuary he'd pawned the parrot off on, then the roadside zoo. Now the car is too warm and I'm falling asleep, but I don't want to blast Ike with the AC. He's playing card games on the console.

Are we leaving so that people can move into our house? Ike asks.

We're going to Ted's Roadside Zoo, I say.

Go fish, Ike says. What's at the zoo?

There's a bird I want to see, I say.

What, he asks, is gin rummy?

We pass a couple in a sedan. The woman is crying and flips down her visor.

It's hard being a single mom, but it's easier than being a miserable wife. I hardly knew Ike's father; he was what I'd call a five-night stand. We used to get coffee at the same place before work. A director of the local college theater, he was a notorious flirt but already married. Separated, he'd claimed. He sends a little money each month, but doesn't want to be *involved*. The upside to our arrangement is simplicity.

I put some pressure on the gas and pass a school bus.

Did I tell you about Louis's mom? Ike says. How she got on the bus last week?

Louis's mom is a born-again Christian with two poodles and a coke habit, the kind of person I avoid at T-ball games and open houses at school.

Tuesday afternoon, Ike says, she boarded the bus with her dogs, raised her fist, and said, "Christ is risen! Indeed, he is risen."

No, I say. Really?

Ike pauses for a minute, as if he needs time to conjure the scene. Really, Ike says. Louis pretended not to know her when she got on, but his mom held on to that chrome bar at the front of the bus and said, "Lord, I've been places where people don't put pepper on their eggs." And she started to dance.

Ike waves his arms in front of his face, fingers spread, imitating Louis's strung-out mother. I see the rust-colored clouds of eczema on his forearms. I want to fix everything. I want him to know nothing but gentle landings. I don't want him to know that people like Louis's mom exist, that people fall into landmines of pain and can't crawl back out.

When Ike was almost a year old, I took him by for Mom to hold while I emptied the old milk from her fridge and scrubbed her toilets. The house was beginning to smell; Mom was not cleaning up after the bird. Suddenly, the woman who'd ironed tablecloths, polished silver, bleached dinner napkins, and rotated mattresses had given up on decorum.

Would you like to hold Ike while I clean? I said.

Mom sat in a brown leather recliner, Carnie in his white lacquered cage a foot away from her—almost always within sight. She was losing weight and I worried she wasn't eating well. I brought cartons of cottage cheese and chicken salad, only to find them spoiled the following month.

Are you trying to sell my house? she said. Are you giving realtors my number? They're calling with offers.

There's a shopping center going in next door, I said. This may be your chance to sell.

I placed Ike in her arms.

It's not hard to lose the baby weight, Mom said, eyeing my waistline, if you try.

I was determined not to fight back. There was heat between us, long-standing arguments we could still feel burning. Should we sell Dad's tools? Should she go to the eye doctor? Who would care for her goddamned bird? Didn't I know how hard they'd worked to give me the right opportunities? Our disagreements were so sharp, so intense that we'd become afraid to engage with each other, and when we stopped fighting, we lost something.

You're like your father now, she said. You never get mad, even when you want to.

It was true—Dad was hard to anger, even when I'd wasted $15,000 of his hard-earned money my freshman year of college at a private school they couldn't afford. The night I came home for the summer, he'd sat with his hands in his lap and a look on his face that was more sad than disappointed. Mom stood behind him, silent and threatening. I knew later she'd berate him for taking it easy on me, and I hated her for it.

I guess you'll need to get a job, he said.

Dad, I said. I made a lot of mistakes this year—

I wanted to give you a good chance, he said, looking down at his fingers.

I remember feeling relieved that he wasn't yelling at me. Now I wish he had.

I'd do it again, he said. But you understand, there just isn't enough money.

I tortured myself imagining each of his hours. He worked at the same plant for twenty-six years making industrial-quality tools—hammers, chisels, knives, clamps. Every day he ate a cold lunch on a bench caked with pigeon shit. I could almost hear the echoes of men moving and talking, their spoken lives bouncing from the plant rafters as their hands worked. The black hole of his effort, the way it would never be enough, or easy—it hung over me, a debt I couldn't pay.

Mom ran her fingers over Ike's cowlick. I emptied the trash can in the kitchen, then the living room.

While you're at it, she said, would you change the newspaper in Carnie's cage? And top off his water?

As I approached the bird's cage, he let out a piercing cry, his black beak open. I held my hand up as if to say "Stop." Cut it, I said.

Put your hand down, Mom said. You're scaring him.

Carnie continued to scream. It was a pleading, horrifying sound, like an alarm. He cocked his head and danced across his bar, shrieking. Ike began to cry.

Never mind, Mom said. I'll do it.

She thrust Ike in my arms and marched toward the cage. When she opened the door, Carnie scampered onto her finger, and she brought him to her shoulder. He was silent. Mom pulled the newsprint from the bottom of his cage with bare hands. Dried birdshit fell to the carpet; she didn't seem to notice.

Let me help you, I said. Sit down. I can do this.

Sit down, Carnie said. Sit down. Sit down.

Mom ignored me and moved to the kitchen, stuffing the soiled papers into the trash can.

You should wash your hands, I said.

Don't tell me what to do, she said.

Sit down, Carnie said. Sit down.

I found Carnie's high-volume pleas disconcerting and worried they agitated Ike, who clung to my shoulder. There were things, once, that I thought I deserved. My parents' money, and certainly their unconditional love. But as years passed, our love had turned into a bartering system, a list of complicated IOUs.

I'm sorry, I said. I don't know about birds.
You'll learn, Mom said. Soon.

Ike and I arrive in Myrtle Beach at eight P.M. I know the zoo will
be closed at this hour, so we find a Day's Inn. There's something
about the hum of an ice machine and waterlogged AstroTurf that
takes me back to childhood.

Ike face-plants onto the bed before I can remove the comforter.

Wait a second, baby, I say. Let me get that dirty thing off.

We get in bed and flip channels. Ike holds the fabric of my
pajama legs with one hand, wraps the other around a blanket my
mother crocheted for me when I was in college. His travel blanket.
I'm racked with sadness every time I see it: the coral and black star-
bursts, the tight knots.

I remember a hotel I stayed in with my mother during her own
mother's funeral. Downtown Norfolk, 1986. There was a rotating
bucket of chicken on a sign pole below our window. I watched it
spin. Even when the lights were off and my mother cried into her
pillow, I watched that bucket of chicken rotate like the world itself.

At the time I thought that moms were not allowed to be sad, that
surely women grew out of sadness by the time they had children.

Mom, Ike says. I don't want to move.

His eyes flicker and he fades. The news is on. A lipstick-shellacked
anchor tells of a new breed of aggressive python in southern Florida that strangled a toddler in his sleep. Maybe one will come to
our hotel, I think. And I will have to fight it off with my pocket
knife, club it with the glass lamp on the bedside table, offer it my
own body.

On our second date, Ike's father showed me a video of an
infant in Andhra Pradesh. The child had rich brown skin and curious eyes. He pulled himself across a grass mat while a cobra,
hood spread, hovered above the boy's soft body. The baby grabbed
after the cobra's tail while the toothless snake struck him repeat-
edly on his downy head, snapping down upon his body like a
whip.

This, Ike's father said, is how you cultivate the absence of fear.
Don't you wish someone had given you that gift?

Fear keeps me safe, I said.

Snakes. Why do I think of these things before I try to fall asleep?
I put one arm across Ike's chest so that I will know if he moves. I

can feel the pattern of his breath, the calm and easy way he sleeps, the simple way he dreams.

When I moved out, Mom had said, I need you to take Carnie.

It was the hundredth time she'd asked. We had her bills and bank statements spread out on the coffee table. Her eyesight was failing and we knew she couldn't live alone much longer. It was time to plan.

Carnie hung upside down in his cage. Empty seed casings and shredded newspaper littered the floor. Occasionally he pecked his image in a foil mirror, rang a bell with his beak.

I don't want the bird, I said. He hates me. He's drawn blood, for Christ's sake.

If you loved me, Mom said, you'd take him. I can't sleep without knowing he's safe and taken care of.

That's what you get, I said, for buying a bird with a life expectancy longer than your own.

You know, she said. Then she stopped, as if she were afraid of what she'd say next.

I'd always felt Mom's vision of perfection was outdated. I was never the ruddy-faced, pure-of-heart Girl Scout with 4-H-approved sheep-grooming skills that she'd been. I failed home ec and took a liking to underground hip-hop and traveling jam bands, dyed my hair blue with Kool-Aid one high school summer. In college I got a tattoo of a purple Grateful Dead bear on the back of my neck, which had infuriated Mom when she saw it. When Ike was little, he used to lift my hair until he found the purple bear hiding underneath. At least someone liked it.

In Mom's eyes, atonement was more than walking the line, more than surfacing from the typical angst-ridden throes of adolescence and early scholastic failures. Atonement included my adoption of a bird I couldn't trust around my son. A bird I'd hated for over a decade.

I don't trust the bird around Ike, and I can't handle the mess, the noise —

Mom was silent. I'll give Carnie to the plumber, Mom said, collecting herself. He's always liked Carnie.

I wish I could take him, I said.

Lying doesn't help, Mom said.

*

Even before I see it, Ted's Roadside Zoo depresses me. We park outside. The entrance is a plaster lion's face. We walk through its mouth. On the lion's right canine, someone has written, *Jenny is a midget whore.*

This place smells like pee, Ike says.

It's nine A.M., but it feels like Ted's place isn't open. I've yet to see an employee. We walk a sand-and-gravel path, faux palm trees overhead.

I've heard stories about these places, how they keep big cats in small enclosures. How the animals often have ingrown nails and zero percent body fat.

I have the urge to call out, *Mom?*—as if I'm coming home after a long day.

We find a man feeding a seal.

Where are your birds? I ask. Specifically, your African gray?

We have two, he says. Over by the vending machines.

I need the one named Carnie, I say. The one you received from the Red Oak Bird Sanctuary.

I think it's the one on the left, he says. They all look alike, you know?

I hone in on Carnie's knowing eye, the white mask. He looked like the same bird, though his eyes had yellowed and his gray feathers had worn thin around his neck.

Carnie, I say. Carnie. Carnie. Good boy. What do you want for dinner? I pull out a pack of sunflower seeds I had purchased at the Zip Mart down the road. I look at the white down on the bird's chest and think, Mom's voice is in there.

Ike closes in on the cage. He waves his hands in front of the parrot's face. The sign on Carnie's cage reads, *African gray parrots are as smart as a three-year-old.*

I don't believe it, Ike says.

Carnie? I ask. Want to sing some Patsy?

For a half-hour, Ike and I coo and speak and dance, but the bird doesn't say a word. Beneath this wall of gray feathers is the last shard of my mother, and I feel myself growing increasingly desperate. How thick was her accent? Was her singing as beautiful as I remember? She always spoke sweetly to Carnie, and I wanted to hear that sugary tone, the one she hadn't used with me in her last years.

How do you know this is the right bird? Ike asks.

I did my research, I say. And he hates me. He's spiting me with silence.

Please talk, Ike says to Carnie. Carnie bobs his head up and down and bites his leg, a gesture that strikes me as the bird equivalent of thumbing one's nose.

Just say something, I think. Anything. Just let me hear her again.

I'm surprised when I remember phone numbers and the alphabetical listing of all fifty states, the way I can summon Deuteronomy like a song on a long run. But I can't recall the funny way Mom said *roof* or *Clorox*. Not the rhyme she used to say about bad breath or the toothpaste jingle she had stuck in her head for two years, not the sound of the way she said good night. The longer Carnie goes without talking, the more I miss her.

The morning we moved Mom into a home, the plumber came for Carnie. Mom's possessions had been boxed up and her furniture sold. She'd prepared a box for Carnie that contained his food, toys, water dish, spare newsprint, and a fabric square from one of her dresses. So he remembers me, she said.

The kids are excited, the plumber said. He was tall and large and moved quickly. I was thankful for his efficiency.

I'll be in the car, Mom said, letting herself out of the house. The screen door shut behind her with metallic resonance, as it had thousands of times. I didn't like letting her descend the steps on her own, but I knew, in this moment, she'd refuse help. I took the box she'd made for Carnie and followed the plumber to his car, dropping a towel over the cage in the back seat of his truck.

I'm always walking, Carnie sang, *after midnight . . .*

I couldn't look at Mom. I knew she was crying. I was relieved to see Carnie go, to have the burden of his welfare hoisted onto someone else's shoulders. But immediately I was brought back to the sadness of the moment, the fact that this day represented a breaking-off point. There was an air of finality—my mother grieving in the car, our small home empty.

After the plumber pulled away, I walked through the house one last time. I could almost hear the place settling, breathing a sigh of relief, coming down from a high. Still, there was a palpable residue of our past lives, as if old fights and parrot tirades had left their marks. I paused over my father's plaster fixes and custom molding, things shaped by his hands that I couldn't take with me. Empty, the house reminded me of a tombstone, a commemoration of my childhood. With the shopping center going up next door, I had the feeling no one else would ever live there again.

I joined Mom in the car. I imagined her stillness and set face belied inner fragility, as if beneath the crust lay a deep well of hurt. As I turned onto the highway, I saw her touch her shoulder, the place where Carnie had so often rested, his remembered weight now a phantom presence on her thinning bones.

We've been driving I-95, toward home, for five hours. Ike has been in and out of naps. We pass a billboard that says, *Jesus Is Watching.*

Jesus makes me nervous, Ike says. Jesus is a spy.

I laugh and then pause, thinking how the statement would have made Mom uncomfortable. The night sets in and Ike gets quiet. I watch his eyes in the rearview. I wonder what he's thinking about.

Will you love me forever? I think to myself. Will you love me when I'm old? If I go crazy? Will you be embarrassed of me? Avoid my calls? Wash dishes when you talk to me on the phone, roll your eyes, lay the receiver down next to the cat?

I realize how badly I need a piece of my mother. A scrap, a sound, a smell—something.

I hunger for the person who birthed me, whose body, I realize, after becoming a mother myself, was overrun with nerve endings that ran straight to her heart, until it was numb with overuse, or until, perhaps, she felt nothing.

One more stop, I say to Ike.

We pull into the dark gravel driveway to my mother's house. There's no neighborhood, no signage. It's just a deserted, plain house for plain folks on what is now a major highway. The white paint peels from the siding. I remember pulling into this driveway when I was past curfew, the light in my mother's bedroom glowing, the way I could simultaneously dread and love the thought of slipping through the front door, pouring a glass of water, and crafting an elaborate lie to explain my late arrival.

Ike is sleepy. He's wearing my rain jacket and has the hood cinched tightly to his face, though it's barely raining. RVs are pulling into the Walmart parking lot for the night. The smell of wet leaves makes me sick to my stomach with nostalgia. The boxwoods are overgrown and shapeless.

Hold my hand, I say to Ike. Stay close.

The screen door is still intact, though the screen itself is punctured and webbed over. I hold it open, stare into the dirty glass of the front door. I try the knob—locked.

I have to go in, I say. Close your eyes.

I break the front door pane with the butt of the knife I carry in my purse and carefully reach in through the mouth of glass teeth to turn the doorknob.

This is weird, Ike says. I'm scared.

I clench his wrist. My knuckles are cold and I worry that my grip on Ike's arm is too tight. But I do not let go.

The damp carpet heaves underneath my feet. The house smells like a cave, and yet like home. Checkered contact paper still lines the pantry shelves. Windows are cracked; sills are covered in dead wasps and crumpled spiders. There is mold on the drywall and water spots on the ceiling. Someone has taken red spray paint to the fireplace and living room wall. The stove and toilet have been ripped out. Ike starts to cry.

It's okay, I say. I just want to stay here a minute.

I lead him to the back of the house, down the hallway which still feels more familiar to me than any I know. My bedroom, with its teal carpet and pale pink walls, looks small. Barren. At first, it is so quiet my teeth ache. My ears strain.

I'm sad that you lived here, Ike says, still crying.

It wasn't that bad, honey, I say. This was a beautiful house.

The crown molding my father installed is still up, though one piece is loose and sags. I remember him getting up early so that he could work on it before heading to the factory. It was my mother's birthday present—crown molding for my room.

My father died on the steps of the tool manufacturing plant, not ten minutes down the road. A heart attack. The doctors said it was a birth defect, that he was born with a weak heart. And now the building is empty, abandoned, as if all his work was for nothing. Mom's grief was as long as a river, endless.

I walk back to the kitchen and climb onto the green plastic countertop. Ike watches me, curious and confused. I remove the valances Mom made in the early eighties, dried bugs falling from

the folds of the fabric into the sink below. These are the things
with which she made a home. Her contributions to our sense of
place were humble and put forth with great intent, crafts which
took weeks of stitching and unstitching, measuring, cutting, gath-
ering. I realize how much in the home was done by hand and sweat.
My father had laid the carpeting and linoleum. Mom had painted
and reupholstered the same dinner chairs twice, sewed all the window treatments. My parents were quick-fix-averse, always in for the
long haul. When the country road in front of their house had been
widened to a highway, they complained but never entertained the
idea of moving.

I scan the kitchen and picture Mom paying bills, her perfect
script, the way she always listed her occupation with pride: home-
maker.

I pull scraps of peeling wallpaper from unglued seams and corners. It comes off slow and steady like skin after a sunburn; the old
adhesive gives easily.

Mementos, I tell Ike. I close my eyes. Now I can hear my mother
everywhere—in the kitchen, in my bedroom, on the front porch.

Turn off the television.

Warm up the stove.

Brush your hair.

Put your father's shoes where I can't see them. In the trash.

On Sunday, as promised, my realtor arrives a half-hour before the
potential buyers and their home inspector.

Your house should look as perfect as possible, he'd said before
I left for the weekend. Ask yourself, What would Jackie Onassis
do?

Ike and I had come home to a spare house; some of our chairs,
photographs, and Ike's art had been relocated, as the realtor had
suggested, to "let the space breathe."

When I see the realtor's convertible in the driveway, I ask Ike,
Think you can box up the mini NASCARs and finger puppets?

Sorry I'm late, our realtor says. He rushes to the kitchen, as if he
has immediately sensed disorder. He strokes the valance over the
kitchen window. I remembered last night, as I was hanging it, that
Mom had found the pattern in *Southern Living*.

Is this velvet? he says. Are these . . . cobwebs?

I have placed scraps of rogue wallpaper next to my stove and another in the bathroom—a repeating pattern of pale brown cornucopias and faded fruit I took from my mother's house.

These must come down, the realtor says. Now.

He pinches the curling shreds with his thumb and forefinger.

Leave it, I say. They add charm.

You'll never sell this house, he says, shaking his head in despair. Crickets on speed and a valance that Elvis made in home economics class. Get serious.

Apple pie? I ask, pulling out a day-old pastry I had purchased from the market's discount bread bin that morning.

I've steeled myself against critique. There are too many things I can't fix.

A couple in a minivan pulls up in front of the house, followed by the home inspector in a pickup truck. They come to the door, their faces already twisted with scrutiny. She is small and blond and he is thick like an old football player.

Hi, I say. Welcome. We're about to head out; the house is all yours.

I stuff some magazines and soda into a canvas bag and look around for Ike. I hear him running up the basement steps. He presents a scrap of siding that is covered in glue and cricket exoskeletons. The couple exchange a glance. The inspector scribbles a note.

I crouch down to the floor and touch Ike's cheeks. You're brave, I say. Thank you.

Ike grins. Together, we can make a solid grilled cheese, prune shrubs, clean house. Together, maybe we're the housewife this house needs. Maybe our best life is here. On a good day, we're just one man short of a catalog-worthy family.

A week before she left for the nursing home, we packed my mother's belongings—robes, slippers, and lotions that could do little good for her sagging face. Her diminished vision made it hard for her to read the labels on the boxes.

Ike had just started kindergarten. Leaving him at a friend's house to spend time with Mom on a Saturday was a miserable tradeoff. I wanted to soak up every last bit of innocence he had left, answer every question, scoop him up for hugs when he'd allow it. But I was the only person Mom would allow in the house; there was no one else around to help.

I held up various tchotchkes for Mom's approval.

Take or toss? I asked.

Mom sat in her recliner. She wore a light blue dress she'd made herself. The fabric was so worn it was nearly transparent. Carnie rested comfortably on her shoulder. I worried that his talons would break her thinning skin, but she moved as if she hardly noticed his weight.

I held up a box of ornaments, plastic apples I'd hand-painted for her as a child.

Toss 'em, she'd said.

I began to wrap her glassware in newspaper.

Make sure to leave plenty of print for lining Carnie's cage, she said.

My mother cupped Carnie with both hands and brought him to her lap. She crossed her legs, then scratched the finger-wide point between Carnie's wings. His eyes, like little black seeds, fell to half-mast as she stroked him. They were accustomed to each other, a pair of sad habits. He was more familiar with her voice and touch than I, more dear to her everyday existence. His transgressions— dirty cage, the occasional nip of her finger—were met with gentle understanding.

Don't call here again, he said. Don't call.

Remember, I told my mother. I'm not *obligated* to look after that bird.

Well, she said, I'm not obligated to look after you.

You are, I'd thought at the time, her words a splinter in my chest. You have to be.

In that moment, I withered. I hated her for her coldness, her stubborn rationale, her ability to come up big in a fight even when she was dog-tired and bird-boned and couldn't see the food on the end of her fork.

There she sat, outmoded in her homemade dress, bird in her lap, shit on her shoulder. Steamrolled by the world, but in the face of defeat, she threatened us all.

Carnie moved back to her shoulder and buried his head into her thin hair. It occurred to me that with her voice inside of him, he would always have more of her to remember.

You don't want to keep these? I asked, giving her a second chance on a box of photographs.

My heart, she'd said. I can turn it off.

For years, I'd believed her.

But I know the truth now. What maniacs we are—sick with love, all of us.

TOM BISSELL

A Bridge Under Water

FROM *Agni*

"SO," HE SAID, after having vacuumed up a plate of penne all'arrabiata, drunk in three swallows a glass of Nero D'Avola, and single-handedly consumed half a basket of breadsticks, "do you want to hit another church or see the Borghese Gallery?"

She had plunged her fork exactly ten times into her strawberry risotto and taken two birdfeeder sips from the glass of Gewürztraminer that her waiter (a genius, clearly) had recommended pairing with it. She glanced up and smiled at him (more or less) genuinely. The man put away everything from foie gras to a Wendy's single with the joyless efficiency of a twelve-year-old. He never appeared to taste anything. The plate now before him looked licked clean. When he return-serve smiled, she tried not to notice his red-pepper-and-wine-stained teeth or the breadcrumbs distributed throughout his short beard. They were sitting on the AstroTurfed outdoor patio of an otherwise pleasing restaurant found right behind the American Embassy in Rome. They had been married for three and a half days.

Again she pushed her fork into the risotto and watched steam rise from its disturbed center. "Think I may be a little churched out."

He snapped up another breadstick, leaned back, and rubbed his mouth. This succeeded, perhaps accidentally, in clearing the perimeter of breadcrumbs around his mouth. He had small eyes whose irises were as hard as green marbles, a crooked wide nose, and an uncommonly large chin. His thick and tinder-dry brown hair sat upon his head with shaggy indifference due to how quickly they had cleared out of their hotel room this morning after his rushed shower. She did not mind that he had overslept. The only reason she had not overslept was that she had never fallen asleep to begin with. His plum-colored linen shirt was unbuttoned to his sternum, showcasing a pearl-white chest covered in pubically corkscrewed hair. She felt a sudden urge to lean forward and button him up but did not want the doing of such small tasks ever to fall to her.

He bit the end off his breadstick. "It's not a church, strictly speaking. It's more like a crypt." Now that he was gesturing, the breadstick resembled a wand. "Mark Twain wrote something really funny about it when he visited Rome. Apparently it's decorated with the bones of all the monks who've lived there. Like four centuries' worth. The chandeliers are bones, the gates, everything. All bones. It's supposed to be really creepy."

"A crypt made of monk bones. Why didn't you say so? Let's do that."

His smile softened in a pleased way that made her realize how falsely polite his earlier, larger smile had been. "Funny girl," he said. The thing he liked most about her, he enjoyed telling people when she was in earshot, was her sense of humor. He was the only man who had ever said she was funny, and she wondered, suddenly, if that was one of the reasons why she married him. She was, in fact, very funny.

It had been a good morning, uncontaminated by the reactor-leak conversation of the previous night. They had hardly talked about things today, but she knew both of them were aware they would have to. It was the lone solid thing in their day's otherwise formless future. It was the train they would have to catch.

"Okay," he said, setting down his breadstick with an air of tragic relinquishment, "I'd really like to see the creepy bone crypt."

She put her hands on her only slightly rounded belly and gave it a crystal-ball rubbing. "Let the record show that the pregnant lady would like to see the Borghese Gallery."

The single drum of his fingers on the tabletop made a sound like a gallop. "One way to settle it."

She slammed her fork to the table with mock finality. "I'm not playing. Seriously. I won't do it."

He was nodding. "One way to settle it."

The man loved games of all kinds. Obscure board games, video games manufactured prior to 1990, any and all word games, but he also enjoyed purely biophysical games such as rock, paper, scissors—the "essential fairness" of which he claimed to particularly admire. He was, however, miserably bad at rock, paper, scissors, the reason being that he almost always took paper. She had once been told, as a girl, by some forgotten Hebrew school playmate, that while playing rock, paper, scissors you were allowed, once in your life, the option of a fourth component. This was fire, which was signified by turning up your hand on the third beat and wiggling your fingers. Fire destroyed everything. That this thermonuclear gambit could be used only once was a rule so mystically stern that its validity seemed impossible to question. She had told him of the fire rule when he first challenged her to rock, paper, scissors on their earliest date, which was not that long ago. At issue had been what movie to go see.

Now she said to him, "You do realize you always lose? You're aware of this."

He readied his playing stance: back against the chair, eyes full of blank concentration, right fist set upon the small shelf of his left hand.

She picked up her fork again and began to eat. Probably she would indulge him. "I'm not playing because it's boring. And it's boring because you always pick paper."

"I like its quiet efficiency. I could ask you why you always take scissors."

"Because you always take paper!"

"I am aware that you believe that, which means I'm actually taking paper to psych you out. Statistically I can't keep it up."

"But you *do*. The last time we played you took paper *four* throws in a *row*."

"I know. And I can't possibly keep it up. Or can I? Now, best out of three. No. Five. Three. Best out of fthree." He was smiling again, his teeth no longer quite so stained by the wine and pepper oil. She loved him, she had to admit, a lot right now.

He threw paper for the first two throws. She threw rock for her first just to make the game interesting. After his second paper she fished an ice cube out of her hitherto untouched water glass and threw it at him. On the third throw she was astonished to see her husband wiggling his fingers.

"Fire," he said, extending his still-wiggling fingers so that they burned harmlessly beneath her nose. What he said next was sung in hair-metal falsetto: "Motherfucking fire!"

She pushed his hand away. "You didn't even know about fire until I told you about it!"

"Look on the bright side," he said. "I can never use it again, and you've still got yours."

"Please, honey, *please* button your shirt."

They descended in silence the zigzag stairs of the apricot building she now knew was called the Capuchin Crypt, passing a dozen American student-tourists sitting on, around, and along its stone balustrade. The boys, clearly suffering the misapplications of energy that distinguished all educational field trips, spoke in hey-I'm-shouting voices to the bare-shouldered and sort of lusciously sweaty girls sitting two feet away from them. She was upsettingly conscious of the adult conservatism of her thinly striped collared shirt and black skirt—she was not yet showing so much that her wardrobe required any real overhaul—and her collar, moreover, had wilted in the heat. She felt like a sunbaked flower someone had overwatered in recompense, and wondered how much older she was than these girls, who seemed less young to her than another species altogether. And yet she was only twenty-six, her husband thirty-four. Two once-unimaginable objects, the first incubating in her stomach and the second closed around her ring finger, made her, she realized, unable to remember what being nineteen or twenty had felt like. Looking into the anime innocence of these American girls' faces was to discover the power of new anxieties and the stubbornness of old ones.

At the bottom of the stairs three tanned and lithe young Italian women walked unknowably by. She often felt herself bend away from people who knew how good they looked, but these women had such costume-party exuberance it seemed a waste not to stare. The belt? Three hundred dollars, easy. She somehow counted five purses among them. She hated the farthest girl's rimless aviatrix sunglasses only because she knew she could never wear them without fearing she looked ridiculous. It seemed impossible to her that the sun that turned these sprites clay brown was the same sun whose apparent gamma rays burned and peeled her. She looked down at her gray, pink-accented Pumas and then over at one of the growingly distant Italian's sassy red pumps. She had worn the Pumas only because she felt marriage should annul the desire to impress strangers, a thought that made her feel at once happy and vaguely condemned.

"That *was* creepy," he said as they turned toward where Via Veneto terminated at Palazzo Barberini. "Those bones actually kind of freaked me out."

She was still staring at her stupid shoes. "We could have spent that time looking at Bernini sculptures."

His hand lit upon her back. "We could still do that. I'd be happy to."

"No, it's okay. I'm tired anyway."

"You want to go back to the hotel?" His hand sprang away from her back as he checked his watch. "It's not even three yet." The hand did not return.

She did not say anything, thus sealing their hotel-bound fate. The next block or so was passed in silence, and they turned onto a tight, unremarkable side street (if any street in Rome could be considered unremarkable) made even tighter by the chaotically fender-to-grill-parked cars along both curbs. This was as residential as central Rome had yet seemed to her: hugely ornate wooden double doors with five-pound brass knockers and black-barred ground-level windows. The only word she could think of to describe it was *post-imperial,* which she knew was not even close to being historically correct. She liked this about Rome: whether you knew anything at all about history—and she knew a little—it forced you to think about history, even if in variously crackpot ways. In many cities, history was a loud voice at a party at which one felt underdressed. In Rome she felt history pressing in on all sides of her but in a pleasant, consensual way. Rome's weight was without expectation.

"Not entirely sure I like it here," he suddenly said.

She turned to him. "That's not a nice thing to say."

"No, no. I like being here with *you.* I mean I'm not sure I like Rome. The city. In and of itself."

She supposed she would have to hear this out but let his opportunity for explanation dangle a moment longer than felt polite. "Why not?"

"It really bothers me that everything is closed from noon to four, for starters, and that if you order a cappuccino after breakfast you're a barbarian. And I realized yesterday that I don't like how Italians talk to one another. Everything is so *emotional.* Like those women sitting next to us on the stairs the other day. Listening to them was like overhearing a plot to kidnap the pope. And when I asked that kid what they'd been talking about, he said, 'Shoes.'"

"I thought that was funny."

"You know my friend who lived in Rome for a while? What I didn't tell you is that his first apartment burned down—I guess the wiring was all fucked up—and after the fire was finally put out he and some firemen went inside to see what survived. Exactly one wall did, in the middle of which was this scorched crucifix that had been hung at the insistence of his landlady. There were any number of reasons why this wall survived the fire, but when they saw it all the firemen dropped to their knees and started praying while my friend just stood there. He made the point that you'd have to be astonishingly simple to believe in a God who'd let someone's apartment burn down but magically intervene to save a three-dollar version of his own likeness. He also told me that Italians are basically the most complicated uninteresting people in the world."

"You're being really interesting yourself right now."

"I'm not trying to be interesting." His voice had a real snarl in it. "I'm trying to objectively describe my impressions and tell you about my friend." Then he calmed down, or at least hid his anger more cunningly. "I'm sorry I made fun of your book last night."

Before their argument, while at a restaurant and while she was in the ladies', he had fished out of her purse the travel book she was reading about Italy. Its author was an American woman. When she returned to the table he began to read aloud certain parts in a dopey voice. "Listen to what she has to say about Rome: 'It's like someone invented a city just to suit my specifications.' Considerate of the preceding twenty-seven hundred years of civilization, wasn't it? This is priceless: 'It's like the whole society is conspiring to teach me Italian. They'll even print their newspapers in Italian while I'm here; they don't mind!'" He tossed the book onto the table and stared at it as though it were an excised tumor. Finally he said, "That is, without question, the stupidest fucking book I've ever seen you read."

The book in question was currently a bestseller, and the only reason she was reading it was that her mother had given it to her, just as she had given her (them) the gift of an Italian honeymoon. He too was a travel writer, though one who had never made it off what he sometimes called the "worstseller list." He had published three books (all before she had met him) and preferred writing about places, he had once said in an interview she was embarrassed for him to have given, with "adrenaline payoffs": Nigeria, Laos, Mongolia. (His honeymoon suggestion? Azerbaijan.) She admired his determination to love the unloved parts of the world, but, like all good qualities, it remained admirable only insofar as it was unacknowledged.

She decided to speak carefully. "I *like* that everything is closed from noon to four. It creates a little oasis in the middle of the day. I *like* that life in this city isn't based around my own convenience. I also like that people talk about dumb, pointless things like shoes with passion here. And I like Italians. They seem like totally lovely people."

"I guess what irks me," he said, speaking just as carefully, "is this fantasy that Italy exists only as a sensory paradise when it's got all these completely obvious *problems*."

"Okay. How about this: I hated your creepy bone church."

"Creepy bone *crypt*."

"In fact, I've hated every stupid church we've walked into." She knew she was asking for it here, and waited. He said nothing. Onward, then, into the dark. "You know I'm not comfortable in churches and yet you keep dragging me into them."

Five pounds of emotion seemed to encumber his face. "Please, let's at least lie down before we start talking about this again."

The hotel was many blocks away.

"Why," she asked, "do you want to take me into places you know I'm not comfortable in?"

His mouth set into an ugly little frown. "Because I think this discomfort of yours is ridiculous. I'm no more a Christian than you are. The ideology you suddenly feel so offended by is an ideology that would have had someone like me burning at the stake right next to you. That you can't separate the objectively aesthetic pleasure of churches from your own—" He stopped himself. Standing there, he began to rub his eyes. "Christ. Just forget it."

"My own what?" Now she had stopped too. They were outside

the gate-lowered entrance of a cheese store, whose owner was probably off banging his noontime mistress about now, and good for
him.

He fixed upon her an envenomed look, clearly resisting what he
wanted to say. *Religion,* she knew, was what he wanted to say.

He recklessly took her hands in his. When she made no effort to
return his clasp he rubbed his thumb along the valley between her
index and middle-finger knuckles. His voice turned soft. "I cannot
understand why you're so attached to being Jewish when you don't
even believe in God. And why all of this is only coming up now. Not
to mention why we keep fighting about it."

"And I cannot understand your difficulty in understanding this.
It has nothing to do with God and your position is absolutely bizarre to me." With this she twisted her hands around so that she
was holding his. "And it makes me, I have to tell you, extremely
worried and sad."

Last night, after the restaurant, after the confrontation over the
stupidest fucking book he had ever seen her read, they had argued,
again, for the first time since the wedding, about their child, due
now in six months. They had told themselves, in the weeks leading up to the wedding, that her accidental pregnancy after four
months of dating was not the reason they had decided to get married. But it was clear to both of them now that this was quite possibly not the case. She knew he felt betrayed. His atheism was one of
the first things he had told her about himself, and once things became serious he had quizzed her about her feelings concerning
God, and she had answered that she had no particular feelings
about God, other than a strong suspicion he did not exist. And this
made him happy at a time when his happiness seemed to her a
most precious and mysterious thing. All of that had begun to un-
spool a week before the wedding, when she had mentioned (in
passing) that it was important (to her) that their child would understand him- or herself (they had agreed on keeping the child's
gender a surprise) as a Jew. She could not even remember the context in which this had come up — *that* was how uncontroversially
she had regarded the matter. At hearing that his child would be
Jewish, her husband had laughed, once and loudly, like a king at
some forced merriment, before realizing his pregnant fiancée was
not kidding. *We'll . . . talk about that later,* he had told her. She did

not let him, saying that it was beyond her ability to fathom how exactly this could bother him. What was there to talk about? She was Jewish, her parents were Jewish, her child would be Jewish. His position: Jewishness was and could be only a religion. It was not a race, because there were Chinese and Turkish and Indian Jews. He had met some himself. It was not a proper culture, because there were Sephardic Jews, for instance, whose culture was completely different from that of Ashkenazi Jews. He described to her—one of his less wise moments—some of those differences. It was not an ethnicity, because the idea of Jewishness being determined by matrilineal descent was a religious concept. Out came his feverishly marginaliaed New Revised Standard for citation. It was, therefore, only and solely a religion, and, he told her, he could not and in fact refused to live within a household, a family, in which religion played any role other than that of an occasionally bashed piñata. She could not argue against this reasoning, which part of her agreed with. She disliked Jewish tribalism as much as anyone and had managed to escape Hebrew school without learning how to read, speak, or write Hebrew. Once, after a nephew's bar mitzvah, the theme of which was Wall Street, and which her uncle had broadcastedly made known cost $22,000, she had actually renounced her Jewishness (for two days). But she was having a child, and while she did not want to raise Menachim Begin, a Chabadnik, or a Settler, she did want to raise a Jew in the way she was a Jew, the formalities of which she knew almost nothing about. Being Jewish was, in her innerland, nothing more than a faint but definite light, and it offered her no more pride or direction than that of a faint but definite light. His refusal to grant her, and their child, that tiny, private awareness seemed to her insane.

Since their first argument, she had found herself doing and thinking things that she previously never could have envisioned: feeling unfamiliar pangs while eating pork, writing *G-d* instead of *god* in e-mails, sneering at strangers' pendant crucifixes, resenting churches, discovering within herself an out-of-nowhere identification with A Certain Small Country She Had Never Been To And Did Not Ever Want To Visit. She had no explanation for these things.

They stood holding each other's hand outside the cheese store. There seemed no place for this already battle-weary argument to go, other than deeper into a bunker, where it might just as well blow its own brains out. Suddenly she was crying. His forehead lurched forward, lightly bumping hers. "Don't cry," he said.

She shook her head. "I feel like I've disappointed you in a way I can't even control."

"I'm not disappointed. Disappointment is a beautiful woman reading Ayn Rand. This is not disappointment. This is something we can get through."

"But what if we can't?"

"Then I guess it's a bridge under water."

At the same time they squeezed each other's hand. His brother, a second lieutenant in the Marine Corps, had over the last five years of his eventful service become quite a collector of military-grade phraseology: *unimprovised road, northeasterlyward, shrapmetal, validify,* and *increasely.* "A bridge under water," which a gunnery sergeant had once used to describe to her husband's brother a particularly bad Ramadi neighborhood, was, as her husband knew, her personal favorite. She loved his brother.

She hugged him now with real love, its smoldering edges suddenly extinguished. "I hope it's not a bridge under water. It would be a real blow to my parade if it were."

His arms reached around her back. When he spoke into her hair his voice was unfamiliarly husky. "No need to reinvent the clock."

When they reached their room she slept in her clothes for the rest of the afternoon and awoke around seven to find him writing in His Notebook. She admired that about him too. He could write anywhere. He claimed to have once written an entire op-ed in the bathroom at a friend's birthday party. But she knew that he had not been writing much lately. He told her a while ago that he felt convinced the time of the American voice was over, which sounded even more pretentious when he said it.

She watched him for a little while, then said, "Hey," a drowsy creak in her voice breaking the word in two. "What are you doing?"

"Writing," he said.

"I gathered. What about?"

"A monkey with an unusual level of curiosity. This gets him into trouble in the short term but consistently results in long-term gains for those around him. I think this is due to the purity of his motivation, though I have to admit, I'm just getting to know the character."

When he got like this she really enjoyed throwing things at him and now launched across the room her big supernaturally downy pillow. He absorbed the blow and continued writing. She sat up and looked around the room, which was absurd, beginning with the fact that it did not have a number but rather a symbol. (The floors did not have numbers either; they had colors; they were on Green.) Their room's symbol resembled a Celtic cross. Upon check-in, they had been given a sheet with peel-away representations of this symbol, which they were supposed to affix to all relevant bills. It was apparently some sort of "art hotel," and everything in the room had a gadgety double function. The shower's clear glass door turned discreetly opaque when the water was running. The wall-hung flat-screen television could be pulled out from its steel rigging on some sort of extender arm and angled this way or that, allowing guests to see the screen from literally any point in the room. The day they arrived they had engaged in a long discussion about whether this last innovation was "worthless" or "next to worthless." The décor itself was Modern Android, everything shiny and smooth, with drawers and closets that made no sound when you opened them. She actually kind of loved it here.

She looked at him. "Do you want to order room service and do it like teenagers?"

He crossed something out, glanced over at her, and frowned in a hard-to-read way. They had not made love since the first night they were here, though they had tried. They had even tried last night, after arguing, and the effort had ended, quite literally for her, in tears. When they first got together it was not unusual for them to do it three times a day. Not that unusual, no, but they did it in cabs, in the kitchen, and once with her leaning out their opened living room window at night with all the lights on. Since the argument, they did it only before bed, and only in bed, and as far as she knew, he had not come once. And this was a man who took the greatest and sincerest pleasure in the sight of his own orgasm of anyone she had ever been with. Post-argument, the moment she came he would kiss her, withdraw, and roll over to sleep. The one time she asked him about this he had denied it, and then, she was sure, began faking his orgasms. Twice now he had made his coming noises and after he fell asleep she had squatted on the toilet with her hand cupped beneath her, to no avail. Last night he had not been able to get hard at all, which he blamed on the wine, and then the argument, and then the wine. She wondered why they were otherwise getting along so well, and had the brief, horrified thought that maybe couples in newly dead marriages got along in a way akin to the cheerfulness of people about to kill themselves.

"Honey?" She was wounded, a little, by his lack of response. "Room service?"

Still writing. "Sure, if you want."

She picked up the phone and listened to the harsh European dial tone, so unlike the organic lushness of the North American dial tone. She thought about what to order, then looked over at him again. "What do you suppose is considered a good tip for room service here? Two Celtic crosses or three?"

He did not look up. "I think you use real money for that, sweetie."

She replaced the phone and began to unbutton her shirt. Off came her skirt. Underwear, be gone. Her socks were last. Amazingly, he had not yet noticed, though two-thirds of his back was to her. She swung her legs to the floor and walked softly over to him, careful now to stay out of his peripheral vision, appalled by the sudden determination of her . . . lust? No. She did not even feel particularly wanton. She just needed to know if he still wanted her. She was self-conscious of her stomach, both proud of and slightly concerned by it (she touched it sometimes, when she was alone, as though it were an heirloom of uncertain provenance), and she wondered if this was why he refused to come, if somewhere within him was an animal self that considered her body territory that had already been marked. She was upon her husband now and began rubbing his shoulders. He had a big dog's dumb love of rubs and scratchings and at once his body went slumpy in his chair. His writing fist opened and his pencil toppled over and rolled to the bottom of the page.

"God," he said. "*Really* needed that."

"Stressed out?" She glanced at the page on which he had been writing and saw her name several times. Unlike him, to turn inward—to focus his writing upon his *wife,* of all people. Maybe the time of the American voice really *was* over. She looked away.

"I don't know. A little." She knew his eyes were closed. That he made no effort to conceal what he was writing made her less worried. "That feels *so* nice."

"It's supposed to."

For a while he did not say anything. Then: "While you were asleep"—his voice had changed, become somehow artificially official—"I was reading the guidebook. And I noticed we're not too far away from Rome's biggest synagogue." She realized that at his mention of "synagogue" she had begun to pincer his deltoid too aggressively. "So what I thought was that maybe tomorrow we could go there together. I thought maybe you'd like that. I'd like it too. Maybe seeing it will make me . . ."

"Make you what?" She was no longer rubbing him but was rather behind him, bent over, her hands behind her back, her chin set upon his shoulder, thrillingly conscious of the secret of her nakedness.

"Maybe it will help us." He started to turn around in his chair. "I should warn you that it's a synagogue designed by two Christian archi—Sweetie. You're naked."

"Sit back," she said.

He smiled in a worried way. "What are you doing?"

"Just sit back."

He did, and she went to her knees. She undid his belt with the poised delicacy of someone who already knew what the gift she was unwrapping contained. Without prompting, he lifted his ass off the seat, allowing her to tug off his jeans. She was relieved to find that he was already hard. It had been a hot day and he smelled like the skin underneath a not-recent bandage. She did not mind. She did not muck around, either. His cock was as warm as a mouthful of blood.

"Jesus," he said, and she felt his whole body flex. She was not a huge fan of performing oral sex and took a fairly workmanlike approach to the act. But now she imagined the inside of her mouth as being florally soft and smooth, and was conscious, suddenly, that she would never know what this felt like, disappearing into the mouth of another. The realization made her bizarrely excited. "Jewish girls like to fuck": a Catholic boyfriend of hers had said that to her once. She certainly liked to fuck. But she had corrected the boyfriend: "Reform Jewish girls like to fuck." (Later, after they broke up but stayed friendly, he began dating a black woman and told her, "Black girls like to fuck." She was devastated.) She wondered if her husband did not want to come in her anymore because she was Jewish.

"Jesus," he said again. He was thrusting lightly. Even the most artful blowjob grows repetitive, and, as a thought experiment, she imagined getting divorced. She supposed she would have to if he refused to allow their child to be Jewish. But she wondered if she could. She knew the story of his parents' divorce. It was one of the first intimate stories about himself he had ever told her. His mother used to put him in the back seat of her caramel-colored Cadillac convertible—a car, he said, as long as a submarine—and drop by Ernie's Party Store (she remembered that name, its small-town perfection) for comic books. On the days she took him to Ernie's she always put the top up, and this was a woman who kept the top down even when it was sprinkling. While he read his comic books his mother parked out in front of a strange house in a neighborhood not terribly far from their house. She made sure to park in the shade, at a discreet diagonal angle from the strange house. She would be gone for only a little while, she would tell him, making sure to roll down his window before leaving him to his crime-fighting mutants and walking hurriedly toward the strange house. On the fifth or sixth time she took him here, he asked whom she was going to see inside the strange house. She said she was going to see a friend. After the eighth or ninth time he asked her what she had been doing with her friend, and she said, *It's a surprise. For Daddy. So please don't tell him.* What kind of surprise? She did not answer, so he had hazarded a child's guess: a surprise party? *Yes,* she had said, and started to cry. He naturally misunderstood her tears, and could not stand—no little boy could stand—being the secret sharer of such exciting information for long. When he told his father about the party, asking him to promise that he would pretend to be surprised, his father said he would, then asked a few short, expert questions, nodded, and walked from the room. His mother left the next day. So it was not surprising that the whole question of divorce was a rather knotty one for him. She wondered if he could divorce her. She had read once that every marriage was between a royal and a peasant, a teacher and a student. She wondered what would have to happen for her to know for certain which one she was. She knew what he thought she was.

And with that, amid the pomp of some magnificent, Sasquatchian sounds, he was coming. She had never let anyone come in her mouth before and was not sure whether to swallow it or what. She was game, but the taste was not at all the seawater harshness she imagined it would be, but was rather something chemically nondegradable, like pool cleaner. Her mouth dropped open and what must have been half a cup of sperm and drool splatted against the carpet with water-balloon density. He looked down at her, breathing, his eyes crazed.

It was a weekday morning, but even so, the night had not been gentle to the streets of Rome. Bits of paper tumbleweeded down the swaybacked sidewalk along the Tiber River, and every twenty yards they came upon a little area that looked as though an ill-disciplined army had bivouacked there: Peroni beer bottles with a single stomach-turning swallow left in them, paper plates made transparent by pizza grease, panino wrappers, even a half-deflated soccer ball. The morning was clear and the sunlight seemed to bronze everything it caught, but the air blew with some strange microscopic grit.

The night had not been gentle with him either. She had actually slept well, but he had awakened her at five A.M. to describe the nightmare he had just experienced. In it he was somehow accepting the best director Academy Award for *Revenge of the Sith,* but no one could hear him speak over the music and then people began laughing at him. When she had told him that she would have laughed too were she in the audience, she could hear him sulk in the darkness.

From a distance it did not much resemble a synagogue. It had a square dome, for one. Closer up it did not much resemble a synagogue either. It kind of looked like a bank. But what did she know? The temples of her youth had looked like junior high schools. She disliked the similarity of Christian churches' bland majesty and had never really believed that they were built with love. There was something arctic about their devotion, and the brutal awe she felt inside the churches of Rome annoyed her—a (more or less) innocent opinion, voiced on their first day here, to which her husband had responded with such a grenade of ire that he had apologized almost instantly.

It occurred to her, as they approached, that she did not really care to see Rome's synagogue. The notion that they might discover anything here together struck her as fancifully at odds with what she knew were his real feelings. She was being sinisterly coddled. She felt unwell. The only thing worse than going into this synagogue would be telling him she did not want to go into this synagogue. Perhaps, in her own way, she was coddling him. It was too soon, she felt, to have this many secret motivations.

Now she was standing before the synagogue and took in the penitentiary inelegance of its surrounding black gates, its eggshell marble, its colonnaded ledges and tiers, and its small but noticeable number of broken windows—no longer a bank at all, but the mansion of some once-wealthy eccentric who had gone broke in the middle of an ambitious and possibly demented renovation. All around the synagogue was a typical Roman neighborhood of sun-bleached buildings with windows covered by parsley-green wooden shutters. This neighborhood, she had read, had once been predominantly Jewish—it was indeed still called the Jewish Ghetto—but in recent years many of the Jews had been getting priced out. On the corner of the synagogue's block stood a Plexiglas box, inside of which a hatless police officer read a newspaper. As they walked toward what they guessed was the proper entrance, several signs let it be known that the Museo Ebraico di Roma was currently under AREA VIDEO SORVEGLIATA.

She waited at the bottom of a stone staircase while he went up to an unpromising black-tinted glass door. Before he could give the handle an experimental pull, a short, bald man, whose near-perfect caricature of squat Semitic brusqueness was offset only by his pink sweater, opened the door and asked, "You pay ticket?" When her husband said no, the man jerked his thumb in a vaguely obscene way toward another gate farther down the block. Here they found a doorbell, which she pressed. She hated doorbells that did not make a corresponding sound for the benefit of the doorbeller and, fearing it was broken, pressed again after fifteen seconds. With a disapproving buzz the gate popped open.

They walked without comment through an open-air, yellow-walled corridor, the walls of which were affixed with chunks of old Sicilian synagogues, pieces of alms boxes, ancient fragments of synagogue doorjambs, all of them stamped with Hebrew letters, some of which she thought she might have recognized. All passed through her with no more moment than that of a parachutist through a cloud. He had already gone ahead into the lobby, where apparently tours were booked. The young woman who sat behind the ticket desk with a modest, makeupless presence informed her that entering the synagogue cost seven euros. "An English tour begins at seven fifteen," she said. "We will call you."

She paid, hoping he had not overhead this, but when she gave him his ticket he was smirking.

"It costs seven euros to get in?"

"It's a museum," she said.

"So's Saint Peter's. They don't charge you to go in there because it's still a functional place of worship."

She concentrated on not being angry. "The bone church cost money to get into."

"The bone *crypt* cost money to get into. The church above it was free. And the bone crypt asked for a donation, not seven euros."

She looked at him, nodding. "So you really plan on being a dick about this."

He winced in the stalwart way of a man being injected with something intended to benefit him. "Permission to apologize?"

"Authorization to forgive is pending." She poked him in the belly. "Behave and it might come through."

The museum's capsule history of Rome's Jewish community was set out on a series of large, thick, spot-glossed poster boards. While they stood before the first of these highly reflective plaques, dim and faceless ghost versions of themselves stared out as though from an inescapable dimension. She read one subject heading ("From Judaei to Jews: The Jews of Rome During the Middle Ages"), noted a quote from a twelfth-century visitor to Rome ("Two hundred Jews live there, who are very much respected"), and was not surprised by how quickly the story turned unhappy ("The burning of the Talmud in 1553 dealt a terrible blow to the tradition of Talmudic studies in Rome").

"I didn't know that," her husband said, reading a different section.

"What's that?"

"*Get* was the term for the segregation of man and woman, and that this may be where the word *ghetto* comes from."

She refocused. It was uncanny: every paragraph was filled with information vague enough to be uninteresting and precise enough to be soporific. She tried again, engaging in a little contest with herself to see how long she could hang in there: "The Italian *minhag* is also known as *minhag Kahal Italiani*. Its origins are closest to the land of Israel as are the German and the Romaniote Greek liturgy as well as an ancient French rite that oh my god oh my god boring boring boring."

She turned to the middle of the room, where a glass display case as high as her belly contained a thick old medieval Pentateuco. A book; it had that going for it, at least. Her husband was now across the room, and she joined him in his study of an old map of the city, done in the quaintly incompetent medieval cartographic style. He moved on, and she followed him to a piecrust-colored tombstone with a menorah on it. Next to it was a large glassed-in display of "The Jewish Home." Inside this was a table freighted with carafes, candleholders, menorahs, dreidels, a platter with what was possibly a real piece of bread on it, a dish of salt, a tiny clasped-shut book. She stood there looking at all these items, trying hard to be fascinated, or at least invested. She failed miserably and walked on past a reconstructed dowry, which *really* did not interest her. She resented not being able to tell him how bored she was. She was interested in the traditions, she thought, sort of, but not in the objects themselves. How could this be? She wondered if her husband might not in fact have a point. What *were* such traditions without the tent pegs of religious belief keeping them in place?

Soon they were called and met their guide back in the lobby. His name was David, pronounced Da-*veed*. He had short brown hair, the hawkish Roman nose that had no Jewish or Gentilic preference, perfect pink ears, hydraulically sincere eyebrows, small, catlike teeth, and a weirdly furrowed brow for someone so young. They joined the ten other English-speaking tourists who had already gathered around David, only two of whom looked American: a blinking, sport-coated father and his exquisitely manqué son, who wore cargo pants and a maroon Roma soccer jersey. They were from one of the overfed states, it looked like.

"Please don't take pictures," David began, "inside or outside. Yarmulkes are provided for the men to cover their heads. Women must cover their shoulders as well." With a smile he handed a shawl to an Asian woman old enough to know that her pink Hello Kitty tank top was one hundred percent unacceptable. The men then fished yarmulkes from a basket that David held out to them. Her husband looked at his with a chuckle and plopped it on his head with good-sport disdain. It looked even sillier on him than she was expecting. David proceeded to escort his troupe downstairs into the building's basement Sephardic synagogue, a room as colorful as a detonated rainbow. They sat in the first two rows of the uncomfortable wooden pews while David stood and waited in the middle of the synagogue.

"So we begin," David began, "our guided tour about the history of our community, which is unique among all the Jews of the West, including the United States. The Ashkenazi-Sephardic distinction does not entirely apply to our community." David spoke on, but she looked around, listening with a sonarlike part of her brain, hearing outlines and occasional distinctions, nothing more.

The altar was draped with bright blue, gold-tasseled rugs. Another rug with a gold menorah sewn onto its face was hung on the wall directly across from the altar. The thrones were cast of mottled red marble, their seats covered with thin red cushions. She had a vague sense that one of the thrones was where the Talmud was read during worship. No. All wrong. It was not an altar but a bema, and it faced east; it was also where the Torah, *not* the Talmud, was read. The thrones were where the Torah was *kept*. She actually had to stop herself from laughing. Years of Hebrew school and her husband doubtlessly knew more about Judaic ritual than she did. She tried to figure out which of her fellow tourists were Jewish and which were not, an impulse she would have found unforgivable in anyone but herself.

David was now taking questions. "Jews lived in the Ghetto for three hundred years," he told the Asian woman. "We Italian Jews also became the only Jewish community to be put back in a ghetto *after* being emancipated in 1798. We had to remain there until 1860, and this was long after almost all other members of European Jewry had been granted full legal rights. Florentine Jews suffered the same fate, earning their emancipation in 1808 but being returned to the ghetto in 1815."

Someone then asked about a gated area behind the pews. "That," David said, "is where women sit." Several hands instantly shot up. David laughed and, without calling on anyone, explained the religious reasons for this. That was when she noticed her husband slip off his yarmulke and search around his immediate area with the finicky distaste of someone working out where to stash a plug of chewed gum. He finally gave up and orphaned his yarmulke on the empty seat next to him.

She elbowed him. "Come on," she whispered. "Put it back on."

He whispered back: "Fuck that. They segregate the sexes? Fuck. That."

"I'm glad," she said, still whispering, "that you've found something to be angry about. But this is an Orthodox synagogue."

"I can't be angry?" He was no longer whispering.

"No, you can. What you're not allowed to be is surprised."

As they were leaving, the stout American father took a picture. David rushed over to him with frantically though still politely waving hands. "No photos, please. For security purposes."

The man said, "I'm just taking one of the rug here."

David smiled in what she recognized as tourist-honed, yeah-it-*is*-crazy ingratiation. "Our synagogue was once attacked, by terrorists, and so security is important to us. Please understand."

The man's mouth opened. "When was the synagogue attacked?"

"In 1982."

Her husband burst out laughing.

"Security is important to us," David said to the man in a loud, dislocated voice she knew was directed at her husband. "Upstairs in the Orthodox synagogue you can see for yourself our broken windows. Those were shattered in the attack, and we have never repaired them to remind us of what happened here."

"Was it Muslims?" the man wanted to know.

David smiled. "Let's go upstairs to the Orthodox synagogue."

The trip took them briefly outside. Their feet made wet splashing noises on the gravel walkway that led to the Orthodox synagogue's wooden doors, which David held open for everyone, nodding in identical welcome at each person as he or she passed. Inside were dozens of rows of wooden pews, the baker's-chocolate-colored joinery of which was truly lovely. David allowed them all a few moments to walk around and explore. She saw that many individual seats were affixed with little gold plaques bearing the name of the worshipper for whom they were reserved. She then noted that the entirety of the synagogue's first row was labeled EX DE-PORTATO. She did not need any Italian to know who sat there and why. She looked up into the square dome, filled with a sparkling airborne cathedral of sunlight. And there they were—the synagogue's broken windows, through which shoots of bamboo-colored light beamed.

David began his tour. The synagogue was inaugurated in 1904. The columns were hewn from some rare marble, the name of which she neglected to catch. From the black candelabras and chandeliers to the boiled-milk marble, you could see that the synagogue's Christian architects had worked in what was called the Syrio-Babylonian style.

"And where do the women sit?" one of the other tourists, a small, bespectacled woman with a round face, asked. She looked the woman over: yellow smoker's fingers, trembling hamster nose, an intense grudge-seeking manner about her.

"Women," David answered, "can sit upstairs, behind the gate, if there's room."

"If there's room," her husband echoed loud enough for David to hear.

David looked at him and was about to answer when he noticed that her husband was no longer wearing his yarmulke. That their exchange would now be one of regulation rather than confrontation seemed to relax David. "Excuse me, sir—there are yarmulkes in back." He moved on to answer another question, but her husband did not budge. She felt her face grow warm as the rest of her body chilled like a licked finger raised into the wind. David looked back to her husband a minute later and, still smiling, said, "Sir, please help yourself to a yarmulke in back."

She said her husband's name and gently pushed him rearward, toward the yarmulke basket. Her hands were on his chest, and she realized he had never buttoned up his shirt. He still refused to move; she felt as though she were pushing one of the synagogue's thick marble columns.

They now had the full interest of the tour group. With a kind of herd-animal practicality, she found herself stepping away from her husband. She had felt their eyes picking holes in him, in her, in *them*. Remarkable: after putting only a few feet between her and her husband, no one was looking at her anymore. She was ashamed by her own relief.

"Sir," David said again. There was no need to say anything else.

Watching her husband prepare for an argument was similar to watching a boxer throw off his robe. She knew what was coming but was still not fully prepared for the brazen impudence of what he said, or the sneering pride with which he said it: "So I'm not going to wear a yarmulke."

David blinked. She wondered if anything like this had happened to him before.

"Sir, you must cover your head."

Her husband answered in the same cruel voice he had used two nights ago to disparage her book. "And what's going to happen to me if I don't?"

She had the sense of watching someone fall down a flight of stairs in slow motion and noting the various stages of injury.

David was no longer smiling. "You will have to leave." His voice was tight; each word had a small, cold exactness.

One member of the group, an Englishman no older than twenty-five who was wearing a red Che Guevara T-shirt, said, "Christ, mate—cover your fucking head."

"Why should he?" This was the short, yellow-fingered woman.

"Out of respect," the young Englishman said.

It was to this young prole that her husband now turned. "I would happily cover my head if this synagogue allowed women to sit with men. It doesn't. I don't respect that or the god our friend David here thinks tells him this is right, so why *should* I cover my head?"

Her hand leapt up and landed with an open-palmed smack against her forehead. She said his name again, and again.

"Sir," David said. "This is our place of worship and community. You are here as our guest. If you don't cover your head, I will have to ask you to leave."

Her husband grinned as though this were exactly the argument he had been waiting for David to mount. "You charged me seven euros to come into your place of worship, so I think you kind of lose the right to tell me what I can or cannot wear while I'm in here."

"How does *that* work?" This was the American father in the sport coat. The man's son, she saw, was laughing.

David sighed and withdrew from his pocket a cellular phone. He speed-dialed, spoke a few words in Italian, then snapped shut the phone—a harsh, guillotine sound. He contemplated her husband now as though from a great height. "You will be escorted from this synagogue if you refuse to cover your head."

Her husband's smile was a fragment from some former, exploded confidence. "You're throwing me out of the synagogue."

David nodded. "You will be escorted from this synagogue if you—"

"Get rid of this douche bag!" The boy who a moment ago had been laughing said this. In fact, he was still laughing, which made her husband's stand seem, at that moment, even more ludicrous. "Dude, like what is the matter with you?"

Her husband said nothing while his eyes wandered from one member of their group to another. He avoided her and David, which she hopefully took as an indication that he was about to apologize. Instead he told the group, with great gravity, "Social justice isn't just about hating George Bush."

The bald man in the pink sweater emerged from a room adjacent to the bema and began to walk toward her husband. At this her husband turned to her in something close to lip-licking panic. Not that he was being forcefully removed from a place of worship—she knew he would tell this story, with certain redactions, for years—but rather at the thought of everything else that had been set into motion here.

The man in the pink sweater was upon him. His lips were wet in a way that made her wonder if his lunch had just been interrupted. The man looked at her husband, then at her, and then back at her husband. "We leave now," he said, relying, for the moment, on his presence as reason enough to leave. Her husband refused to look at the man. Instead he shook his head and muttered, "I paid my seven euros. I'm seeing the synagogue. Not leaving." The man in the pink sweater, who seemed both covetous of and frightened by the opportunity to use force, was then summoned by David. They spoke in hushed, spiralingly fast Italian. David's opinion, whatever that might be, seemed to win the day. The man in the pink sweater shook his head while David made another phone call. Soon enough, the hatless police officer from the corner cubicle outside entered the synagogue—and, oddly, crossed himself.

At the sound of the door opening, her husband turned. At the sight of the approaching, expressionless officer, he sighed. "Come on," he said to her. His tone was light; she could nearly hear his mind rearranging what had just happened into nothing more than an amusing misunderstanding. "Let's get thrown out of the synagogue together at least."

He stuck out his hand: his old trick. She took the hand and walked with him past the officer. As the box of daylight at the end of the synagogue aisle grew larger and brighter, she was surprised by how quiet it was—and she knew this, this sound, this sound of different hopes collapsing, of separate divinities forming, of exclusion, of closed doors, of one story's end.

JENNIFER EGAN

Out of Body

FROM *Tin House*

YOUR FRIENDS ARE PRETENDING to be all kinds of stuff, and
your special job is to call them on it. Drew says he's going straight
to law school. After practicing a while, he'll run for state senator.
Then U.S. senator. Eventually, president. He lays all this out the
way you'd say, "After Modern Chinese Painting I'll go to the gym,
then work in Bobst until dinner," if you even made plans anymore,
which you don't—if you were even in school anymore, which you
aren't, although that's supposedly temporary.

You look at Drew through layers of hash smoke floating in the
sun. He's leaning back on the futon couch, his arm around Sasha.
He's got a big, hey-come-on-in face and a head of dark hair, and
he's built—not with weight-room muscle like yours, but in a basic
animal way that must come from all that swimming he does.

"Just don't try and say you didn't inhale," you tell him.

Everyone laughs except Bix, who's at his computer, and you feel
like a funny guy for maybe half a second, until it occurs to you that
they probably only laughed because they could see you were *trying*
to be funny, and they're afraid you'll jump out the window onto
East Seventh Street if you fail even at something so small.

Drew takes a long hit. You hear the smoke creak in his chest. He
hands the pipe to Sasha, who passes it to Lizzie without smoking any.

"I promise, Rob," Drew croaks at you, holding in smoke, "if anyone asks, I'll tell them the hash I smoked with Robert Freeman Junior was excellent."

Was that "Junior" mocking? The hash is not working out as

planned: you're just as paranoid as with pot. You decide, no, Drew doesn't mock. Drew is a believer—last fall, he was one of the die-hards passing out leaflets in Washington Square and registering students to vote. After he and Sasha got together, you started help-ing him—mostly with the jocks, because you know how to talk to them. Coach Freeman, aka your pop, calls Drew's type "woodsy." They're loners, Pop says—skiers, woodchoppers—not team play-ers. But you know all about teams; you can talk to people on teams (only Sasha knows you picked NYU because it hasn't had a football team in thirty years). On your best day you registered twelve team-playing Democrats, prompting Drew to exclaim, when you gave him the paperwork, "You've got the *touch*, Rob." But you never reg-istered yourself, that was the thing, and the longer you waited, the more ashamed of this you got. Then it was too late. Even Sasha, who knows all your secrets, has no idea that you never cast a vote for Bill Clinton.

Drew leans over and gives Sasha a wet kiss, and you can tell the hash is getting him horny because you feel it too—it makes your teeth ache in a way that will only let up if you hit someone or get hit. In high school you'd get in fights when you felt like this, but no one will fight with you now—the fact that you hacked open your wrists with a box cutter three months ago and nearly bled to death seems to be a deterrent. It functions like a force field, para-lyzing everyone in range with an encouraging smile on their lips. You want to hold up a mirror and ask, How exactly are those smiles supposed to help me?

"No one smokes hash and becomes president, Drew," you say. "It'll never happen."

"This is my period of youthful experimentation," he says, with a sincerity that would be laughable in a person who wasn't from Wis-consin. "Besides," he says, "who's going to tell them?

"I am," you say.

"I love you too, Rob," Drew says, laughing.

Who said I loved you? you almost ask.

Drew lifts Sasha's hair and twists it into a rope. He kisses the skin under her jaw. You stand up, seething. Bix and Lizzie's apart-ment is tiny, like a dollhouse, full of plants and the smell of plants (wet and planty), because Lizzie loves plants. The walls are cov-ered with Bix's collection of Last Judgment posters—naked, baby-

ish humans getting separated into good and bad, the good ones
rising into green fields and golden light, the bad ones vanishing into mouths of monsters. The window is wide open, and
you climb onto the fire escape. The March cold crackles your si-
nuses.

Sasha climbs out on the fire escape a second later. "What are you
doing?" she asks.

"Don't know," you say. "Fresh air." You wonder how long you can
go on speaking in two-word sentences. "Nice day."

Across East Seventh Street, two old ladies have folded bath towels on their windowsills and are resting their elbows on them while
they peer down at the street below. "Look there," you say, pointing.
"Two spies."

"It makes me nervous, Bobby," Sasha says. "You out here." She's
the only one who gets to call you that; you were Bobby until you
were ten, but according to your pop it's a girl's name after that.

"How come?" you say. "Third floor. Broken arm. Or leg. Worst
case."

"Please come in."

"Relax, Sash." You park yourself on the grille steps leading up to
the fourth-floor windows.

"Party migrate out here?" Drew origamis himself through the living room window onto the fire escape and leans over the railing
to look down at the street. From inside, you hear Lizzie answer the
phone—"Hi, Mom!"—trying to fluff the hash out of her voice.
Her parents are visiting from Texas, which means that Bix, who's
black, is spending his nights in the electrical engineering lab where
he's doing his PhD research. Lizzie's parents aren't even staying
with her—they're at a hotel. But if Lizzie is sleeping with a black
man in the same city where her parents are, they will just *know.*

Lizzie pokes her torso out the window. She's wearing a tiny blue
skirt and tan patent leather boots that go up higher than her knees.
To herself, she's already a costume designer.

"How's the bigot?" you ask, realizing with chagrin that the sentence has three words.

Lizzie turns to you, startled. "Are you referring to my mother?"

"Not me."

"You can't talk that way in my apartment, Rob," she says, using
the Calm Voice they've all been using since you got back, a voice

that leaves you no choice but to see how hard you have to push before it cracks.

"I'm not." You indicate the fire escape.

"Or on my fire escape."

"Not yours," you correct her. "Bix's too. Actually, no. The city's."

"Fuck you, Rob," Lizzie says.

"You too," you say, grinning with satisfaction at the sight of real anger on a human face. It's been a while.

"Calm down," Sasha tells Lizzie.

"Excuse me? I should calm down?" Lizzie says. "He's being a total asshole. Ever since he got back."

"He's been back two weeks," Sasha says. "That's not very long."

"I love how they talk about me like I'm not here," you observe to Drew. "Do they think I'm dead?"

"They think you're stoned."

"They're correct."

"Me too." Drew climbs the fire escape until he's a few steps above you and perches there. He takes a long breath, savoring it, and you take one too. In Wisconsin, Drew has shot an elk with a bow and arrow, skinned it, cut off the meat into sections, and carried it home in a backpack, wearing snowshoes. Or maybe he was kidding. He and his brothers built a log cabin with their bare hands. He grew up next to a lake, and every morning, even in winter, Drew swam there. Now he swims in the NYU pool, but the chlorine hurts his eyes and it's not the same, he says, with a ceiling over you. Still, he swims there a lot, especially when he's troubled or stressed or in a fight with Sasha. "You must've grown up swimming," he said when he first heard you were from Florida, and you said, Of course. But the truth is you've never liked the water—something only Sasha knows about you.

You lurch from the steps to the other end of the fire escape platform, where a window looks into the little alcove where Bix's computer lives. Bix is in front of it, dreadlocks thick as cigars, typing messages to other graduate students that they'll read on their computers, and reading messages they send back. According to Bix, this computer-message-sending is going to be *huge*—bigger than the telephone. He's big on predicting the future, and you haven't really challenged him—maybe because he's older, maybe because he's black.

Bix jumps at the sight of you looming outside his window in your baggy jeans and football jersey, which you've taken to wearing again, for some reason. "Shit, Rob," he says, "what are you doing out there?"

"Watching you."

"You've got Lizzie all stressed out."

"I'm sorry."

"So get in here and tell her that."

You climb in through Bix's window. There's a Last Judgment poster hanging right over his desk, from the Albi Cathedral. You remember it from your Intro to Art History class last year, a class you loved so much you added art history to your business major. You wonder if Bix is religious.

In the living room Sasha and Lizzie are sitting on the futon couch, looking grim. Drew is still out on the fire escape. "I'm sorry," you tell Lizzie.

"It's okay," she says, and you know you should leave it there—it's fine, leave it alone, but some crazy engine inside you won't let you stop: "I'm sorry your mom is a bigot. I'm sorry Bix has to have a girlfriend from Texas. I'm sorry I'm an asshole. I'm sorry I make you nervous because I tried to kill myself. I'm sorry to get in the way of your nice afternoon . . ." Your throat tightens up and your eyes get wet as you watch their faces go from stony to sad, and it's all kind of moving and sweet except that you're not completely there—a part of you is a few feet away, or above, thinking, Good, they'll forgive you, they won't desert you, and the question is, which one is really "you," the one saying and doing whatever it is, or the one watching?

You leave Bix and Lizzie's with Sasha and Drew and head west, toward Washington Square. The cold spasms in the scars on your wrists. Sasha and Drew are a braid of elbows and shoulders and pockets, which presumably keeps them warmer than you. When you were back in Tampa, recovering, they took a Greyhound to Washington, D.C., for the inauguration and stayed up all night and watched the sun rise over the Mall, at which point (they both say) they felt the world start to change right under their feet. You snickered when Sasha told you this, but ever since, you find yourself watching strangers' faces on the street and wondering if they feel it too; a change having to do with Bill Clinton or something even bigger that's everywhere—in the air, underground—obvious to everyone but you.

At Washington Square you and Sasha say goodbye to Drew, who peels off to take a swim and wash the hash from his head. Sasha's wearing her backpack, heading for the library.

"Thank God," you say. "He's gone." You can't seem to *stop* talking in two-word sentences now, even though you'd like to.

"Nice," Sasha remarks.

"I'm kidding. He's great."

"I know."

Your high is wearing off, leaving a box of lint where your head should be. Getting high is new for you—your *not* getting high was the whole reason Sasha picked you out the first day of classes last year, in Washington Square. Blocking your sun with her henna-red hair, smart, quick eyes looking at you from the side rather than head-on. "I'm in need of a fake boyfriend," she said. "Are you up for it?"

"How about your real one?" you said.

She sat down beside you and laid things out: in high school, back in L.A., she'd run away with the drummer for a band you'd never heard of, left the country and traveled alone in Europe and Asia—never even graduated. Now, a freshman, she was almost twenty-one. Her stepfather had pulled every string to get her in here. Last week he'd told her he was hiring a detective to make sure she "toed the line" on her own in New York. "Someone could be watching me right now," she said, looking across the square, crowded with kids who all seemed to know each other. "I feel like someone is."

"Should I put my arm around you?"

"Please."

You've heard somewhere that the act of smiling makes people feel happier; putting your arm around Sasha made you want to protect her. "Why me?" you asked. "Out of curiosity."

"You're cute," she said. "Plus, you don't look druggy."

"I'm a football player," you said. "Was."

You and Sasha had books to buy; you bought them together. You visited her dorm, where you caught Lizzie, her roommate, mugging approval when your back was turned. At five thirty you were both loading your cafeteria trays, you going heavy on the spinach because everyone says football muscle turns to Jell-O when you stop playing. You both got your library cards, went back to your dorms, then met at the Apple for drinks at eight o'clock. It was packed with students. Sasha kept glancing around, and you figured she was thinking about the detective, so you put your arm around her and kissed the side of her face and her hair, which had a nice burned smell, the not-realness of it all relaxing you in a way you'd never managed to be with girls at home. At which point Sasha explained Step Two: each of you had to tell the other something that would make it impossible for you ever to really go out.

"Have you done this before?" you asked, incredulous.

She'd drunk two white wines (which you'd matched two-to-one with beers) and was starting on her third. "Of course not."

"So . . . I tell you I used to torture kitty cats, and that stops you from wanting to jump my bones?"

"Did you?"

"Fuck, no."

"I'll go first," Sasha said.

She'd started shoplifting at thirteen with her girlfriends, hiding beaded combs and sparkly earrings inside their sleeves, seeing who could get away with more, but it was different for Sasha—it made her whole body glow. Later, at school, she'd replay every step of what had happened, counting the days until they could do it again. The other girls were nervous, competitive, and Sasha struggled to show only that much.

In Naples, when she ran out of money, she stole things from stores and sold them to Lars the Swede, waiting her turn on his kitchen floor with other hungry kids holding tourists' wallets, costume jewelry, American passports. They grumbled about Lars, who never gave them what they deserved. He'd played the flute in concerts back in Sweden, supposedly, but the source of that rumor might have been Lars himself. They weren't allowed beyond his kitchen, but someone had glimpsed a piano through a closing door, and Sasha often heard a baby crying. Her first time, Lars made Sasha wait longer than anyone, holding a pair of spangly platform shoes she'd taken from a boutique. And when everyone else was paid and gone, he had squatted beside her on the kitchen floor and unbuttoned his pants.

For months she'd done business with Lars, arriving sometimes without having managed to take anything, just needing money. "I thought he was my boyfriend," she said. "But I think I wasn't thinking anymore." She was better now, hadn't stolen anything in two years. "That wasn't me, in Naples," she told you, looking out at the room. "I don't know who it was. I feel sorry for her."

And maybe from a sense that she'd dared you, or that anything at all could be said in the chamber of truth where you and Sasha now found yourselves, or that she'd blown out a vacuum some law of physics required that you fill, you told her about James, your teammate: how one night, the two of you took out two girls in your pop's car, and after you'd brought them home (early—it was a game night), you and James drove to a secluded place and spent maybe an hour alone in the car. It happened just that one time, without discussion or agreement; the two of you had barely spoken after that. At times you'd wondered if you'd made it up.

"I'm not a fag," you told Sasha.

It wasn't you in the car with James. You were somewhere else, looking down, thinking, That fag is fooling around with another guy. How can he do that? How can he want it? How can he live with himself?

In the library, Sasha spends two hours typing a paper on Mozart's early life and sneaking sips of a Diet Coke. Being older, she feels behind—she's taking six courses a semester plus summer school so she can graduate in three years. She's a business/arts double major, like you, but in music. You rest your head in your arms on the table and sleep until she's done. Then you walk together through the dark to your dorm, on Third Avenue. You smell popcorn from the elevator—sure enough, all three suitemates are home, along with Pilar, a girl you quasi-dated last fall to distract yourself after Sasha paired off with Drew. The minute you walk in, the Nirvana volume drops and the windows fly open. You now seem to be in the same category as a professor or a cop: you make people instantly nervous. There's got to be a way to enjoy this.

You follow Sasha into her room. Most students' rooms are like hamster burrows lined with scraps and tufts of home—pillows and stuffed doggies and plug-in pots and furry slippers—but Sasha's room is practically empty; she showed up last year with nothing but

a suitcase. In one corner is a rented harp she's learning to play.
You lie face-up on her bed while she gathers her shower bag and
green kimono and goes out. She comes back quickly (not wanting
to leave you alone, you have a feeling), wearing the kimono, her
head in a towel. You watch from the bed as she shakes out her long
hair and uses a wide-tooth comb to get the snarls out. Then she
slips out of the kimono and starts getting dressed: lacy black bra
and panties, torn jeans, a faded black T-shirt, Doc Martens. Last
year, after Bix and Lizzie got together, you started spending nights
in Sasha's room, sleeping in Lizzie's empty bed, three feet away
from Sasha's. You know the scar on her left ankle from a break that
had to be operated on when it didn't heal right; you know the Big
Dipper of reddish moles around her bellybutton and her mothball
breath when she first wakes up. Everyone assumed you were a couple—it was that deep between you and Sasha. She would cry in her
sleep, and you'd climb in her bed and hold her until her breathing got regular and slow. She felt so light in your arms. You'd fall
asleep holding her and wake up with a hard-on and just lie there,
feeling this body you knew so well, its skin and smells, alongside
your own need to fuck someone, waiting for the two to merge into
one impulse. *Come on, pull this all together and act like someone normal
for a change,* but you were scared to put your lust to the test, not
wanting to ruin it with Sasha if things went wrong. It was the biggest mistake of your life, not fucking Sasha—you saw this with brutal clarity when she fell in love with Drew, and it clobbered you with
such remorse that you thought at first you couldn't survive it. You
might have held on to Sasha and become normal at the same time,
but you didn't even try—you gave up the one chance God threw
your way and now it's too late.

Out in the world, Sasha would grab your hand or throw her arms
around you and kiss you—that was for the detective. He could
be anywhere, watching you toss snowballs in Washington Square,
Sasha jumping onto your back, her fluffy mittens leaving fibers
on your tongue. He was the invisible companion you saluted over
bowls of steamed vegetables at Dojo ("I want him to see me eating healthy food," she said). Occasionally you raised practical questions about the detective—Had her stepfather mentioned him
again? Did she know for certain it was a man? How long did she
think the surveillance would last?—but this line of thinking

seemed to irritate Sasha, so you let it go. "I want him to know I'm happy," she said. "I want him to see me well again—how I'm still normal, even after everything." And you wanted that too.

When she met Drew, Sasha forgot about the detective. Drew is detective-proof. Even her stepfather likes him.

It's after ten by the time you and Sasha meet up with Drew on Third Avenue and St. Marks Street. His eyes are bloodshot from swimming, his hair is wet. He kisses Sasha like they've been apart for a week. "My older woman," he calls her sometimes, and loves the fact that she's been on her own in the wider world. Of course, Drew knows nothing about how bad things got for Sasha in Naples, and lately you have the feeling she's starting to forget, begin over again as the person she is to Drew. This makes you sick with envy; why couldn't you do that for Sasha? Who's going to do it for you?

On East Seventh you pass Bix and Lizzie's, but the lights are off—Lizzie is out with her parents. The streets are full of people, most of whom seem to be laughing, and you wonder again about that change Sasha felt when the sun rose in Washington, D.C.— whether these people feel it too, and their laughter is connected to that.

On Avenue A, the three of you stand outside the Pyramid Club, listening. "Still the second band," Sasha says, so you walk up the street for egg creams at the Russian newsstand and drink them on a bench in Tompkins Square Park, which just reopened last summer.

"Look," you say, opening your hand. Three yellow pills. Sasha sighs; she's running out of patience.

"What are they?" Drew asks.

"E."

He has an optimist's attraction to everything new—a faith that it will enrich him, not hurt him. Lately you've found yourself using this quality in Drew, scattering breadcrumbs for him one by one. "I want to do it with *you*," he tells Sasha, but she shakes her head. "I missed your druggie moment," he says wistfully.

"Thank God," Sasha says.

You pop one of the pills and put the other two back in your pocket. You start to feel the E as soon as you enter the club. The Pyramid is jammed. The Conduits have been big on college cam-

puses for years, but Sasha is convinced their new album is total genius and will go multiplatinum. She likes to get right up against the
stage, the band in her face, but you need more distance. Drew stays
close to Sasha, but when the Conduits' nutcase of a lead guitarist,
Bosco, starts flinging himself around like a berserk scarecrow, you
notice him edging back.

You've entered a state of tingling, stomachy happiness that feels
the way you hoped adulthood would be as a kid: a blur of lost bear-
ings, release from the drone of meals and homework and church
and That's not a nice way to talk to your sister, Robert Junior. You
wanted a brother. You want Drew to be your brother. Then you
could have built the log cabin together and slept inside it, snow pil-
ing up outside the windows. You could have slaughtered the elk,
and afterward, slick with blood and fur, peeled off your clothes together beside a bonfire. If you could see Drew naked, even just
once, it would ease a deep, awful pressure inside you.

Bosco is getting tossed over your head, his shirt gone, skinny
torso slimed with beer and sweat. Your hands slip over the flinty
muscles of his back. He's still playing his guitar, hollering without a
microphone. Drew spots you and moves closer, shaking his head.
He'd never been to a concert before he met Sasha. You shimmy
one of the remaining yellow pills from your pocket and push it into
his hand.

Something was funny a while ago, but you can't remember what.
Drew doesn't seem to know either, although you're both convulsed
with helpless hysterics.

Sasha thought you would wait for her inside after the show, so it
takes her a while to find the two of you out on the pavement.
Her eyes move between you in the acid streetlight. "Ah," she says.
"I get it."

"Don't be mad," Drew says. He's trying not to look at you—if
you look at each other, you're gone. But you can't stop looking at
Drew.

"I'm not mad," Sasha says. "I'm bored." The Conduits' producer,
Bennie Salazar, has invited her to a party. "I thought we could all
go," she tells Drew, "but you're too high."

"He doesn't want to go with you," you bellow, your nose running
with laughter and snot. "He wants to come with me."

"That's true," Drew says.

"Fine," Sasha says angrily. "Then everyone's happy."

The two of you reel away from her. Hilarity keeps you busy for several blocks, but there's a sickness to it, like an itch that, if you keep on scratching, will grind straight through skin and muscle and bone, shredding your heart. At one point you both have to stop walking and sit on a stoop, leaning against each other, half sobbing. You buy a gallon of orange juice and guzzle it with Drew on a corner, juice gushing over both your chins and soaking your puffy jackets. You hold the carton upside down above your mouth, catching the last drops in the back of your throat. When you toss it away, the city rises darkly around you. You're on Second Street and Avenue B. People are exchanging little vials in their handshakes. But Drew stretches out his arms, feeling the E in his fingertips. You've never seen him afraid; only curious.

"I feel bad," you say, "about Sasha."

"Don't worry," Drew says. "She'll forgive us."

After your wrists had been stitched and bandaged and someone else's blood had been pumped inside you and your parents were waiting at the Tampa Airport for the first flight out, Sasha pushed aside the IV coils and climbed into your bed at St. Vincent's. Even through the painkillers, there was a thudding ache around your wrists.

"Bobby?" she whispered. Her face was almost touching yours. She was breathing your breath and you were breathing hers, malty from fear and lack of sleep. It was Sasha who found you. Ten more minutes, they said.

"Bobby, listen to me."

You opened your eyes and Sasha's green eyes were right up against them, your lashes interlocking. "In Naples," she said, "there were kids who were just lost. You knew they were never going to get back to what they'd been, or have a normal life. And then there were other ones who you thought, maybe they will."

You tried to ask which kind Lars the Swede was, but it came out a mush.

"Listen," she said. "Bobby. In a minute, they're going to kick me out."

You opened your eyes, which you hadn't realized were shut. "What I'm saying is, *We're the survivors*," Sasha said.

She spoke in a way that briefly cleared your head of the sweet cloudy things they were pumping inside you: like she'd opened an envelope and read a result that you urgently needed to know. Like you'd been caught offside and had to be straightened out.

"Not everyone is. But we are. Okay?"

"Okay."

She lay alongside you, every part of you touching, like you'd done so many nights before she met Drew. You felt Sasha's strength seeping into your skin. You tried to hold her, but your hands were stuffed-animal stumps, and you couldn't move them.

"Which means you can't do that again," she said. "Ever. Ever. Ever. Ever. Do you promise me, Bobby?"

"I promise." And you meant it. You wouldn't break a promise to Sasha.

"Bix!" Drew shouts. He charges up Avenue B, boots clobbering the pavement. Bix is alone, hands in the pockets of his green army jacket.

"Whoa," he says, laughing when he sees from Drew's eyes how high he is. Your own high is just beginning to teeter. You've been planning to take that last pill, but you offer it to Bix instead.

"I don't really do this anymore," Bix says, "but rules are for bending, right?" A custodian made him leave the lab; he's been walking around for two hours.

"And Lizzie's asleep," you say, "in your apartment."

Bix gives you a cold look that empties your good mood. "Let's not get started on that."

You walk together, waiting for Bix to come onto the E. It's after two A.M., the hour when (it turns out) normal people go home to bed, and drunk, crazy, fucked-up people stay out. You don't want to be with those people. You want to go back to your suite and knock on Sasha's door, which she leaves unlocked when Drew isn't spending the night.

"Earth to Rob," Bix says. His face is soft and his eyes are shiny and bewitched.

"I was thinking I might go home," you say.

"You can't!" Bix cries. Love for his fellow creatures pulses from within him like an aura; you can feel its glow on your skin. "You're central to the action."

"Right," you mutter.

Drew slings his arm around you. He smells like Wisconsin—woods, fires, ponds—although you've never been near it. "Truth, Rob," he says, serious. "You're our aching, pounding heart."

You wind up at an after-hours club Bix knows about on Ludlow, crowded with people too high to go home. You all dance together, subdividing the space between now and tomorrow until time seems to move backward. You share a strong joint with a girl whose bangs are very short, leaving her bright forehead exposed. She dances near you, her arms around your neck, and Drew shouts in your ear over the music, "She wants to go home with you, Rob." But eventually the girl gives up, or forgets—or you forget—and she disappears.

The sky is just getting light when the three of you leave the club. You walk north together to Leshko's, on Avenue A, for scrambled eggs and piles of fried potatoes, then stagger, stuffed, back onto the groggy street. Bix is between you and Drew, one arm around each of you. Fire escapes dangle off the sides of buildings. A croupy church bell starts up, and you remember: it's Sunday.

Someone seems to be leading the way toward the Sixth Street overpass to the East River, but really you're all moving in tandem, like on a Ouija board. The sun blazes into view, spinning bright and metallic against your eyeballs, ionizing the water's surface so you can't see a bit of pollution or crud underneath. It looks mystical, biblical. It raises a lump in your throat.

Bix squeezes your shoulder. "Gentlemen," he says, "good morning."

You stand together at the river's edge, looking out, the last patches of old snow piled at your feet. "Look at that beautiful water," Drew says. "I wish I could swim in it." After a minute he says, "Let's remember this day, even when we don't know each other anymore."

You look over at Drew, squinting in the sun, and for a second the future tunnels away, some version of "you" at the end of it, looking back. And right then you feel it—what you've seen in people's faces on the street—a swell of movement, like an undertow, rushing you toward something you can't quite see.

"We'll know each other forever," Bix says. "The days of losing touch are almost gone."

"What does that mean?" Drew asks.

"We're going to meet again in a different space," Bix says. "Everyone we've lost, we'll find. Or they'll find us."

"Where? How?" Drew asks.

Bix hesitates, like he's held this secret so long he's afraid of what will happen when he releases it into the air. "I picture it like Judgment Day," he says finally, his eyes on the water. "We'll rise up out of our bodies and find each other again in spirit form. We'll meet in that new place, all of us together, and first it'll seem strange, and pretty soon it'll seem strange that you could ever lose someone, or get lost."

Bix knows, you think—he's always known, in front of that computer, and now he's passing the knowledge on. But what you say is, "Will you finally get to meet Lizzie's parents?"

The surprise lands cleanly in Bix's face, and he laughs, a big, billowing noise. "I don't know, Rob," he says, shaking his head. "Maybe not—maybe that part will never change. But I like to think so." He rubs his eyes, which look suddenly tired, and says, "Speaking of which. Time to head back home."

He walks away, hands in the pockets of his army jacket, but it's a while before it feels like he's really gone. You pull your last joint from your wallet and smoke it with Drew, walking south. The river is quiet, no boats in sight, a couple of toothless geezers fishing under the Williamsburg Bridge.

"Drew," you say.

He's looking at the water with that stoned distraction that makes anything seem worth studying. You laugh, nervous, and he turns. "What?"

"I wish we could live in that cabin. You and me."

"What cabin?"

"The one you built. In Wisconsin." You see confusion in Drew's face, and you add, "If there is a cabin."

"Of course there's a cabin."

Your high granulates the air, then Drew's face, which reconstitutes with a new wariness in it that frightens you. "I would miss Sasha," he says slowly. "Wouldn't you?"

"You don't really know her," you say, breathless, a little desperate. "You don't know who you'd be missing."

A massive storage hangar has intervened between the path and the river, and you walk alongside it. "What don't I know about Sasha?" Drew asks in his usual friendly tone, but it's different—you sense him already turning away, and you start to panic.

"She was a hooker," you say. "A hooker and a thief—that's how she survived in Naples."

As you speak these words, a howling starts up in your ears. Drew stops walking. You're sure he's going to hit you, and you wait for it.

"That's insane," he says. "And fuck you for saying it."

"Ask her," you shout, to be heard above the howling. "Ask about Lars the Swede who used to play the flute."

Drew starts walking again, his head down. You walk beside him, your steps narrating your panic: *What have you done? What have you done? What have you done? What have you done?* The FDR is over your heads, tires roaring, gasoline in your lungs.

Drew stops again. He looks at you through the dim, oily air as if he's never seen you before. "Wow, Rob," he says. "You are really and truly an asshole."

"You're the last to know."

"Not me. Sasha."

He turns and walks quickly away, leaving you alone. You charge after him, seized by a wild conviction that containing Drew will seal off the damage you've done. *She doesn't know,* you tell yourself, *she still doesn't know. As long as Drew is in sight, she doesn't know.*

You stalk him along the river's edge, maybe twenty feet between you, half running to keep up. He turns once: "Go away! I don't want to be near you!" but you sense his confusion about where to go, what to do, and it reassures you somehow. *Nothing has happened yet.*

Between the Manhattan and Brooklyn Bridges, Drew stops beside what might be called a beach. It's made entirely out of garbage: old tires, trash, splintered wood and glass and filthy paper and old plastic bags tapering gradually into the East River. Drew stands on this rubble, looking out, and you wait a few feet behind him. Then he begins to undress. You don't believe it's happening at first; off comes his jacket, his sweater, his two T-shirts and undershirt. And there is Drew's bare torso, strong and tight as you'd imagined, though thinner, the dark hair on his chest in the shape of a spade.

In jeans and boots, Drew picks his way to where garbage and water meet. An angular slab of concrete juts out, the failed foundation of something long forgotten, and he scrambles on top of it.
He unlaces his boots and removes them, then kicks off his jeans
and boxers. Even through your dread, you feel a faint appreciation
for the beauty and inelegance of a man undressing.

He glances back at you, and you glimpse his naked front, the
dark pubic hair and strong legs. "I've always wanted to do this," he
says in a flat voice, and takes a long, leaping, shallow dive, slamming the East River's surface and letting out something between a
scream and a gasp. He surfaces, and you hear him trying to catch
his breath. It can't be more than forty-five degrees out.

You climb the slab of concrete and start taking off clothes, sodden with dread but moved by a flickering sense that if you can master this dread it will mean something, prove something about you.
Your scars twang in the cold. Your dick has shriveled to the size
of a walnut and your football bulk is starting to slide, but Drew
isn't even watching you. He's swimming: strong, clear swimmer's
strokes.

You make a clumsy leap, your body crashing onto the water, your
knee hitting something hard under the surface. The cold locks in
around you, knocking out your breath. You swim crazily to get away
from the garbage, which you picture underneath, rusty hooks and
claws reaching up to slash your genitals and feet. Your knee aches
from whatever it hit.

You lift up your head and see Drew floating on his back. "We can
get back out of here, right?" you yell.

"Yes, Rob," he answers in that new, flat voice. "Same way we
got in."

You don't say anything else. It takes all your strength to tread
water and yank in breath. Eventually, without your noticing, the
cold begins to feel almost tropically warm against your skin. The
shrieking in your ears subsides, and you can breathe again. You
look around, startled by the mythic beauty of what surrounds you:
Water encircling an island. A distant tugboat jutting out its rubbery lip. The Statue of Liberty. A thunder of wheels on the Brooklyn Bridge, which looks like the inside of a harp. Church bells, meandering and off-key, like the chimes your mother hangs on the
porch. You're moving fast, and when you look for Drew you can't

find him at first. The shore is far away. A person is swimming near it, but at such a distance that when the swimmer pauses, waving frantic arms, you can't see who it is. You hear a faint shout— *"Rob!"*—and realize you've been hearing that voice for a while. Panic scissors through you, bringing crystalline engagement with physical facts: you're caught in a current—there are currents in this river—you knew that—heard it somewhere and forgot—you shout, but feel the smallness of your voice, the seismic indifference of the water around you—all this in an instant.

"Help! Drew!"

As you flail, knowing you're not supposed to panic—panicking will drain your strength—your mind pulls away as it does so easily, so often, without your even noticing sometimes, leaving Robert Freeman Junior to manage the current alone while you withdraw to the broader landscape, the water and buildings and streets, the avenues like endless hallways, your dorm full of sleeping students, the air thick with their communal breath. You slip through Sasha's open window, floating over the sill lined with artifacts from her travels: a white seashell, a small gold pagoda, a pair of red dice. Her harp in one corner with its small wood stool. She's asleep in her narrow bed, her burned red hair dark against the sheets. You kneel beside her, breathing the familiar smell of Sasha's sleep, whispering into her ear some mix of *I'm sorry* and *I believe in you* and *I'll always be near you, protecting you,* and *I will never leave you, I'll be curled around your heart for the rest of your life,* until the water pressing my shoulders and chest crushes me awake and I hear Sasha screaming into my face: Fight! Fight! Fight!

NATHAN ENGLANDER

Free Fruit for Young Widows

FROM *The New Yorker*

WHEN THE EGYPTIAN PRESIDENT Gamal Abdel Nasser took control of the Suez Canal, threatening Western access to that vital route, an agitated France shifted allegiances, joining forces with Britain and Israel against Egypt. This is a fact neither here nor there, except that during the 1956 Sinai Campaign there were soldiers in the Israeli Army and soldiers in the Egyptian Army who ended up wearing identical French-supplied uniforms to battle.

Not long into the fighting, an Israeli platoon came to rest at a captured Egyptian camp to the east of Bir Gafgafa, in the Sinai Desert. There Private Shimmy Gezer (formerly Shimon Bibberblat, of Warsaw, Poland) sat down to eat at a makeshift outdoor mess. Four armed commandos sat down with him. He grunted. They grunted. Shimmy dug into his lunch.

A squad mate of Shimmy's came over to join them. Professor Tendler (who was then only Private Tendler, not yet a professor, and not yet even in possession of a high school degree) placed the tin cup that he was carrying on the edge of the table, taking care not to spill his tea. Then he took up his gun and shot each of the commandos in the head.

They fell quite neatly. The first two, who had been facing Professor Tendler, tipped back off the bench into the sand. The second pair, who had their backs to the professor and were still staring open-mouthed at their dead friends, fell face down, the sound of their skulls hitting the table somehow more violent than the report of the gun.

Shocked by the murder of four fellow soldiers, Shimmy Gezer

tackled his friend. To Professor Tendler, who was much bigger than Shimmy, the attack was more startling than threatening. Tendler grabbed hold of Shimmy's hands while screaming, "Egyptians! Egyptians!" in Hebrew. He was using the same word about the same people in the same desert that had been used thousands of years before. The main difference, if the old stories are to be believed, was that God no longer raised his own fist in the fight.

Professor Tendler quickly managed to contain Shimmy in a bear hug. "Egyptian commandos—confused," Tendler said, switching to Yiddish. "The enemy. The enemy joined you for lunch."

Shimmy listened. Shimmy calmed down.

Professor Tendler, thinking the matter was settled, let Shimmy go. As soon as he did, Shimmy swung wildly. He continued attacking, because who cared who those four men were? They were people. They were human beings who had sat down at the wrong table for lunch. They were dead people who had not had to die.

"You could have taken them prisoner," Shimmy yelled. "Halt!" he screamed in German. "That's all—halt!" Then, with tears streaming and fists flying, Shimmy said, "You didn't have to shoot."

By then Professor Tendler had had enough. He proceeded to beat Shimmy Gezer. He didn't just defend himself. He didn't subdue his friend. He flipped Shimmy over, straddled his body, and pounded it down until it was level with the sand. He beat his friend until his friend couldn't take any more beating, and then he beat him some more. Finally he climbed off his friend, looked up into the hot sun, and pushed through the crowd of soldiers who had assembled in the minutes since the Egyptians sat down to their fate. Tendler went off to have a smoke.

For those who had come running at the sound of gunfire to find five bodies in the sand, it was the consensus that a pummeled Shimmy Gezer looked to be in the worst condition of the bunch.

At the fruit-and-vegetable stand that Shimmy Gezer eventually opened in Jerusalem's Mahane Yehuda Market, his son, little Etgar, asked about the story of Professor Tendler again and again. From the time he was six, Etgar had worked the *duchan* at his father's side whenever he wasn't in school. At that age, knowing only a child's version of the story—that Tendler had done something in

one of the wars that upset Etgar's father, and Etgar's father had
jumped on the man, and the man had (his father never hesitated
to admit) beat him up very badly—Etgar couldn't understand why
his father was so nice to the professor now. Reared, as he was, on
the laws of the small family business, Etgar couldn't grasp why he
was forbidden to accept a single lira from Tendler. The professor
got his vegetables free.

After Etgar weighed the tomatoes and the cucumbers, his father
would take up the bag, stick in a nice fat eggplant, unasked, and
pass it over to Professor Tendler.

"Kach," his father would say. "Take it. And wish your wife well."

As Etgar turned nine and ten and eleven, the story began to fill
out. He was told about the commandos and the uniforms, about
shipping routes and the Suez, and the Americans and the British and the French. He learned about the shots to the head. He
learned about all the wars his father had fought in—'73, '67, '56,
'48—though Shimmy Gezer still stopped short of the one he'd
first been swept up in, the war that ran from 1939 to 1945.

Etgar's father explained the hazy morality of combat, the split-
second decisions, the assessment of threat and response, the nature of percentages and absolutes. Shimmy did his best to make
clear to his son that Israelis—in their nation of unfinished borders
and unwritten constitution—were trapped in a gray space that was
called real life.

In this gray space, he explained, even absolutes could maintain
more than one position, reflect more than one truth. "You too,"
he said to his son, "may someday face a decision such as Professor Tendler's—may you never know from it." He pointed at the
bloody stall across from theirs, pointed at a fish below the mallet,
flopping on the block. "God forbid you should have to live with the
consequences of decisions, permanent, eternal, that will chase you
in your head, turning from this side to that, tossing between wrong
and right."

But Etgar still couldn't comprehend how his father saw the story
to be that of a fish flip-flopping, when it was, in his eyes, only ever
about that mallet coming down.

Etgar wasn't one for the gray. He was a tiny, thoughtful, buck-
toothed boy of certainties. And every Friday when Tendler came by

the stand, Etgar would pack up the man's produce and then run through the story again, searching for black-and-white.

This man had saved his father's life, but maybe he hadn't. He'd done what was necessary, but maybe he could have done it another way. And even if the basic schoolyard rule applied in adult life—that a beating delivered earns a beating in return—did it ever justify one as fierce as the beating his father had described? A pummeling so severe that Shimmy, while telling the story, would run Etgar's fingers along his left cheek, to show him where Professor Tendler had flattened the bone.

Even if the violence had been justified, even if his father didn't always say, "You must risk your friend's life, your family's, your own, you must be willing to die—even to save the life of your enemy—if ever, of two deeds, the humane one may be done," it was not his father's act of forgiveness but his kindness that baffled Etgar. ·

Shimmy would send him running across Agrippas Street to bring back two cups of coffee or two glasses of tea to welcome Professor Tendler, telling Etgar to snatch a good-sized handful of pistachios from Eizenberg's cart along the way. This treatment his father reserved only for his oldest friends.

And absolutely no one but the war widows got their produce free. Quietly and with dignity, so as to cause these women no shame, Etgar's father would send them off with fresh fruit and big bags of vegetables, sometimes for years after their losses. He always took care of the young widows. When they protested, he'd say, "You sacrifice, I sacrifice. All in all, what's a bag of apples?"

"It's all for one country," he'd say.

When it came to Professor Tendler, so clear an answer never came.

When Etgar was twelve, his father acknowledged the complexities of Tendler's tale.

"Do you want to know why I can care for a man who once beat me? Because to a story there is context. There is always context in life."

"That's it?" Etgar asked.

"That's it."

At thirteen, he was told a different story. Because at thirteen Etgar was a man.

"You know I was in the war," Shimmy said to his son. The way he said it Etgar knew that he didn't mean '48 or '56, '67 or '73. He did not mean the Jewish wars, in all of which he had fought. He meant the big one. The war that no one in his family but Shimmy had survived, which was also the case for Etgar's mother. This was why they had taken a new name, Shimmy explained. In the whole world, the Gezers were three.

"Yes," Etgar said. "I know."

"Professor Tendler was also in that war," Shimmy said.

"Yes," Etgar said.

"It was hard on him," Shimmy said. "And that is why, why I am always nice."

Etgar thought. Etgar spoke.

"But you were there too. You've had the same life as him. And you'd never have shot four men, even the enemy, if you could have taken them prisoner, if you could have spared a life. Even if you were in danger, you'd risk—" Etgar's father smiled, and stopped him.

"*Kodem kol,*" he said, "a similar life is not a same life. There is a difference." Here Shimmy's face turned serious, the lightness gone. "In that first war, in that big war, I was the lucky one," he said. "In the Shoah, I survived."

"But he's here," Etgar said. "He survived, just the same as you."

"No," Etgar's father said. "He made it through the camps. He walks, he breathes, and he was very close to making it out of Europe alive. But they killed him. After the war, we still lost people. They killed what was left of him in the end."

For the first time, without Professor Tendler there, without one of Shimmy's friends from the ghetto who stopped by to talk in Yiddish, without one of the soldier buddies from his unit in the reserves, or one of the kibbutzniks from whom he bought his fruits and his vegetables, Etgar's father sent Etgar across Agrippas Street to get two glasses of tea. One for Etgar and one for him.

"Hurry," Shimmy said, sending Etgar off with a slap on his behind. Before Etgar had taken a step, his father grabbed his collar and popped open the register, handing him a brand-new ten-shekel bill. "And buy us a nice big bag of seeds from Eizenberg. Tell him to keep the change. You and I, we are going to sit awhile."

Shimmy took out the second folding chair from behind the register. It would also be the first time that father and son had ever sat down in the store together. Another rule of good business: a customer should always find you standing. Always there's something you can be doing—sweeping, stacking, polishing apples. The customers will come to a place where there is pride.

This is why Professor Tendler got his tomatoes free, why the sight of the man who beat Shimmy made his gaze go soft with kindness in the way that it did when one of the *miskenot* came by—why it took on what Etgar called his father's free-fruit-for-young-widows eyes. This is the story that Shimmy told Etgar when he felt that his boy was a man:

The first thing Professor Tendler saw when his death camp was liberated was two big, tough American soldiers fainting dead away. The pair (presumably war-hardened) stood before the immense, heretofore unimaginable brutality of modern extermination, frozen, slack-jawed before a mountain of putrid, naked corpses, a hill of men.

And from this pile of broken bodies that had been—prior to the American invasion—set to be burned, a rickety skeletal Tendler stared back. Professor Tendler stared and studied, and when he was sure that those soldiers were not Nazi soldiers he crawled out from his hiding place among the corpses, pushing and shoving those balsa-wood arms and legs aside.

It was this hill of bodies that had protected Tendler day after day. The poor Sonderkommandos who dumped the bodies, as well as those who came to cart them to the ovens, knew that the boy was inside. They brought him the crumbs of their crumbs to keep him going. And though it was certain death for these prisoners to protect him, it allowed them a sliver of humanity in their inhuman jobs. This was what Shimmy was trying to explain to his son—that these palest shadows of kindness were enough to keep a dead man alive.

When Tendler finally got to his feet, straightening his body out, when the corpse that was Professor Tendler at age thirteen—"your age"—came crawling from that nightmare, he looked at the two Yankee soldiers, who looked at him and then hit the ground with a thud.

Professor Tendler had already seen so much in life that this was not worth even a pause, and so he walked on. He walked on naked through the gates of the camp, walked on until he got some food and some clothes, walked on until he had shoes and then a coat. He walked on until he had a little bread and a potato in his pocket—a surplus.

Soon there was also in that pocket a cigarette and then a second; a coin and then a second. Surviving in this way, Tendler walked across borders until he was able to stand straight and tall, until he showed up in his childhood town in a matching suit of clothes, with a few bills in his pocket and, in his waistband, a six-shooter with five bullets chambered, in order to protect himself during the nights that he slept by the side of the road.

Professor Tendler was expecting no surprises, no reunions. He'd seen his mother killed in front of him, his father, his three sisters, his grandparents, and, after some months in the camp, the two boys that he knew from back home.

But home—that was the thing he held on to. Maybe his house was still there, and his bed. Maybe the cow was still giving milk, and the goats still chewing garbage, and his dog still barking at the chickens as before. And maybe his other family—the nurse at whose breast he had become strong (before weakened), her husband who had farmed his father's field, and their son (his age), and another (two years younger), boys with whom he had played like a brother—maybe this family was still there waiting. Waiting for him to come home.

Tendler could make a new family in that house. He could call every child he might one day have by his dead loved ones' names.

The town looked as it had when he'd left. The streets were his streets, the linden trees in the square taller but laid out as before. And when Tendler turned down the dirt road that led to his gate, he fought to keep himself from running, and he fought to keep himself from crying, because, after what he had seen, he knew that to survive in this world he must always act like a man.

So Tendler buttoned his coat and walked quietly toward the fence, wishing that he had a hat to take off as he passed through the gate—just the way the man of the house would when coming home to what was his.

But when he saw her in the yard—when he saw Fanushka his nurse, their maid—the tears came anyway. Tendler popped a precious button from his coat as he ran to her and threw himself into her arms, and he cried for the first time since the trains.

With her husband at her side, Fanushka said to him, "Welcome home, son," and "Welcome home, child," and "We prayed," "We lit candles," "We dreamed of your return."

When they asked, "Are your parents also coming? Are your sisters and your grandparents far behind?," when they asked after all the old neighbors, house by house, Tendler answered, not by metaphor, and not by insinuation. When he knew the fate, he stated it as it was: beaten or starved, shot, cut in half, the front of the head caved in. All this he related without feeling — matters, each, of fact. All this he shared before venturing a step through his front door.

Looking through that open door, Tendler decided that he would live with these people as family until he had a family of his own. He would grow old in this house. Free to be free, he would gate himself up again. But it would be his gate, his lock, his world.

A hand on his hand pulled him from his reverie. It was Fanushka talking, a sad smile on her face. "Time to fatten you up," she said. "A feast for first dinner." And she grabbed the chicken at her feet and twisted its neck right there in the yard. "Come in," she said, while the animal twitched. "The master of the house has returned."

"Just as you left it," she said. "Only a few of our things."

Tendler stepped inside.

It was exactly as he remembered it: the table, the chairs, except that all that was personal was gone.

Fanushka's two sons came in, and Tendler understood what time had done. These boys, fed and housed, warmed and loved, were fully twice his size. He felt, then, something he had never known in the camps, a civilized emotion that would have served no use. Tendler felt ashamed. He turned red, clenched his jaw tight, and felt his gums bleeding into his mouth.

"You have to understand," Etgar's father said to his son. "These boys, his brothers, they were now twice his size and strangers to him."

The boys, prodded, shook hands with Tendler. They did not know him anymore.

"Still, it is a nice story," Etgar said. "Sad. But also happy. He makes it home to a home. It's what you always say. Survival, that's what matters. Surviving to start again."

Etgar's father held up a sunflower seed, thinking about this. He cracked it between his front teeth.

"So they are all making a dinner for Professor Tendler," he said. "And he is sitting on the kitchen floor, legs crossed, as he did when he was a boy, and he is watching. Watching happily, drinking a glass of goat's milk, still warm. And then the father goes out to slaughter that goat. 'A feast for dinner,' he says. 'A chicken's not enough.' Professor Tendler, who has not had meat in years, looks at him, and the father, running a nail along his knife, says, 'I remember the kosher way.'"

Tendler was so happy that he could not bear it. So happy and so sad. And, with the cup of warm milk and the warm feeling, Tendler had to pee. But he didn't want to move now that he was there with his other mother and, resting on her shoulder, a baby sister. A year and a half old and one curl on the head. A little girl, fat and happy. Fat in the ankle, fat in the wrist.

Professor Tendler rushed out at the last second, out of the warm kitchen, out from under his roof. Professor Tendler, a man whom other men had tried to turn into an animal, did not race to the outhouse. It didn't cross his mind. He stood right under the kitchen window to smell the kitchen smells, to stay close. And he took a piss. Over the sound of the stream, he heard his nurse lamenting.

He knew what she must be lamenting — the Tendler family destroyed.

He listened to what she was saying. And he heard.

"He will take everything," is what she said. "He will take it all from us — our house, our field. He'll snatch away all we've built and protected, everything that has been — for so long — ours."

There outside the window, pissing and listening, and also "disassociating," as Professor Tendler would call it (though he did not then have the word), he knew only that he was watching himself from above, that he could see himself feeling all the disappointment as he felt it, until he was keenly and wildly aware that he had felt nothing all those years, felt nothing when his father and mother were shot, felt nothing while in the camps, nothing, in fact, from the moment he was driven from his home to the moment he returned.

In that instant, Tendler's guilt was sharper than any sensation he had ever known.

And here, in response to his precocious son, Shimmy said, "Yes, yes, of course it was about survival—Tendler's way of coping. Of course he'd been feeling all along." But Tendler—a boy who had stepped over his mother's body and kept walking—had, for those peasants, opened up.

It was right then, Professor Tendler later told Shimmy, that he became a philosopher.

"He will steal it all away," Fanushka said. "Everything. He has come for our lives."

And her son, whom Tendler had considered a brother, said, "No." And Tendler's other almost-brother said, "No."

"We will eat," Fanushka said. "We will celebrate. And when he sleeps we will kill him." To one of the sons she said, "Go. Tell your father to keep that knife sharp." To the other she said, "You get to sleep early, and you get up early, and before you grab the first tit on that cow I want his throat slit. Ours. Ours, not to be taken away."

Tendler ran. Not toward the street but back toward the outhouse in time to turn around as the kitchen door flew open, in time to smile at the younger brother on his way to find his father, in time for Tendler to be heading back the right way.

"Do you want to hear what was shared at such a dinner?" Shimmy asked his son. "The memories roused and oaths sworn? There was wine, I know. 'Drink, drink,' the mother said. There was the chicken and a pot of goat stew. And, in a time of great deprivation, there was also sugar for the tea." At this, Shimmy pointed at the bounty of their stand. "And, as if nothing, next to the baby's basket on the kitchen floor sat a basket of apples. Tendler hadn't had an apple in who knows how long."

Tendler brought the basket to the table. The family laughed as he peeled the apples with a knife, first eating the peels, then the flesh, and savoring even the seeds and the cores. It was a celebration, a joyous night. So much so that Professor Tendler could not by its end, belly distended, eyes crossed with drink, believe what he knew to have been said.

There were hugs and there were kisses, and Tendler—the master of the house—was given his parents' bedroom upstairs, the two boys across the hall, and below, in the kitchen ("It will be warmest"), slept the mother and the father and the fat-ankled girl.

"Sleep well," Fanushka said. "Welcome home, my son." And, sweetly, she kissed Tendler on both eyes.

Tendler climbed the stairs. He took off his suit and went to bed. And that was where he was when Fanushka popped through the door and asked him if he was warm enough, if he needed a lamp by which to read.

"No, thank you," he said.

"So formal? No thanks necessary," Fanushka said. "Only 'Yes, Mother,' or 'No, Mother,' my poor reclaimed orphan son."

"No light, Mother," Tendler said, and Fanushka closed the door.

Tendler got out of bed. He put on his suit. Once again without any shame to his actions, Tendler searched the room for anything of value, robbing his own home.

Then he waited. He waited until the house had settled into itself, the last creak slipping from the floorboards as the walls pushed back against the wind. He waited until his mother, his Fanushka, must surely sleep, until a brother intent on staying up for the night—a brother who had never once fought for his life—convinced himself that it would be all right to close his eyes.

Tendler waited until he too had to sleep, and that's when he tied the laces of his shoes together and hung them over his shoulder. That's when he took his pillow with one hand and, with the other, quietly cocked his gun.

Then, with goose feathers flying, Tendler moved through the house. A bullet for each brother, one for the father and one for the mother. Tendler fired until he found himself standing in the warmth of the kitchen, one bullet left to protect him on the nights when he would sleep by the side of the road.

That last bullet Tendler left in the fat baby girl, because he did not know from mercy, and did not need to leave another of that family to grow to kill him at some future time.

"He murdered them," Etgar said. "A murderer."

"No," his father told him. "There was no such notion at the time."

"Even so, it is murder," Etgar said.

"If it is, then it's only fair. They killed him first. It was his right."

"But you always say—"

"Context."

"But the baby. The girl."

"The baby is hardest, I admit. But these are questions for the philosopher. These are the theoretical instances put into flesh and blood."

"But it's not a question. These people, they are not the ones who murdered his family."

"They were coming for him that night."

"He could have escaped. He could have run for the gate when he overheard. He didn't need to race back toward the outhouse, race to face the brother as he came the other way."

"Maybe there was no more running in him. Anyway, do you understand 'an eye for an eye'? Can you imagine a broader meaning of *self-defense?*"

"You always forgive him," Etgar said. "You suffered the same things—but you aren't that way. You would not have done what he did."

"It is hard to know what a person would and wouldn't do in any specific instance. And you, spoiled child, apply the rules of civilization to a boy who had seen only its opposite. Maybe the fault for those deaths lies in a system designed for the killing of Tendlers that failed to do its job. An error, a slip that allowed a Tendler, no longer fit, back loose in the world."

"Is that what you think?"

"It's what I ask. And I ask you, my Etgar, what you would have done if you were Tendler that night?"

"Not kill."

"Then you die."

"Only the grownups."

"But it was a boy who was sent to cut Tendler's throat."

"How about killing only those who would do harm?"

"Still it's murder. Still it is killing people who have yet to act, murdering them in their sleep."

"I guess," Etgar said. "I can see how they deserved it, the four. How I might, if I were him, have killed them."

Shimmy shook his head, looking sad.

"And whoever are we, my son, to decide who should die?"

It was on that day that Etgar Gezer became a philosopher himself. Not in the manner of Professor Tendler, who taught theories up at the university on the mountain, but, like his father, practical and concrete. Etgar would not finish high school or go to college, and except for his three years in the army, he would spend his life—happily—working the stand in the *shuk*. He'd stack the fruit into pyramids and contemplate weighty questions with a seriousness of thought. And when there were answers Etgar would try employing them to make for himself and others, in whatever small way, a better life.

It was on that day too that Etgar decided Professor Tendler was both a murderer and, at the same time, a *misken*. He believed he understood how and why Professor Tendler had come to kill that peasant family, and how men sent to battle in uniform—even in the same uniform—would find no mercy at his hand. Etgar also came to see how Tendler's story could just as easily have ended for the professor that first night, back in his parents' room, in his parents' bed, a gun with four bullets held in a suicide's hand—how the first bullet Tendler ever fired might have been into his own head.

Still, every Friday Etgar packed up Tendler's fruit and vegetables. And in that bag Etgar would add, when he had them, a pineapple or a few fat mangos dripping honey. Handing it to Tendler, Etgar would say, "*Kach*, Professor. Take it." This, even after his father had died.

ALLEGRA GOODMAN

La Vita Nuova

FROM *The New Yorker*

THE DAY HER FIANCÉ LEFT, Amanda went walking in the Colonial cemetery off Garden Street. The gravestones were so worn
that she could hardly read them. They were melting away into the
weedy grass. You are a very dark person, her fiancé had said.

She walked home and sat in her half-empty closet. Her vintage
1950s wedding dress hung in clear asphyxiating plastic printed
"NOT A TOY."

She took the dress to work. She hooked the hanger onto a grab
bar on the T and the dress rustled and swayed. When she got out
at Harvard Square, the guy who played guitar near the turnstiles
called, "Congratulations."

Work was at the Garden School, where Amanda taught art, including theater, puppets, storytelling, drumming, dance, and now
fabric painting. She spread the white satin gown on the art-room
floor. Two girls glued pink feathers all along the hem. Others
brushed the skirt with green and purple. A boy named Nathaniel
dipped his hand in red paint and left his little handprint on the
bodice as though the dress were an Indian pony. At lunchtime, the
principal asked Amanda to step into her office.

You are like living with a dark cloud, Amanda's fiancé had told
her when he left. You're always sad.

I'm sad now, Amanda had said.

The principal told Amanda that for an educator, boundaries
were an issue. "Your personal life," said the principal, "is not an appropriate art project for first grade. Your classroom," said the principal, "is not an appropriate forum for your relationships. Let's
pack up the wedding dress."

"It's still wet," Amanda said.

Her mother could not believe it. She had just sent out all the invitations. Her father swore he'd kill the son of a bitch. They both asked how this could have happened, but they remembered that they had had doubts all along. Her sister, Lissa, said she could not imagine what Amanda was going through. She must feel so terrible. Was Amanda going to have to write to everyone on the guest list? Like a card or something? She'd have to tell everybody, wouldn't she?

I waited all this time because I didn't want to hurt you, Amanda's fiancé had said.

After school, she went for a drink with the old blond gym teacher, Patsy. They went to a bar called Cambridge Common and ordered gin and tonics. Patsy said, "Eventually you're going to realize that this is a blessing in disguise."

"We had too many differences," said Amanda.

Patsy lifted her glass. "There you go."

"For example, I loved him and he didn't love me."

"Don't be surprised," said Patsy, "if he immediately marries someone else. Guys like that immediately marry someone else."

"Why?" Amanda asked.

Patsy sighed. "If I knew that, I'd be teaching at Harvard, not teaching the professors' kids."

Amanda tried writing a card or something. She wrote that she and her fiancé had decided not to marry. Then she wrote that her fiancé had decided not to marry her. She said that she was sorry for any inconvenience. She added that she would appreciate gifts anyway.

Her parents told her not to send the card. They said that they were coming up for a week. She said that they couldn't come, because she was painting her apartment. She did not paint the apartment.

In the winter, Amanda cut her hair short like a boy's.

"Oh, your hair," said Patsy. "Your beautiful curls."

In the spring, the principal told Amanda that, regretfully, she was not being renewed for the following year, because the art program at the Garden School was moving in a different direction.

In the summer, Amanda's fiancé married someone else.

*

When school ended, Amanda took a job babysitting Nathaniel, the boy with the red handprint. Nathaniel's mother asked for stimulating activities, projects, science. No TV. Nathaniel's father didn't ask for anything.

Their first day together, Amanda asked Nathaniel, "What do you want to do?"

"Nothing."

She said, "You read my mind."

They ate chocolate mice at Burdick's and then they stood in front of the Harvard Coop and listened to Peruvian musicians. They explored the cemetery, and Amanda told Nathaniel that the gravestones were dragons' teeth. They walked down to the river and she said, "If you trace the river all the way to the beginning, you'll find a magic cave." They took the T to Boston and stood in line for the swan boats in the Public Garden. She said, "At night, these boats turn into real swans."

Nathaniel said, "You have a great imagination."

His mother lived in a Victorian house on Buckingham Street. She worked at the Media Lab at MIT and she had deadlines. The house had a garden full of flowers, but Nathaniel didn't play there, because you couldn't really dig.

His father lived in an upside-down town house on Chauncy Street. The bedrooms were on the bottom floors, and the kitchen and living room on top. His father was writing a book and he came home late.

Amanda and Nathaniel had pizza delivered to Chauncy Street and watched Charlie Chaplin movies from Hollywood Express. Sometimes they spread a sheet over the couch and ate a big bowl of popcorn.

It's hard to be with you, her fiancé had said. I feel like I'm suffocating.

Open a window, Amanda had said.

When the movie was done, Amanda gathered the sheet and stepped onto the balcony, where she shook out the crumbs.

Amanda and Nathaniel had play-dates with his friends at Walden Pond. They went canoeing on the Charles, and Nathaniel dropped his paddle in the water. Amanda almost tipped the boat, trying to fish it out. They wrote a book about pirates. Nathaniel told the stories and Amanda typed them on the computer in his father's study. "Aarrr, matey," she typed, "I'm stuck on a ship."

When his father stayed out past Nathaniel's bedtime, Amanda tucked Nathaniel in, and then she read books in the study. The books were about American history. She read only a few pages of each, so she didn't learn anything.

If you ever stopped to listen, her fiancé had said, then you would understand.

She stood on a chair and pulled out some small paperbacks from the top shelf. Dante, *The Divine Comedy*, in a new translation. Boccaccio, *The Decameron*, Chaucer's *Canterbury Tales*, complete and unabridged. Dante again, *La Vita Nuova*.

La Vita Nuova explained how to become a great poet. The secret was to fall in love with a perfect girl but never speak to her. You should weep instead. You should pretend that you love someone else. You should write sonnets in three parts. Your perfect girl should die.

Amanda's mother said, "You have your whole life ahead of you."

She fell asleep on the couch waiting for Nathaniel's father to come home. When she woke up, she saw him kneeling in front of her. She said, "What's wrong?"

He said, "Nothing's wrong. I'm sorry. I didn't want to wake you."

But he did wake her. She went home and stayed awake all night.

"Let's go somewhere," she told Nathaniel the next day.

"Where?"

"Far away."

They took the T to Ashmont, at the end of the Red Line. They sat together in the rattling car and talked about doughnuts.

"I like cinnamon doughnuts, but they make me cough," Nathaniel said.

She slept lightly. She dreamed she was walking with Nathaniel in a pine forest. She was telling him not to step on the dead hummingbirds. The birds were sapphire-throated, brilliant blue. She stole *La Vita Nuova*. It was just a paperback.

Her sister called to check in. Her friend Jamie said she knew someone she'd like Amanda to meet. Amanda said, "Soon."

Jamie said, "What exactly are you waiting for?"

Nathaniel's father pretended not to look at her. Amanda pretended not to notice his dark eyes.

"The question is what you're going to do in September," Amanda's mother told her on the phone.

"The question is what you're going to do with your life," her father said.

Dante wrote, "O you who on the road of Love pass by / Attend and see / If any grief there be as heavy as mine."

"When was the last time you painted anything?" her mother asked. "Apart from your apartment?"

Her father said, "I paid for Yale."

All day Amanda and Nathaniel studied the red ants of Buckingham Street. They experimented with cake crumbs and observed the ants change course to eat them. Nathaniel considered becoming an entomologist when he grew up.

The next day he decided to open his own ice cream store.

They hiked to Christina's, in Inman Square. Nathaniel pedaled in front on his little bike. Amanda pedaled behind on her big bike and watched for cars.

At Christina's, Nathaniel could read almost all the flavors on the board: adzuki bean, black raspberry, burnt sugar, chocolate banana, chocolate orange, cardamom. Nathaniel said, "I'll have vanilla." They sat in front near the bulletin board with ads for guitar lessons, tutoring, transcendental meditation.

"What's an egg donor?" Nathaniel said.

I want to be with you for the rest of my life, her fiancé had told her once. You are my best friend, he had written on her birthday card. You make me smile, you make me laugh. "Love weeps," Dante wrote.

"Could I have a quarter for a gumball?" Nathaniel asked Amanda.

"You just had ice cream," she said.

"Please."

"No! You just had ice cream. You don't need candy."

"Please, please, please," he said.

"You're lovely," Nathaniel's father whispered to Amanda late that night. She was just leaving, and he'd opened the door for her.

"You're not supposed to say that," Amanda whispered back. "You're supposed to write a sonnet."

Nathaniel said that he knew what to do when you were upset. She said, "Tell me, Nathaniel."

He said, "Go to the zoo."

Nathaniel studied the train schedule. They took the Orange

Line to Ruggles Station and then the No. 22 bus to the Franklin Park Zoo. They watched orangutans sitting on their haunches, shredding newspapers, one page at a time. They climbed up on viewing platforms to observe the giraffes. They ran down every path. They looked at snakes. They went to the little barnyard and a goat frightened Nathaniel. Amanda said the goat was just curious. She said, "Goats wouldn't eat you."

Nathaniel fell asleep on the T on the way home. He leaned against Amanda and closed his eyes. The woman sitting next to Amanda said, "He's beautiful."

Amanda's friend Jamie had a party in Somerville. The wine was terrible. The friend that Jamie wanted Amanda to meet was drunk. Amanda got drunk too, but it didn't help.

She was late to work the next day. She found Nathaniel waiting on his mother's porch. "I thought you were sick," he said.

"I was," she told him.

They walked to Harvard Square and watched the street magicians. They went to Le's and shared vegetarian summer rolls and Thai iced tea.

"This tastes like orange chalk," Nathaniel said.

They went to a store called Little Russia and looked at the lacquered dolls there. "See, they come apart," Amanda told Nathaniel. "You pop open this lady, and inside there's another, and another, and another."

"Do not touch, please," the saleslady told them.

They walked down to the river and sat on the grass under a tree and talked about their favorite dogs.

"Labradoodle," Amanda said.

Nathaniel giggled. "No, schnoodle."

"Golden streudel."

Nathaniel said, "Is that the kind you had when you were young?"

She dreamed that she was a Russian doll. Inside her was a smaller version of herself, and inside that an even smaller version.

She ordered a set of blank wooden dolls online and began painting them. She covered the dolls with white primer. Then she painted them with acrylics and her finest brushes.

First, a toddler only an inch high, in a gingham bathing suit.

Second, a fingerling schoolgirl, wearing glasses.

Third, an art student, with a portfolio under her arm.

Fourth, a bride in white with long flowing hair.

Fifth, a babysitter in sandals and sundress. She painted Nathaniel standing in front of her in his gecko T-shirt and blue shorts. He stood waist high, with her painted hands on his shoulders.

When the paint was dry, she covered each doll with clear gloss. After that coat dried, she glossed each doll again until the reds were as bright as candy apples, the blues sparkled, and every color looked good enough to eat.

She bought another set of blanks and began all over. She stayed up late each night painting.

"Why are you so sleepy?" Nathaniel asked her in the afternoons.

In the mornings, his mother asked her, "Why are you always late?"

She fell asleep with Nathaniel at eight o'clock. She curled up next to him in his captain's bed and woke when his father came in and touched her cheek.

"I was wondering if you could come to the Cape with us," Nathaniel's father said as they tiptoed out into the hall.

She shook her head.

"Just for a few days in August."

His voice was low. His eyes were almost pleading. You are so beautiful, her fiancé had said.

She painted Nathaniel's father on a set of Russian dolls.

First, she painted a toddler in a romper.

Second, she painted a boy in a little Catholic school uniform with short pants and a tie.

Third, she painted a bridegroom, dashing in a dark suit with white stephanotis for his boutonnière.

Fourth, she painted a new father, with a baby Nathaniel in his arms.

Fifth, she painted a gray-haired man in reading glasses. She painted Nathaniel's father older than he was, and stouter. Not handsome, as he was in real life, but grandfatherly, with a belly following the contours of the bell-shaped doll.

As before, she coated each painted doll with clear gloss until the colors gleamed. As before, she made each doll a perfect jewel-like object, but she spent the most time on the biggest, oldest doll.

After that, she bought more blanks and painted more sets: people she knew, people she didn't know. People she met. Portraits in series, five dolls each. She painted Patsy, blonder and blonder in each incarnation. She painted her fiancé as a boy, as an athlete, as a law student, as a paunchy bald guy, as a decrepit old man. She didn't kill him, but she aged him.

She lined up the dolls and photographed them. She thought about fellowships. She imagined group shows, solo shows. Refusing interviews.

She took Nathaniel to swimming lessons. She went down to the harbor with him and they threw popcorn to seagulls that caught the kernels in midair.

Nathaniel had his seventh birthday party on Castle Island. He and his friends built a walled city of sandcastles with a moat. Nathaniel was the architect. Amanda was his assistant. His father was the photographer. His mother served the cake.

At the end of the party, Amanda gathered the presents. Nathaniel was leaving for the Cape with his father, and then his mother was going to take him to the Vineyard for Labor Day weekend. Nathaniel said, "When we come back, it will be September."

She said, "You're right."

He said, "Could you come with me?"

Amanda said, "I can't. I'm painting my apartment."

He said, "What color?"

She said, "Actually, I'm moving."

"Moving away?"

She told him, "You can talk to me on the phone."

Nathaniel started to cry.

His mother said, "Honey!"

He held on to Amanda and cried. "Why can't you be my babysitter anymore?"

"I'm going to New York," she said.

"Why?"

Because your mother doesn't like me, she told him silently. Because your father wants to sleep with me. Because the only reason I came to Boston was my fiancé. Because the question is what I'm going to do with my life. But all she said aloud was, "That's where I'm from."

She knelt down and gave him a map she'd drawn. She'd singed the edges of the parchment to make it look old.

The map showed the cave at the source of the Charles River, the swan boats flying away, the chocolate mice at Burdick's. Christina's Ice Cream, Ashmont, the cemetery with dragons' teeth.

Nathaniel's mother said, "This is gorgeous."

Nathaniel's father said, "You're really very talented."

Nathaniel said that he didn't want a map. He said that he would rip it up.

His mother said, "Nathaniel, is that any way to treat a gift?"

His father said, "Come here."

Nathaniel tore a big piece out of the map. He screamed at his parents, "I don't want you!"

"He's tired," Nathaniel's mother told Amanda. "He's exhausted. Too much excitement in one day."

"I'm not tired!" Nathaniel screamed, and he wouldn't let go of Amanda. He held on to her, half strangling her with his arms around her neck.

"Look, Nathaniel—" his father began.

His mother interrupted. "You're making it worse!"

Nathaniel was crying harder. He cried with his whole body. No one could get him to stop.

Amanda closed her eyes. She said she was sorry. She said, "Please stop." Finally, she rocked him in her arms and said, "I know. I know."

EHUD HAVAZELET

Gurov in Manhattan

FROM *TriQuarterly*

ON A JANUARY DAY, a little before nine in the morning, this was
the situation: Sokolov, fifty-two, lecturer in Russian literature at
Lehman College in the Bronx, two years post-transplant for leuke-
mia, stood on Riverside Drive looking north to Canada, while Lermontov, his suffering aged wolfhound, tried with trembling exer-
tions to relieve himself, looking south toward New Orleans. The
day was cold, scrubbed clear, one of the January days in New York
that slice through you and deride your hopes that winter will ever
open its fist. The vet, a young woman with auburn hair braided
and an athlete's bony litheness, the kind who caught Sokolov's eye
(the kind whose eye *he* used to catch — alas, no longer), told him
dogs Lermontov's size were lucky to reach ten, eleven. If, as Sokolov
said, he was thirteen, it was a miracle, and she smiled at the dog
tenderly while Sokolov (she didn't know him) thought sourly that
only the carelessly youthful and naive (the healthy) could have the
gall to think surviving is blessing enough.

It had not snowed in a week and the last storm's remnants were
pocked glacial outcroppings crusted with soot and cigarette ends
and animal droppings (alas again: none Lermontov's). In the trees
along the drive half-a-dozen crows perched without a sound.
Sokolov chanced a quick peek. The dog had an intestinal block-
age, perhaps a tumor, and on top of the diabetes was too old for
surgery. (Thirteen, Sokolov had said. Could be thirty-five for all he
knew. He was Kelly's dog, and Kelly wasn't there to ask, was she?) If
he didn't somehow (more miracles) come through in the next few
days, it wasn't fair to let him suffer. Again, Sokolov stared broadly

at the pretty young face that hadn't more than glanced at his in passing since he hauled the reluctant dog through the office door. Let him suffer, as if she knew, as if anybody knew the tipping point between life's durance and life's ending. Ten years ago this might have been his opening, the moment he'd inject a wry observation, oblique, evocative, European.

This morning he'd simply said, "How many?"

Still looking at the dog (maybe if he set himself on fire . . .), she'd said, "How many what?"

"Days."

Then she did look, as if that fact, the number, and Sokolov's bringing it up, was tactless indeed, and made her unwillingly see him: gruff, bothered, indifferent. (Balding, gaunt, nearing tooth-lessness.) He was past caring what she thought. He'd been given numbers once, a lot of them, none good. He'd wanted to know, and now he assumed Lermontov wanted it also.

"I don't know exactly," the doctor said. "Let's say two."

"Two," Sokolov answered, barely noticing she ignored the witti-cism. He paid at the desk, stopped by the door to give the dog a couple of good whomping pats to the side, the way he liked it, then made the ten-block walk to their corner, where they, Sokolov look-ing one direction, the dog another, waited for what was next.

Time was, Sokolov wanted everything. Now he wanted less. Or, more precisely, this is what Sokolov wanted: to want less. Coming to this country with dreams not all that different from or more re-alistic than the conquistadors' visions of El Dorado, he'd thought that the combination of his past (Leningrad, gray), his education (doctoral thesis: "Response to the Pastoral in Theodore Dreiser," laughingly wrongheaded, unpublished), his genealogy (rabbis, radicals, a thunderous drunk or two), and his, by general report, Slavic handsomeness and insouciant Old World charm ensured he would be welcomed, transformed from the young man with an old man's maladies (melancholy, dyspepsia), free to wander in this big fat orchard America and pluck its ripest fruit.

Two unfinished novels and an incinerated memoir later, a dozen-odd ignored applications to schools out of the city, floored by the hoof of a Cossack horse-kick by cancer, left alive but with tingling blue-edged fingers, toes, riotous bowels, hair not only grayed and thinning but matted like a horsehair blanket, he was an old man with an old man's maladies. And alone. Kelly, after three years, was gone, and Sokolov still couldn't believe how quickly, how briskly, how efficiently this woman he'd lived with had disappeared from his life, leaving only her declining dog as remembrance.

How long would Lermontov take? As pathetic as his silent clenching was, he'd dutifully stand there and try for an hour if Sokolov didn't, with a flick of the leash, release him. Were it warmer, or Lermontov younger, maybe he'd leave him tied to the meter outside the coffee shop, continue his lacerating study of the waitress there, Amity. Chancing another bleak glance, he saw Lermontov motionless, maybe done, but then beginning again the stiffening hopeless crouch, the shakes working from the legs up that indicated he was still—who could blame him?—trying.

How had they met (he, Kelly, the dog)? It was, for once, something actually out of a book. Sokolov on his midafternoon stroll, after what was probably a fruitless morning laboring over an essay, banging his head against the lunacy of American academic prose (thicket of colons, slashed made-up new words, snide allusive jargon of a boys' club), lunch a quick sandwich and black, scalding coffee, he had come out to give his frustrations some air. There on a bench, Kelly reading a thick hardback, long-limbed in red pants, brown sweater, lissome even in silhouette, massed jet-black hair untidily stirruped over a shoulder; Lermontov, younger then, regally bored, looking straight ahead as if nothing he'd seen warranted a turn of the eye, immediately gaining Sokolov's admiration. Bored as the dog, Sokolov figured, What else do I have going today?, and after sitting on the bench's far edge, patting the dog once, twice, ventured, "You know, there's a famous Russian story about two people meeting over a dog."

Kelly took a moment, as if she needed first to finish a sentence in her book, then turned on Sokolov two astonishing brown eyes. "Yes," Kelly said. "But the dog was white, and small. And it didn't turn out too well for the lovers."

He'd not used the term, intentionally. "Didn't it?" Sokolov said, assuming his best devil-may-care, roguish grin.

And that was that. Kelly was finishing a doctoral course at the university, comp lit and women's studies. She was what Sokolov pretended to be but disagreeably knew he really wasn't—anarchic and determined and free of constraint. When they made love she entered into it with such vigorous abandon he wondered if she remembered he was there; the same night she cooked an enormous lamb stew he could still summon the taste of. She had drunk at least as much of three bottles of wine as Sokolov, and by the time she perused his heaped bookshelves and piles of untidy notes with a scholar's proprietary eye, wearing just panties and one of his button-downs, then settling into the easy chair (Sokolov's favorite) with a new translation of Turgenev he'd been meaning to get to, Sokolov was, as they liked to say here, head over heels. When he saw and commented on her studio apartment (shabby, unlit), it seemed only natural for her to pack up and move in with him. It was two months into their relationship, Kelly was already calling him Gurov (he superstitiously desisting from calling her Anna), Sokolov had found a true friend in Lermontov, another refugee cast below his station in life, also not a complainer, and they had lugged her boxes and plants and fancy Scandinavian mattress up in the cramped service elevator. Kelly bought new shower curtains and lined his dusty shelves with paper, a three-foot ficus that immediately began the business of dying in the thin airshaft light, and they started: three years of life, desultory happiness maybe, a restiveness almost welcome for the torrential manner in which Kelly would respond to it. Conferences (hers: San Francisco, Montreal; his: Camden, Baltimore), a wild trip through the Adirondacks (this was early) drinking chilled vodka from the bottle and listening to Chaliapin on Sokolov's old tapes, eight days in Key West unconvincingly joining the resident vacationers who gathered at the pier each night to pay homage to the sunset, drinking too much at Hemingway's bar, talking to everyone (this was later) but each other, waking with pounding headaches and the brittle realization they were sullen, disconsolate, exhausted.

So? Tolstoy had hated no one as much as his wife and they stayed together. Chekhov, based on geographical evidence, enjoyed his actress wife more through the mail than in the house. Who, in his right mind, expected everything?

Sokolov, apparently.

Then the illness, life slamming its lid on him, and Kelly, who had perhaps considered many experiences would come to her at twenty-eight, but caring for a terrified middle-aged Russian who clung to her harder the more his terror rose, was certainly not one of them. Yes, Sokolov was no model patient. Yes, he tolerated the sunny prattle of the nurses with ill-concealed impatience. Yes, he raged, yes, cursed and wept, yes when the drugs wrecked his stomach and the radiation stripped his mouth and tongue bare he allowed himself great waves of pity and remorse and yes yes yes he behaved nothing like what he would have written for himself (if he still wrote): not the moody doomed poetry of Pushkin but the frantic unmanned panic of the clerk in Gogol's story, which Sokolov had always dismissed as sentimental, a febrile hallucination until one day he found himself living it.

Kelly had stayed. He would not forget. Stayed through the treatments and the endless doctors' visits, the biopsies and tests, the nights on morphine when Sokolov dreamed a landscape of tiny men burrowing with axes in his brain, the fevers and chills, when, had he the strength, he would have wished to die. Kelly had stayed.

So then? When for the fourth six-month interval his biopsies were clear, when she had asked every possible responsible question of the doctors and nurses and pharmacists and social workers, after an uncharacteristically quiet (relaxed, Sokolov, idiot, had thought) dinner, she announced she had accepted a position at a women's college in Virginia, and would be leaving, now Sokolov was all right.

All right?

Floored, flummoxed (he had again drunk too much wine and his ruined innards were letting him know what they thought about it), Sokolov searched for his old poise like a man fumbling through a closet in the dark. What of the Chekhov story? Didn't she remember? Gurov, Anna, the hard part? What if they had survived that, the hard part? What if now would be easy?

But Kelly was a student of literature, a better one, Sokolov knew, than he, and she looked at him in pain and weary apology but unshaken in the knowledge of what he knew as well—Chekhov hadn't written this story—and when he had returned from answering his intestines' calamitous summons, she had a suitcase out and the ficus (grandson to the first, also deceased) was poking spindly branches at Sokolov from the trash bin where Kelly had tossed it.

A shift in the breeze scooped even colder air from the river as a rich man in a camelhair coat talked into a phone and followed two galumphing bassets across 108th. They paused by Lermontov, who,

after a halfhearted sniff, ignored them, and the man, who kept telling somebody on the phone, "That's not what I said. I never said
anything like that," was hauled on his leashes past Sokolov up the
drive. The crows, now as if struggling to stay awake, flapped a wing
or shifted position in the branches. Lermontov and his owner regarded each other a wordless moment, then Sokolov, not bother-
ing to examine his motives, turned himself and the dog toward
Broadway and the odd pleasurable torment of contemplation and
regret that awaited him daily at the coffee shop.

Amity was her name (it would have to be), she'd been there six
weeks (four since Kelly had traveled south), midtwenties, briskly
attractive, blond, toned (she rode a bike to work, even in this
weather), with lit blue eyes that stopped Sokolov in his tracks every
time. What would it be to have those eyes look at you?
    A forensic sociologist, self-appointed, Sokolov (failed writer) had
made a study of the issue. What alchemical burst in the cortex,
what detonation of the synapses, what pheremonal heaving in
every nerve and muscle, was set off by beauty? Made the male animal tense with opportunity, recognition before awareness, led just
by instinct's unwavering dowser? What symmetry of feature or ca-
dence of glance and response, what shimmer of illuminata in a
passing eye, would become suddenly Beatrice, Helen, your Tatyana
or Anna or Dolores Haze? What, in your hollow, dried-up reced-
ing, made you feel, suddenly, alive?
    A turning point in his reckonings had come when he first saw
the girl. She was on break, at the counter on the rotating stools,
reading a paper. Sokolov was paying his bill—coffee, soup, a hard
roll—when he saw her and something wheeling in him froze. Amity (he'd learn her name the next day), the loose disregarded hair,
the perfect chin and shoulder, then the blue eyes suggesting behind them an empyrean, spring, eternity, joy. He stood there like
a gawker at a country fair and she eventually looked up, took him
in in a second, and returned to page six. Nothing had cut him so
deeply in years: Sokolov, Old World conqueror, who had held the
gaze of every woman in his novels class, who had wooed dozens just
by a line from Herzen or a pose struck thoughtfully looking out a
window, who had slept with half the humanities faculty at Lehman,
knew all at once age, irrelevance, invisibility. And standing there
with a five-dollar bill in his hand, for the first time since the terrify-

ing clap of mortality when the doctor pronounced the diagnosis, felt the brush of the dark angel's wing on his neck.

And since, he had returned daily to verify the sensation, rage, and concede and quietly wonder at the many ways we pass into insubstantiality. An old fool in love.

Lermontov, who in his nimble youth would bound at traffic, particularly cabs, as if their presence in his street were outrageous, now stood on the west side of the avenue, looking back uncertainly at Sokolov. Just a quick cup of coffee, Sokolov assured him, then for you a big bowl of soup. North on the avenue the light was dimmer, a gray haze suggesting more snow. Not quite dragging the dog, Sokolov made it across the street, bent to tie the aggrieved animal to the parking meter in front of Tom's, assured him with a pat and a word or two, turned to go inside.

And there she was, Amity, talking with another waitress through the smeared half-steamed window, at the counter, maybe five feet from where Sokolov and his dog stood watching. It was like watching a scene from a movie, Lubitsch, maybe. She was crying, or had been, and the other waitress, a broad-backed matron who must have been here when La Guardia came looking for free pie, had her arm on Amity, gently rubbing the muscled back of her black leotard. And then it happened. Sokolov, who for weeks had been wanting nothing more than a look of interest, of open feeling, of vulnerability from this young woman, got it. Through the window she locked eyes with him, and the look she gave was of such fresh youthful misery that it was Sokolov, voyeur emeritus, who turned away.

As the movie shifted scenes, his visions, one by one, drifted toward him and disappeared: Amity turning her head when he finally found the right thing to say, about to laugh; Amity on his couch, cradling a big glass of wine; Amity in his bed, flushed, exhausted, satisfied, Borodin on the stereo, or, if she was another Kelly, Shostakovich. Amity. Such an odd enclosed crystalline word. He knew nothing about her.

It was much easier getting the dog back across Broadway. Maybe he had heard Sokolov's telepathic offer of soup. Maybe he just wanted to get out of the cold. Passing the bank and the falafel stand and the cut-rate sundries shop, Sokolov felt himself relent, slipped into a quiet sadness of relief and withdrawal, of repudiation. He remembered the moment in the Chekhov where Gurov, having gotten what he wanted from Anna, pauses to eat a watermelon on the table. "There followed at least a half-hour of silence," the story read.

Sokolov's teachers had seen this as further proof of Gurov's heartlessness: done with his conquest, why not a fortifying snack? But this reading never sat quite right with Sokolov, who was sounder in his doubts than in his disorganized assertions regarding them. Was it possible Gurov, knowing only the buoyant pulse of seduction, had here first actually seen the woman whose life he was about to change? And his own, internally shifting from snatched, temporary, disposable affection to something else — deeper, permanent, at so much greater cost?

This is what swept through Sokolov's head as he followed Lermontov — the old dog suddenly moving fast, nearly racing — past the sleepy doormen and people rushing toward the subway. What had he to offer this girl, this stranger? He remembered no poetry. He could give her no advice about whoever had made her cry (at least it wasn't Sokolov). Face it, old man, he told himself, reflecting on his once ever-spry organ, now a flabby curled-up pasha who would, since the chemo, never again see reason to stir himself. When Sokolov closed his eyes at night, trilobites swam in the darkness before him. What had he to offer? Nothing: let her live her life. And an image of Kelly, on a campus someplace warmer, carrying books from the library — Kelly too.

At their corner Sokolov, ready for a nap, moved toward the stairs, but Lermontov pulled him back to the soiled bank of snow. Why not? Sokolov scanned the branches, but the crows that had seemed immovable earlier now were gone. East somewhere, over Garden City, Mineola, the sun, angled low, broke a moment through the clouds, and Sokolov saw his shadow and the crouching dog's stretched westward into the street, then vanish when the sun again drew back. Lermontov, with what might be pride, or relief, or happy fatigue, stood before a small cluster of curled brown turds. Sokolov found the plastic bag in his pocket, cleaned up, gave the dog a solid pat, another, looked back at Broadway a moment, over at the river and New Jersey, then followed the straining dog up the broad cement stairs toward their apartment and the promised bowl of soup.

CAITLIN HORROCKS

The Sleep

FROM *The Atlantic Fiction for Kindle*

THE SNOW CAME EARLY that first year, and so heavy that when Albert Rasmussen invited the whole town over, we had to park around the corner from his unplowed street. We staggered through the drifts, across the lawns, down the neat sidewalks where a few of Al's neighbors owned snowblowers. Mr. Kajaamaki and the Lutven boys were still out huffing and puffing with shovels. We waved as we passed, and they nodded.

Al stood that November in his family room, arms outstretched, knee-deep in a nest of mattresses and bedding: flannels and florals mixed with Bobby Rasmussen's NASCAR pillowcases, Dee's Disney-princess comforter. The sideboard had a hot plate and an electric kettle plugged into a power strip. Al opened drawers filled with crackers, tinned soup, bags of pink-frosted animal cookies, vitamin C pills and canned juice to prevent scurvy. "Hibernation," he announced. "Human hibernation."

This was before the cameras, before the sleep, before the outsiders, and the plan sounded as strange to us then as it would to anybody. Our town had always wintered the way towns do: gas bills and window plastic, blankets and boots. We bought cream for our cracked skin and socks for our numb feet. We knew how we felt when our extremities faded temporarily away, and we knew how much we hurt when they prickled back to life.

Al showed off a heater he'd built that ran on used grease, and the filter that sieved out the hash browns and hamburger. Al had always been handy. He'd been the smartest kid in school, back when Bounty still had its own high school. He was the senior everyone called "college material" until he decided to stay, and then we called him "ours." Our Albert, Albert and his girl Jeannie, who were confident that everything they could want in the world was right here in Bounty. We went to their wedding, the Saturday after graduation, and then stood by, helpless, when Albert's parents lost the farm three years later. Maybe the family should have gotten out then, moved away and never looked back. Al might have found a job that paid better than fence repair, and Jeannie might not have been killed by Reggie Lapham, seventeen years old and driving drunk on Highway 51 eight months before Al's November invitation. Al might never have struck on hibernation, and we might all have gone along the way we'd been going, for better or worse.

But they had stayed, and Jeannie had died, and Reggie had been sent to a juvenile detention facility downstate. The accident happened in early spring, when patches of snow were still dissolving on the roads, and what no one would say within Al's earshot was that the weather had killed her as much as Reggie had. Al needed something small enough to blame, and Reggie, skinny as a weed and driving his father's truck, served as well as anything could. Al had always seemed older than he was, had transitioned easily from high school basketball star to assistant coach. Now, in his thirties, he looked twenty years older, bent and exhausted. We wondered if the weight on his shoulders was truly Jeannie, or if he'd been carrying, for more years than we'd realized, some piece of Bounty, and he'd invited us over to make sure we understood that he was putting it down.

We'd all stayed in Bounty the way Al had stayed, had carried it as best we could. When our high school shut down, we sent our children to the next town over, then to the county consolidated when that one closed too. They came home with their textbooks about westward expansion, about the gold rush, the tin rush, the copper rush, the wheat farms, the corn farms, the feedlots. About land that gave until it couldn't give, and the chumps who kept trying to live on it. Our children came home and told us that we were the suckers of the last century.

"But what if you love it here?" we asked them. "What if you don't want to leave?"

"What's to love?" our children asked, in surly disbelief: What kind of morons hustle for jobs that don't even pay for cable television? What kind of people spend twenty years buying beer at the Hop-In and drinking in the quarry, the next thirty drinking at the Pointes, the last sodden ten at the Elks Lodge?

Our kind of people, we thought.

"Sleep," Al said, there in his living room, and explained how in the old days in Russia people sacked out around a stove when the snows came, waking to munch a piece of rye bread, feed the fire, slump back into sleep. Only so much food could be laid in, and the thinking went that unless a man could come up with something to do in the cold and the dark that justified the calories he'd expend doing it, he was better off doing nothing. The Russians would wake up skinny and hungry, but they'd wake up alive.

We worried that maybe the Rasmussens were harder up than we had thought. Times were tough for everybody, but others weren't shutting down their houses and lives and planning to warm their kids with burger grease. "What do we do all winter?" Al asked, the kind of question we knew he considered rhetorical. "Why work like dogs all summer to keep the television on, the furnace cranked, noodles on the stove? Why scrape off the car to burn fuel to go to the store to buy more noodles? That's pointless."

Mrs. Pekola, of Pekola Downtown Antiques, opened her mouth for a moment, as if she were going to point out that that routine wasn't much different from plenty of people's autumns and springs and maybe summers, in which case Al was saying that we might as well all blow our brains out and have done with it. But she stayed silent, probably because she thought of many things we didn't need to hear.

"What about Christmas?" Mrs. Drausmann, the librarian, offered.

"We're staying awake for it. Just doing a two-month trial run this year, January and February," Al explained.

"School," Bill and Valeer Simmons said. "Your kids."

Al shrugged. Both his kids were bright and ahead of their classes. At seven, Dee read at a sixth-grade level. Bobby was nine and the best speller at Bounty Elementary. Al had picked up copies of the upcoming curriculum: long division, suffixes, photosynthesis, cursive.

"We're having a sleepover instead," Dee said.

"You know what Mrs. Fiske has planned for February? Fractions!"

Bobby yelled, and the kids bopped around the room until Al chased them upstairs.

"They'll get caught up in spring," Al said. "I don't think they'll have difficulty."

He looked around at us, his old compatriots, the parents of the handful of children still enrolled at the school, and apologized. "I didn't mean anything by that," he said. "I don't think they're special. But they probably won't miss much."

We nodded. Being the children of a dying town had taught us that none of us was special. Whatever our various talents, we'd all ended up here, in the Rasmussens' family room.

"Don't try to convince me anything worthwhile happens in this town during January and February. I've lived here as long as you have," Al said. We could tell he meant to joke, but nobody laughed. "I'm not crazy. NASA studies this stuff. They're planning for astronauts to hibernate through long voyages. So they don't go stir-crazy and kill each other, bust out the shuttle walls." Al's fingers twitched a bit, and we looked at his walls: scuffed beige paint, three china plates with pictures of Holsteins, a family portrait taken at the JCPenney in Bullhorn when Jeannie was still alive, and a single round hole at the height of a man's fist, sloppily covered with paint and plaster. His walls looked a lot like our walls, and all of a sudden we were tempted to jam our fists in and pull them down.

"You think we're like that?" Nils Andersen asked from the back of the crowd, all the way in the front foyer, and people parted to let him come closer. He'd been a point guard to Al's shooting guard on the old high school basketball team. The two still sometimes took practice shots into the hoop on Al's garage.

"Like what?"

"Russians and astronauts. You think we've got two options, asleep or dead?"

Al started to shake his head, because we're not a town that likes to offend. Then he paused, ran his big hands through his hair, and let them drop to his sides. Fair and broad and tall, like his parents and grandparents and Norwegian great-grandparents, like a lot of the rest of us, he looked suddenly large and unwieldy. As if he could only ever fit in this little room curled up asleep, and we'd all been crazy to hope otherwise. He hunched his shoulders and looked down at the floor. "Maybe," he said. "This is about my family. I never meant any of you had to be involved. But maybe."

We'd thought our town's silence had been stoic; we glimpsed now how much we simply hadn't wanted to say. We rustled in the blankets but kept our mouths shut, put on our shoes, and drifted out into the snow. Some of us drove straight home. Others took longer routes down Main Street, past First Lutheran, the Pointes, the Elks Lodge, Mrs. Pekola's antiques store, the single-screen movie theater with the marquee still announcing CLOSED, as if the closing were news. The public library was housed in the old pharmacy; we checked out our books at the prescriptions counter and bought our prescriptions thirty miles down the road. We looked at all the shuttered stores and tried to remember what each one had sold.

We cruised back and forth like bored teenagers on Saturday nights, watching the road run quickly from empty storefronts to clapboard frame houses and tiny brick ranches. We turned around at the Hop-In at the west end of town, near the park with its silent gray bandstand. We drove east until we passed the elementary school and empty high school, then turned into the parking lot of the old farm supply store, the beams of its collapsed roof poking skyward and its windows like eyes. Bounty had never been a pretty town, but we'd tried to be proud of it. Now we examined it carefully, looking for new reasons to stay awake. One by one we gave up, peeled off, and drove home. We turned into our shoveled driveways in the tiny grid of residential streets, or took spokes of blacktop and gravel out to scattered farmhouses in little islands of yard, their old acreage spreading behind them like a taunt. Bounty was an assertion, an act of faith. It looked best left unexamined.

A few of us met back at the Pointes that night for beer and darts. The hours went by, but no one said a thing about Al Rasmussen, and we were all waiting for it. "Fucking *grease*," Nils finally said. "Like fucking *Russians*." We were able to laugh then and walk out to the parking lot, slapping each other's backs and leaving trails of footprints in the snow. We felt better about ourselves, sitting side by side in our idling cars, waiting for the engines to warm.

On New Year's Day, the Rasmussens made neighborhood rounds, dropping off house keys and perishables: a gallon of milk and some apples for the Lutven boys, carrots for Valeer Simmons, a bag of shredded cheese and half a loaf of bread for Mr. Kajaamaki. We wished them luck and hung the keys on pegs.

We could have robbed them blind while they slept, but we knew they didn't have anything worth taking. We tiptoed in ones and twos to watch the family sleep, to see how this hibernation thing was working out. The kids looked peaceful. The food disappeared in barely perceptible increments. The room was stuffy by late February, smelling of night sweat and canned soup, but the Rasmussens didn't seem to mind. Mrs. Pekola lit a lavender-scented candle on the sideboard and found it blown out the next day. All in all, they looked cozy.

In March the children woke first, bounding out the front door in their pajamas. Spring hadn't really started yet; dirty snow was still melting into mud. But the fiercest part of winter was over. Al looked rested for the first time since Jeannie's death, the terrible tension gone from his shoulders. His body looked more like that of the man most of us had known for years, but his eyes looked like a stranger's. No one could place the expression, except those of us whose children or grandchildren had left Bounty, gone off for college or work. When the children came back, we said, their eyes looked like that, like departure. *Imagine*, we thought: *Albert had found that look in his sleep.*

He asked for all the updates. A blizzard in early February had blown the roof off the old hardware store. Mr. Fiske had had a heart attack one morning in the barn with his livestock. One of the grain elevator operators had died of cirrhosis, and half the town had applied for his job. The youngest Suarez boy had tried to hitch home from work at the rendering plant in Piric one evening, but nobody stopped. He decided to walk and disappeared into the snow. We drove poles down, walking across the fields in formation, bracing ourselves to strike flesh. We never found him; now that spring had come, we probably would.

"Anything good?" Al asked.

We struggled. We hadn't thought about how dark the winter had been when we were in its midst. "One of the Thao girls had a baby," we said.

Al smiled, although half of the town thought the Thaos belonged to us, and half wanted nothing to do with them. "That's something."

"What did *you* do?" we asked, and before he could say "I slept," we specified: "What was it like? How did it feel?"

"I had these long dreams," he said. "Unfolding over days. I dreamed I was in Eden, but it was mine. My farm. I picked pineapples every day."

Al Rasmussen had wintered in Eden, we thought. We started to feel a little like suckers.

Bobby and Dee had boundless energy, and spent a lot of it recounting dreams to their schoolmates. Soon many of the children were planning for their own long sleep, and the ones who weren't were calculating how scary empty classrooms might get, how the forest of raised hands would thin and they'd get called on over and over, expected to know the right answers. They pictured how lonely the playground would be, all lopsided seesaws and unpushed swings, and soon all the children of Bounty were begging to spend the next winter asleep.

Quite a few of them got their way. The Lutven boys were happy not to catch the bus in the dark, standing around in 20 below. The pudgy Sanderson girl, all bushy hair and braces, woke up with her teeth straighter and her belly flat. She showed off her new smile for Lucy Simmons, and Lucy confessed that her period had started sometime in early February. How easily, they thought, so much of the hard work of growing up had happened while they were asleep, while no one could make fun of them for it.

Mrs. Sanderson fit into clothes she hadn't worn since high school. The styles had changed, but she paraded around in her high-waisted, acid-washed jeans just so we could admire what sleep had done for her. Mr. Sanderson had started off awake, reporting to the John Deere dealership north of town at nine every morning, the way he'd done for years. But suddenly he saw the unfairness, his creaking out of bed while his wife rolled over with a slack, content smile. "Our food costs were way down," he said at the Pointes one night the next spring. "The heat bills. Gas. For once my daughter wasn't pestering for a new pair of jeans. I asked for a temporary leave. They said sales were down so far I'd be doing them a favor."

A lot of us lived in houses our parents or grandparents had owned; mortgages weren't usually our problem. Just the daily costs of living, and the closer those got to zero, the less we needed to work. John Deere lost three more before the winter was over. Other folks didn't have any employers to apologize to. The families that still kept animals thought we were all a bunch of pansies, at least according to Nils, but then we imagined him slogging to the barn every morning at five for the feeding and the milking, his fingers stiff and snot frozen in his mustache, and we mostly just felt smart.

Mrs. Drausmann, the town librarian, hated the sleep even more than Nils. She cornered Bobby and Dee after story time, near the shelves that once held skin creams and now held paperbacks, and threatened: "This will be like Narnia under the White Witch. Always winter and never Christmas."

"After Christmas," Dee asked her, "what's there to like? What do *you* do?"

"I keep the library open," she said. "So everyone has books. They come and use the computers and get their music and their movies."

"If you're dreaming, you have your own movies," Dee said gravely, and Mrs. Drausmann sighed. We tried to make it up to her, registered for her summer reading program and attended fall story time. But Dee was right. Sleeping folk needed almost nothing—a little food, a little water, air, and warmth. They definitely didn't need DVDs.

That second winter, the road crews noticed less traffic, and some of the plow drivers' hours were cut. Several decided to screw it and just sleep, and by the time the county and the drivers were done sniping at each other, the budget for next year's salting and plowing was half what it had been. The harder leaving your driveway was, the easier the choice to stay home.

The third year, a family died of carbon monoxide poisoning from an unventilated gas heater. An electric space heater started a fire at the Simmonses'. They got out, but the house was a loss. Al staggered into the snow bleary-eyed, called his neighbors dumbasses, and then invited them to pile on into his family room. When he woke up for real in March, he announced that if we were all going to do this thing, we should do it right. He didn't have enough old grease for everyone, so he charged hourly for consultations about different compact heating systems, then for assembly and installation, and soon he was doing well enough to quit fence repair.

We were glad Al had the new business, because that October, Reggie Lapham came home. He'd been seventeen when he hit Jeannie three and a half years earlier, and as young as that was, as much as we remembered the ice on the road and the evenings we'd gotten behind the wheel when we shouldn't have, we weren't sure how to forgive him. Our hearts went out to Reggie and then to Jeannie and then to Al and Bobby and Dee and then back to Reggie, until we couldn't keep our hearts straight and peaceful in our own chests. They were all ours, and we were too much like all of them. We needed men like Al to lead us, and we needed young people like Reggie to stay. We looked to Al for permission to take Reggie back.

But Reggie seemed to know Al wasn't going to give it, at least not that autumn, because he walked from his parents' van into his house and wouldn't come out again. We spoke to Mrs. Lapham at the Hop-In. "He's looking forward to the sleep," she said. "That's really all he wants to do. I don't think he would have come back if he had to—"

She broke off, and we wondered, *Had to what? Leave the house? Talk to people? Get a job?* The family went to bed a few days after Thanksgiving. Mrs. Lapham said that seemed like the easiest way to get through what had to be gotten through. Then we heard that Al had put his kids to bed early too, without Christmas, and then some of us started calculating the money we could save not buying presents. Those of us without small children, or without extended families, had to admit that the holidays were a downer as often as not. We knew that the Laphams and Rasmussens weren't sleeping for the healthiest of reasons, but we understood the urge.

Mrs. Drausmann called in to a radio psychologist when everyone woke up the next spring, about whether sleeping through four months of strife was sanity or just denial. She talked her way past the producers, but Dr. Joe wouldn't believe her. "Sure, excessive sleeping is a sign of depression," he said. "But no one hibernates." Then he hung up.

Several of us heard the call, and it prompted some soul-searching, both about why so many of us were listening to *The Dr. Joe Show* and about what our town might look like to outsiders. We started to wonder if Reggie Lapham should maybe be talking to somebody. If Al and Reggie needed help, we weren't giving it to them, because sleeping was easier for us too.

A woman from the *Piric Gazette* heard *The Dr. Joe Show* that night and came to ask Mrs. Drausmann some questions. We braced ourselves for the story, but the reporter apparently couldn't figure out whom to believe or what the heck was going on, and before she hit on the answer, the Gannett Company shut down the paper. We saw Nils Andersen and Al having a beer together at the Pointes a few weeks later, the first time they'd been social together in years. "She came to interview me," Nils said. "I told her the hibernation business was bullshit."

"I know you think the sleeping's bullshit," Al said. "You don't need to tell me."

"I told her Drausmann was bullshit. I told her nothing was going on in this town that was any of Dr. Joe's business or the *Piric Gazette*'s. I told her to leave you alone." Nils shook his head and clinked the neck of his bottle against Al's. "I figured you've always known what you needed. Crazy fucker."

A few weeks later, we watched the grease heater leave the Rasmussen house in parts, the foam-taped exhaust pipe, the burger filter. The mattresses came out, Bobby's and Dee's sheets, graduated now from NASCAR and Disney to plain solids, navy and lavender. We worried Al was abandoning the cause, until we found out he'd reassembled it all at the Andersen farm. With more people to share shifts taking care of the animals, Al explained, everyone could get some sleep.

More people economized like this, throwing in their lots with friends, neighbors. The Simmonses rebuilt their burned house with a single large room on the ground floor, an energy-efficient heat stove in the center, with nonflammable tile around the base. They went to ask Al's permission and then invited the Laphams to spend the next winter. They knew what a chill felt like, they said, as well as to be given shelter when nothing but cold was around you.

Mrs. Drausmann stayed awake. She had her books; she had her own kind of dreaming. She and Mrs. Pekola would walk up and down the streets, Mrs. Drausmann's snow boots and Mrs. Pekola's orthopedics the only prints for miles. Mrs. Pekola's faith wouldn't let her sleep. She walked to the Lutheran church every December 24 to light the Christ candle. "I'm sorry," she whispered to God. "They don't mean anything by it. They don't mean to disrespect you." She tried to tell us in spring how lonely our church looked, a single candle alight in the empty sanctuary.

In the first years, the reverend turned the electricity back on whenever the temperature hit 45, but then someone hit on the idea of Easter. We flipped the switch on the day that Christ rose. "Alleluia, alleluia," we sang, uttering the word we had denied ourselves for Lent, one of the first words to pass our lips since waking. The Rasmussens and the Laphams stood in their old pews, just across the aisle from each other. They didn't embrace at the greeting-neighbors part of the service, didn't say "Peace be with you" or "And also with you," but they didn't flee. Al stood between his children, with an arm draped over each of them, and we realized with surprise that Bobby was fourteen now and nearly as tall as his father. He would have been good at basketball too, if he'd been awake for the season. Dee's pale hair had darkened to a dirty blond, and her face was spotted with acne. The kids leaned into their father, facing forward, until Dee looked to her right and nodded at Mrs. Lapham. Just then, Reggie turned his head to peer anxiously over his mother, and we saw Dee freeze and then slowly nod at him too. We all nodded our pale faces at each other, and that seemed like enough.

In the end, the Hop-In is what brought the outsiders. Corporate couldn't understand why winter-quarter sales were down 95 percent from five years earlier. A regional manager came out, and then his supervisors, and finally news crews from Fargo. The satellite vans were hard to miss, and we stayed up that night for the eleven o'clock news. We hadn't expected the story they chose to tell: it wasn't a human-interest piece about ingenuity or survival. Our hibernation practice was horrible, the anchors announced, from up and down the state, then across the country. Horrifying. Another product of the recession. A new economic indicator: in addition to tumbling home prices and soaring unemployment, a town was going to sleep. A blond reporter asked the Sandersons if they were making a statement.

"We get tired," they said. "Is that a statement?"

We were annoyed at how they filmed the shabbiest parts of our town, until we flipped through the newscasts and realized that together they'd filmed nearly all of our town and that it all looked equally shabby. We were used to our potholes and tumbledown barns, and now alongside those were cracked sidewalks and collapsing houses. The gray bandstand in the park leaned heavily to one side; the flat roof of the old high school had caved in under last year's snow. Raccoons and groundhogs hibernated in some of the downtown buildings and chased each other up and down Main Street in their spring excitement. A few had gotten into Mrs. Pekola's antiques store, either for burrow bedding or just to be troublesome, and we were plagued by a video clip of skinny raccoons bursting out the store's front door, trailing gnawed-up christening dresses and crib quilts. A badger birthed a spring litter in the church basement on a pile of old Sunday school workbooks. We told ourselves that none of this mattered. We weren't using the buildings anyway: the barns, the high school, most of downtown. We reminded ourselves that Bounty had never been a pretty place. It was built for function, not ornament, and as long as it functioned the way we wanted, we shouldn't be ashamed. We had never had any great architecture in Bounty, and the certainty that we never would didn't seem a sacrifice.

We might have become a tourist attraction, except that getting to us when we were sleeping was so hard. The snow accumulated in giant drifts. We put a big stick out by the WELCOME TO BOUNTY sign and let it measure how deeply we were buried. People could come in on the highway, as far as the county plowed it, and then see a wall of snow taller than their car greeting them at the entrance.

That was the establishing shot, a tiny car next to a wall of snow, when the documentary was released. On the tenth anniversary of the sleep, the state public television channel contacted us and said they planned to take a more balanced approach than the news crews. We liked that they promised to hold the premiere in Bounty, projected after dark onto the wall of the farm supply store, since the old movie theater had been condemned.

They interviewed Bobby in his dorm room in the last weeks of the fall semester. The state university had offered him a small baseball scholarship. He was a one-sport kid. "I'm not sure where I'll go for Christmas break," he said. "I haven't had Christmas in years. My dad and my sister won't even be awake." He was broad like his father, a young man there in his cramped college room, and we wondered if Jeannie would even have recognized him.

The Lutven boys had already finished college, worked for a year in St. Paul, and then come home. They liked the pace of life here, they said. They liked the way winter gave you a chance to catch your breath. One of them married the Sanderson girl, who'd taken over the antiques store and chased the raccoons out. Even after two Lutven babies, ten-pound Scandinavian boys, she fit into the shop's old clothes, the slim, fitted dresses. She liked the quiet way her boys were growing up, she said, polite and calm and curled for five months like warm puppies at her side.

Mrs. Pekola had passed away, which we knew, but we hadn't known her family blamed us. Her eldest daughter was living in Florida, and the filmmakers had gone down to interview her about how her mother had died alone in a church pew, frozen to death in a wool coat and orthopedic shoes. "No one found her till spring," the woman said, her anger fresh and righteous.

Mrs. Fiske had taught all the Pekola girls over the years. "Fractions," she whispered in the audience. "That girl just hated fractions."

Dee had never left Bounty, never expressed any interest in going anywhere else. She was "ours," like her father before her, despite her faraway look most days, her eyes the color of the ice that froze over the flooded quarry. Her dirty-blond hair had darkened to brown, and her teenage acne had faded into a nearly translucent paleness. She volunteered at the library with Mrs. Drausmann and took over story time. The film showed her sitting in a rocking chair with books far too advanced for the children gathered cross-legged around her. "He heard the snow falling faintly through the universe and faintly falling, like the descent of their last end, upon all the living and the dead," she read, as the children squirmed. She wasn't very good at story time, but Mrs. Drausmann had grown hoarse and weary over the years.

One by one we tried to explain for the cameras. Why stay? What is Bounty worth? Three months? Four? Half your life spent asleep? Our people had moved to Bounty because the land was there and it was empty, and now all we had was the emptiness and each other. We had a wide sky and tall grass and a sun that felt good when you'd waited for it half the year. We had our children, the ones we'd feared for, feared their boredom and their recklessness and their hunger for somewhere else. We'd feared becoming Jeannie Rasmussen, and we'd feared becoming Reggie Lapham. We'd feared wanting too much and ending up with less than what we already had. Now Al and Nils dreamed of the sound of a basketball bouncing off the warped, snow-soaked floor of the high school gymnasium. Al dreamed of nights asleep in Jeannie's arms. Reggie Lapham probably dreamed his life differently too, but he seemed content with what he had: he was interviewed with his son on his lap, a boy who had never made a snowman, never opened a Christmas present. He spoke about that first year back, about how the sleep had saved him, and when his voice foundered, his wife, Nkauj Thao-Lapham, reached over to squeeze his hand.

Dr. Joe, interviewed, said that the sleep was profoundly unhealthy, that legislation should be passed before the custom could spread. The documentary included interviews with American history professors at the state university, experts on westward expansion, on what had happened to our county over the past two centuries. Someone in a bow tie said he was dismayed by what had happened to our immigrant spirit, to our desire to press on and out to something better. Our congressman pointed out that the immigrant spirit might have pushed us all the way on out of the state, further west or back east. Instead, we'd found a way to stay, and the census didn't ask if you were awake or asleep. It just asked where you lived, and now, more than ever, we were proud to say we lived in Bounty.

"*Sisu,*" old Mr. Kajaamaki grunted for the camera, with his hand held in front of his mouth; his teeth had fallen out, but he'd never bothered with dentures, and we felt a bit guilty that no one had insisted on driving him to Piric to get some fitted. Our people were shabby, like our houses, our streets, our ancient coats and boots. But our ancestors had come, and they had stopped, and we persisted. Persistence, Mr. Kajaamaki's old-world word for it. The endurance of a people who had once starved and eaten bark and come across an ocean to a flat sea of snow, to make new ways of life when the old ones seemed insufficient.

"But do you regret their decision? Your father's?" the interviewer, off-camera, prodded. The film cut back to Dee and Al standing together. They were outside, walking down the shuttered main street of our town, the sky blue and endlessly wide. Dee squinted in the light, and Al squinted at his daughter. He'd been quiet in front of the cameras, tentative to the point of taciturn, and as we watched the movie from lawn chairs in the farm supply store parking lot, we could see him fidgeting, turning his head to check the expression on his children's faces, turning around in his seat to look at the people he'd led into sleep.

"I barely remember what our life was like before. I remember being cold."

"And now?"

Dee looked baffled, not able to find words sufficient to explain half her life, the happier, more perfect half. The camera turned to Al, but his face was unreadable. "Now?" Dee said. "Now I guess we're not."

Now we are the people of Bounty, the farmers of dust and cold, the harvesters of dreams. After the lumber, after the mines, after the railroad, after the interstate, after the crops, after the cows, after the jobs. We're better neighbors in warm beds than we ever were awake. The suckers of the last century, but not of this one.

BRET ANTHONY JOHNSTON

Soldier of Fortune

FROM *Glimmer Train*

HER NAME WAS Holly Hensley, and except for the two years when her father was transferred to a naval base in Florida, her family lived across the street from mine. This was on Beechwood Drive, in Corpus Christi, Texas. Our parents held garage sales together, threw hurricane parties, went floundering in the shallow, bottle-green water under the causeway. If the Hensleys were working overtime and Holly was staying late for pep-squad practice — which meant grinding against Julio Chavez in the back seat of his Sky-lark — my mother would pick up Holly's younger brother from daycare and watch him until they got home. Sam had been born while they were living in Florida. ("My old man got one past the goalie," Holly liked to say. "There's nothing more disgusting.") In 1986, the year everything happened at the Hensley house, Sam was three. Holly was eighteen, a senior at King High School, and I was a freshman, awkward and shy and helpless with love.

Most mornings we walked to school together. Holly's hair would be wet from the shower, her eyes wide and glassy with fatigue; she'd yawn and say, "What's buzzin', cousin?" She liked to drag her fingers along the chain-link fences we passed, and to stop at Maverick Market to buy Diet Cokes and steal candy bars. I waited outside, worrying she'd get caught. We talked about what she'd do after graduation — some days she planned to enroll at the beauty college, others she wanted to dance at the Fox's Den out by the oil refineries — and about Roscoe, the collie she'd adopted in Florida. She told me how her little brother preferred her Aggie sweatshirt to his baby blanket. I invented stories of girls I'd been with, wild

things named Rhonda and Mandy and Anastasia who attended different schools and who, I hoped, might make Holly jealous. Usually she'd just bump me with her hip and say, "You're more of a slut
than I am." We never talked about the rumors that she and Julio
had let a crowd of kids watch them in bed at a homecoming party,
or that she'd recently been spotted leaving the Sea Ranch Motel
with Mr. Mitchell, the geology teacher. Even my parents had heard
about Mr. Mitchell. My mother said Holly was just trying to get her
parents' attention, acting out because of the new baby. My father
said she was trouble and if he caught me alone with her, he'd whip
my ass. But I rarely saw her after we got to campus. Holly would
disappear onto the school's smoking patio, a dismal slab of concrete where stringy-haired surfers and kids with safety pins through
their eyebrows loitered, and I would go find Matt Rickard.

Matt and I had been friends since elementary. We'd played on
the same soccer team, joined and quit Boy Scouts together, leaned
despondently against the gym bleachers and watched couples sway
at the junior-high dances our parents made us attend. In our freshman year, Matt wore sleeveless shirts and tucked the cuffs of his
camouflage pants into military boots; he had a pair of fatigues for
every day of the week—desert camo, woodland and blue woodland, tiger-stripe and black tiger-stripe. For a while we'd been into
guerrilla warfare. We bought *Soldier of Fortune* magazines, made
blowguns from copper tubing, slathered our faces with mud when
we crept under the lacy mesquite trees behind his house. We saved
our allowances for the gun expos at the Bayfront Auditorium and
loaded up on Chinese throwing stars and bandoliers of blank bullets, butterfly knives and pamphlets on chokeholds, and MREs that
tasted like gluey chalk. We ate meals with the forks and spoons attached to our Swiss Army knives. Over the summer, though, I'd
grown bored and embarrassed by the warfare stuff—my walls had
been draped with camouflage netting, and over my bed I'd had
a poster of one ninja roundhousing another—but Matt still liked
it, so I'd recently told him he could have my cache. He was disappointed in me, I knew, as if I'd defected to the enemy, and probably the reason he hadn't yet come to collect my stuff was the hope
that I'd change my mind. But I'd already packed everything into
my army duffel, and each afternoon I waited for Matt to take it
away. I didn't think we'd stay friends much longer.

When my father came into my room on a Friday night in early October, I thought he'd say Matt was on the porch. I was on my bed, staring at the acoustic ceiling where the ninja poster had been and listening to my stereo. My father crossed the room and lowered the volume. He wore a short-sleeved shirt and a clip-on tie; he'd just gotten off work. He gazed through my window and into the backyard.

"Is Matt here?" I asked.

"You need to take care of Holly's dog for a few days."

"Roscoe," I said.

"Make sure he has food and water. Maybe play with him a little."

I sat up on my bed. My father's voice sounded frayed, as if I were hearing him from far away. His hands were clasped behind his back. I thought I smelled cigarette smoke on him, but then I realized it was floating down the hall from the kitchen.

"Are they heading out of town?" I asked. The Hensleys had a van and sometimes drove to Comfort or Falling Water in the Hill Country.

"Don't go over there tonight," he said. "You can just start in the morning."

"Okay," I said. A wind gusted outside. Tallow branches scraped against the side of the house.

"If the dog shits on their patio, spray it down with the hose."

"Is Mom smoking again?"

"She might be, Josh," he said, and put his hand against the window. "Yes, that might be happening."

In 1986 my father worked at the naval air station—most everyone's father did, including Holly's and Matt's—but he was also moonlighting at Sears, selling radial tires and car batteries, which he blamed on Reagan. It was the year the president denied trading arms for hostages in Iran and the space shuttle *Challenger* exploded and Halley's Comet scorched through the sky. It was the year I loved a reckless girl, the year being around my best friend made me lonely. It was the year my mother was working at the dry-cleaning plant and trying to quit smoking. I knew she occasionally snuck cigarettes—I'd seen her in the backyard on evenings when my father was at Sears—but she hadn't smoked in our house for months. On that night in October, when the filmy scent of smoke wafted into my room, I could only think that Holly's family was moving again. The last time her father had gotten news of his transfer, they were gone within a week.

But they weren't leaving. There'd been an accident earlier that day, something involving Sam, Holly's little brother. My father only knew that Sam had been taken away in an ambulance and the Hensleys would likely spend a few nights with him at the hospital. He relayed the information in a detached tone, as if summarizing a movie he didn't want me to watch. He'd moved from the window to sit on my bed, where he looked small. He said their mail would be held and there was a key under the ceramic cow skull on their porch. I tried to remember the last time I'd seen Sam, but couldn't—maybe the previous weekend, when he and Holly drew on their driveway with colored chalk, or maybe when Mr. Hensley was watering the yard with Sam on his shoulders. In my room, my father kept dragging his hand over his face, as if trying to wake himself up. I asked if he knew how Holly was doing, and he said, "She's hurting, Josh. They're all hurting like hell."

My mother baked all night—brownies and lemon bars, biscuits and an enchilada casserole. She fried chicken and sliced vegetables and made salami-and-cheese sandwiches that she quartered into triangles. When I went into the kitchen on Saturday morning, the counter was crowded with foil-covered dishes. My mother was wall-eyed. She poured me a glass of orange juice and put two pieces of cold fried chicken on my plate. "Breakfast of champions," she said.

With all the foil, the kitchen was bright and strange. The table was tacky with humidity. My mother shook a cigarette from a pack, then lit it from a burner on the stove. I heard it sizzle.

"Liz called last night," she said, and exhaled smoke toward the ceiling. Liz was Mrs. Hensley, Holly's mother. My mother said, "Little Sam is sedated in intensive care."

"I don't know what's happening," I said.

"He burned himself," she said. "He's scalded all over the front of his little body."

Sam, my mother explained, had woken with a fever, so Mrs. Hensley kept him home from daycare. He spent the morning watching cartoons and napping on the living room couch. While he slept, Mrs. Hensley was cleaning the house and washing clothes, then decided to make tuna salad for lunch. She put water on to boil eggs. She checked on Sam on the couch, then stepped into the garage to put a load of laundry in the dryer. They had an attached garage, so she left the kitchen door open in case Sam woke up and called for her. She got sidetracked looking for dryer sheets and stayed out there longer than she'd intended. Then she heard her son screaming: he'd pulled the pot of boiling water down onto himself.

I felt cored out, not like I was going to vomit but like I already had. I pushed my plate away. At Sam's last birthday party, my parents and I had given him a toy garbage truck. Holly gave him a baseball cap that read, *I Wasn't Born In Texas, But Got Here As Soon As I Could.* He'd been wearing it when Mr. Hensley watered their lawn.

My mother opened the oven, looked inside, and then closed the door. Her cigarette was in an ashtray on the counter, smoke ribboning toward the open window.

"That poor family," my mother said.

"They're behind the eightball," I said. It was a phrase my father used.

"They sure are," she said. "Liz couldn't find Holly until very late. She thought she was off with that Julio."

"She had pep-squad practice," I lied. "I saw her when I walked home."

"You did?"

"There's a game this weekend," I said. "A big one."

"Then that's a relief. I worried she was with the teacher again."

"I don't think that really happened, the stuff with Mr. Mitchell," I said.

"I know you don't, sweetheart."

I took another bite of chicken, drained my orange juice. I said, "Matt might come over today. I'm giving him all my war stuff."

"I'll leave some chicken for you two," she said. "Your father and I are taking the rest to the hospital."

"I want to go," I said.

She brought her cigarette to her lips, then stubbed it out. She said, "No, Joshie, I don't think you do."

Their house had always been nicer than ours, and bigger. Over the years, workers had renovated the Hensleys' kitchen and added two rooms on the house's backside, a study and a game room. They had a bumper-pool table, thick carpet and Saltillo tile, lights with dimmer switches, and a fireplace. "Who needs a fireplace in Corpus?" my father had said one night. He was squinting through the peephole in our front door, watching smoke rise from the Hensleys' chimney. "Don't try to be something you're not, boy," he told me, and then told me again when they bought an aboveground pool for their backyard right before Mr. Hensley was transferred to Florida. I'd assumed the transfer was a demotion or punishment, but my father said Hensley had applied for it. (By way of explanation, he'd only said, "They're Republicans, Joshie.") While they were away, the Hensleys rented the house to a Catholic deacon and his wife, and when they returned, they paid to have new vinyl siding installed. It was gray with white and black trim, the shades of a lithograph.

Until that October weekend, I'd never been alone in their house. It seemed illicit, like when Matt and I paged through his father's *Playboy*s. The darkened rooms made me anxious. I had the sense I would do something I shouldn't, the dangerous and disappointing feeling that I couldn't be trusted. Had there been a route for me to bypass the house and still reach the garage where Roscoe's food was, I would've taken it, but I didn't have their garage-door opener—their automatic door was another extravagance my father resented—so I had to cut through the kitchen. I went twice on Saturday, three times on Sunday. I moved like a thief on each visit, never lingering or touching what I didn't have to. The air in the house smelled of potpourri, cloistered and spiced, and I tried not to breathe. I averted my gaze from the familiar and mysterious artifacts of the Hensleys' lives.

And yet I couldn't keep from seeing the coffee table Mrs. Hensley had pulled over to the couch so Sam wouldn't roll off, Holly's Aggie sweatshirt spread over the cushions, little red high-top shoes upturned on the carpet. I pretended not to know the Hensleys and tried to piece together a different family based on evidence they'd left behind. *Their son is an only child*, I thought. *His parents have taken him to a swimming lesson.* Or I imagined all of the Hensleys were home and hiding, waiting for me to break or steal something. My heart pumped in my ears. I left the lights off. In the kitchen, the floor tile gleamed; Holly's father had come home briefly Friday night, mopped up the spilled water, and grabbed fresh clothes for everyone at the hospital. The copper-bottomed pot was in the sink. Four unopened cans of tuna were stacked on the counter.

In the backyard, Roscoe always barreled into my legs and knocked me sideways. He jumped as high as my shoulders and scratched my chest through my shirt and licked my hand with his warm tongue. I let him chase me around the pool, and I threw pinecones for him to catch. We wrestled in the grass the way Holly had said he liked, then I scratched the scruff of his neck until he snored. I fed him more than I should. Before school on Monday morning, maybe because I'd been hoping Holly would appear on her porch and we'd walk to school together, I opened one of the cans of tuna and let Roscoe eat it from a spoon. That evening there was diarrhea all over the patio.

At school, the story kept changing. Sam wasn't scalded, he'd drowned in the Hensleys' pool. He'd slipped on a wet floor and hit his head. His brain was swelling. He'd been hit by a car, he'd eaten roach poison. Someone claimed to have seen the geology teacher taking flowers to the hospital, and someone else said they'd been in the faculty parking lot and found him weeping in his truck. On Wednesday, Matt said he'd heard the whole thing was a lie to cover up how Sam had accidently shot himself with his father's unregistered pistol.

We were standing by the statue of a mustang, the school mascot. Matt was in his blue woodland camos. He said, "I bet it was the Luger she showed us. If it was, the kid's toast."

Shortly after she returned from Florida, Holly had taken me and Matt into her parents' bedroom and showed us her father's pistol. She'd been babysitting Sam, and we'd been climbing the retama tree in my front yard. We were wearing our camouflage with pellet rifles slung over our shoulders, pretending to be mercenaries. She'd called across the street, "Y'all want to see something cool?" The pistol was a German Parabellum 1908, a semiautomatic Luger. We'd read about them in our magazines.

"He burned himself," I told Matt. "He's sedated in intensive care, but he's going to pull through." I made up the last part. The night before, I'd asked my father about Sam and he told me to concentrate on my schoolwork and not to give Roscoe any more tuna.

"I heard he did it in the game room," Matt said. "I heard there's a gnarly bloodstain under the pool table."

"You heard from who?"

"Jeff Deyo," Matt said.

"You don't know Jeff Deyo," I said. Jeff Deyo was a red-eyed senior, a friend of Julio's who'd gotten held back. He wore the same flannel shirt every day, unbuttoned and tattered, and when I passed him in the hall, I smelled the smoker's patio.

"We've been hanging out," Matt said. "We've been getting high. If you tell, I'll kick your ass."

"You need to come get all of my gear. If you don't want it, I'll throw it away."

"Don't take it out on me just because your girlfriend's brother blew his face off."

"She's not my girlfriend," I said.

"Right," he laughed. "She's dating Mr. Mitchell and you're with Anastasia from across town."

"You're an asshole."

"Check the game room," he said. "I heard the stain looks like a pot leaf."

Later that night, Mrs. Hensley called. My father was working his shift at Sears, and I was watching television on the couch while my mother smoked beside me. After answering, my mother handed me the receiver and told me to hang up once she switched to the kitchen phone. While she made her way down the hall, I told Mrs. Hensley about Roscoe catching the pinecones I tossed. She thanked me and said Holly would call me once things calmed down with Sam. Then my mother said, "Okay, Joshie, I got it."

"Okay," I said, but I just pushed the mute button and stayed on the line. I wanted to hear if Mrs. Hensley would say anything more about Holly, if she'd mention Mr. Hensley's Luger.

"We're going to Houston," Mrs. Hensley said. "They're moving him to the burn unit at the Shriners Hospital."

"Okay," my mother said. "Okay."

"I don't know. I don't know if it's okay."

"Are the doctors saying anything else?"

"You're going to Houston, that's what they're saying. They're saying, We can't help him here."

I checked out the game-room carpet on Saturday morning, then crept through the rest of the house that night. I knew I wouldn't find a bloodstain, just as I knew stealing through their hallways was a betrayal, but I couldn't stop myself. The moonlight canting through the blinds was bright enough in most rooms, but I also used the angle-head flashlight I'd bought at a gun expo. In the near dark, the Hensleys' house seemed smaller, not bigger, which surprised me. A fine layer of dust on the surfaces—the marble-topped dressers, the pool table's rails, the framed pictures on the walls—shone in the light, reflected it, and made me think of silt on a riverbed. Moving through their rooms gave me a jumpy, underwater feeling, as if I were swimming through the wreckage of a sunken ship, paddling from one ruined space to another. I avoided Sam's room.

And I'd told myself I wouldn't go into Holly's room, but on Sunday night I did. The moon hung low in the sky, a lurid glow seeping through her curtains and puddling on the carpet. The room smelled of lavender. I'd been in there before, but stripped of noise and electric light, the layout seemed unexpected. Her bed was made, piled high with frilly pillows and stuffed animals—open-armed bears, mostly, and a plush snake stretching the length of her mattress. Four silver-framed photos topped her vanity: Holly and Sam in an orange grove, Julio on Padre Island flexing his arms and smirking, Roscoe licking Holly's face with her eyes closed, and a picture of Holly when she was younger, eating ice cream with a fork. Green and white streamers were tacked to her closet door, and when I moved too quickly, they fluttered and startled me. She had a banana-shaped phone on her nightstand, and I began worrying it would ring. Or I thought my father would silently appear in her doorway, his eyes narrow with disgust. *Leave,* I thought. *Go home.* In my chest, my heart was wild as a trapped, frantic bird.

And yet I stayed. Outside, Roscoe trotted around the pool; his tags tinkled. Once, he started barking and I dropped to the floor and shimmied under Holly's bed. The Hensleys, I knew, had returned from Houston. I imagined Holly coming into her room and calling someone—Julio or maybe even Mr. Mitchell—to relay news about Sam. I imagined her turning off the lights and weeping and falling asleep with me under her. I considered bolting, trying to climb out the window and into the backyard, but knew I'd make too much racket. Roscoe kept barking. He was racing from one fence to another. I held my breath. I listened to phantom footfalls, the murmur of floorboards and studs behind the walls, the sad and random noises of an empty house at night. My hands were trembling, so I tucked them between my chest and the carpet. I still had the same underwater feeling, though now it was as if I were sinking, watching the surface grow blurry and distant. I waited to hit the bottom, to be discovered in the darkness.

But the lights in Holly's room never came on, and eventually Roscoe settled down. I pulled myself out from under the bed. I thought of how Matt and I used to crawl on our bellies in the brush behind his house, our faces obscured with mud. It occurred to me that while I was hiding in the Hensleys' house, he might be getting high with Jeff Deyo, and I felt suddenly and intensely alone. I had an odd sense of erasure, as if I were seeing the set for a play be dismantled. It was disorienting. And now that I'd crossed into Holly's room, I knew I'd return every night. The knowledge left me feeling resigned and melancholy, but also shot through with boldness. Before leaving, I dialed Matt's number on the banana phone, and when he answered, I didn't say a word.

My father was off from Sears that Thursday, so when he got home from the base, we mowed the Hensleys' lawns. Maybe my mother had asked him to do it, or maybe he'd gotten the idea after finishing our yard. I hoped it meant the Hensleys would return soon. As he pushed our lawnmower across the street—the engine idling, the blades scattering debris like when a Chinook lifts off—I followed him with the rake and bag of clippings.

A cold front had silvered the sky, unraveled the clouds. The air smelled briny, and every so often a wind would gust and eddy the fallen leaves. I waited for my father to announce the Hensleys were driving back from Houston, but he never did. While he swept the back patio, I said, "Maybe when Sam comes home Mom will quit smoking."

He leaned the broom against the house and fished his handkerchief out of his pocket, wiped his forehead. Roscoe was snortling along the fenceline. I looked at my shoes, flecked with cut grass.

I said, "Maybe she'll be less stressed and—"

"Josh," he interrupted, "when Sam comes home, he might not look the same. We need to start preparing ourselves for that."

I nodded and dragged the rake across the grass; the trimmings jumped like grasshoppers. I thought of the picture in the silver frame on Holly's dresser, the one of her and her brother in the orange grove. Originally I'd assumed they were in Florida, but now I believed they might have been in the Rio Grande Valley. In the picture, they're holding hands and heading away from the camera so their faces are invisible. It had become my favorite thing in Holly's room. Since Sunday night, I'd lain on Holly's bed, opened her closet to press my nose into her clothes, even spritzed her perfume on my Windbreaker so I could inhale her at home. I'd dialed every number I could think of on her banana phone—my mother at the dry cleaner, my father at the base and Sears, the secretary at King and the principal and my own house—then hung up when anyone answered. I never looked in her drawers, and I never stole anything, but every night I considered taking the orange-grove picture. I could stare at it for hours, imagining where they might go once they stepped beyond the aperture.

"He's behind the eight ball," I said.

"This kind of thing can tear up a family," my father said. "It can rip even a strong family to shreds. It's not easy to watch."

"They need our help," I said. "You're saying we need to—"

"We'll help however we can, Josh, but what I'm saying is we're not going to let them drag us into their problems."

"I understand," I said, though I didn't.

"What I'm saying is when Holly needs a shoulder to cry on, don't let it be yours."

But the Hensleys didn't come home. Mrs. Hensley, I knew, called my mother late at night every couple of days, and I kept hoping to wake up and see their van in their driveway, but it never appeared. One night I overheard my parents talking about skin grafts and a neoprene bodysuit that would keep Sam's flesh hydrated, compressed. Their voices were hushed and somber. My father also mentioned how Mr. Hensley's sick leave and vacation days were long gone. Another night I thought they were talking about Sam again, but they were just discussing the breakdown of talks between President Reagan and Gorbachev in Iceland. The neighborhood started getting ready for Halloween, carved pumpkins appearing on porches and cardboard witches hanging in windows, and the temperature was dropping, especially in the evenings. In Corpus, the fall is damp and glomming. I laid out a pallet of blankets for Roscoe in the garage and started pouring warm water over his food. I used the copper-bottomed pot that Holly's father had left in the sink.

I'd barely seen Matt since the day we talked about the bloodstain. He'd been skipping school a lot, and on those days when I did glimpse him in the hall, I hid behind my locker door or ducked into the bathroom. With the changing weather, he'd taken to wearing a plaid flannel shirt with his fatigues. He hung out on the smoker's patio in the mornings and afternoons. I called his house every night from Holly's banana phone and never said anything. Sometimes Matt hung up right away, others he'd lay the receiver beside a radio he'd tuned to a Tejano station, or he'd read classified ads from *Soldier of Fortune* into the phone: *The survival knife you've been waiting for, ten-inch blade and hollow compass-topped handle. Bounty hunting is legal and profitable! Silent firepower: crossbows and slingshots.* The duffel bag with all of my warfare stuff was still in my room, and though I no longer expected Matt to take it away, I also hadn't unpacked it.

So on the morning when he waved me over to the smoker's patio and said he'd pick up the duffel that afternoon, I should have been relieved. There were a few other students on the patio, sallow-skinned seniors I'd seen with Holly, and who'd always intimidated me. I was surprised by how easily Matt fit in, saddened by it. He was wearing his tiger-stripe camos, toeing out a cigarette with his combat boot. He blew smoke over his shoulder, the way my mother sometimes did, and said, "Is that cool? Jeff said he'd give me a ride."

"I threw it away," I said.

"No way," he said, his voice light with disappointment, as if I'd forgotten his birthday.

"I didn't think you were coming. I was tired of seeing it."

"That really sucks, Josh."

"And there wasn't a bloodstain," I said.

"What?"

"At Holly's house," I said. "Sam didn't shoot himself."

"That's what this is about?"

"I looked. There's no bloodstain," I said. "He burned himself with a pot of water. He'll probably have a skin graft."

Matt nodded, his eyes downcast and thoughtful. A small wind

picked up, wafting the acrid smell of put-out cigarettes. I thought Matt was thinking of something kind to say about Sam. Once, when I got stung by an asp behind his house, he broke off a piece of aloe from his mother's plant and rubbed it on the wound.

Now, though, he just grinned and said, "I bet his face looks like melted cheese, all stretched and gooey. He won't need a mask for Hallowe—"

My fist connected right above Matt's temple. "Oh shit," a girl said, and a crowd of smokers cinched around us. Before Matt knew what was happening—before *I* knew what was happening—I'd hit him again, on his mouth. Already there was blood on his teeth, in the corners of his lips. Then I was on top of him and we were falling to the patio and he was trying to cover his face with his forearms and saying, "Dude, come on, please no," and I was waiting for someone to stop me, to pull me off him, to save both of us.

The principal called my mother at the dry cleaners to pick me up from school; he'd suspended me for three days. I expected her to be angry or embarrassed, but when I apologized to her, she said, "Oh, Joshie, we always thought Matt was a twerp."

We drove to the bayfront and sat on the seawall. Although we were out in the open—the bay seething in front of us, the docked sailboats bobbing in the marina to the west—I felt as if we were hiding, staking out a place to plot our next move. The tide heaved. Waves walloped the barnacled pylons; the dirty foam spread and dissolved. Eventually a crisp, salted wind nosed ashore and my mother scooted closer to me. I kept expecting her to light a cigarette.

"Sometimes I snoop in the Hensley house," I said.

"I know."

"You do?"

"I watch your little flashlight beam from our window," she said. "It reminds me of a fly trying to get out."

"I don't take anything," I said. "I just look."

"I know that too."

A white gull hovered over us, then banked off and wheeled over the surf. I could hear cables clanging against hollow masts in the marina, the wind soughing through the dry palm trees that loomed along the seawall. Behind us stood the Bayfront Auditorium, where the gun expos took place. My knuckles ached.

"Dad says Sam might look different when he comes home," I said.

My mother nodded. She was watching the gull. It had landed on a pylon, its head moving around in twitches.

"And he said I should stay away from Holly."

"Her life's already sewn up," she said, her gaze still trained on the gull. "Matt's is too. And now probably Sam's."

"I don't understand," I said.

"Good," my mother said, resting her head on my shoulder. "Good, I'm glad."

Now I think of 1986 as the year my life pivoted away from what it had been, maybe the year when all of our lives pivoted. It was the year my parents spoke in low, furtive tones and I strained to hear what they weren't saying. It was the year I surrendered the weapons of my youth—the morning after I fought Matt, I *did* throw out my duffel bag—and the year Holly Hensley shocked everyone by dropping out of school and joining the coast guard. This happened right after Thanksgiving. Her enlisting, I remember, was met with disillusionment and disdain—it seemed selfish and rash—but she found her footing in the military and enjoyed a distinguished career. After the coast guard, she moved to the army and was stationed in Hawaii, Guam, and, until her chopper went down two days ago, Afghanistan. According to the short obituary my mother just e-mailed me, Holly is survived by two sons and a husband, and she achieved the rank of staff sergeant. I hadn't seen her in almost twenty years. Funeral arrangements are being made in Corpus. I'll send flowers, and if I can find it, I'll make a copy of the orange-grove photo and mail it to her family.

The night after I got suspended, I decided to steal that picture of Holly and her brother. I'd been lying on my bed earlier that day—my father had taken away my stereo and television privileges, and until my suspension ended, I was only allowed out of the house to feed Roscoe—and I'd thought having the orange-grove photo might quell my desire to sneak into Holly's room. I'd also started thinking Mr. Hensley would return soon, so my access to the house felt fleeting, like a journey to a foreign country—a deployment—was coming to an end. I wanted a souvenir.

The moon was full that night, lamping the Hensleys' backyard and rimming the curtains in Holly's room. Everything else lay in deep shadow; I clicked my flashlight on and off to see, and wondered if my mother was watching from across the street. I suspected she was and didn't mind. The house still smelled of potpourri, a little dank. I'd debated over grabbing another picture from Holly's parents' room to replace the one I wanted to take, but finally decided I'd just cluster the remaining three photos and hope Holly would have forgotten what had been there before. It seemed possible.

I was standing in front of her dresser, trying to visualize the most inconspicuous way to rearrange the pictures, when from behind me I heard, "What's buzzin', cousin?"

I spun around, knocked into the dresser. The frames toppled. My heart kicked in my chest. Holly was on her bed, lying on her side among the stuffed animals. Even when I looked straight at her, her image was obscured in the dark.

"I didn't take anything," I said.

"You should have," she said. "I would."

"I just like the picture of you and Sam in the orange grove."

"I do too," she said. "What you can't see is that the oranges are frozen solid. It was last year, right before we came back, and there was this massive cold snap that killed everything."

I clasped my hands behind my back; they were trembling again. I said, "I'm sorry for sneak—"

"We're alone here, if you're wondering," she said, shifting on the bed. "My parents are still in Houston with Sam. Julio came to get me. If I don't go back to school, I won't graduate."

"I'm suspended," I said.

"And Matt's a bloody mess."

"You heard?"

"I heard you were defending Sam," she said. "I almost went to your house to thank you, but then I saw the grass clippings on the carpet and figured you'd be back."

"I never looked in your drawers," I said.

"You'll do better next time," she said.

A raft of clouds floated past the moon, shrouding the room for a moment. I looked at the ceiling and couldn't see it. I could hear myself breathing.

"I wanted the orange-grove picture," I said. "I was going to steal it."

"You can't have that one, but I'll make you a copy," she said. "Want anything else?"

"I want Sam to get better."

"Me too. He's trying. Anything else?"

"I want to know about Mr. Mitchell," I said.

Holly rolled onto her back. She tossed a stuffed white bear into the air, caught it, then did it again. She said, "I'll tell you, but you only get three wishes. You're sure this is how you want to use your last one?"

I wasn't sure of anything at that moment. I felt as if I were balancing on a precipice, and I needed to think clearly. I tried to imagine how disappointed my father would be if he knew where I was, tried to understand what my mother had meant about everyone's lives being sewn up. I thought of how Sam used Holly's sweatshirt for a blanket, and the baseball cap she'd given him for his birthday. I wondered how it would feel to live outside Texas, what it would be like to walk through a frozen orange grove or to douse yourself with boiling water or to see your young son lying in a coma and not recognize him.

And then, like that, I understood. Before I could stop myself, I said, "He's yours, isn't he? Sam is."

Holly tossed the bear again, higher. In the air, it spiraled and looked like a silver fish flashing through murky water. She did it again, higher still. I thought she was trying to hit the ceiling I could barely see.

"That's why you went to Florida," I said. "Your parents didn't want—"

"Josh," she said.

"Yes?"

"Stop talking," she said.

"I won't tell anyone."

"Come here," Holly said. "Just come here."

I thought I would lie beside her and she would whisper the trajectory of Sam's life to me, explain who else knew her secrets and who his father was. It gave me a sensation of inertia, of countless mysteries parting around me like currents. But Holly offered none of this. She just lifted the comforter and I took off my shoes and she pulled me on top of her. We kicked her stuffed animals to the carpet, stripped off our clothes, tangled into each other. Roscoe barked in the backyard and ran along the fence; Holly said, "He chases possums." The house groaned. I shivered. I thought of the Luger in her parents' bedroom and wondered where Matt was at that late hour. I worried my father would come looking for me, but also felt certain my mother would run interference. Soon Holly said, "I just want him to be okay," and started sobbing against my chest. I was fourteen years old, scared and inexperienced and mystified by the luck of my life, and though I could think of nothing to say, I held her close, as tight as I could. Eventually her breathing slowed so completely I wondered if she'd gone to sleep. I hoped so. I was wide awake, my eyes open and adjusted to the darkness. The edges of her curtains were again framed in moonlight, and in the shallow glow, our skin looked new and smooth and unblemished, ready for the scars that were lying, somewhere, in ambush.

CLAIRE KEEGAN

Foster

FROM *The New Yorker*

EARLY ON A SUNDAY, after first mass in Clonegal, my father, instead of taking me home, drives deep into Wexford toward the coast, where my mother's people came from. It is a hot August day, bright, with patches of shade and greenish sudden light along the road. We pass through the village of Shillelagh, where my father lost our red shorthorn in a game of forty-five, and on past the mart in Carnew, where the man who won her sold her not long afterward. My father throws his hat on the passenger seat, winds down the window, and smokes. I shake the plaits out of my hair and lie flat on the back seat, looking up through the rear window. I wonder what it will be like, this place belonging to the Kinsellas. I see a tall woman standing over me, making me drink milk still hot from the cow. I see another, less likely version of her, in an apron, pouring pancake batter into a frying pan, asking would I like another, the way my mother sometimes does when she is in good humor. The man will be her size. He will take me to town on the tractor and buy me red lemonade and crisps. Or he'll make me clean out sheds and pick stones and pull ragweed and docks out of the fields. I wonder if they live in an old farmhouse or a new bungalow, whether they will have an outhouse or an indoor bathroom with a toilet and running water.

An age, it seems, passes before the car slows and turns into a tarred, narrow lane, then slams over the metal bars of a cattle grid. On either side, thick hedges are trimmed square. At the end of the lane, there's a white house with trees whose limbs are trailing the ground.

"Da," I say. "The trees."

"What about them?"

"They're sick," I say.

"They're weeping willows," he says, and clears his throat.

On the housefront, tall, shiny windowpanes reflect our coming. I see myself looking out from the back seat, wild as a tinker's child, with my hair all undone, but my father, at the wheel, looks just like my father. A big, loose hound lets out a few rough, halfhearted barks, then sits on the step and looks back at the doorway, where the man has come out to stand. He has a square body like the men my sisters sometimes draw, but his eyebrows are white, to match his hair. He looks nothing like my mother's people, who are all tall, with long arms, and I wonder if we have not come to the wrong house.

"Dan," he says, and tightens himself. "What way are you?"

"John," Da says.

They stand looking out over the yard for a moment and then they are talking rain: how little rain there is, how the priest in Kilmuckridge prayed for rain this very morning, how a summer like this was never before known. There is a pause, during which my father spits, and then the conversation turns to the price of cattle, the EEC, butter mountains, the cost of lime and sheep dip. I am used to it, this way men have of not talking: they like to kick a divot out of the grass with a boot heel, to slap the roof of a car before it takes off, to sit with their legs wide apart, as though they do not care.

When the woman comes out, she pays no heed to the men. She is even taller than my mother, with the same black hair, but hers is cut tight like a helmet. She's wearing a printed blouse and brown, flared trousers. The car door is opened and I am taken out, and kissed.

"The last time I saw you, you were in the pram," she says, and stands back, expecting an answer.

"The pram's broken."

"What happened at all?"

"My brother used it for a wheelbarrow and the wheel fell off."

She laughs and licks her thumb and wipes something off my face. I can feel her thumb, softer than my mother's, wiping whatever it is away. When she looks at my clothes, I see my thin cotton dress, my dusty sandals through her eyes. Neither one of us knows what to say. A queer, ripe breeze is crossing the yard.

"Come on in, *a leanbh.*"

She leads me into the house. There's a moment of darkness in the hallway; when I hesitate, she hesitates with me. We walk through into the heat of the kitchen, where I am told to sit down, to make myself at home. Under the smell of baking, there's some disinfectant, some bleach. She lifts a rhubarb tart out of the oven and puts it on the bench. Pale yellow roses are still as the jar of water they are standing in.

"So how is your mammy keeping?"

"She won a tenner on the prize bonds."

"She did not."

"She did," I say. "We all had jelly and ice cream and she bought a new tube for the bicycle."

I feel, again, the steel teeth of the comb against my scalp earlier that morning, the strength of my mother's hands as she wove my plaits tight, her belly at my back, hard with the next baby. I think of the clean pants she packed in the suitcase, the letter, and what she must have written. Words had passed between my mother and father:

"How long should they keep her?"

"Can't they keep her as long as they like?"

"Is that what I'll say?"

"Say what you like. Isn't it what you always do."

Now the woman fills an enamel jug with milk.

"Your mother must be busy."

"She's waiting for them to come and cut the hay."

"Have ye not the hay cut?" she says. "Aren't ye late?"

As the men come in from the yard, it grows momentarily dark, then brightens once again when they sit down.

"Well, missus," Da says, pulling out a chair.

"Dan," she says, in a different voice.

"There's a scorcher of a day."

"'Tis hot, surely." She turns her back to watch the kettle, waiting.

"Wasn't it a great year for the hay all the same. Never saw the like of it," Da says. "The loft is full to capacity. I nearly split my head on the rafters pitching it in."

I wonder why my father lies about the hay. He is given to lying about things that would be nice, if they were true. Somewhere farther off, someone has started up a chain saw, and it drones on like a big, stinging wasp for a while. I wish I was out there, working. I am unused to sitting still and do not know what to do with my hands. Part of me wants my father to leave me here while another wants him to take me back, to what I know. I am in a spot where I can neither be what I always am nor turn into what I could be.

The kettle rumbles up to the boiling point, its steel lid clapping. Kinsella gets a stack of plates from the cupboard, opens a drawer and takes out knives and forks, teaspoons. He opens a jar of beetroot and puts it on a saucer with a little serving fork, leaves out sandwich spread and salad cream. Already there's a bowl of tomatoes and onions chopped fine, a fresh loaf, ham, a block of red cheddar.

"And what way is Mary?" the woman says.

"Mary? She's coming near her time."

"I suppose the last babby is getting hardy?"

"Aye," Da says. "He's crawling. It's feeding them that's the trouble. There's no appetite like a child's, and believe you me, this one is no different."

"Ah, don't we all eat in spurts, the same as we grow," the woman says, as though this is something he should know.

"She'll ate but you can work her."

Kinsella looks up at his wife. "There'll be no need for any of that," he says. "The child will have no more to do than help Edna around the house."

"We'll keep the child gladly," the woman echoes. "She's welcome here."

When we sit in at the table, Da tastes the ham and reaches for the beetroot. He doesn't use the serving fork but pitches it onto the plate with his own. It stains the pink ham, bleeds. Tea is poured. There's a patchy silence as we eat, our knives and forks breaking up what's on our plates. After some little scraps of speech, the tart is cut. Cream falls over the hot pastry, into warm pools.

Now that my father has delivered me and eaten his fill, he is anxious to light his fag and get away. Always, it's the same: he never stays in any place long after he's eaten, not like my mother, who would talk until it grew dark and light again. This, at least, is what my father says but I have never known it to happen. With my mother it is all work: us, the butter-making, the dinners, the washing up and getting up and getting ready for mass and school, weaning calves, and hiring men to plow and harrow the fields, stretching the money and setting the alarm for a time before the sun rises. But this is a different type of house. Here there is room to think. There may even be money to spare.

"I'd better hit the road," Da says.

"What hurry is on you?" Kinsella says.

"The daylight is burning, and I've yet the spuds to spray."

"There's no fear of blight these evenings," the woman says, but she gets up anyway, and goes out the back door with a sharp knife. A silence climbs between the men while she is gone.

"Give this to Mary," she says, coming in. "I'm snowed under with rhubarb, whatever kind of year it is."

My father takes the rhubarb from her, but it is as awkward as the baby in his arms. A stalk falls to the floor and then another. He waits for her to pick them up, to hand them to him. She waits for him to do it himself. In the end, it's Kinsella who stoops. "There now," he says.

Out in the yard, my father throws the rhubarb onto the back seat, gets in behind the wheel, and starts the engine. "Good luck to ye," he says. "I hope this girl will give no trouble." He turns to me. "Try not to fall into the fire, you."

I watch him reverse, turn into the lane, and drive away. Why did he leave without so much as a goodbye or ever mentioning when he would come back for me?

"What's ailing you, child?" the woman says.

I look at my feet, dirty in my sandals.

Kinsella stands in close. "Whatever it is, tell us. We won't mind."

"Lord God Almighty, didn't he go and forget all about your wee bits and bobs!" the woman says. "No wonder you're in a state. Well, hasn't he a head like a sieve, the same man."

"Not a word about it," Kinsella says. "We'll have you togged out in no time."

When I follow the woman back inside, I want her to say something, to put me at ease. Instead she clears the table, picks up the sharp knife, and stands at the window, washing the blade under the running tap. She stares at me as she wipes it clean and puts it away.

"Now, girleen," she says. "I think it's nearly time you had a bath."

She takes me upstairs to a bathroom, plugs the drain, and turns the taps on full. "Hands up," she says, and pulls my dress off.

She tests the water and I step in, trusting her, but the water is too hot, and I step back out.

"Get in," she says.

"It's too hot."

"You'll get used to it."

I put one foot through the steam and feel, again, the same rough scald. I keep my foot in the water, and then, when I think I can't stand it any longer, my thinking changes, and I can. The water is deeper than any I have ever bathed in. Our mother bathes us in what little she can, and makes us share. After a while, I lie back and through the steam watch the woman as she scrubs my feet. The dirt under my nails she scrapes out with tweezers. She squeezes shampoo from a plastic bottle, lathers my hair, and rinses the lather off. Then she makes me stand and soaps me all over with a cloth. Her hands are like my mother's hands but there is something else in them too, something I have never felt before and have no name for. This is a new place, and new words are needed.

"Now your clothes," she says.

"I don't have any clothes."

"Of course you don't." She pauses. "Would some of our old things do you for now?"

"I don't mind."

"Good girl."

She takes me to a bedroom, at the other side of the stairs, and looks through a chest of drawers.

"Maybe these will fit you."

She is holding a pair of old-fashioned trousers and a new plaid shirt. The sleeves and legs are a bit too long but the waist tightens with a canvas belt, to fit me.

"There now," she says.

"Mammy says I have to change my pants every day."

"And what else does your mammy say?"

"She says you can keep me for as long as you like."

She laughs at this and brushes the knots out of my hair, and turns quiet. The windows are open and I see a stretch of lawn, a vegetable garden, edible things growing in rows, spiky yellow dahlias, a crow with something in his beak which he slowly breaks in two and eats.

"Come down to the well with me," she says.

"Now?"

"Does now not suit you?"

Something about the way she says this makes me wonder if it's something that we are not supposed to do.

"Is this a secret?"

"What?"

"I mean, am I not supposed to tell?"

She turns me around, to face her. I have not really looked into her eyes until now. Her eyes are dark blue, pebbled with other blues. In this light she has a mustache.

"There are no secrets in this house, do you hear?"

I don't want to answer back but feel she wants an answer.

"Do you hear me?"

"Yeah."

"It's not 'yeah.' It's 'yes.' What is it?"

"It's yes."

"Yes, what?"

"Yes, there are no secrets in this house."

"Where there's a secret," she says, "there's shame, and shame is something we can do without."

"Okay." I take big breaths so I won't cry.

She puts her arm around me. "You're just too young to understand."

As she says this, I realize that she is just like everyone else, and I wish I was back at home so that the things I do not understand could be the same as they always are.

Downstairs, she fetches a zinc bucket from the scullery. At first I feel uneasy in the strange clothes, but walking along, I forget. Kinsella's fields are broad and level, divided with electric fences that she says I must not touch, unless I want a shock. When the wind blows, sections of the longer grass bend over, turning silver. On one strip of land, bony Friesian cows stand all around us, grazing. They have huge bags of milk and long teats. I can hear them pulling the grass up from the roots. Neither one of us talks, the way people sometimes don't, when they are happy. As soon as I have this thought, I realize that its opposite is also true. We climb over a stile and follow a dry path through the grass to a small iron gate, where stone steps run down to a well. The woman leaves the bucket on the grass and comes down with me.

"Look," she says. "There's not a finer well in the parish. Who'd ever know there wasn't so much as a shower since the first of the month?"

I go down steps until I reach the water.

"Taste it," she says.

Hanging above us is a big ladle, a shadow cupped in the steel. I reach up and take it from the nail. She holds the belt of my trousers so I won't fall in.

"It's deep," she says. "Be careful."

I dip the ladle and bring it to my lips. This water is as cool and clean as anything I have ever tasted. I dip it again and lift it level with the sunlight. I drink six measures of water and wish, for now, that this place without shame or secrets could be my home. She takes me back up the steps, then goes down alone. I hear the bucket floating on its side for a moment before it sinks and swallows, making a grateful sound, a glug, before it's pulled out and lifted.

That night, I expect her to make me kneel down, but instead she tucks me in and tells me that I can say a few little prayers in my bed, if that is what I ordinarily do. The light of the day is still bright and strong. She is just about to hang a blanket over the curtain rail, to block it out, when she pauses. "Would you rather I left it?"

"Yeah," I say. "Yes."

"Are you afraid of the dark?"

I want to say that I am afraid but am too afraid to say so.

"Never mind," she says. "It doesn't matter. You can use the toilet past our room, but there's a chamber pot here too, if you'd prefer."

"I'll be all right," I say.

"Is your mammy all right?"

"What do you mean?"

"Your mammy. Is she all right?"

"She used to get sick in the mornings but now she doesn't."

"Why isn't the hay in?"

"She hasn't enough to pay the man. She only just paid him for last year."

"God help her." She smooths the sheet across me, sighs. "Do you think she'd be offended if I sent her a few bob?"

"Offended?"

"Would she mind?"

I think about this for a while. "She wouldn't, but Da would."

"Ah, yes," she says. "Your father."

She kisses me, a plain kiss, then says good night. I sit up when she is gone and look around the room. Trains of every color race across the wallpaper. There are no tracks for these trains, but here and there a small boy stands off in the distance, waving. He looks happy, but some part of me feels sorry for every version of him. I roll onto my side and, though I know that she wants neither, wonder if my mother will have a girl or a boy this time. I think of my sisters, who will not yet be in bed. I stay awake for as long as I can, then make myself get up and use the chamber pot, but only a dribble comes out. I go back to bed, more than half afraid, and fall asleep. At some point later in the night—it feels much later—the woman comes in. I grow still and breathe as though I have not wakened. I feel the mattress sinking, the weight of her on the bed. Quietly, she leans over me. "God help you, child. If you were mine, I'd never leave you alone with strangers."

All through the day, I help the woman around the house. She shows me the big white machine that plugs in, a freezer, where what she calls "perishables" can be stored for months without rotting. We make ice cubes, go over every inch of the floors with a hoovering machine, dig new potatoes, make coleslaw and two loaves, and then she takes the clothes in off the line while they are still damp and sets up a board and starts ironing. She does it all without rushing but she never really stops. Kinsella comes in and makes tea for us out of the well water and drinks it standing up, with a handful of Kimberley biscuits, then goes back out. Later he comes in again, looking for me. "Is the wee girl there?" he calls.

I go to the door.

"Can you run?"

"What?"

"Are you fast on your feet?" he says.

"Sometimes," I say.

"Well, run down there to the end of the lane, as far as the box, and run back."

"The box?" I say.

"The postbox. You'll see it there. Be as fast as you can."

I take off, racing, to the end of the lane and find the box and get the letters and race back. Kinsella is looking at his watch. "Not bad," he says, "for your first time."

He takes the letters from me. "Do you think there's money in any of these?"

"I don't know."

"Ah, you'd know if there was, surely. The women can smell money. Do you think there's news?"

"I wouldn't know," I say.

"Do you think there's a wedding invitation?"

I want to laugh.

"It wouldn't be yours anyhow," he says. "You're too young to be getting married. Do you think you'll get married?"

"I don't know," I say. "Mammy says I shouldn't take a present off a man."

Kinsella laughs. "She could be right there. Still and all, there's no two men the same. And it'd be a swift man that would catch you, Long Legs. We'll try you again tomorrow and see if we can't improve your time."

"I've to go faster?"

"Oh, aye," he says. "By the time you're ready for home you're to be as fast as a reindeer, so there'll not be a man in the parish will catch you without a long-handled net and a racing bike."

After supper and the nine o'clock news, when Kinsella is reading his newspaper in the parlor, the woman sits me on her lap and idly strokes my bare feet.

"You have nice long toes," she says. "Nice feet."

She makes me lie down with my head on her lap and, with a hair clip, cleans the wax out of my ears.

"You could have planted a geranium in what was there," she says.

When she takes out the hairbrush, I can hear her counting under her breath to a hundred before she stops and plaits it.

And so the days pass. I keep waiting for something to happen, for the ease I feel to end, but each day follows on much like the one

before. We wake early with the sun coming in and have eggs of one
kind or another with porridge and toast for breakfast. Kinsella puts
on his cap and goes out to the yard to milk the cows, and myself
and the woman make a list out loud of the jobs that need to be
done: we pull rhubarb, make tarts, paint the skirting boards, take
all the bedclothes out of the hot press, hoover out the spiderwebs,
and put all the clothes back in again, make scones, scrub the bathtub, sweep the staircase, polish the furniture, boil onions for onion
sauce and put it in containers in the freezer, weed the flower beds,
and, when the sun goes down, water things. Then it's a matter of
supper and the walk across the fields to the well. Every evening the
television is turned on for the nine o'clock news and then, after
the forecast, I am told that it is time for bed.

One afternoon, while we are topping and tailing gooseberries
for jam, Kinsella comes in from the yard and washes and dries his
hands and looks at me in a way he has never looked before.

"I think it's past time we got you togged out, girl."

I am wearing a pair of navy-blue trousers and a blue shirt that
the woman pulled out of the chest of drawers.

"What's wrong with her?" the woman says.

"Tomorrow's Sunday, and she'll need something more than that
for mass," he says. "I'll not have her going as she went last week."

"Sure, isn't she clean and tidy?"

"You know what I'm talking about, Edna." He sighs. "Why don't
you go up and change and I'll run us into Gorey."

The woman keeps on picking the gooseberries from the colander, stretching her hand out, but a little more slowly each time, for
the next one. At one point I think she will stop, but she keeps on
until she is finished and then she gets up and places the colander
on the sink and lets out a sound I've never heard anyone make,
and slowly goes upstairs.

Kinsella looks at me and smiles a hard kind of a smile. His eyes
are not quite still in his head. It's as though there is a big piece of
trouble stretching itself out in the back of his mind. He toes the
leg of a chair and looks over at me. "You should wash your hands
and face before you go to town," he says. "Didn't your father even
bother to teach you that much?"

I freeze in the chair, waiting for something much worse to happen, but Kinsella just stands there, locked in the wash of his own

speech. As soon as he turns, I race for the stairs, but when I reach the bathroom the door won't open.

"It's all right," the woman says after a while from inside, and then, shortly afterward, opens it. "Sorry for keeping you." She has been crying, but she isn't ashamed. "It'll be nice for you to have some clothes of your own," she says then, wiping her eyes. "And Gorey is a nice town. I don't know why I didn't think of taking you there before now."

Town is a crowded place with a wide main street. Outside the shops, many different things are hanging in the sun. There are plastic nets full of beach balls, blow-up toys, and beds that float. A see-through dolphin looks as though he is shivering in a cold breeze. There are plastic spades and matching buckets, molds for sandcastles, grown men digging ice cream out of tubs with little plastic spoons, a van with a man calling, "Fresh fish!"

Kinsella reaches into his pocket and hands me something. "You'll get a choc ice out of that."

I open my hand and stare at the pound note.

"Couldn't she buy half a dozen choc ices out of that," the woman says.

"Ah, what is she for, only for spoiling?" Kinsella says.

"What do you say?" the woman says.

"Thanks," I say. "Thank you."

"Well, stretch it out and spend it well," Kinsella says, laughing.

The woman takes me to the draper's and picks out five cotton dresses and some pants and trousers and a few tops. We go behind a curtain so that I can try them on.

"Isn't she tall?" the assistant says.

"We're all tall," the woman says.

"She's the spitting image of her mammy. I can see it now," the assistant says, and then decides that the lilac dress is the best fit and the most flattering. Mrs. Kinsella agrees. She buys me a printed blouse too, with short sleeves, blue trousers, and a pair of black leather shoes with a little strap and a buckle, some pants, and white ankle socks. The assistant hands her the docket, and she takes out her purse and pays for it all.

"Well may you wear," the assistant says. "Isn't your mammy good to you?"

I don't know how to answer.

Out in the street, the sun feels strong again, blinding. We meet people the woman knows. Some of them stare at me and ask who I am. One has a new baby in a pushchair. The woman bends down and coos, and he slobbers a little and starts to cry.

"He's making strange," the mother says. "Pay no heed."

We meet a woman with eyes like picks, who asks whose child I am. When she is told, she says, "Ah, isn't she company for you all the same, God help you."

Mrs. Kinsella stiffens, then says, "You must excuse me but this man of mine is waiting, and you know what these men are like."

"Like fecking bulls, they are," the woman says. "Haven't an ounce of patience."

"God forgive me but if I ever run into that woman again it will be too soon," Mrs. Kinsella says, when we have rounded the corner.

Before we go back to the car she leaves me loose in a sweetshop. I take my time choosing what I want.

"You got a right load there," she says, when I come out.

Kinsella has parked in the shade and is sitting with the windows open, reading the newspaper. "Well?" he says. "Did ye get sorted?"

"Aye," she says.

"Grand," he says.

I give him the choc ice and her the Flake and lie on the back seat eating the wine gums, careful not to choke as we cross over bumps in the road. I listen to all the change rattling around in my pocket, the wind rushing through the car, and the little pieces of speech, scraps of gossip, being shared between them in the front.

When we turn into the yard, another car is parked outside the door. A woman is on the front step, pacing, with her arms crossed.

"Isn't that Harry Redmond's girl?"

"I don't like the look of this," Kinsella says.

"Oh, John," she says, rushing over. "I'm sorry to trouble you but didn't our Michael pass away and there's not a soul at home. They're all out on the combines and won't be back till God knows what hour, and I've no way of getting word to them. We're rightly stuck. Would you ever come down and give us a hand digging the grave?"

"I don't know that this'll be any place for you but I can't leave you here," the woman says, later the same day. "So get ready and we'll go, in the name of God."

I go upstairs and change into my new dress and my ankle socks and shoes.

"Don't you look nice," she says, when I come down. "John's not always easy but he's hardly ever wrong."

Walking down the road, we pass houses with their doors and windows wide open, long, flapping clotheslines, graveled entrances to other lanes. Outside a cottage, a black dog with curls all down his back comes out and barks at us, hotly, through the bars of a gate. At the first crossroads we meet a heifer, who panics and races past us, lost. All through the walk, the wind blows hard and soft and hard again, through the tall, flowering hedges, the high trees. In the fields, the combines are out cutting the wheat, the barley, and the oats, saving the corn, leaving behind long rows of straw. Farther along, we meet two bare-chested men, their eyes so white in faces that are tanned and dusty. The woman stops to greet them and tells them where we are going.

"Well, it must be a relief to the man, to be out of his misery."

"Sure, didn't he reach his three score and ten?" the other says. "What more can any of us hope for?"

We keep on walking, standing in tight to the hedges, the ditches, letting things pass.

"Have you been to a wake before?" the woman asks.

"I don't think so."

"Well, I might as well tell you. There will be a dead man in a coffin and lots of people and some of them might have a little too much taken."

"What will they be taking?"

"Drink," she says.

When we come to the house, several men are leaning against a low wall, smoking. There's a black ribbon on the door, but when we go in, the kitchen is bright and packed with people who are talking. The woman who asked Kinsella to dig the grave is there, making sandwiches. There are bottles of red and white lemonade and stout, and, in the middle of all this, a big wooden box with a dead old man lying inside it. His hands are joined, as though he had died praying, a string of rosary beads around his fingers. Some of the men are sitting around the coffin, using the part that's closed as a counter on which to rest their glasses. One of these is Kinsella.

"There she is," he says. "Long Legs. Come over here."

He pulls me onto his lap and gives me a sip from his glass. "Do you like the taste of that?"

"No."

He laughs. "Good girl. Don't ever get a taste for it. If you start, you might never stop, and then you'd wind up like the rest of us."

He pours red lemonade into a cup for me. I sit on his lap, drinking it and eating queen cakes out of the biscuit tin and looking at the dead man, hoping that his eyes will open.

The people drift in and out, shaking hands, drinking and eating and looking at the dead man, saying what a lovely corpse he is, and doesn't he look happy now that his end has come, and who was it who laid him out? They talk of the forecast and the moisture content of corn, of milk quotas and the next general election. I feel myself getting heavy on Kinsella's lap. "Am I getting heavy?"

"Heavy?" he says. "You're like a feather, child. Stay where you are."

I put my head against him but I'm bored and wish there were things to do, other girls who would play.

"She's getting uneasy," I hear the woman say.

"What's ailing her?" another says.

"Ah, it's no place for the child, really," she says. "It's just I didn't like not to come, and I wouldn't leave her behind."

"Sure, I'll take her home with me, Edna. I'm going now. Can't you call in and collect her on your way?"

"Oh," she says. "I don't know should I."

"Mine'd be a bit of company for her. Can't they play away out the back? And that man there won't budge as long as he has her on his knee."

Mrs. Kinsella laughs. I have never really heard her laugh till now.

"Sure, maybe, if you don't mind, Mildred," she says. "What harm is in it? And we'll not be long after you."

"Not a bother," Mildred says.

When we are out on the road and the goodbyes are said, Mildred strides on into a pace I can just about keep, and as soon as she rounds the bend the questions start. Hardly is one answered before the next is fired: "Which room did they put you into? Did Kinsella give you money? How much? Does she drink at night? Does he? Are they playing cards up there much? Do ye say the rosary? Does she put butter or margarine in her pastry? Where does the old dog sleep? Is the freezer packed solid? Does she skimp on things or is she allowed to spend? Are the child's clothes still hanging in the wardrobe?"

I answer them all easily, until the last. "The child's clothes?"

"Aye," she says. "If you're sleeping in his room you must surely know. Did you not look?"

"Well, she had clothes I wore for all the time I was here, but we went to Gorey this morning and bought new things."

"This rig-out you're wearing now? God Almighty," she says. "Anybody would think you were going on for a hundred."

"I like it," I say. "They told me it was flattering."

"Flattering, is it? Well. Well," she says. "I suppose it is, after living in the dead's clothes all this time."

"What?"

"The Kinsellas' young lad, you dope. Did you not know?"

I don't know what to say.

"That must have been some stone they rolled back to find you. Sure, didn't he follow that auld hound of theirs into the slurry tank and drown? That's what they say happened anyhow," she says.

I keep on walking and try not to think about what she has said, even though I can think of little else. The time for the sun to go down is hours from now, but the day feels like it is ending. I look at the sky and see the sun, still high, and, far away, a round moon coming out.

"They say John got the gun and took the hound down the field but he hadn't the heart to shoot him, the softhearted fool."

We walk on between the bristling hedges, in which small things seem to rustle and move. Chamomile grows along these ditches, wood sage and mint, plants whose names my mother somehow found the time to teach me. Farther along, the same heifer is still lost, in a different part of the road. Soon we come to the place where the black dog is barking through the gate. "Shut up and get in, you," she says to him.

It's a cottage she lives in, with uneven slabs of concrete outside the front door, overgrown shrubs and red-hot pokers growing tall. Here I must watch my head, my step. When we go in, the place is cluttered and an older woman is smoking at the cooker. There's a baby in a highchair. He lets out a cry when he sees the woman and drops a handful of marrowfat peas over the edge. "Look at you," she says. "The state of you."

I'm not sure if it's the woman or the child she is talking to. She takes off her cardigan and sits down and starts talking about the wake: who was there, the type of sandwiches that were made, the queen cakes, the corpse who was lying up crooked in the coffin and hadn't even been shaved properly, how they had plastic rosary beads for him, the poor fucker.

I don't know whether to sit or stand, to listen or leave, but just as I'm deciding what to do the dog barks and the gate opens and Kinsella comes in, stooping under the doorframe. "Good evening all," he says.

"Ah, John," the woman says. "You weren't long. We're only in the door. Aren't we only in the door, child?"

"Yes."

Kinsella hasn't taken his eyes off me. "Thanks, Mildred. It was good of you to take her home."

"It was nothing," the woman says. "She's a quiet young one, this."

"She says what she has to say, and no more. May there be many like her," he says. "Are you ready to come home, Petal?"

I follow him out to the car, where the woman is waiting.

"Were you all right in there?" she says.

I say I was.

"Did she ask you anything?"

"A few things, nothing much."

"What did she ask you?"

"She asked me if you used butter or margarine in your pastry."

"Did she ask you anything else?"

"She asked me was the freezer packed tight."

"There you are," Kinsella says.

"Did she tell you anything?" the woman asks.

I don't know what to say.

"What did she tell you?"

"She told me you had a little boy who followed the dog into the slurry tank and died, and that I wore his clothes to mass last Sunday."

When we get home, the hound comes out to the car to greet us, and I realize that I've not yet heard either one of them call him by his name. Kinsella sighs and goes off, stumbling a little, to milk. When he comes inside, he says he's not ready for bed. He puts what I realize is the boy's jacket on me.

"What are you doing now?" the woman says.

"I'm taking her as far as the strand."

"You'll be careful with that girl, John Kinsella," she says. "And don't you go without the lamp."

"What need is there for a lamp on a night like tonight?" he says, but he takes it anyhow, as it's handed to him.

There's a big moon shining on the yard, chalking our way onto the lane and along the road. Kinsella takes my hand in his. As he does, I realize that my father has never once held my hand, and some part of me wants Kinsella to let me go, so I won't have to think about this. It's a hard feeling, but as we walk along, I settle and let the difference between my life at home and the one I have here be.

When we reach the crossroads, we turn right, down a steep hill. The wind is high and hoarse in the trees, tearing fretfully, making the dry boughs rise and swing. It's sweet to feel the open road falling away under us, knowing that we will, at its end, come to the sea. Kinsella says a few meaningless things along the way, then falls quiet, and time passes without seeming to pass, and then we are in a sandy, open space where people must park their cars. It is full of tire marks and potholes, a rubbish bin that seems not to have been emptied in a long time.

"We're almost there now, Petal."

He leads me up a hill, where tall rushes bend and shake. Then we are standing on the crest of a dark place where the land ends and there is a long strand and water, which I know is deep and stretches all the way to England. Far out, in the darkness, two bright lights are blinking.

Kinsella lets me go and I race down the dune to the place where the black sea hisses up into loud, frothy waves. I run toward them as they back away, and run back, shrieking, when they crash in. Kinsella catches up and takes my shoes off, then his own. We walk along the edge of the sea as it claws at the sand under our bare feet. At one point, he holds me on his shoulders and we go in until the water is up to his knees. Then he walks me back to the tide line, where the dunes begin. Many things have washed up here: plastic

bottles, sticks and floats, and, farther on, a stable door whose bolt
is broken.

"Some man's horse is loose tonight," Kinsella says. "You know
the fishermen sometimes find horses out at sea. A man I know
towed a colt in once and the horse lay down for a long time and
then got up. And he was perfect.

"Strange things happen," he says. "A strange thing happened to
you tonight, but Edna meant no harm. It's too good, she is. She
wants to believe in the good in others, and sometimes her way of
finding out is to trust them, hoping she'll not be disappointed, but
she sometimes is."

I don't know how to answer.

"You don't ever have to say anything," he says. "Always remember that. Many's the man lost much just because he missed a perfect opportunity to say nothing."

He laughs then, a queer, sad laugh.

Everything about the night feels strange: to walk to a sea that's
always been there, to see it and feel it and fear it in the half-dark, to
listen to this man telling me things—about horses being towed in
from the deep, about his wife trusting others so she'll learn whom
not to trust—things that I don't fully understand, things that may
not even be intended for me.

As we turn to head back along the beach, the moon disappears
behind a cloud and we cannot see where we are going. At this
point, Kinsella lets out a sigh, stops, and lights the lamp.

"Ah, the women are nearly always right, all the same," he says.
"Do you know what the women have a gift for?"

"What?"

"Eventualities. A good woman can look far down the line and
smell what's coming before a man even gets a sniff of it."

He shines the light along the strand to find our footprints and
follow them back, but the only prints he can find are mine. "You
must have carried me there," he says.

I laugh at the thought of my carrying him, at the impossibility,
then realize that it was a joke, and I got it.

When the moon comes out again, he turns the lamp off and
we easily find the path we took through the dunes. We stop at the
top and he puts my shoes back on and then his own and knots the
laces. We turn and look at the water.

"See, there's three lights there now, where there was only two before."

I look out across the sea. There, the two lights are still blinking, but with another, steady light, shining in between.

"Can you see it?" he says.

"I can," I say. "It's there."

And that is when he puts his arms around me and gathers me into them as though I were his.

After a week of rain, on a Thursday, the letter comes. It is not so much a surprise as a shock. Already I have seen the signs: the shampoo for head lice in the chemist's shop, the fine-tooth combs. In the gift gallery there are copybooks stacked high, Biros, rulers, mechanical drawing sets. In the hardware, the lunchboxes and satchels and hurling sticks are left out front, where the women can see them.

We come home and take soup, dipping our bread, breaking it, slurping a little, now that we know one another. Afterward, I go with Kinsella out to the hay shed, where he makes me promise not to look while he is welding. I am following him around, I realize, but I cannot help it. It is past the time for the post to come but he does not suggest that I fetch it until evening, after the cows are milked and the milking parlor is swept and scrubbed. "I think it's time," he says, washing his boots with the hose.

I get into position, using the front step as a starting block. Kinsella looks at the watch and pulls down his handkerchief as if it was a flag. I race down the yard to the lane, make a tight corner, open the box, get the letters, and race back to the step, knowing that my time was not as fast as yesterday's.

"Nineteen seconds faster than your first run," Kinsella says. "And a two-second improvement on yesterday, despite the heavy ground. It's like the wind, you are." He takes the letters and goes through them, but today, instead of making jokes about what's inside of each, he pauses.

"Is that from Mammy?"

"You know," he says, "I think it could be."

"Do I have to go home?"

"Well, it's addressed to Edna, so why don't we give it in to her and let her read it."

We go into the parlor, where she is sitting with her feet up, looking through a book of knitting patterns. Kinsella slides the letter onto her lap. She opens it and reads it. It's one small sheet with writing on both sides. She puts it down, then picks it up and reads it again.

"Well," she says, "you have a new brother. Nine pounds two ounces. And school starts on Monday. Your mother has asked us to leave you up at the weekend so she can get you togged out and all."

"I have to go back, then?"

"Aye," she says. "But sure didn't you know that?"

I nod.

"You couldn't stay here forever with us two old forgeries."

I stand there and stare at the fire, trying not to cry. I don't so much hear as feel Kinsella leaving the room.

"Don't upset yourself," the woman says. "Come over here."

She shows me pages with knitted jumpers and asks me which pattern I like best, but all the patterns seem to blur together and I just point to one, a blue one, that looks like it might be easy.

"Well, you would pick the hardest one in the book," she says. "I'd better get started on that this week or you'll be too big for it by the time it's knitted."

Now that I know I must go home, I almost want to go. I wake earlier than usual and look out at the wet fields, the dripping trees, the hills, which seem greener than they did when I came. Kinsella hangs around all day, doing things but not really finishing anything. He says he has no disks for his angle grinder, no welding rods, and he cannot find the vise grip. He says that he got so many jobs done in the long stretch of fine weather that there's little left to do.

We are out looking at the calves, who have been fed. With warm water, Kinsella has made up their milk replacement, which they suck from long rubber teats. They look content lying there in a fresh bed of straw.

"Could ye leave me back this evening?"

"This evening?" Kinsella says.

I nod.

"Any evening suits me," he says. "I'll take you whenever you want, Petal."

I look at the day. It is like any other, with a flat gray sky hanging over the yard and the wet hound on watch outside the front door.

"Well, I had better milk early, so," he says. "Right." And goes on down the yard past me as though I am already gone.

The woman gives me a brown leather bag. "You can keep this old thing," she says. "I never have a use for it."

We fold my clothes and place them inside, along with the Ladybird books we found on the stand at Webb's in Gorey: *The Three Billy Goats Gruff, The Ugly Duckling, Snow-White and Rose-Red.* I can remember how the lines go, can match my memory of the words with the words that are written there. She gives me a bar of yellow soap and my facecloth, and the hairbrush she bought for me. As we gather all these things together, I remember where we got them, what was said, the days we spent, and how the sun, for most of the time, was shining.

Just then a car pulls into the yard. I am afraid to look, afraid it is my father, but it's a neighboring man. "Edna," he says, in a panic. "Is John about?"

"He's out at the milking," she says. "He should be finishing up now."

He runs across the yard, heavy in his Wellington boots, and minutes later Kinsella sticks his head around the door. "Joe Fortune needs a hand pulling a calf," he says. "Would you ever run out and finish the parlor off? I have the herd out."

"I will, surely," she says.

"I'll be back just as soon as I can."

"Don't I know you will."

She puts on her anorak and I watch her go down the yard. I wonder if I should go out to help but I come to the conclusion that I'd only be in the way. I sit in the armchair and look out to where a watery light is shining off the zinc bucket in the scullery. I could go to the well for water for her tea. It could be the last thing I do.

I put on the boy's jacket, take up the bucket, and walk down the fields. I know the way, could find the well with my eyes closed. When I cross the stile, the path does not look like the same path we followed on that first evening here. The way is muddy now and slippery in places. I trudge on along toward the little iron gate and down the steps. The water is much higher these days. I was on the fifth step that first evening here, but now I stand on the first and see the surface of the water reaching up and just about sucking the edge of the step that's one down from me. I bend with the bucket, letting it float then sink, as the woman does, but when I reach out to lift it another hand just like mine seems to come out of the water and pull me in.

It is not that evening or the following one but the evening after, on the Sunday, that I am taken home. When I come back from the well, soaked to the skin, the woman takes one look at me and turns very still before she gathers me up and takes me inside and makes up my bed again.

The following morning I do not feel hot, but she keeps me upstairs, bringing me warm drinks with lemon and cloves and honey, aspirin.

"'Tis nothing but a chill, she has," I hear Kinsella say.

"When I think of what could have happened."

"If you've said that once, you've said it a hundred times."

"But—"

"Nothing happened, and the girl is grand. And that's the end of it."

I lie there with the hot-water bottle, listening to the rain and looking through my books, making up something slightly different to happen at the end of each, each time.

On Sunday I am allowed to get up, and we pack everything again, as before. Toward evening, we have supper and wash and change into our good clothes. The sun has come out, is lingering in long, cool slants, and the yard is dry in places. Sooner than I would like, we are ready and in the car, turning down the lane, going up through Gorey and on, along the narrow roads through Carnew and Shillelagh.

"That's where Da lost the red heifer playing cards," I say.

"Wasn't that some wager?" the woman says.

"It was some loss for him," Kinsella says.

When we get to our lane, the gates are closed and Kinsella gets out to open them, then closes them behind us, and drives on very slowly to the house. I feel, now, that the woman is trying to make up her mind whether she should say something to me, but I don't really have any idea what it is, and she gives me no clue. The car stops in front of the house, the dogs bark, and my sisters race out. I see my mother through the window, with what is now the second youngest in her arms.

Inside, the house feels damp and cold. The lino is tracked over with dirty footprints. Mammy stands there with my little brother, and looks at me. "You've grown," she says.

"Yes," I say.

"'Yes,' is it?" she says, and raises her eyebrows.

She bids the Kinsellas good evening and tells them to sit down—if they can find a place to sit—and fills the kettle from the bucket under the kitchen table. We move playthings off the car seat under the window and sit down. Mugs are taken off the dresser, a loaf of bread is sliced, butter and jam left out.

"Oh, I brought you jam," the woman says. "Don't let me forget to give it to you, Mary."

"I made this out of the rhubarb you sent down," Ma says. "That's the last of it."

"I should have brought more," the woman says. "I wasn't thinking."

"Where's the new addition?" Kinsella asks.

"Oh, he's up in the room there. You'll hear him soon enough."

"Is he sleeping through the night for you?"

"On and off," Ma says. "The same child could crow at any hour."

My sisters look at me as though I am an English cousin, coming over to touch my dress, the buckles on my shoes. They seem different, thinner, and have nothing to say. We sit in to the table and eat the bread and drink the tea. When a cry is heard from upstairs, Ma gives my brother to Mrs. Kinsella and goes up to fetch the baby. He is pink and crying, his fists tight. He looks bigger than the last, stronger.

"Isn't there a fine child, God bless him," Kinsella says.

Ma pours more tea with one hand and sits down and takes her breast out for the baby. Her doing this in front of Kinsella makes me blush. Seeing me blush, Ma gives me a long, deep look.

"No sign of himself?" Kinsella says.

"He went out there earlier, wherever he's gone," Ma says.

A little bit of talk starts up then, little balls of speech they seem to kick uneasily back and forth. Soon after, a car is heard outside. Nothing more is said until my father appears and throws his hat on the dresser.

"Evening, all," he says.

"Dan," Kinsella says.

"Ah, there's the prodigal child," he says. "You came back to us, did you?"

I say I did.

"Did she give trouble?"

"Trouble?" Kinsella says. "Good as gold, she was, the same girl."

"Is that so?" Da says, sitting down. "Well, isn't that a relief."

"You'll want to sit in," Mrs. Kinsella says, "and get your supper."

"I had a liquid supper," Da says, "down in Parkbridge."

I sneeze then, and reach into my pocket for my handkerchief, and blow my nose.

"Have you caught cold?" Ma asks.

"No," I say, hoarsely.

"You haven't?"

"Nothing happened."

"What do you mean?"

"I didn't catch cold," I say.

"I see," she says, giving me another deep look.

"The child's been in bed for the last couple of days," Kinsella says. "Didn't she catch herself a wee chill."

"Aye," Da says. "You couldn't mind them. You know yourself."

"Dan," Ma says, in a steel voice.

Mrs. Kinsella looks uneasy.

"You know, I think it's nearly time that we were making tracks," Kinsella says. "It's a long road home."

"Ah, what's the big hurry?" Ma says.

"No hurry at all, Mary, just the usual. These cows don't give you any opportunity to have a lie-in."

He gets up then and takes my little brother from his wife and gives him to my father. My father takes the child and looks across at the baby suckling. I sneeze and blow my nose again.

"That's a right dose you came home with," Da says.

"It's nothing she hasn't caught before and won't catch again," Ma says. "Sure, isn't it going around?"

"Are you ready for home?" Kinsella asks.

Mrs. Kinsella stands then, and they say their goodbyes. I follow them out to the car with my mother, who still has the baby in her arms. Mrs. Kinsella takes out the cardboard box with the pots of jam. Kinsella lifts a four-stone sack of potatoes out of the boot. "These are floury," he says. "Queens they are, Mary."

My mother thanks them, saying it was a lovely thing they did, to keep me.

"The girl was welcome and is welcome again, anytime," the woman says.

"She's a credit to you, Mary," Kinsella says. "You keep your head in the books," he says to me. "I want to see gold stars on them copybooks next time I come up here." He gives me a kiss then, and the woman hugs me. I watch them getting into the car and closing the doors and I feel a start when the engine turns and the car begins to move away.

"What happened at all?" Ma says, now that the car is gone.

"Nothing," I say.

"Tell me."

"Nothing happened." This is my mother I am speaking to, but I have learned enough, grown enough, to know that what happened is not something I need ever mention. It is my perfect opportunity to say nothing.

I hear the car braking on the gravel in the lane, the door opening, and then I am doing what I do best. It's nothing I have to think about. I take off from standing and race on down the lane. My heart feels not so much in my chest as in my hands. I am carrying it along swiftly, as though I have become the messenger for what is going on inside of me. Several things flash through my mind: the boy on the wallpaper, the gooseberries, that moment when the bucket pulled me under, the lost heifer, the third light on the water. I think of my summer, of now, of a tomorrow that I can't entirely believe in.

As I am rounding the bend, reaching the point where I daren't look, I see him there, closing the gate, putting the clamp back on. His eyes are down, and he seems to be looking at his hands, at what he is doing. My feet batter on along the rough gravel, the strip of tatty grass in the middle of our lane. There is only one thing I care about now, and my feet are carrying me there. As soon as he sees me, he grows still. By the time I reach him, the gate is open and I am smack against him and lifted into his arms. For a long stretch, he holds me tight. I feel the thumping of my heart, my breaths coming out, then my heart and my breaths settling differently. At a point, which feels much later, a sudden gust blows through the trees and shakes big, fat raindrops over us. My eyes are closed now and I can feel him, the heat of him coming through his good clothes, can smell the soap on his neck. When I finally open my eyes and look over his shoulder, it is my father I see, coming along strong and steady, his walking stick in his hand. I hold on as though I'll drown if I let go, and listen to the woman, who seems, in her throat, to be taking it in turns sobbing and crying, as though she is crying not for one but for two now. I daren't keep my eyes open and yet I do, staring up the lane, past Kinsella's shoulder, seeing what he can't. If some part of me wants with all my heart to get down and tell the woman who has minded me so well that I will never, never tell, something deeper keeps me there in Kinsella's arms, holding on.

"Daddy," I keep warning him, keep calling him. "Daddy."

SAM LIPSYTE

The Dungeon Master

FROM *The New Yorker*

THE DUNGEON MASTER has detention. We wait at his house by
the county road. The Dungeon Master's little brother Marco puts
out corn chips and orange soda.

Marco is a paladin. He fights for the glory of Christ. Marco has
been many paladins since winter break. They are all named Valentine, and the Dungeon Master makes certain they die with the least
possible amount of dignity.

It's painful enough when he rolls the dice, announces that a
drunken orc has unspooled some of Valentine's guts for sport.
Worse are the silly accidents. One Valentine tripped on a floor
plank and cracked his head on a mead bucket. He died of trauma
in the stable.

"Take it!" the Dungeon Master said that time. Spit sprayed over
the top of his laminated screen. "Eat your fate," he said. "Your
thread just got the snippo!"

The Dungeon Master has a secret language that we don't quite
understand. They say he's been treated for it.

Whenever the Dungeon Master kills another Valentine, Marco
runs off and cries to their father. Dr. Varelli nudges his son back
into the study, sticks his bushy head in the door, says, "Play nice, my
beautiful puppies."

"Father," the Dungeon Master will say, "stay the fuck out of my
mind realm."

"I honor your wish, my beauty."

Dr. Varelli says things like that. It's not a secret language, just an
embarrassing one. Maybe that's why his wife left him, left Marco

and the Dungeon Master too. It's not a decent reason to leave, but as the Dungeon Master hopes to teach us, the world is not a decent place to live.

Now we sit, munch chips.

"If they didn't say corn, I wouldn't think of them as corn," Brendan says.

He's a third-level wizard.

"Detention?" Cherninsky says, and stands, squats, stands, sits. He's got black bangs and freckles, suffers from that disease where you can't stay in your chair.

"He chucked a spaz in Spanish," I say. "I heard one of the seniors."

"The teacher rides him," Marco says. Marco despises the Dungeon Master but loves his brother. I like Marco, but I'm no fan of Valentine. I'm a third-level ranger. I fight for the glory of me.

The door smacks open.

"Ah, the doomed." The Dungeon Master strides past us, short and pasty with a fine brown beard.

He sits behind his screen, which he's ordered us never to touch. We never do, not even when he's at detention. He shuffles some papers—his maps and grids. Dice click in his stubby hand. Behind him, on the wall, hang Dr. Varelli's diplomas. The diplomas say that he's a child psychiatrist, but he never brings patients here, and I'm not sure he ever leaves the house.

"When last we met," the Dungeon Master begins, "Olaf the thief had been caught stealing a loaf of pumpernickel from the village bakery. A halfling baker's boy had cornered our friend with a bread knife. Ready to roll?"

"I don't want to die this way," Cherninsky says.

Cherninsky always dies this way—we all do, or die of something like it—but he seems pretty desperate this afternoon. Maybe he's thinking of people who really have died, like his baby sister. She drowned in the ocean. Nobody ever mentions it.

"This situation begs the question," the Dungeon Master says, and sips from a can of strawberry milk. "Is bread the staff of life or the staff of death?"

"What does that mean?" Cherninsky asks.

"Read more," the Dungeon Master says. "Enrich yourself."

"We all read," Brendan says.

"I mean books," the Dungeon Master says. "I can't believe you're a wizard."

"Don't kill me in a bakery," Cherninsky says.

"Don't steal bread."

"What do you want? I'm a thief."

"Roll."

Cherninsky rolls, dies, hops out of his chair.

"So why'd you get detention?" he says.

"When did I get detention?"

"Today," I say. "You got it today."

The Dungeon Master peers at me over his screen.

"Today, bold ranger, I watched a sad little pickpocket bleed out on a bakery floor. That's the only thing that has happened today. Get it?"

"Got it," I say.

I know that he is strange and not as smart as he pretends, but at least he keeps the borders of his mind realm well patrolled. That must count for something.

"Now," the Dungeon Master says, "any of you feebs want to take on the twerp with the kitchen utensil? Or would you rather consider a back-alley escape?"

"Back-alley escape," Marco says.

"Valentine the Twenty-seventh?" the Dungeon Master says.

"Twenty-ninth."

"Don't get too attached, brother."

There are other kids, other campaigns. They have what teachers call imaginations. Some of them are in gifted. They play in the official afterschool club.

"I've got a seventeenth-level elf wizard," Eric tells me in our freshman homeroom. "She flies a dragon named Green Star. We fought an army of frost giants last week. What about you?"

"We never even see a dragon, let alone fly one. You have a girl character?"

"You play with that psycho senior, what's-his-face."

"The Dungeon Master," I say.

"He calls himself that? Like it's his name?

"He doesn't call himself anything."

"I heard that when he was little he hit some kid with an aluminum bat. Gave him brain damage."

"Completely made up," I say, though I'm pretty sure it's true. "He's very smart."

"He's not in gifted," Eric says.

"Neither am I."

"Good point," Eric says, and turns to talk to Lucy Mantooth.

Most days we play until we're due home for dinner. But sometimes, if we call our houses for permission, Dr. Varelli cooks for us—hamburgers, spaghetti—and, if it's not a school night, we sleep over. In the morning it's pancakes, bacon, eggs, toast.

"Eat, eat, my puppies."

We puppies eat in the study. Since we die so often, we take breaks while one of us makes a new character.

One day, while Marco rolls Valentine the Thirty-second into being, I wander out to the parlor. Dr. Varelli sits on the divan with a shiny wooden guitar. His fingers flutter over the strings, and he sings something high and weepy. He stops, looks up.

"It's an Italian ballad." There is shame in his voice, but it's not about the song.

I follow his gaze to an old photograph on the wall. A young woman poses beside a fountain. Pigeons swoop off its stone rim. Marco once told me that this woman is his mother.

"So beautiful," I say.

"Of course," Dr. Varelli says. "Rome is a beautiful city."

Later we gather in the study for a new adventure. Our characters rendezvous at an inn called the Jaundiced Chimera. We've all died here before, in brawls and dagger duels, of poisoned ale, or even just of infections borne on unwashed steins. But the Dungeon Master insists the place has the best shepherd's pie this side of the Flame Lakes.

We befriend a blind man. Cherninsky steals his silver, but the poor sap doesn't notice, so we befriend him some more. He tells us of a cave near the top of Mt. Total Woe, of a dragon in the cave and a hoard beneath the dragon.

"Sounds dangerous," Marco says.

"That's the point," I say.

"It's a tough decision," Brendan says. I barely know Brendan. He met Marco at swim class or something. He's nice, for the most part, and kind of dim. Wherever he goes to school, I doubt people notice him enough to bully him.

Not true of Cherninsky. He makes a habit of asking for it, though some tormentors hang back. There's something feral and untutored about his schoolyard ways. You sense that he might take a bully's punches to the death. He's the kid people whisper has no mother or father at home, but of course he does, they're just old and stopped raising him years ago, maybe when his sister drowned. He always plays a thief, and even outside of the game, when he's just Cherninsky, he steals stuff from the stores on Main. He and the Dungeon Master are not so different, or this town hurts them the same, which is probably why they sometimes hate each other.

"Damn it, Brendan," Cherninsky says now. "A tough decision? I say we go to that cave and get the gold. And then we get wenches."

"Wenches?" Brendan says.

"Tarts," Cherninsky says. "Elf beaver."

It's all a charade, because there is no decision. There is no alternative. We shall scale Mt. Total Woe or die trying. Most likely the latter.

"We're going to grease that dragon," I say.

"Grease?" Brendan says.

"Vietnam," I say.

"Oh, right."

But now the Dungeon Master has a mysterious appointment, which Dr. Varelli leans in to remind his beautiful puppy of, and the game adjourns.

Cherninsky and I head home. Soon we're near the reservoir, and we squish ourselves under the fence. We stumble down a rock embankment and start throwing things into the water, whatever we can find — rocks, bottles, old toys, parts of cars. We've all grown up doing this. I guess it's our child psychiatry.

Cherninsky drags a shredded tire toward the shoreline. He waves off my offer to help.

"So what's your opinion?" he asks. "Think this Mt. Woe thing is going to be any different?"

The tire wobbles in the water, then pitches over with a splash. I whip a golf ball at its treads.

"Maybe," I say. "It could be."

"Saddest thing is how Marco and Brendan are so scared of dying. It's just a game, but he's playing with their minds. He's been to Bergen Pines. Did you know that? Certified mental. I'm quitting soon. This game is for dorks, gaylords, and psychos, no offense."

"None taken," I lie.

Cherninsky claps my neck.

"Want to smoke weed?"

"No thanks."

"Want to watch my neighbor take a shower? She usually does it around now. She takes care of herself in there."

"What do you mean?"

"You know what I mean. Oh, forget it. You want to start a band? I have all the equipment."

"Where'd you get the equipment?"

"Don't worry about that. We'd need a name."

"How about Elf Beaver?"

"That's pretty stupid," Cherninsky says. "The fact that you thought of that could be a sign you're a nimrod. Help me with this other tire."

We eat leftover London broil from my mother's last catering job. My father, home from human resources, has his home-from-work work shirt on. He slices cucumbers for the cucumber salad, his specialty, while my mother pulls a tray from the stove. Upstairs, my sister squeals. She's all phone calls and baggy sweaters.

Today my ranger nearly got the snippo. A giant warthog jumped him in the woods. Is there even a warthog in the game manual? My ranger—his name is Valium, just to tease Marco—cut the beast down, but lost a lot of hit points. Even now I can picture him bent over a brook, cupping water onto his wounds. Later he rests in the shade of an oak. The warthog crackles on a spit.

"How's it going over there?" my mother asks.

"Here?" I say. "Great."

"Awesome," my sister says, joining us. "Dead cow. Is there anything veggie?"

"Cucumber salad," my father says.

"Way to experiment with new dishes, Dad."

"Way to employ sarcasm," my father says.

"Not here," my mother says. "There."

"Where?" I say.

"The Varelli house."

"It's going fine," I say.

"Is it fun?" my mother asks. "I want you to have fun, you know."

"Yeah, it's fun, I guess."

My mother gives my father one of those meaningful looks which mean nothing to me yet.

"What?" I say.

"The Varelli kid," my sister says. "Isn't he the one who flashed those girls at the ice rink? And set his turds on fire in the school parking lot?"

"That was a long time ago," I say.

"It was kind of cool," my sister says. "In a sicko way."

"Poor Varelli," my father says. "His wife."

"That's the thing about it," my mother says.

"The thing about what?" I say.

My father turns to my sister and me as though he had something to say but has forgotten it and is now trying to come up with something else.

"I put something special in the cucumber salad. Can you taste it?"

"Veal?" my sister asks.

"I've got nothing against you having fun and using your imagination," my mother says. "But it's just too crucial a time in your life to get sidetracked with games. They write those articles. And this one's a little creepy. They write articles about that too."

"My grades are good," I say.

"It's middle track, honey. Of course your grades are good. But we're trying not to be middle-track people."

Later my father and I do the dishes, scour the pans—our pans, the catering pans.

"Don't worry," he says. "Everything will be okay."

Maybe he's that guy at the office too—the reassurance dispenser, the diplomat. The middleman with the middle-track son.

"Are you guys getting a divorce?" I ask for no reason.

"Funny you should say that."

My father inspects the sudsy platter in his gloved hand.

"Yes," he says finally, "we are getting a divorce."

I stand there for a stunned moment, and then his weird chirpy laugh kicks in.

"Gotcha!"

He must be the human-resources jokester as well, though maybe I had it coming. Now he gets serious. My mother's catering gigs are drying up, and the raise he was counting on has fallen through.

My sister and I will have to find afterschool jobs if we mean to keep ourselves in candy and movies and rock 'n' roll, he says.

"There's still some time," he adds. "Enjoy your game. We're just saying you might want to find some better things to do while you can. You're going to be plenty busy."

I don't really have better things to do. I could do what I did before I started going to the Varellis'. I could come home and eat too much peanut butter and hide in my room. I could lie in bed and think about Lucy Mantooth, stroke a batch off, nap until dinnertime. I could watch TV and fake doing my homework. But I'm not sure that those are better things.

We tramp past the tree line of Mt. Total Woe, reach a stony ridge shrouded in mist. We hear odd bleats on the wind, and our weapons are wet with the blood of minor beasts we've slain along the trail. Deathbirds squawk overhead. Valentine the Whatever scans the rock face for possible points of ingress.

It's hard to see far in the mist.

"I could weave a spell to clear it," Brendan says.

"What if the goats are shape-shifters?" Cherninsky says.

"What goats?" Brendan asks.

"Those are goats. Only goats bleat."

"Sheep bleat," Marco says.

"And anyway," Cherninsky says, "why should we believe that blind guy at the inn?"

"I think he was chaotic good," I say. "I recognize my own kind."

"I'm sure you do," Marco says.

Marco's character is lawful good. It makes for what you'd call personality clashes. But today's game is too good to waste bickering. We smite the fanged and scaly, stalk the untold riches the blind man did, in fact, tell us about. Meanwhile, no runaway oxcart smears us into the road. We are not nipped by rabid squirrels. We do not succumb slowly, like one early Valentine, to rectal cancer. This must be what the official afterschool game is like — gifted children dreaming up splendors, not middle-trackers squirming beneath a nutso's moods.

What has come over the Dungeon Master? He seems almost happy behind his screen.

"Brendan's spell works," he says. "The mist is clearing. About a hundred yards closer to the top you can see an outcropping and the mouth of a cave. Guarded, yes, by goats."

"We're going into that mountain," I say. "I can't believe we're going into that mountain. Let's stove some heads."

"And get the gold," Cherninsky says.

"Stove?" Brendan says.

"He reads," the Dungeon Master says, and shoots me a grin so rare it's a benediction. I decide not to tell him that I stole *stove* from a whaling movie.

Now we're at the cave mouth. The goats sing their goat songs and part at our approach. Valentine takes a prayerful knee.

"Enough," Cherninsky says. "You can rim Christ on the way out."

"Infidel," Marco says.

"I'm a humanist," Cherninsky says.

"Is that like human resources?" I ask.

"Maybe."

"Okay," I say. "Let's go into the fucking cave."

We go into the fucking cave. It's dark and we light torches, listening to bats flap off. We hunch and shuffle through the tunnel maze. Putrid fiends lurk at every dead end. That's how you know it's a dead end: something that smells like rotten sausage pops up and claws at your eyeballs. This is what we always wanted: the top-shelf monsters, hydras and griffins, basilisks, giant worms. The thief and the wizard set traps and decoys, cast spells of misdirection. Valentine and Valium, that suddenly ferocious duo, berserk right in with morning stars and swords of dwarven steel. We bash and slice. Monsters fall in quivering, sushilike chunks.

The Dungeon Master, he almost roots for us. He lets each situation develop, refrains from his dire lessons, his murderous intrusions. We're steeped in the dire. We want to stab beasts.

We turn a granite corner, and there, lo and behold, we behold him. The dragon lounges, obscenely, atop a great apron of stone, his vermilion scales ablaze. Rainbow flames snake from his nostrils with each dozy breath. He regards us through the slits of his slimy amber eyes.

The dragon's treasure spills out from beneath him—gold, silver, rubies, jade. Just what's heaped around our feet at the threshold of the chamber is a princely sum.

"Let's take that," Cherninsky says.

"Take what?" Marco asks.

"What's around our feet. Just scoop it up and run."

"Not fight the dragon?" the Dungeon Master asks.

"I like it," Brendan says. "That's strategy."

"The dragon could really kill the hell out of us," Marco, who will never learn, explains.

"No, let's fight the dragon," I say, and the Dungeon Master nods. "It's part of the game. Maybe we can tame him and ride him."

"Ride him?" Cherninsky says. "Are you out of your mind?"

"People do it."

"It would be cool," Brendan says.

"I got one thing to say," Cherninsky declares, out of his chair now and pacing. "I'm not going to die here."

"Take a chance," I say. "Otherwise it's just boring. You're the one who said we shouldn't be afraid to die."

"When did I say that?"

"Down at the reservoir."

"The reservoir," the Dungeon Master says. "You guys talk about the campaign down there? You suck each other's little bird dicks and talk tactics?"

"Yeah," Cherninsky says. "We did it Bergen Pines style."

"Guys," I say. "Stop it. Come on. Let's decide about the dragon. You really want to bail?"

"Better safe than sorry," Marco says.

"Is that an old paladin saying?"

"You're outvoted," Cherninsky says to me.

"Fine."

"Okay," Cherninsky says to the Dungeon Master. "We'll just scoop up what's near our feet and not rile the dragon. Can you roll for not riling the dragon?"

"Sure you want to do this?" the Dungeon Master asks. "This moment might never come again."

"We're sure."

"Listen," the Dungeon Master says. "I know I've been hard on all of you. I want to be more easygoing from now on. I want you to have fun."

"This is fun," Brendan says. "Really. Thank you. This is so exciting. But I think right now we should just grab a little gold and leave the cave."

"This is pathetic," I say. "It's weenis."

"You don't know anything about real violence," Brendan says.

"What?"

"You heard."

"It's a dragon, man!"

I notice Cherninsky slide a scrap of paper over to the Dungeon Master. The Dungeon Master drops dice in his leather cup, the one reserved for the most fateful rolls. The dice thump on the desk blotter.

"Consider the dragon officially riled."

"No," Brendan says. "No, no."

"Get the gold!" Cherninsky says.

I draw my two-handed sword and brandish it at the dragon while the others shovel treasure and flee.

"Come on!" they call.

"Go," I say. "I'll catch up. I've got a sudden craving for dragon burgers."

A smile wavers on the Dungeon Master's face. Because I am brave, I realize, he will spare me.

I charge the dragon, leap with my sword for his throat. Rainbow flames pour over my magic chain mail.

The Dungeon Master flicks his eyes at my roll.

"You're dead. Deep-fried."

"Huh?"

"A craving for dragon burgers? You think you're in a movie?"

"No," I say. "A game. And I have magic chain mail."

"Bogus magic chain mail," the Dungeon Master says. "You bought it off that wino monk."

"It's held up okay until now."

"You thought you could kill a dragon? Sorry, my friend. Long may we honor the memory of Valium."

"This is bullshit."

"Bullshit?" the Dungeon Master says. He's wound up. He really isn't that well. "It's not bullshit. It's probability. What, you gonna kwy? You gonna kwy like my little bratha? Life is nasty, brutish, and, more to the point, it sucks. Get it, bird dick? How's your two-handed bird dick now?"

"It's okay," I say.

The remainder of the group makes it out of the mountain maze, but the goats turn out to be shape-shifters, just as Cherninsky warned. They transform into ogres with huge spiked maces. It's hardly a fight. Before he dies, Cherninsky's thief does manage to stick an ogre with his dirk. The ogre turns back into a goat, then into Cherninsky's dead sister, drenched, draped in seaweed.

"Just a little girl," the Dungeon Master says.

"You freak," I say.

Cherninsky's got his pen out, and I think he's about to go for the Dungeon Master's neck, but then he starts to bawl.

"Cry it out, sweetheart," the Dungeon Master says.

"Leave him alone," I say.

"This doesn't concern you," the Dungeon Master says. "Just back off. You have no clue."

"Okay," Marco says. "It'll be okay."

He sounds like my father.

"The hell it will," the Dungeon Master says.

The Dungeon Master holds up the note Cherninsky passed him.

"Wait till you hear this," he says. "Your pal was planning to steal everybody's gold. He wanted me to roll for it."

"He's a thief," I say.

"Go ahead, defend him."

"I am."

Brendan freezes in his chair. Cherninsky keeps weeping. Marco bobs up and down, mumbles a prayer of okay.

I stand, whack the screen off the Dungeon Master's desk, see the dice, the sheets of graph paper, the manuals and numerical tables. There are doodles on the blotter. Giant vaginas with angel wings, mostly. They soar through ballpoint clouds.

"I said never touch the screen," the Dungeon Master hisses.

"And I say don't flash girls you will never have at the ice rink. Don't set fire to your shits in the parking lot. You're a mental case. They should have kept you locked up."

The Dungeon Master comes around the desk and I think he's about to make a speech, but he lowers his head and spears me in the gut. We crash together to the floor. He squeezes my throat. I palm his chin and push. Marco screams, and I'm almost out of air when Brendan climbs the Dungeon Master's back and bites his head. They both tumble away. The door bangs open and Dr. Varelli leans in.

"Play nice, you goddamn puppies!" he bellows, then shuts the door.

We lie there, heaving. My wrist throbs. I smell raspberry soda in the carpet.

The Dungeon Master paws at the blood on his head. Brendan rubs his tooth.

"You children," the Dungeon Master says, then rises, and lumbers off. We hear him scream at his father in the kitchen. He calls him a loser, a lesbian.

"It's been a little difficult around here," Marco says.

I crawl over to the window. In the next yard, some kids kick a ball. It looks amazing.

My broken wrist takes a long time to heal. I stay clear of the Varelli house, and at school only Eric signs my cast. He puts his initials on it, as though his full name would announce too heavy an association. The deal is that I don't have to get a job until the cast comes off.

I join the afterschool club, roll a ranger called Valium the Second, but nobody thinks it's funny. Why would they? Lucy Mantooth plays a wizard-thief. It's clear that she doesn't want me in the club.

Eric lives near me, and sometimes we walk part of the way home together. He likes to cut through some trees on a path near the Varellis' house, and I don't say anything. One day we see the Dungeon Master's Corvette in the driveway. His father bought it for him last year, but the Dungeon Master has never driven it. He doesn't even have a license.

"You like our game so far?" Eric asks.

"It's cool."

It is cool, despite the death stares from Lucy Mantooth. We fly dragons, battle giants, build castles, raise armies and families and crops. But something is missing. No goblin child will shank you for your coin pouch. You'll never die from a bad potato.

"I think Lucy likes you," Eric says.

"What's the giveaway? The fact that she never talks to me or that she rolls her eyes whenever I say anything?"

"Both."

"I guess I don't know much about girls."

"You'll learn," Eric says. "You've been hanging out with those weirdos."

"Everything's weird if you stare at it," I say.

"I don't know about that," Eric says. "We're sponsored by the school, just like the chess team."

I get bored with Eric's game. Lucy Mantooth never warms up. Her wizard-thief leaves me for dead in a collapsing wormhole. Was there something I was supposed to say? I resume my old routine: peanut butter, batch, nap.

One day I'm headed home to do just that. A sports car pulls up to the sidewalk, a midnight-blue Corvette.

"Need a ride?" the Dungeon Master asks.

I don't, but slide in anyway. I've never been in a Corvette.

We drive around town for a while, past my school, the hobby shop.

"Thought you didn't have a license," I say.

"Who said I do?"

The Dungeon Master smiles.

"There are rumors and there is the truth and there are true rumors. You want the rundown?" he asks. "Here's the rundown. Hit a kid with a bat and gave him brain damage, yes. Flashing, yes. Burning my bowel movements, no. Have I been to the bughouse? I've been to the bughouse. Am I insane? Does my opinion even count? Remember all the newspaper stories about how the game makes kids crazy? Makes them do horrible things?"

"My mom clips them for me."

"Love those. Take, for example, suicides. The game doesn't create suicides. If anything, it postpones them. I mean, the world gives you many reasons to snuff it, got to admit."

"I'm fourteen," I say. "I don't know what I admit."

"In another age you could be a father already. In another neighborhood, even."

We drive for a while. We're a few towns east.

"Nobody's seen you lately," the Dungeon Master says. "Marco says you play with some snotty faggots at school."

"I stopped."

"You hear about Cherninsky? He got caught with all this stolen musical stuff in his garage. Amps and guitars and drums, the whole deal. Tried to dump it in the reservoir, but the cops got most of it. Now his dad might go to jail."

"His dad?" I say.

"Harsh, right? Anyway, we're into war-gaming now. Real technical shit. It's not the same. Brendan can barely handle it. We're doing Tobruk. I'm Rommel."

"The Desert Fox."

"You read," the Dungeon Master says, though I picked up the name from an old tank movie. "That's what I like about you. That's why I thought I could teach you."

"Teach me what?"

We pull into a scenic lookout, the Palisades. Past the bushes in front of us the cliff drops sheer to some rocks in the Hudson. The Corvette idles, and I wonder if I made a mistake when I accepted this ride. The Dungeon Master looks off across the river as though ready to jump it.

"Teach me what?" I ask.

The Dungeon Master guns the engine. I turn to him—that pale skin, the fine-spun beard, the bright, bitter eyes.

"Teach me what?"

His answer is another rev. His fingers drum on the gear knob. We're going to fly a dragon, after all. Part of me is ready. Maybe it's the part that kept me in Dr. Varelli's study so long.

"Whoa," the Dungeon Master laughs. "You're shaking."

He shifts into reverse and swings the car around. Soon we're back on town streets.

"Had you shitting," he says.

"You did."

"I'm doing that for real at some point."

"Oh," I say.

"But not for a while."

"That's good."

"My dad's kicking me out after graduation. I think it'll be better for Marco. That kid needs to bloom."

"Where will you go? Your mom's house?"

"My mom doesn't have a house. She died when Marco was born."

"Really? I'm sorry. I figured she just left."

"Well, guess that's true in a way. No, I've got a cousin in Canada. We might room together."

"That'll be cool."

"Probably not. Here we are."

"Okay," I say. "Thanks for the lift."

"You were almost home when I picked you up."

"Still, thanks."

I'm cutting across the yard when the Dungeon Master calls my name.

"No hard feelings, okay?" he says.

I stop, picturing him there behind me with his ridiculous head sticking out of the passenger-side window, but I cannot turn around. I'm still trembling from our drive. Do I have an almost uncanny sense in this instant of what's to come, some cold swirling vision whose provenance I do not comprehend but in which I see the Dungeon Master, blue-cheeked, hanging by his communion tie in Dr. Varelli's study, and Cherninsky, his dad in prison, panhandling with the scrawny punks, the pin-stuck runaways in Alphabet City, and me, Burger Castle employee of the month for the month of October, degunking the fryolator in the late autumn light?

Of course I don't.

"Really," the Dungeon Master calls again. "No hard feelings."

It must be the dumbest thing he's ever said. No hard feelings? What could ever be harder than feelings?

I want to tell him this, but even as I turn back the Corvette peels away.

REBECCA MAKKAI

Peter Torrelli, Falling Apart

FROM *Tin House*

WHEN CARLOS ASKED WHY I would risk my whole career for
Peter Torrelli, I told him he had to understand that in those last
three years of high school, Peter and I were the only two gay boys
in Chicago. Because I really believed it, back then, and twenty-five
years of experience proving otherwise was nothing in the face of
that original muscle memory: me and Peter side by side on the
hard pew during chapel, not listening, washed blind by the sun
from the high windows, breathing in sync. It didn't matter that we
weren't close anymore, I told Carlos. The point was, he'd been my
first love. I'd never actually loved him, but still, listen, believe me,
there's another kind of first love.

It was during one of those long lectures or concerts or assem-
blies that Peter and I had discovered our common neurosis: the
fear of magically switching bodies with the speaker or singer or
priest, and then having to improvise an exit. I would slide toward
Peter on the pew, open a hymnal, and above "A Mighty Fortress Is
Our God" scribble in pencil: "Tuba player?" Peter would look up
to the stage to watch the fat Winnetka sophomore puff his cheeks
like a blowfish and write back: "Stop playing—no one misses a
tuba." "1st Violin?" I wrote. "Feign a swoon," he'd write back. And
then he'd mouth it to me, relishing the *oooo* of *swoon*. We joked
about this fear, but really I think it bothered us both—this idea
that we might suddenly be thrust in front of our peers and examined. It doesn't take a psychotherapist to figure out why. Peter later
claimed the whole reason he became an actor was that the only way
he could enjoy a play was from the inside.

Everyone else knew it was his looks. I hadn't understood until we were sixteen what it meant to turn heads. I'd considered it a figurative expression. But when we stood in line at Manny's, or walked down Dearborn toward the bus, he was a human magnet. He was the North Pole. The girls at school would feel his sweater and tug his necktie. He said he had a girlfriend back east, that she was Miss Teenage Delaware, and everyone believed it. How could he *not* be onstage with that dark, sad face, that ocean of black hair, those sarcastic eyes? By the time we graduated, he'd done two seasons of professional summer stock. I was the varsity soccer goalie, and he was a movie star walking among us. When we sat together in chapel we looked like the kings of the school, and nobody knew any different.

And then the next day we were thirty-eight years old, and Peter fell to pieces. During a matinee of *Richard III,* in the middle of the second act, my friend abruptly and forever lost the ability to act. He said later it was something about the phrase "jolly thriving wooer," the strangeness of those words as they left his mouth, the pause a second too long before Ratcliffe entered. Since Peter told me all this, I've read the page twenty times in my Signet Classic—which is how I know that Peter's next line, as Richard, was "Good or bad news, that thou com'st in so bluntly?" It was a line he'd have made foul jokes about backstage. "And I said it," he told me. "But it came out in this voice, like all the costumes had fallen away, like I was some kid in eighth-grade English and I had to read my poem out loud. It was just *me,* and there was no character, no play, just these words I had to say. You know our whole thing about leapfrogging into someone else's body? It was like that, but like I suddenly leapfrogged into myself." He said he could see each face in the audience, every one of them at once, smell what they'd eaten for lunch. He could feel every pore of his own skin, and the ridiculous hump strapped to his back. Backstage, they knew something was wrong even before he started to shake. By the end of the next scene, the understudy was dressing.

Peter told me this the next week over lunch. Actually, he told me many times, over many lunches in the following year, as if through the retelling he could undo something. We met every other Thursday at the Berghoff, where he'd have root beer and

I'd have two pale ales and we'd both eat enormous plates of bratwurst and chicken schnitzel and noodles with butter sauce. We had set these lunches up two years earlier, very formally. We'd been in and out of touch for ages when we found ourselves alone on the living room futon of a boring party in Hyde Park, drunk, wondering aloud if knowing each other when we had acne was the reason we'd never dated as adults. We had kissed just once, sophomore year, when we stayed behind after a SADD meeting to pick up the leftover fliers. I didn't know he was gay. I hardly knew *I* was. He came over with the green fliers in a stack as if to hand them to me, but when I took hold of the papers he pulled them back and me with them. The only person I'd ever kissed before was a girl named Julie Gleason. Afterward he said, "You're pretty dense, aren't you." That was it. We didn't talk for two weeks, and then we were best friends again, before the paper cuts on my palm had even fully healed.

I had looked at him that night at the party—beautiful and grown up, with a beer bottle sweating against the leg of his jeans—and said, "I never see you anymore."

He said, "Yes, I'm slowly becoming invisible." Peter was the kind of guy who would try for any joke, any chance to flash his perfect orthodontia. Even when it wasn't funny, you had to appreciate the showmanship. And then he looked at me seriously, which was rare at the time. "We *should* get together and talk. I mean regularly, because I miss you. It would be like therapy." I should have known I would always be the therapist. I told him once that he was the Gatsby to my Nick Carraway. He flashed his teeth and said, "Yes, but I throw *much* wilder parties."

And like stupid little Nick, I ended up trying to fix things. If I hadn't spent American Lit distracted by Zach Moretti and his amazing forearms, I might have registered that these stories never end well.

Let me say, Peter had been brilliant. Chicago breeds its own stage stars who stay local even if they're good enough to go to New York, and he was one of them. When I saw his Hamlet at Chicago Shakespeare, all memories of Mel and Lord Larry vanished in a celluloid fog. He was the right age, the right build, and those eyes could turn like lightning from irony to terror. I wonder how that colored our friendship, that I saw him simultaneously as Peter and

Hamlet. If nothing else, it made me more tolerant of his ramblings and neuroses.

After the night he froze up ("The Night of Which We Shall Not Speak," he called it whenever he spoke of it, which was constantly), he took sick leave for a week, then tried again. If anything, he was worse. He quit before they could fire him, and spent the next two months looking for work. He walked into each audition knowing everyone in the room had heard about his big dry-up. It couldn't have helped.

A few months later, Peter moved to southern Wisconsin and took a job doing dinner theater, and our lunches became less frequent. In late November 2005, almost a year after The Night of Which We Tended to Speak Obsessively, we sat near a window in the Berghoff and watched the year's first snow collect in the street. He told me about his new role as Bob Cratchit in something called *Let's Sing a Christmas Carol!* The director wanted British accents from everyone. Peter could do a perfect one, of course, but not without sinking further into the hollow cadences, the glazed eyes, the strangling sense of the ridiculous.

"Most of them sound southern, it's terrible," he said. He was on caffeine or something worse. He was literally bouncing on the springy seat of the booth. "The eleven o'clock number is, I shit you not, called 'God Bless Us, Every One.' Jesus Christ, you should hear it, it sounds like Scrooge drops by Tara for pecan pie." Every time I saw him he talked faster, as if he were running out of time. He still flashed the smile, but perfunctorily, as if displaying his incisors for the dentist.

When our food came, he finally asked me a question so he could stop talking and eat his schnitzel. "How's life in phone-a-thon land? Are you giving away thousands of tote bags?"

I worked in special events for NPR, and for several years before we officially reconnected, Peter and I would run into each other in the restaurants of the monstrous tourist trap on Navy Pier where Chicago Shakespeare and Chicago Public Radio both live. Once, after we'd drifted apart for a few months, our lunch parties at Riva joined together, and when someone introduced us and said we might hit it off, we started laughing so hard Peter dropped his wineglass.

"We're doing better than last year," I answered.

"I've been telling everyone in the Land of Moo about the Republicans trying to shut you down. I'm going to assemble an army of cheeseheads for your defense."

"Thank you, Peter. That's thoughtful."

Peter started mixing all the food on his plate: schnitzel, potato, creamed spinach, kraut.

"So, what about trying my shrink?" I said. "She's good. I wouldn't lie to you."

The old Peter would have cued up his German psychiatrist impersonation, drawing the attention of everyone around us, but the new Peter just stared at his mixed-up food. "She might be good, but how far is she from Kenosha, the epicenter of the theatrical world?"

"She's here in the city, and that would be good for you."

He agreed to call her and then told me about his great-uncle, who, after undergoing electroshock, became obsessed with licking copper objects. I wanted him to ask about me, to ask about Carlos, who was moving out of my apartment in gradual increments and breaking my heart in painful slow motion. I'd have to find someone else to complain to.

"Listen, though," said Peter, "I'm on the mend. If I had more serious roles again, that might do it. I mean, I was never a comedian, and that's what they're asking me to do."

As much as I didn't believe his optimism, I was glad he wasn't giving up. I constantly pictured him hanging himself from the closet rod of his cold little apartment, or drinking something medieval and poisonous. Maybe I'd just watched his Romeo too many times.

"I've got an offer for you," I said. I'd thought about it in the car on the way there, and decided I couldn't ask him. I decided it several times, in fact, but now here it was, coming out of my mouth. "I want you to do some on-air work for me." He nodded, eyes wide, as he mashed his food and listened to me explain the project: in cooperation with the Art Institute, we'd commissioned twenty local poets and authors to write short works relating to the museum's crown jewels—a mystery writer casting one of the little Thorne rooms as a crime scene, a Pulitzer-winning poet extolling Picasso's man with the blue guitar in sonnet. The poems and stories would hang beside the art, and my job was to find actors to read them aloud at the gala opening and then record them for NPR and for the museum audio tour that people could rent with headphones. My brilliant idea had launched a two-year nightmare of collaboration with a hateful little man I'd come to call Institute Steve, and somehow I'd ended up in charge of the reading part. "It's December thirtieth, if your show is done. The thing is," I said, grabbing for the only available out, "the other actors might be people you knew."

"People I know, Drew." His face stilled itself long enough to shoot me one of his complicated, devastating looks: part annoyance, part sarcasm, part glee that he'd caught me saying what I really thought. "I'll do it, if you don't think I'd embarrass you."

And so the Rubicon was crossed.

He left with Dr. Zeller's business card in his pocket and both of our leftovers in Styrofoam boxes. He was eating plenty despite his meager paycheck because he got free food at the dinner theater, but every night he had to choose between chicken à la king and Lake Superior whitefish.

I stayed behind to pay the bill, and as I waited for the busboy to come back, I pressed my cheek to the dirty, cold glass of the window beside me. I felt like I needed to wake myself up. I had just risked my career on his ability to be Peter again, to jump back into himself, and I strongly doubted he could do it.

The next time we met for dinner was before the Art Institute event. I had more important things to do, but I'd been in earlier to see that my interns were on task, and I wanted to make sure Peter was ready and calm. The Berghoff was right around the corner, and I knew neither of us would get a chance to eat the shrimp and strawberries at the reception. He'd been down a couple of weeks before to record at the studio, and I'd been relieved at how good he was, at least without an audience. I'd invited him over then for dinner with Carlos, who was still hanging around to see what further damage he could inflict on my psyche, but Peter had an audition in Milwaukee with the Kinnickinnick Players for *The Night of January Sixteenth*. He hadn't gotten the part.

Tonight Peter looked skinnier and pale and had a soft stubble he might have been growing for insulation, the way he sat there in his coat and hat, his jaw shaking against the cold. To put it delicately, he looked like a few friends I had in the 1980s who are not with us anymore. I got the waitress to bring us some tea as soon as we sat down. He held the cup, letting it warm his hands, but didn't drink any. It was all over the news that the Berghoff would be closing in a couple of months. We'd stood outside in the cold for forty minutes just to get a table. People around us were taking pictures, touching the menus as if they were the faces of dying lovers.

"I went to your shrink," he said. "Twice. You didn't tell me she was beautiful. Like Juliette Binoche. And we're very optimistic." He was warming up enough to lay his woolly hat on the table.

"Great," I said. I couldn't keep from staring at how his brow and cheekbones stuck out sharply from his face, how his skin stretched over them, shiny and translucent. He went on and on about the therapy, about opening himself up to pain, about finding his core. I barely listened.

"So, how's Carlos?" he said once we'd ordered dessert.

It was too late in the meal, and he was too far behind on the story. "Not great, but you know," I said, confident he didn't care enough to press further. To be safe, though, I changed the subject. I said, "So, I had a dream about the Berghoff last night. I was running around downtown, trying to give everyone vitamin shots because of this disease I'd exposed them to. It was wartime, with tanks in the streets, and if people didn't get these shots they were going to die. I had to find everyone I ever slept with and get them to come to the Berghoff to get this shot. So I'm knocking on doors, but people have moved, and by the time I find Carlos he tells me he won't take the shot, he'd rather die. He's lying there in the snow, dying, and he goes, 'You can't save them all, Drew.' And I woke up screaming. I mean, what the hell *is* that?"

"Dreams don't mean anything," he said. "I used to believe they did, but they really don't. Random synapses." As I signed the bill, he dug into his apple tart like someone just rescued from the wilderness, his eyes wide with the wonder of sugar and crust. He chewed so fast it looked like his teeth were chattering. He gestured behind me with a jerk of his eyes, and I turned to look at the next table, pretending to get something out of my jacket pocket. I assumed he meant the teenage girl with a roll of fat hanging over the back of her low jeans. She was with her parents. "What would you do?" he said. His mouth was full of tart.

Sometime after high school, the game had evolved away from musicians and actors, and we (or at least Peter) had begun obsessing about leaping into regular people's lives, about how to fool their families. I was tired of it after twenty-five years, but this wasn't the day to put him in a bad mood. "Okay. Pretend to get sick so I don't have to go to school, and spend the whole time doing aerobics. I could get fifteen pounds off, at least. Do I get to be myself again after?"

"Presumably."

"Then I finish reading Proust."

Peter took a sip from his root beer, and I noticed his hand shaking. I wondered briefly if it was Parkinson's, if the whole personality shift was that easy to explain—but Peter was such a hypochondriac, he'd have thought of that already. "You're so fucking boring," he said. "I'd run that fat little ass right into the street right now and see if I could stop traffic. I'd see how many laws I could break."

"You could do it right now," I said. "You could run out there and just ruin your life. Nothing stopping you."

He put his napkin on his plate and stood up. "I thought that's what the museum was for."

As we entered the front doors of the Art Institute, the last regular museum visitors of the night were bundling past the stone lions and out into the cold. "Did you ever read that book when you were a kid?" Peter said as we walked through the emptying halls. "The one where the kids run away and live in the Met?"

"And they bathe in the fountain," I said.

"That's my new plan. I want to camp out under some dinosaur bones and just . . ." He let his sentence trail off, as if the suits of armor we were passing would explain the rest. I imagined them as a hundred failed geniuses, hiding behind the glass, starved down to thin, steel exoskeletons. They knew what he meant.

We stopped at the Chagall windows, stood for a minute in the warmth of their thick blue light, then headed into the special exhibit hall. I left Peter staring at a messy Klee while I talked to Lauren, my boss, who had hated the idea of this event from the time I brought it up two years before and was waiting for everything to fall apart. Her overplucked little eyebrows arched up her forehead as she asked me why half the writers weren't there yet. I went to check on the champagne, and once the evening started moving I lost track of Peter among the tablecloths and microphones and whining interns, and finally among the rush of people and coats. Half were Art Institute supporters with vintage bracelets or Frank Lloyd Wright neckties, and half were NPR junkies with professor haircuts. Some might have been both, God bless them.

I knew I should have introduced Peter to the other actors, told him where to be, but leaving him alone was my small way of shaking him by the shoulders, of telling him to grow up. When I saw him again, he was talking to one of the actresses he knew from Chicago Shakespeare, a woman who'd just returned from off-Broadway and chopped her hair short. She was laughing at something he said, and he was teetering back and forth on his feet, as if he might at any second lose a lifelong battle with gravity. He was laughing too, but the way his skin stretched on his jaws, he looked deathly.

I took the microphone and welcomed everyone, but my voice could never command a room; people still milled and talked and jostled for position. I introduced the five actors, and it wasn't until they came and stood beside me that I noticed Peter still had his puffy green coat on, his hands shoved down in its pockets. I wondered if he was punishing me for leaving him alone, or if he was so thin under there that he didn't want to frighten people. In high school, he would take his shirt off at every opportunity, claiming it was hot out at sixty degrees. I'd assumed back then that his dark skin was from Italian genes, but now I saw it must have just been the sun.

The two other men were dressed in sleek sweaters, and the two women wore silk blouses and pants. Audition outfits, like Peter used to have dozens of. He looked now as if we'd found him on the street at the last minute.

We started with the first painting, Caillebotte's *Paris Street, Rainy Day*, and the short-haired actress read a brief story by Stuart Dybek called "Rainy Day Chicago." When she finished, the crowd moved across the gallery to a tiny Picasso, where one of the men read a poem called "Triangle Woman." We'd pulled a miracle, getting the Art Institute to move so many of its own crowd-pleasers into one exhibit; they'd wanted to highlight lesser-known works, things they would pull from some vault, but most of the writers had agreed to the commission only if they could choose the painting. We'd asked the writers to e-mail us their wish lists, and *Nighthawks* topped almost every one. It was something about the loneliness, the coffee, the silence—everyone wanted to lay private claim to that one desolate corner of the universe. In the end, no one got it because it was on loan in New York. How could this one object embody loneliness, I wondered, when people crowded shoulder to shoulder around it, shared it, traded it, paraded it around? If Hopper's little coffee counter was lonely, it was in the way a prostitute was lonely. Or an actor.

I had a hard time paying attention, and I stood there thinking how flat the readers all were, how little grace they showed compared to Peter in his prime. He played Edgar in *Lear* one summer up in Evanston, in the park by the beach. He was beautiful in a red shirt, and his voice made every line sound like something you'd been on the verge of remembering, if you'd only had time.

Peter's first reading was for my least favorite story, as well as my least favorite painting in the entire museum. A very young, way-too-hip fiction writer from Bucktown named Sam Demarr had e-mailed us that the only painting he felt like writing on was "the one with the giant gum." I'd actually loved it as a child—that enormous pack of gum floating over the city skyline. Now I hated how the gum hovered there, out of proportion. It had nothing to do with the city below it, no shared color palette, the garish green wrapper rendering the brown skyline drab and uniform. On one of our first dates, Carlos and I had stood there joking that it was based on a true story, the Giant Gum Crash of '72. Since then, I'd always thought of the gum as about to land, to flatten the unsuspecting workers below, so I'd found it particularly funny that the story Sam Demarr had submitted was called "The Gum Flew Away." Demarr himself was standing there at the side of the room in dirty khakis, smirking at his wineglass.

Peter pulled a tube of papers from his coat pocket and unrolled it so he could read the top one. The other actors held theirs in the black folders we'd sent them in. "First, all the gum flew off," he read, "leaving Chicago in its spearmint dust. Then the department stores floated away." Aside from the fact that his papers were visibly shaking, Peter sounded like himself, strong-voiced and in full control of the English language. This story suited his flat, ironic delivery. I'd chosen it for him specifically because it was monochromatic and free from dialogue. "The hot dog stands were next," I heard him say. For all my daydreaming about finding myself stranded onstage, this was the closest I'd come to feeling as if it were my own energy propelling an actor, as if when I stopped focusing, the whole thing would fall apart. Peter was gesturing around now, with the still-shaking papers, backing toward the wall and away from the old ladies in the front row. Even his legs were bouncing, and it finally occurred to me that maybe it was drugs making his limbs and voice and eyes jump around like that. It didn't seem like something he'd do, but who was I, anymore, to say what Peter would do?

And then as he read the line about the mayor launching himself off the Hancock tower, Peter actually put the back of his hand against the painting and swept it up the canvas. The gasp from the crowd was so loud and so high that I couldn't tell where it stopped and the alarm started. A security guard I'd barely noticed trotted from the room, and another stepped forward, speaking into a radio. Peter froze, and I could feel his stomach flip. I could feel the sweat sticking the papers to his hand. The alarm was turned off, and people started talking quietly.

"And this is why we didn't broadcast live," Lauren whispered beside me. She was glaring at me as if I'd done it myself. The institute coordinators were talking in a cluster while two guards and a woman in a suit came hurrying in, asking Peter to step aside so they could inspect the painting for damage.

The crowd just looked embarrassed, all touching their faces but waiting politely for the reading to resume. Sam Demarr seemed to find the whole thing hilarious. Peter had stepped aside, but he was still up there in front of everyone, the only movement coming from his eyes, which jumped around liquidly, looking for their chance to leap free from his face once and for all. One of the guards talked with him in what should have been a whisper, but everyone could hear. He asked for his name, his driver's license, copied everything down on a big clipboard. If the guard took any notice of the waiting audience at all, it was as an audience for his own fine performance.

And I thought, maybe that's what I would have done, if I'd leapfrogged up there into Peter's body, if I needed to get away before anyone realized I was a fraud: I'd hit the painting and make the show stop. But Peter had his lines right there, and he knew what to do.

It was a good five minutes before the woman in the suit stepped away from the painting and signaled that we could continue. She stayed there, though, in the corner of the room, frowning. I assumed she'd have a long night of paperwork ahead of her now, a lot of calls to make. I felt bad for her.

I took the mike again and said, with a big fundraising grin, "Now you've seen what fine security your contributions support!" Lauren was at the front of the crowd, shaking her head at me over and over to show how disappointed she was, as if I hadn't gotten the message yet. "We're going to try that one again." I waited for a meek laugh from the audience and then turned toward the actors. Peter looked at me with those blank, jumpy eyes. He hadn't done it on purpose, or at least he didn't think he had. He looked like he didn't even recognize me, like I was just another blurred member of his audience, watching and breathing and waiting for him to fail. I'm still not sure what I felt, standing there. Maybe I felt my heart break, or maybe I felt Peter's heart break. When you've known someone that long, when you formed yourself around his personality, back when you were just a fourteen-year-old lump of clay, isn't it really the same thing? Aren't his heart and your own somehow conjoined? Perhaps that's what I could never explain to Carlos: ours was a kind of first love that wasn't aimed at each other, but somehow out at the world. We were forever side by side on the chapel bench, watching the show. Peter whispered something to the short-haired actress and handed her his papers. He held up his open hands to the audience in apology, ten pale, bony fingers, then walked around the people and out of the exhibit.

"The Gum Flew Away," the woman read, the clarity of her voice a reassurance, a wiping away. "By Sam Demarr. First, all the gum flew off, leaving Chicago in its spearmint dust. Then the department stores floated away."

I thought of following Peter out. I'd done it so many times before, chasing him down as he stormed from a party, calling his name five times until he finally turned to look at me, tear-streaked or red-faced on the wet sidewalk. "He didn't mean it," I'd usually say, or "You're just drunk," or "We all love you." I never said that *I* did. Just all of us, meaning everyone at the party, everyone he'd ever met, everyone who'd ever seen him from across the street. It wasn't true anymore; the world didn't love him, just I did, and I had the feeling that even if I could say that, it wouldn't be enough. And even if it were, then what? What would I do with that responsibility? And now Lauren, who was still my boss if I was lucky, was finally shooting me a look of conspiratorial relief. *"Actors,"* said her face. "I know," said mine.

It hit me like a wall of cold water that I wouldn't see Peter again, that he'd avoid my calls until he drifted to another city to try again and fail. Someone would hire him at a third-tier regional theater on the basis of his résumé, and he'd last one show, if that. He probably wouldn't know how to give up.

After the readings, I propped myself up at the microphone and said my bit about membership and shortening the pledge drive with early donations, and Institute Steve said something I couldn't follow in his nasally little whine, and I got a drink in my hand. It was cold enough outside that I wanted to drink just so I wouldn't feel the bone chill on the way home. I chatted up as many people as I could stomach over the wine and shrimp. People didn't want to talk to me, though. What they wanted was to meet the actors, these instant, small celebrities who had become important merely by commanding attention for twenty minutes and possessing nice faces. "I saw you in *Phaedra* at the Court," a woman said to one of the actresses, who smiled graciously. "It was just gorgeous. You wore that red dress. Tell me your name again."

Another woman asked the actor who'd read the Stuart Dybek piece to sign her program. She didn't seem to notice Dybek himself standing a few feet away, laughing with a friend and wiping his glasses on his tie. If the actor found the request strange he didn't show it, signing his name on the margin of the paper. Peter would have written something like "Peter Torrelli is *fabulous*. Love and kisses, Pablo P." Or the old Peter would have, the one who knew magic.

I felt the wine go to my head, and I felt relief that the whole thing was over. I drank more wine to shut out the suspicion that I was glad Peter had left. I got through the next hour and walked out into the cold, relieved to be drunk and half expecting to find Peter there on the sidewalk, eighteen years old and scribbling in ballpoint pen on the knee of his khakis. He was gone, and there were just people waiting for buses and people waiting for taxis, everybody waiting to leave.

It was like that after our kiss sophomore year, the way I stood frozen thirty seconds and then ran after him into the cold night, one of my duck boots untied, my left palm bleeding in parallel papercut stripes. He was gone, and I'd stood under the school's archway entrance looking to see his breath in the air, thinking it would tell me which way he went. I thought, *If he ran back inside I'll follow him, and I'll kiss him again. If he got a cab, there's nothing I can do.*

He *had* found a cab that night, as he probably had now. Or maybe he'd slouched all the way down Adams, his parka blurring him into the frozen crowd, the crowd sweeping him onto the train, the train shooting him up north and off the face of my earth.

This is the way it happens: First, my friend floats away, leaving Chicago in his dust. Then he leaves me—no breath above the concrete, no voice in the air to catch and hold so I can jump into him, so I can steer him back. Then the Berghoff closes, and the radio stations all shut down. The school chapel folds its benches and windows and flies away. The frozen sidewalks peel up like strips of gum. The skyscrapers drift like icebergs into the lake, up the St. Lawrence and out to sea. The citizens grab for something to save, but it's all too cold to touch. The mayor holds a press conference. "We can't save it all," he says.

In a month, they've all forgotten. Standing in the empty streets of their empty city, the people look up and say to no one in particular, "Something used to be here, something beautiful and towering that overshadowed us all, and it seemed very important at the time. And now look: I can't even remember its name."

ELIZABETH McCRACKEN

Property

FROM *Granta*

THE AD SHOULD HAVE SAID, *For rent, six-room hovel. Quarter-filled Mrs. Butterworth's bottle in living room, sandy sheets throughout, lingering smell.*

Or, *Wanted: gullible tenant for small house, must possess appreciation for chipped pottery, mid-1960s abstract silk-screened canvases, mouse-nibbled books on Georgia O'Keeffe.*

Or, *Available June 1 — shithole.*

Instead, the posting on the website called the house at 55 Bay-berry Street old and characterful and sunny, furnished, charm-ing, on a quiet street not far from the college and not far from the ocean. Large porch; separate artist's studio. Not bad for the young married couple, then, Stony Badower and Pamela Graff, he thirty-nine, redheaded, soft-bellied, long-limbed, and beaky, a rare and possibly extinct waterbird; she blond and soft and hotheaded and German and sentimental. She looked like the plump-cheeked naughty heroine of a German children's book having just sawed off her own braids with a knife. Her expression dared you to teach her a lesson. Like many sentimentalists, she was estranged from her family. Stony had never met them.

"America," she said that month. "All right. Your turn. Show me America." For the three years of their courtship and marriage they'd moved every few months. Berlin, Paris, Galway, near Odense, near Edinburgh, Rome, and now a converted stone barn in Nor-mandy that on cold days smelled of cowpats and on hot days like the lost crayons of tourist children. Soon enough it would be sum-mer and the barn would be colossally expensive and filled with

English people. Now it was time for Maine, where Stony had accepted a two-year job, cataloguing a collection of 1960s underground publications: things printed on rice paper and Popsicle sticks and cocktail napkins. It fell to him to find the next place to live.

"We'll unpack my storage space," he said. "I have things."

"Yes, my love," she said. "I have things too."

"You have a duffel bag. You have clothing. You have a saltshaker shaped like a duck with a chipped beak."

She cackled a very European cackle, pride and delight in her ownership of the lusterware duck, whose name was Trudy. "The sole exhibit in the museum. When I am dead, people will know nothing about me." This was a professional opinion: she was a museum consultant. In Normandy she was helping set up an exhibition in a stone cottage that had been owned by a Jewish family deported during the war. In Paris, it had been the atelier of a minor artist who'd been the longtime lover of a major poetess; in Denmark, a workhouse museum. Her speciality was the air of recent evacuation: you knew something terrible had happened to the occupants, but you hoped it might still be undone. She set contemporary spectacles on desktops and snuggled appropriate shoes under beds and did not overdust. Too much cleanliness made a place dead. In Rome she arranged an exhibit of the commonplace belongings of Ezra Pound: chewed pencils, drinking glasses, celluloid dice, dog-eared books. Only the brochure suggested a connection to greatness. At the Hans Christian Andersen House in Odense, where they were mere tourists, she lingered in admiration over Andersen's upper plate and the length of rope that he traveled with in his suitcase in case of hotel fire. "You can tell more from dentures than from years of diaries," she'd said then. "Dentures do not lie." But she herself threw everything out. She did not want anyone to exhibit even the smallest bit of her.

Now Stony said, solemnly, "I never want to drink out of Ikea glasses again. Or sleep on Ikea sheets. Or—and this one is serious—cook with Ikea pans. Your husband owns really expensive pans. How about that?"

"I am impressed, and you are bourgeois."

"Year lease," he said.

"I am terrified," said Pamela, smiling with her beautiful angular un-American teeth, and then, "Perhaps we will afford to have a baby."

She was still, as he would think of it later, casually alive. In two months she would be, according to the doctors, *miraculously* alive, and, later still, alive in a nearly unmodifiable twilight state. Or too modifiable: *technically* alive. Now she walked around the barn in her bra, which was as usual a little too small, and her underpants, as usual a little too big, though she was small-breasted and big-bottomed. Her red-framed glasses sat on her face at a tilt. "My ears are not plumb," she always said. It was one of the reasons they belonged together: they were flea-market people, put together out of odd parts. She limped. Even her name was pronounced with a limp, the accent on the second syllable. For a full month after they met he'd thought her name was Camilla, and he never managed to say it aloud without lining it up in his head beforehand—pa-MILLa, paMILLa—the way he had to collect German words for sentences ahead of time and then properly distribute the verbs. In fact he did that with English sentences too, when speaking to Pamela, when she was alive.

He e-mailed the woman who'd listed the house—she was not the owner, she was working for the owners—and after a month of wrangling (she never sent the promised pictures; he was third in line, behind a gaggle of students and a clutch of summer people; if they rented for the summer they could make a lot more money), managed to talk her out of a yearlong lease, starting June 1.

The limp, it turned out, was the legacy of a stroke Pamela'd had in her early twenties that she'd never told him about. She had another one in the barn two weeks before they were supposed to move; she hit her head on the metal counter as she fell. Stony's French was good enough only to ask the doctors how bad things were, but not to understand the answer. Pamela spoke the foreign languages; he cooked dinner, she proclaimed it delicious. In the hospital her tongue was fat in her mouth and she was fed through a tube. Someone had put her glasses on her face so that she would look more herself. A nurse came in hourly to straighten them. They did this as though her glasses were the masterpiece and all of Pamela the gallery wall—palms flat and gentle, leery of gravity. He sat in a molded green chair and dozed. One night he woke to the final nurse, who was straightening the glasses and then the bed sheets. She turned to Stony. The last little bit of French he possessed drained out through the basin of his stomach.

"No?" he said.

This nurse was a small brown rabbit. Even her lips were brown. She wobbled on her feet as though deciding whether it would be better if the mad husband caught and ate her now or there should be a chase. Then she shrugged.

When someone dies it is intolerable to be shrugged at. He went back to the barn to pack. First his suitcase, an enormous green nylon item with fretful, overworked zippers. Then Pamela's, that beige strap-covered duffel bag that looked like a midcentury truss. He had to leave France as soon as possible. He stuffed the bag with the undersized bras and oversized pants, her favorite pair of creased black patent-leather loafers, an assortment of embroidered handkerchiefs. He needed a suitcase and a computer bag and then any number of plastic bags to move from place to place, he collected souvenirs like vaccinations, but all of Pamela's belongings fit in her bag. When he failed to find the duck, he remembered the words of the lovely Buddhist landlady in Edinburgh, when he'd apologized for breaking a bowl: "We have a saying — it was already broken." Even now he wasn't sure if *we* meant Buddhists or Scots. He would leave a note for the landlady concerning the duck, but of course the loss of the duck could not break his heart.

The weight of the bag was like the stones in a suicide's pocket. Stony e-mailed his future boss, the kindly archivist, asked if he could straighten things out with the real estate agent — he would come, he would definitely come, but in the fall. *My wife has died,* he wrote, in rotten intelligible English. He'd wept already, and for hours, but suddenly he understood that the real thing was coming for him soon, a period of time free of wry laughter or distraction. The bag he put in the closet for the French landlady to deal with. The ashes from the mortuary came in an urn, complete with a certificate that explained what he was to show to customs officials. These he took with him to England, where he went for the summer, to drink.

The Not Owner of the house was a small, slightly creased, ponytailed blond woman in a baseball cap and a gleaming black exercise suit that suggested somewhere a husband dressed in the exact same outfit. She waved at him from the front porch. For the past month she'd sent him cheerful e-mails about getting the lovely house ready for him, all of which came down to this: What did he need? What did he own?

Books, art, cooking equipment. And a collection of eccentric but unuseful tables. That was it. He'd chosen this house because it was not a sabbatical rental: even before—a word he now pronounced as a spondee, like BC—he'd longed to be reunited with his books, art, dishes, the doctor's table, the old diner table, the various card catalogs, the side table made from an old cheese crate. He didn't want to live inside someone else's life, and sabbatical houses were always like that. You felt like a teenager who'd been given too much responsibility. Your parents were there frowning at you in the very arrangement of the furniture.

The house wasn't Victorian, as he'd for some reason assumed, but an ordinary wood-framed house painted toothpaste blue. Amazing, how death made petty disappointments into operatic insults.

"Hello!" The woman whooshed across toward him. "I'm Carly. You're here. At last! It seems like ages since we started talking about you and this house!"

The porch was psoriatic and decorated with a series of lawn chairs.

"I'm glad you found summer people," said Stony.

Carly nodded. "Yes. The last guy moved out this morning."

"Ah," said Stony, though they'd discussed this via e-mail over the last week. It was his ingratiating way, as a lifelong renter, to suggest unnecessary, helpful things, and he had said he'd arrive on the fourth instead of the third so she'd have more time to arrange for cleaners.

"Fireplace," she said. "Cable's still hooked up. Maybe you'll be lucky and they won't notice." A round-jawed teenager sat on a leather settee with a hand-held video game, frowning at the screen like a Roman emperor impatient with the finickiness of his lions. "It's a nice room. These old houses have such character. This one—do you believe it?—it's a Sears, Roebuck kit. You picked it out of the catalog and it was delivered and assembled."

He could hear Pamela's voice: this is not an old house. The barn in Normandy was eighteenth century, the apartment in Rome even older. The walls were lined with homemade bookshelves, filled with paperback books: Ionesco, the full complement of Roths.

"Fireplace work?"

"There was a squirrel incident," said Carly vaguely. She swished into the dining room. "Dining room. The lease, I'm sure you'll remember, asks you to keep the corner cupboard locked."

The cupboard in question looked filled with eyecups and egg cups and mustache cups. In the corner, a broken Styrofoam cooler had been neatly aligned beneath a three-legged chair; a white melamine desk had papers stuck in its jaw. Kmart furniture, he thought. Well, he'd have the movers take it down to the basement.

"Kitchen's this way."

The kitchen reminded him of his 1970s childhood, and the awful taste of tongue depressors at the back of the throat. It looked as though someone had taken a potting shed and turned it inside out. A pattern of faux shingles crowned the honey-colored cupboards; the countertop Formica was patterned like a hospital gown. A round, fluorescent light fixture lit up a collection of dead bugs. High above everything, a terra-cotta sun smiled down from the shingles with no sense of irony, or shame, whatsoever.

The smell of Febreze came down the stairs, wound around the smell of old cigarettes and something chemical, and worse.

"Four bedrooms," said Carly.

She led him up the stairs into one of the front rooms, furnished with a double mattress on a brown wooden platform. It looked like the sort of thing you'd store a kidnapped teenage girl underneath. The café curtains on the windows were badly water-stained and lightly cigarette-burned.

"Listen!" said Carly. "It's a busy street, but you can't even hear it! Bedclothes in the closets. I need to get going," she said. "Tae kwon do. Settle in and let me know if there's anything else I can do for you, all right?"

He had not stood so close to a woman all summer, at least not while sober. He wanted to finger her ponytail and then yank on it like a schoolyard bully.

"Can I see the artist's studio?" he asked.

"Forgot!" she said. "Come along."

They walked through the scrubby backyard to a half-converted garage.

"Lock sticks," said Carly, jiggling a door with a rice-paper cataract over its window. "Looks dark in here till you turn on the lights."

The art studio was to have been Pamela's: she was a sometime jeweler and painter. Stony did not know whether it made things better or worse that this space was the most depressing room he'd ever seen. The old blinds seemed stitched together from moth wings. A picture of Picasso, clipped from a newspaper, danced on a bulletin board to a smell of mildew that was nearly audible. Along one wall a busted door rested on sawhorses, and across the top a series of shapes huddled together as though for warmth. Pots, vases, bowls, all clearly part of the same family, the bluish gray of expensive cats. He expected them to turn and blink at him.

"My father was a potter," said Carly.

It took him a moment. "Ah! Your parents own this place?"

"My mom," said Carly. "She's an ob-gyn. Retired. She's in New York now. You can't go anywhere in this town without meeting kids my mother delivered. She's like an institution. There's a wheel, if you're interested. Think it still works. Potter's."

"No, thank you."

She sighed and snapped off the light. They went back to the house. "All right, pumpkin," she said, and the teenager stood up and revealed herself to be a girl, not a boy, with a few sharp, painful-looking pimples high on her cheeks, a long nose, and a smile that suggested that not everything was right with her. She shambled over to her tiny mother and the two of them stood with their arms around each other.

Was she awkward, just? Autistic? Carly reached up and curled a piece of hair behind her daughter's ear. It was possible, thought Stony, that all American teenagers might appear damaged to him these days, the way that all signs in front of fast-food restaurants—MAPLE CHEDDAR COMING SOON! MCRIB IS BACK—struck him as mysterious and threatening.

"You okay?" Carly asked.

The girl nodded and cuddled closer. The air in the Sears, Roebuck house—yes, he remembered now, that was something he would normally be intrigued by, a house built from a kit—felt tender and sad. My wife has died, he thought. He wondered whether Carly might say something. Wasn't now the time? *By the way, I'm*

sorry. I'm so sorry, what happened to you. He had that thought sometimes these days. It wasn't grief, which he could be subsumed in at
any moment, which like water bent all straight lines and spun whatever navigational tools he owned into nonsense—but a rational,
detached thought: wasn't that awful, what happened to me, one,
two, three months ago? That was a terrible thing for a person to go
through.

Carly said, "Tae kwon do. Call if you need me."

An empty package of something called Teddy Lasker. A half-filled
soda bottle. Q-tips strewn on the bathroom floor. Mrs. Butterworth's, sticky, ruined, a crime victim. Cigarette butts in one window well. Three condom wrappers behind the platform bed. Rubber bands in every drawer and braceleting every doorknob—why
were old rubber bands so upsetting? The walls upstairs bristled
with pushpins and the ghosts of pushpins and the square-
shouldered shadows of missing posters. Someone had emptied several boxes of mothballs into the bedclothes that were stacked in
the closets, and had thrown dirty bedclothes on top, and the idea
of sorting through clean and dirty made him want to weep. The
bathmat looked made of various flavors of old chewing gum.
Grubby pencils lolled on desktops and in coffee mugs and snuggled along the baseboards. The dining room tablecloth had been
painted with scrambled egg and then scorched. The walls upstairs
were bare and filthy, the walls downstairs covered in old art. The
bookshelves were full. On the edges in front of the books were coffee rings and—there was no other word for it—detritus: part of a
broken key ring, more pencils, half-packs of cards. He had relatives
like this. When he was a kid he loved their houses because of how
nothing ever changed, how it could be 1974 outside and 1936 inside, and then he got a little older and realized that it was the same
Vicks VapoRub on the bedside table, noticed how once a greeting
card was stuck on a dresser mirror it would never be moved, understood that the jars of pennies did not represent possibility, as he'd
imagined, but only jars and only pennies.

The landlords had filled the house with all their worst belongings and said, *This will be fine for other people.* A huge snarled antique
rocker sat under an Indian print; the TV cart was fake wood and
slightly broken. The art on the walls—posters, silk-screened can-

vases—had been faded by the sun, but that possibly was an improvement.

The kitchen was objectively awful. Old bottles of oil with the merest skim at the bottom crowded the counters. Half-filled boxes of a particularly cheap brand of biscuit mix had been sealed shut with packing tape. The space beneath the sink was filled, back to front, with mostly empty plastic jugs for cleaning fluids. After he opened the kitchen garbage can and a cloud of flies flew out, he called Carly from his newly purchased cell phone. Her voice was cracked with disappointment.

"Well, I can come back and pick up the garbage—"

"The house," said Stony, "is dirty. It's dirty. You need to get cleaners."

"I don't think Mom will go for that. She paid someone to clean in May—"

Pamela would have said, *Walk out.* Sue for the rent and the deposit. That is, he guessed she would. Then he was furious that he was conjuring up her voice to address this issue.

"The point," he said, "is not that it was clean in May. It's not clean now. It's a dirty house, and we need to straighten this out."

"I have things I have to do," said Carly. "I'll come over later."

Then the movers arrived, two men who looked like middle-aged yoga instructors. The boss exuded a strange calm that seemed possibly like the veneer over great rage. He whistled at the state of the house, and Stony wanted to hug him.

"Don't lose your cool," said the mover. "Hire cleaners. Take it out of the rent."

They unloaded all of Stony's old things: boxes of books, boxes of dishes, all the things he needed for his new life as a bourgeois widower. He really lived here. He felt pinned down by the weight of his belongings and then decided it was not a terrible feeling. From the depths of his e-mail program he dug up an e-mail from Carly that cc'd Sally Lasker, to whom he'd written the rent check. If he sat on the radiator at the back of the room and leaned, he could catch just a scrap of a wireless connection, and so he sat, and leaned, and wrote what seemed to him a firm but sympathetic e-mail to Sally Lasker, detailing everything but her unfortunate taste in art.

Sally wrote back:

We cleaned the house in May, top to bottom. It took me a long time to dust the books, I did it myself. I cleaned the coffee rings off the bookcase. We laundered all the bedclothes. I'm sorry that the house is not what you expected. I'm sorry that the summer people have caused so much damage. That can't have been pleasant for you. But it seems that you are asking a great deal for a nine-month rental. We lived modestly all our lives, I'm afraid, and perhaps this is not what you pictured from Europe. I do feel as though we have bent over backward for you so far.

He went over this in a confused rage. What difference did it make that the house was clean in May? That there had been coffee rings before where coffee rings were now? He'd turned forty over the summer and it reminded him of turning eighteen. *I am not a child!* he wanted to yell. *I do not sleep on homemade furniture! I do not hide filthy walls with posters and Indian hangings!*

What did she mean, bent over backward?

He stalked into the sweet little Maine town and had two beers in a sports bar, then stalked back. All the while he wrote to Sally in his head, and told her he was glad she'd found summer renters who'd made up the rent and maybe she had not heard what exactly had delayed his arrival.

When he found the wireless again, there was a new e-mail:

Hire the cleaners. Take the total out of the rent. I am sorry, and I hope this is the end of the problems. If you want to store anything precious, put it in the studio, not the basement. The basement floods.

So he couldn't even send his righteous e-mail.

That night he boxed up Sally's kitchen and took it to the basement, pulled the art from the walls and put it in the dank studio. He couldn't decide on what was a more hostile act, packing the filthy bathmat or throwing it away. Packing it, he decided, and so he packed it. He tumbled the mothball-filled bedclothes into garbage bags. He moved out the platform bed and slept on the futon sofa and went the next day to the nearby mall to buy his very own bed. The following Monday the cleaners came, looking like a *Girls in Prison* movie (missing teeth, tattoos, denim shorts, cleavage), and declared without prodding that the house was disgusting, and he felt a small surge of actual happiness: yes, disgusting, it was, anyone could see it. He was amazed at how hard they worked. They cleaned out every cupboard. They hauled all those bottles to the curb. He tipped them extravagantly. One of the cleaners left her number on several pieces of paper around the house — PERSONAL HOUSECLEANING CALL JACKIE $75 — and the owner of the cleaning service called the next day to say that she'd heard one of the girls was offering to clean privately, was that true, it wasn't allowed, and Stony accidentally said yes, and was heartbroken, that the perfect transaction of cleaning had been ruined. Then he called back and said he'd misunderstood, she hadn't. Everything had been perfect.

That night he wrote Sally an e-mail explaining where everything was: kitchen goods boxed in basement, linens and art in the studio.

He painted the upstairs walls and hung his own art. He boxed up some of the books. Slowly he moved half the furniture to the studio and replaced it with things bought at auction. The kindly archivist, his boss, came by the house.

"My God!" he said. "This place! You've made it look great. You know, I tried to get you out of the lease last May, but Sally wouldn't go for it. I tried to find you someplace nicer. But you've made it nice. Good for you."

At work he cataloged the underground collection, those beautiful daft objects of passion, pamphlets and buttons, broadsides. What would the founders of these publications make of him? What pleasure, to describe things that had been invented to defy description — but maybe he shouldn't have. The inventors never imagined these things lasting forever, filling phase boxes, the phase boxes filling shelves. He was a cartographer, mapping the unmappable, putting catalog numbers and provenance where once had been only waves and the profiles of sea serpents. Surely some people grieved for those sea serpents.

He didn't care. He kept at it, constructing his little monument to impermanence.

By March he was dating a sociology lecturer named Eileen, a no-nonsense young woman who made comforting, stodgy casseroles and gave him back rubs. He realized he would never know what his actual feelings for her were. She was not a girlfriend; she was a side effect of everything in the world that was Not Pamela. The house too. Every now and then he thought, out of the blue, But what did that woman mean, she bent over backward for me? And all day long, like a telegraph, he received the following message: *My wife has died, my wife has died, my wife has died.* Quieter than it had been; he could work over it now. He could act as though he were not an insane person with one single thought.

In April he got a tattoo at a downtown parlor where the students got theirs, a piece of paper wafting as though windswept over his bicep with a single word in black script: *Ephemera.*

Then it was May. His lease was over. Time to move again.

Through some spiritual perversity, he'd become fond of the house: its Sears, Roebuck feng shui, its square squatness, the way it got light all day long. Sally sent him e-mails, dithering over move-out dates, and for a full week threatened to renew the lease for a year. Would he be interested? He consulted his heart and was astounded to discover that yes, he would. Finally she decided she would move back to the house on June first to get it ready to sell. Did he want to buy it? No, ma'am. Well then: May thirtieth.

He found an apartment with a bit of ocean view, a grown-up place with brand-new appliances and perfect arctic countertops that reminded him of no place: not the stone barn in Normandy, nor the beamed Roman apartment, nor the thatched cottage near Odense. As he packed up the house he was relieved to see its former grubbiness assert itself, like cleaning an oil painting to find a murkier, uglier oil painting underneath. He noticed the acoustic tiles on the upstairs ceilings and the blackness of the wooden floors. He took up the kilim he'd put down in the living room and replaced the old oriental; he packed his flat-screen TV, a splurge, into a box and found in the basement the old mammoth remoteless TV and the hobbled particleboard cart. He cleaned the house as he'd never cleaned before, because he was penitent and because he suspected Sally would use any opportunity to hold on to his security deposit; he washed walls and the insides of cupboards and baseboards and doorjambs. She had no idea how much work she had ahead of her, he thought. The old rocker was a pig to wrestle back into the house; he covered it with the Indian throw, so she would have someplace to sit, but he left the art off the walls, and he did not restock the kitchen, because that would have made more work for her.

And besides.

Besides, why should he?

Those boxes were time machines: if he even thought about them, all he could remember was the fury with which he packed them. These days he was pretending to be a nice, rational man.

He bought a bunch of daffodils and left them in a pickle jar in the middle of the dining room table with a note that reminded Sally of the location of her kitchenware and bed linen, and signed his name, and added his cell-phone number. Then he went away for the weekend, up the coast, so he could take a few days off from things, boxes, the fossil record of his life.

In the morning, the first cell-phone message was Sally, who wanted to know where her dishcloths were.

The second: bottom of the salad spinner.

The third: her birth certificate. She'd left it in the white desk that had been in the dining room and where was that?

The fourth: What on earth had happened to the spices? Had he put them in a separate box?

The reception in this part of the state was miserable. He clamped the phone over one ear and his hand over the other.

"Sally?" he said.

She said, "Who's this?"

"Stony Badower."

There was silence.

"Your tenant—"

"I know," she said, in a grande dame voice. Then she sighed.

"Are you all right?" he asked.

"It's been more daunting moving back in than I'd thought," she said.

"But you're all right."

"I found the dishcloths," she said. "And the desk."

"And the birth certificate?" he asked.

"Yes." More silence.

"Why don't I come over this evening when I get back," he said, "and I can—"

"Yes," she said. "That would be nice."

He'd imagined a woman who looked spun on a potter's wheel, round and glazed and built for neither beauty nor utility. Unbreakable till dropped from a height. But the door was answered by a woman as tall as him, five feet ten, in her late sixties, more ironwork than pottery, with the dark hair and sharp nose of her granddaughter. She shook his hand. "Stony, hello." Over a flowered T-shirt she wore the sort of babyish bright blue overalls that Berlin workmen favored, that no American grown-up would submit to (or so he'd have thought). They showed off the alarmingly beautiful small of her back as she retreated to the kitchen. Already she'd dug out some of the old pottery and found a new tablecloth to cover the cigarette-burned oilcloth on the dining room table.

"What I don't understand . . . ," she said.

In each hand as she turned was a piece of a salad spinner: the lid with the cord that spun it like a gyroscope, the basket that turned. Her look described the anguish of the missing plastic bowl with the point at the bottom. His own salad spinner was waiting in a box in the new apartment. It worked by a crank.

"Who packed the kitchen?" she asked.

"I did," he said.

"What I don't understand," she said again, "was that these were in *separate* boxes. And the bottom? Gone."

"Oh," he said.

She gestured to the wooden shelf — Murphy Oil Soaped and bare — by the window. "What about the spices?"

"That's my fault," he said, though before he'd come over he'd Googled *how long keep spices* and was gratified by the answer. He could see them still, sticky, dusty, greenish brown grocery-store spice jars, the squat plastic kind with the red tops. He'd thrown them out with everything else that had been half used. "I got rid of them. They were dirty. Everything in the kitchen was."

She shook her head sadly. "I wiped them all down in May."

"Sally," he said. "Really, I promise, the kitchen was dirty. It was so, so filthy." Was it? He tried to remember, envisioned the garbage can of flies, took heart. "Everything. It's possible that I didn't take time to pick out exactly what was clean and what wasn't, but that was how bad things were."

She sighed. "It's just — I thought I was moving back home."

"Oh," he said. "So — when did you move out?"

"Four years ago. When I retired. Carly grew up here. She didn't tell you? I was always very happy in this house."

"No," he said. He'd thought they'd moved ten years ago. Twenty.

"Listen, I have some favors to ask you. If you could help me move some furniture back in."

"Of course," he said.

"There's an armchair in the studio I'd like upstairs. So I have something to sit on. I was looking for my bed, you know. That really shouldn't have been moved."

"I said, I think—"

"It's all right. Amos made it. He made a lot of the furniture here—the shelves, the desks. He was a potter."

"I'm so sorry," he said, because after Pamela died, he'd promised himself that if anyone told him the smallest, saddest story, he would answer, *I'm so sorry.* Meaning, *Yes, that happened.* You couldn't believe the people who believed that not mentioning sadness was a kind of magic that could stave off the very sadness you didn't mention—as though grief were the opposite of Rumpelstiltskin, and materialized only at the sound of its own name.

"That asshole," she said. "*Is a* potter, I should say." She looked around the kitchen. "It's just," she said, "the bareness. I wasn't expecting that."

She turned before his eyes from an iron widow into an abandoned wife.

"I figured you were selling the house," he said.

She scratched the back of her neck. "Yes. Come," she said in the voice of a preschool teacher. "Studio."

It was raining and so she put on a clear raincoat, another childish piece of clothing. She even belted it. They went out the back door that Stony had almost never used. In the rainy dusk, the transparent coat over the blue, she looked alternately like an art deco music box and a suburban sofa wrapped against spills.

The doorknob stuck. She pushed it with her hip. "Can you?" she asked, and he manhandled it open and flicked on the light.

Here it was again: the table covered with pots, Picasso dancing, though now Picasso was covered up to his waist in mold. The smell was terrible. He saw the art he'd brought out nine months before, which he'd stacked carefully but no doubt had been ruined by the damp anyhow. He felt the first flickers of guilt and tried to cover them with a few spadefuls of anger: if it hadn't happened to her things, it would have happened to his.

"Here everything is," she said. She pointed in the corner. "Oh, I love that table. It was my mother's."

"Well, you said not the basement."

"You were here for only nine months," she said. She touched the edge of the desk that the blue pots sat on, then turned and looked at him. "It's a lot to have done, for only nine months."

She was smiling then, beautifully. Raindrops ran down her plastic-covered bosom. She stroked them away and said, "When I walked in, it just felt as though the twenty-five years of our residency here had been erased."

Oh, lady, he wanted to say, you rented me a house, a house, not a museum devoted to you and to Laskeriana and the happiness and failure of your marriage. You charged me market rent, and I paid it so I could *live* somewhere. But he realized he'd gotten everything wrong. She had not left her worst things behind four years ago, but her best things, her beloved things. She'd left the art, hoping it would bring beauty into the lives of the students and summer renters and other wayward subletters, all those people unfortunate enough not to have made a home here yet. She loved the terra-cotta sun that he'd taken down from the kitchen the first day. She loved the bed made for her in the 1970s by that clever, wretched man her husband. She bought herself a cheap salad spinner so her tenants could use this one which worked so well. If Pamela had been with him that day nine months ago, she would have known. She would have seen the pieces of key chain and clucked over the dirty rug and told him the whole story. This was a house abandoned by sadness, not a war or epidemic but the end of a marriage, and kept in place to commemorate both the marriage and its ruin.

"It was such a strange feeling, to see everything gone," she said. "As though ransacked. You know?"

He'd never even called the French landlady to ask about Trudy the lusterware duck, and right now that seemed like the biggest lack in his life, worse than Pamela, whom he knew to be no longer on this earth. He should have carried the duck to America, though he'd scattered Pamela's ashes on the broads in Norfolk. He should have flown to Bremen, where she was from, to startle her mother and sisters, demanded to see her childhood bed, tracked it down if it was gone from whatever thrift store or relative it had been sent to—Pamela was the one who taught him that a bed on display is never just furniture, it is a spirit portrait of everyone who has ever slept in it, been born in it, had sex in it, died in it. *Look,* she said. *You can see them if you look.* He had done everything wrong.

"I know," he said. "I'm sorry," he said, and then, "It was already broken."

STEVEN MILLHAUSER

Phantoms

FROM *McSweeney's*

The Phenomenon

THE PHANTOMS OF OUR TOWN do not, as some think, appear
only in the dark. Often we come upon them in full sunlight, when
shadows lie sharp on the lawns and streets. The encounters take
place for very short periods, ranging from two or three seconds
to perhaps half a minute, though longer episodes are sometimes
reported. So many of us have seen them that it's uncommon to
meet someone who has not; of this minority, only a small number
deny that phantoms exist. Sometimes an encounter occurs more
than once in the course of a single day; sometimes six months pass,
or a year. The phantoms, which some call Presences, are not easy
to distinguish from ordinary citizens: they are not translucent, or
smokelike, or hazy, they do not ripple like heat waves, nor are they
in any way unusual in figure or dress. Indeed they are so much
like us that it sometimes happens we mistake them for someone
we know. Such errors are rare, and never last for more than a moment. They themselves appear to be uneasy during an encounter
and swiftly withdraw. They always look at us before turning away.
They never speak. They are wary, elusive, secretive, haughty, un-
friendly, remote.

Explanation #1

One explanation has it that our phantoms are the auras, or visible traces, of earlier inhabitants of our town, which was settled in

1636. Our atmosphere, saturated with the energy of all those who have preceded us, preserves them and permits them, under certain conditions, to become visible to us. This explanation, often fitted out with a pseudo-scientific vocabulary, strikes most of us as unconvincing. The phantoms always appear in contemporary dress, they never behave in ways that suggest earlier eras, and there is no evidence whatever to support the claim that the dead leave visible traces in the air.

History

As children we are told about the phantoms by our fathers and mothers. They in turn have been told by their own fathers and mothers, who can remember being told by their parents—our great-grandparents—when they were children. Thus the phantoms of our town are not new; they don't represent a sudden eruption into our lives, a recent change in our sense of things. We have no formal records that confirm the presence of phantoms throughout the diverse periods of our history, no scientific reports or transcripts of legal proceedings, but some of us are familiar with the second-floor Archive Room of our library, where in nineteenth-century diaries we find occasional references to "the others" or "them," without further details. Church records of the seventeenth century include several mentions of "the devil's children," which some view as evidence for the lineage of our phantoms; others argue that the phrase is so general that it cannot be cited as proof of anything. The official town history, published in 1936 on the three hundredth anniversary of our incorporation, revised in 1986, and updated in 2006, makes no mention of the phantoms. An editorial note states that "the authors have confined themselves to ascertainable fact."

How We Know

We know by a ripple along the skin of our forearms, accompanied by a tension of the inner body. We know because they look at us and withdraw immediately. We know because when we try to follow them, we find that they have vanished. We know because we know.

Case Study #1

Richard Moore rises from beside the bed, where he has just finished the forty-second installment of a never-ending story that he tells each night to his four-year-old daughter, bends over her for a good-night kiss, and walks quietly from the room. He loves having a daughter; he loves having a wife, a family; though he married late, at thirty-nine, he knows he wasn't ready when he was younger, not in his doped-up twenties, not in his stupid, wasted thirties, when he was still acting like some angry teenager who hated the grown-ups; and now he's grateful for it all, like someone who can hardly believe that he's allowed to live in his own house. He walks along the hall to the den, where his wife is sitting at one end of the couch, reading a book in the light of the table lamp, while the TV is on mute during an ad for vinyl siding. He loves that she won't watch the ads, that she refuses to waste those minutes, that she reads books, that she's sitting there waiting for him, that the light from the TV is flickering on her hand and upper arm. Something has begun to bother him, though he isn't sure what it is, but as he steps into the den he's got it, he's got it: the table in the side yard, the two folding chairs, the sunglasses on the tabletop. He was sitting out there with her after dinner, and he left his sunglasses. "Back in a sec," he says, and turns away, enters the kitchen, opens the door to the small screened porch at the back of the house, and walks from the porch down the steps to the backyard, a narrow strip between the house and the cedar fence. It's nine-thirty on a summer night. The sky is dark blue, the fence lit by the light from the kitchen window, the grass black here and green over there. He turns the corner of the house and comes to the private place. It's the part of the yard bounded by the fence, the side-yard hedge, and the row of three Scotch pines, where he's set up two folding chairs and a white ironwork table with a glass top. On the table lie the sunglasses. The sight pleases him: the two chairs, turned a little toward each other, the forgotten glasses, the enclosed place set off from the rest of the world. He steps over to the table and picks up the glasses: a good pair, expensive lenses, nothing flashy, stylish in a quiet way. As he lifts them from the table he senses something in the skin of his arms and sees a figure standing beside the third Scotch pine. It's darker here than at the back of the house, and he can't see her all that well: a tall, erect woman, fortyish, long face, dark dress. Her expression, which he can barely make out, seems stern. She looks at him for a moment and turns away—not hastily, as if she were frightened, but decisively, like someone who wants to be alone. Behind the Scotch pine she's no longer visible. He hesitates, steps over to the tree, sees nothing. His first impulse is to scream at her, to tell her that he'll kill her if she comes near his daughter. Immediately he forces himself to calm down. Everything will be all right. There's no danger. He's seen them before. Even so, he returns quickly to the house, locks the porch door behind him, locks the kitchen door behind him, fastens the chain, and strides to the den, where on the TV a man in a dinner jacket is staring across the room at a woman with pulled-back hair who is seated at a piano. His wife is watching. As he steps toward her, he notices a pair of sunglasses in his hand.

The Look

Most of us are familiar with the look they cast in our direction before they withdraw. The look has been variously described as proud, hostile, suspicious, mocking, disdainful, uncertain; never is it seen as welcoming. Some witnesses say that the phantoms show slight movements in our direction, before the decisive turning away. Others, disputing such claims, argue that we cannot bear to imagine their rejection of us and misread their movements in a way flattering to our self-esteem.

Highly Questionable

Now and then we hear reports of a more questionable kind. The phantoms, we are told, have grayish wings folded along their backs; the phantoms have swirling smoke for eyes; at the ends of their feet, claws curl against the grass. Such descriptions, though rare, are persistent, perhaps inevitable, and impossible to refute. They strike most of us as childish and irresponsible, the results of careless observation, hasty inference, and heightened imagination corrupted by conventional images drawn from movies and television.

Whenever we hear such descriptions, we're quick to question them and to make the case for the accumulated evidence of trustworthy witnesses. A paradoxical effect of our vigilance is that the phantoms, rescued from the fantastic, for a moment seem to us normal, commonplace, as familiar as squirrels or dandelions.

Case Study #2

Years ago, as a child of eight or nine, Karen Carsten experienced a single encounter. Her memory of the moment is both vivid and vague: she can't recall how many of them there were, or exactly what they looked like, but she recalls the precise moment in which she came upon them, one summer afternoon, as she stepped around to the back of the garage in search of a soccer ball and saw them sitting quietly in the grass. She still remembers her feeling of wonder as they turned to look at her, before they rose and went away. Now, at age fifty-six, Karen Carsten lives alone with her cat in a house filled with framed photographs of her parents, her nieces, and her late husband, who died in a car accident seventeen years ago. Karen is a high school librarian with many set routines: the TV programs, the weekend housecleaning, the twice-yearly visits in August and December to her sister's family in Youngstown, Ohio, the choir on Sunday, dinner every two weeks at the same restaurant with a friend who never calls to ask how she is. One Saturday afternoon she finishes organizing the linen closet on the second floor and starts up the attic stairs. She plans to sort through boxes of old clothes, some of which she'll give to Goodwill and some of which she'll save for her nieces, who will think of the collared blouses and floral-print dresses as hopelessly old-fashioned but who might come around to appreciating them someday, maybe. As she reaches the top of the stairs she stops so suddenly and completely that she has the sense of her own body as an object standing in her path. Ten feet away, two children are seated on the old couch near the dollhouse. A third child is sitting in the armchair with the loose leg. In the brownish light of the attic, with its one small window, she can see them clearly: two barefoot girls of about ten, in jeans and T-shirts, and a boy, slightly older, maybe twelve, blond-haired, in a dress shirt and khakis, who sits low in the chair with his neck bent up against the back. The three turn to look at her and at once rise and walk into the darker part of the attic, where they are no longer visible. Karen stands motionless at the top of the stairs, her hand clutching the rail. Her lips are dry, and she is filled with an excitement so intense that she thinks she might burst into tears. She does not follow the children into the shadows, partly because she doesn't want to upset them, and partly because she knows they are no longer there. She turns back down the stairs. In the living room she sits in the armchair until nightfall. Joy fills her heart. She can feel it shining from her face. That night she returns to the attic, straightens the pillows on the couch, smooths out the doilies on the chair arms, brings over a small wicker table, sets out three saucers and three teacups. She moves away some bulging boxes that sit beside the couch, carries off an old typewriter, sweeps the floor. Downstairs in the living room she turns on the TV, but she keeps the volume low; she's listening for sounds in the attic, even though she knows that her visitors don't make sounds. She imagines them up there, sitting silently together, enjoying the table, the teacups, the orderly surroundings. Now each day she climbs the stairs to the attic, where she sees the empty couch, the empty chair, the wicker table with the three teacups. Despite the pang of disappointment, she is happy. She is happy because she knows they come to visit her every day, she knows they like to be up there, sitting in the old furniture, around the wicker table; she knows; she knows.

Explanation #2

One explanation is that the phantoms *are not there*, that those of us who see them are experiencing delusions or hallucinations brought about by beliefs instilled in us as young children. A small movement, an unexpected sound, is immediately converted into a visual presence that exists only in the mind of the perceiver. The flaws in this explanation are threefold. First, it assumes that the population of an entire town will interpret ambiguous signs in precisely the same way. Second, it ignores the fact that most of us, as we grow to adulthood, discard the stories and false beliefs of childhood but continue to see the phantoms. Third, it fails to account

for innumerable instances in which multiple witnesses have seen
the same phantom. Even if we were to agree that these objections
are not decisive and that our phantoms are in fact not there, the
explanation would tell us only that we are mad, without revealing
the meaning of our madness.

Our Children

What shall we say to our children? If, like most parents in our town,
we decide to tell them at an early age about the phantoms, we
worry that we have filled their nights with terror or perhaps have
created in them a hope, a longing, for an encounter that might
never take place. Those of us who conceal the existence of phantoms are no less worried, for we fear either that our children will
be informed unreliably by other children or that they will be dan-
gerously unprepared for an encounter should one occur. Even
those of us who have prepared our children are worried about
the first encounter, which sometimes disturbs a child in ways that
some of us remember only too well. Although we assure our children that there's nothing to fear from the phantoms, who wish
only to be left alone, we ourselves are fearful: we wonder whether
the phantoms are as harmless as we say they are, we wonder
whether they behave differently in the presence of an unaccompa-
nied child, we wonder whether, under certain circumstances, they
might become bolder than we know. Some say that a phantom, en-
countering an adult and a child, will look only at the child, will let
its gaze linger in a way that never happens with an adult. When
we put our children to sleep, leaning close to them and answering their questions about phantoms in gentle, soothing tones, until
their eyes close in peace, we understand that we have been preparing in ourselves an anxiety that will grow stronger and more aggressive as the night advances.

Crossing Over

The question of "crossing over" refuses to disappear, despite a history of testimony that many of us feel ought to put it to rest. By

"crossing over" is meant, in general, any form of intermingling between us and them; specifically, it refers to supposed instances in
which one of them, or one of us, leaves the native community and
joins the other. Now, not only is there no evidence of any such re-
grouping, of any such transference of loyalty, but the overwhelming testimony of witnesses shows that no phantom has ever remained for more than a few moments in the presence of an
outsider or given any sign whatever of greeting or encouragement.
Claims to the contrary have always been suspect: the insistence of
an alcoholic husband that he saw his wife in bed with *one of them*,
the assertion of a teenager suspended from high school that a
group of phantoms had threatened to harm him if he failed to
obey their commands. Apart from statements that purport to be
factual, fantasies of crossing over persist in the form of phantom
tales that flourish among our children and are half believed by naive adults. It is not difficult to make the case that stories of this kind
reveal a secret desire for contact, though no reliable record of contact exists. Those of us who try to maintain a strict objectivity in
such matters are forced to admit that a crossing of the line is not
impossible, however unlikely, so that even as we challenge dubious
claims and smile at fairy tales we find ourselves imagining the sudden encounter at night, the heads turning toward us, the moment
of hesitation, the arms rising gravely in welcome.

Case Study #3

James Levin, twenty-six years old, has reached an impasse in his
life. After college he took a year off, holding odd jobs and traveling all over the country before returning home to apply to grad
school. He completed his coursework in two years, during which
he taught one introductory section of American history, and then
surprised everyone by taking a leave of absence in order to read for
his dissertation ("The Influence of Popular Culture on High Culture in Post–Civil War America, 1865–1900") and think more carefully about the direction of his life. He lives with his parents in his
old room, dense with memories of grade school and high school.
He worries that he's losing interest in his dissertation; he feels he
should rethink his life, maybe go the med-school route and do

something useful in the world instead of wasting his time wallow-
ing in abstract speculations of no value to anyone; he speaks less
and less to his girlfriend, a law student at the University of Michigan, nearly a thousand miles away. Where, he wonders, has he
taken a wrong turn? What should he do with his life? What is the
meaning of it all? These, he believes, are questions eminently suit-
able for an intelligent adolescent of sixteen, questions that he himself discussed passionately ten years ago with friends who are now
married and paying mortgages. Because he's stalled in his life, because he is eaten up with guilt, and because he is unhappy, he has
taken to getting up late and going for long walks all over town, first
in the afternoon and again at night. One of his daytime walks leads
to the picnic grounds of his childhood. Pine trees and scattered
tables stand by the stream where he used to sail a little wooden tugboat—he's always bumping into his past like that—and across the
stream is where he sees her, one afternoon in late September. She's
standing alone, between two oak trees, looking down at the water.
The sun shines on the lower part of her body, but her face and
neck are in shadow. She becomes aware of him almost immediately,
raises her eyes, and withdraws into the shade, where he can no
longer see her. He has shattered her solitude. Each instant of the
encounter enters him so sharply that his memory of her breaks
into three parts, like a medieval triptych in a museum: the moment
of awareness, the look, the turning away. In the first panel of the
triptych, her shoulders are tense, her whole body unnaturally still,
like someone who has heard a sound in the dark. Second panel:
her eyes are raised and staring directly at him. It can't have lasted
for more than a second. What stays with him is something severe in
that look, as if he's disturbed her in a way that requires forgiveness.
Third panel: the body is half turned away, not timidly but with a
kind of dignity of withdrawal, which seems to rebuke him for an
intrusion. James feels a sharp desire to cross the stream and find
her, but two thoughts hold him back: his fear that the crossing will
be unwelcome to her, and his knowledge that she has disappeared.
He returns home but continues to see her standing by the stream.
He has the sense that she's becoming more vivid in her absence, as
if she's gaining life within him. The unnatural stillness, the dark
look, the turning away—he feels he owes her an immense apology.
He understands that the desire to apologize is only a mask for his

desire to see her again. After two days of futile brooding he returns
to the stream, to the exact place where he stood when he saw her
the first time; four hours later he returns home, discouraged, rest-
less, and irritable. He understands that something has happened
to him, something that is probably harmful. He doesn't care. He
returns to the stream day after day, without hope, without pleasure. What's he doing there, in that desolate place? He's twenty-six,
but already he's an old man. The leaves have begun to turn; the air
is growing cold. One day, on his way back from the stream, James
takes a different way home. He passes his old high school, with
its double row of tall windows, and comes to the hill where he used
to go sledding. He needs to get away from this town, where his
childhood and adolescence spring up to meet him at every turn;
he ought to go somewhere, do something; his long, purposeless
walks seem to him the outward expression of an inner confusion.
He climbs the hill, passing through the bare oaks and beeches and
the dark firs, and at the top looks down at the stand of pine at the
back of Cullen's Auto Body. He walks down the slope, feeling the
steering bar in his hands, the red runners biting into the snow, and
when he comes to the pines he sees her sitting on the trunk of a
fallen tree. She turns her head to look at him, rises, and walks out
of sight. This time he doesn't hesitate. He runs into the thicket,
beyond which he can see the whitewashed back of the body shop,
a brilliant blue front fender lying up against a tire, and, farther
away, a pickup truck driving along the street; pale sunlight slants
through the pine branches. He searches for her but finds only a
tangle of ferns, a beer can, the top of a pint of ice cream. At home
he throws himself down on his boyhood bed, where he used to
spend long afternoons reading stories about boys who grew up to
become famous scientists and explorers. He summons her stare.
The sternness devastates him, but draws him too, since he feels it
as a strength he himself lacks. He understands that he's in a bad
way; that he's got to stop thinking about her; that he'll never stop
thinking about her; that nothing can ever come of it; that his life
will be harmed; that harm is attractive to him; that he'll never return to school; that he will disappoint his parents and lose his girlfriend; that none of this matters to him; that what matters is the
hope of seeing once more the phantom lady who will look harshly
at him and turn away; that he is weak, foolish, frivolous; that such

words have no meaning for him; that he has entered a world of dark love, from which there is no way out.

Missing Children

Once in a long while, a child goes missing. It happens in other towns, it happens in yours: the missing child who is discovered six hours later lost in the woods, the missing child who never returns, who disappears forever, perhaps in the company of a stranger in a baseball cap who was last seen parked in a van across from the elementary school. In our town there are always those who blame the phantoms. They steal our children, it is said, in order to bring them into the fold; they're always waiting for the right moment, when we have been careless, when our attention has relaxed. Those of us who defend the phantoms point out patiently that they always withdraw from us, that there is no evidence they can make physical contact with the things of our world, that no human child has ever been seen in their company. Such arguments never persuade an accuser. Even when the missing child is discovered in the woods, where he has wandered after a squirrel, even when the missing child is found buried in the yard of a troubled loner in a town two hundred miles away, the suspicion remains that the phantoms have had something to do with it. We who defend our phantoms against false accusations and wild inventions are forced to admit that we do not know what they may be thinking, alone among themselves, or in the moment when they turn to look at us, before moving away.

Disruption

Sometimes a disruption comes: the phantom in the supermarket, the phantom in the bedroom. Then our sense of the behavior of phantoms suffers a shock: we cannot understand why creatures who withdraw from us should appear in places where encounters are unavoidable. Have we misunderstood something about our phantoms? It's true enough that when we encounter them in the aisle of a supermarket or clothing store, when we find them sitting on the edge of our beds or lying against a bed pillow, they behave as they always do: they look at us and quickly withdraw. Even so, we feel that they have come too close, that they want something from us that we cannot understand, and only when we encounter them in a less frequented place, at the back of the shut-down railroad station or on the far side of a field, do we relax a little.

Explanation #3

One explanation asserts that we and the phantoms were once a single race, which at some point in the remote history of our town divided into two societies. According to a psychological offshoot of this explanation, the phantoms are the unwanted or unacknowledged portions of ourselves, which we try to evade but continually encounter; they make us uneasy because we know them; they are ourselves.

Fear

Many of us, at one time or another, have felt the fear. For say you are coming home with your wife from an evening with friends. The porch light is on, the living room windows are dimly glowing before the closed blinds. As you walk across the front lawn from the driveway to the porch steps, you become aware of something, over there by the wild cherry tree. Then you half see one of them, for an instant, withdrawing behind the dark branches, which catch only a little of the light from the porch. That is when the fear comes. You can feel it deep within you, like an infection that's about to spread. You can feel it in your wife's hand tightening on your arm. It's at that moment you turn to her and say, with a shrug of one shoulder and a little laugh that fools no one, "Oh, it's just one of them!"

Photographic Evidence

Evidence from digital cameras, camcorders, iPhones, and old-fashioned film cameras divides into two categories: the fraudulent and the dubious. Fraudulent evidence always reveals signs of tampering. Methods of digital-imaging manipulation permit a wide range of effects, from computer-generated figures to digital clones; sometimes a slight blur is sought, to suggest the uncanny. Often the artist goes too far, and creates a hackneyed monster-phantom inspired by third-rate movies; more clever manipulators stay closer to the ordinary, but tend to give themselves away by an exaggeration of some feature, usually the ears or nose. In such matters, the temptation of the grotesque appears to be irresistible. Celluloid fraud assumes well-known forms that reach back to the era of fairy photographs: double exposures, chemical tampering with negatives, the insertion of gauze between the printing paper and the enlarger lens. The category of the dubious is harder to disprove. Here we find vague, shadowy shapes, wavering lines resembling ripples of heated air above a radiator, half-hidden forms concealed by branches or by windows filled with reflections. Most of these images can be explained as natural effects of light that have deceived the credulous person recording them. For those who crave visual proof of phantoms, evidence that a photograph is fraudulent or dubious is never entirely convincing.

Case Study #4

One afternoon in late spring, Evelyn Wells, nine years old, is playing alone in her backyard. It's a sunny day; school is out, dinner's a long way off, and the warm afternoon has the feel of summer. Her best friend is sick with a sore throat and fever, but that's all right: Evvy likes to play alone in her yard, especially on a sunny day like this one, with time stretching out on all sides of her. What she's been practicing lately is roof-ball, a game she learned from a boy down the block. Her yard is bounded by the neighbor's garage and by thick spruces running along the back and side; the lowest spruce branches bend down to the grass and form a kind of wall. The idea is to throw the tennis ball, which is the color of lime Kool-Aid, onto the slanted garage roof and catch it when it comes down. If Evvy throws too hard, the ball will go over the roof and land in the yard next door, possibly in the vegetable garden surrounded by chicken wire. If she doesn't throw hard enough, it will come right back to her, with no speed. The thing to do is make the ball go almost to the top, so that it comes down faster and faster; then she's got to catch it before it hits the ground, though a one-bouncer isn't terrible. Evvy is pretty good at roof-ball—she can make the ball go way up the slope, and she can figure out where she needs to stand as it comes rushing or bouncing down. Her record is eight catches in a row, but now she's caught nine and is hoping for ten. The ball stops near the peak of the roof and begins coming down at a wide angle; she moves more and more to the right as it bounces lightly along and leaps into the air. This time she's made a mistake—the ball goes over her head. It rolls across the lawn toward the back and disappears under the low-hanging spruce branches not far from the garage. Evvy sometimes likes to play under there, where it's cool and dim. She pushes aside a branch and looks for the ball, which she sees beside a root. At the same time she sees two figures, a man and a woman, standing under the tree. They stare down at her, then turn their faces away and step out of sight. Evvy feels a ripple in her arms. Their eyes were like shadows on a lawn. She backs out into the sun. The yard does not comfort her. The blades of grass seem to be holding their breath. The white wooden shingles on the side of the garage are staring at her. Evvy walks across the strange lawn and up the back steps into the kitchen. Inside, it is very still. A faucet handle blazes with light. She hears her mother in the living room. Evvy does not want to speak to her mother. She does not want to speak to anyone. Upstairs, in her room, she draws the blinds and gets into bed. The windows are above the backyard and look down on the rows of spruce trees. At dinner she is silent. "Cat got your tongue?" her father says. His teeth are laughing. Her mother gives her a wrinkled look. At night she lies with her eyes open. She sees the man and woman standing under the tree, staring down at her. They turn their faces away. The next day, Saturday, Evvy refuses to go outside. Her mother brings orange juice, feels her forehead, takes her temperature. Outside, her father is mowing the lawn. That night she doesn't sleep. They are standing under the tree, looking at her with their shadow-eyes. She can't see their faces. She doesn't remember their clothes. On Sunday she stays in her room. Sounds startle her: a clank in the yard, a shout. At night she watches with closed eyes: the ball rolling under the branches, the two figures standing there, looking down at her. On Monday her mother takes her to the doctor. He presses the silver circle against her chest. The next day she returns to school, but after the last bell she comes straight home and goes to her room. Through the slats of the blinds she can see the garage, the roof, the dark green spruce branches bending to the grass. One afternoon Evvy is sitting at the piano in the living room. She's practicing her scales. The bell rings and her mother goes to the door. When Evvy turns to look, she sees a woman and a man. She leaves the piano and goes upstairs to her room. She sits on the throw rug next to her bed and stares at the door. After a while she hears her mother's footsteps on the stairs. Evvy stands up and goes into the closet. She crawls next to a box filled with old dolls and bears and elephants. She can hear her mother's footsteps in the room. Her mother is knocking on the closet door. "Please come out of there, Evvy. I know you're in there." She does not come out.

Captors

Despite widespread disapproval, now and then an attempt is made to capture a phantom. The desire arises most often among groups of idle teenagers, especially during the warm nights of summer, but is also known among adults, usually but not invariably male, who feel menaced by the phantoms or who cannot tolerate the unknown. Traps are set, pits dug, cages built, all to no avail. The nonphysical nature of phantoms does not seem to discourage such efforts, which sometimes display great ingenuity. Walter Hendricks, a mechanical engineer, lived for many years in a neighborhood of split-level ranch houses with backyard swing sets and barbecues; one day he began to transform his yard into a dense thicket of pine trees, in order to invite the visits of phantoms. Each tree was equipped with a mechanism that was able to release from the branches a series of closely woven steel-mesh nets, which dropped swiftly when anything passed below. In another part of town, Charles Reese rented an excavator and dug a basement-sized cavity in his yard. He covered the pit, which became known as the Dungeon, with a sliding steel ceiling concealed by a layer of sod. One night, when a phantom appeared on his lawn, Reese pressed a switch that caused the false lawn to slide away; when he climbed down into the Dungeon with a high-beam flashlight, he discovered a frightened chipmunk. Others have used chemical sprays that cause temporary paralysis, empty sheds with sliding doors that automatically shut when a motion sensor is triggered, even a machine that produces flashes of lightning. People who dream of becoming captors fail to understand that the phantoms cannot be caught; to capture them would be to banish them from their own nature, to turn them into us.

Explanation #4

One explanation is that the phantoms have always been here, long before the arrival of the Indians. We ourselves are the intruders. We seized their land, drove them into hiding, and have been careful ever since to maintain our advantage and force them into postures of submission. This explanation accounts for the hostility that many of us detect in the phantoms, as well as the fear they sometimes inspire in us. Its weakness, which some dismiss as negligible, is the absence of any evidence in support of it.

The Phantom Lorraine

As children we all hear the tale of the Phantom Lorraine, told to us by an aunt, or a babysitter, or someone on the playground, or perhaps by a careless parent desperate for a bedtime story. Lorraine is a phantom child. One day she comes to a tall hedge at the back of a yard where a boy and girl are playing. The children are running through a sprinkler, or throwing a ball, or practicing with a hula hoop. Nearby, their mother is kneeling on a cushion before a row of hollyhock bushes, digging up weeds. The Phantom Lorraine is moved by this picture, in a way she doesn't understand. Day after day she returns to the hedge, to watch the children playing. One day, when the children are alone, she steps shyly out of her hiding place. The children invite her to join them. Even though she is different, even though she can't pick things up or hold them, the children invent running games that all three can play. Now every day the Phantom Lorraine joins them in the backyard, where she is happy. One afternoon the children invite her into their house. She looks with wonder at the sunny kitchen, at the carpeted stairway leading to the second floor, at the children's room with the two windows looking out over the backyard. The mother and father are kind to the Phantom Lorraine. One day they invite her to a sleepover. The little phantom girl spends more and more time with the human family, who love her as their own. At last the parents adopt her. They all live happily ever after.

Analysis

As adults we look more skeptically at this tale, which once gave us so much pleasure. We understand that its purpose is to overcome a child's fear of the phantoms, by showing that what the phantoms really desire is to become one of us. This of course is wildly inaccurate, since the actual phantoms betray no signs of curiosity and rigorously withdraw from contact of any kind. But the tale seems to many of us to hold a deeper meaning. The story, we believe, reveals our own desire: to know the phantoms, to strip them of mystery. Fearful of their difference, unable to bear their otherness, we imagine, in the person of the Phantom Lorraine, their secret sameness. Some go further. The tale of the Phantom Lorraine, they say, is a thinly disguised story about our hatred of the phantoms, our wish to bring about their destruction. By joining a family, the Phantom Lorraine in effect ceases to be a phantom; she casts off her nature and is reborn as a human child. In this way, the story expresses our longing to annihilate the phantoms, to devour them, to turn them into us. Beneath its sentimental exterior, the tale of the Phantom Lorraine is a dream tale of invasion and murder.

Other Towns

When we visit other towns, which have no phantoms, often we feel that a burden has lifted. Some of us make plans to move to such a town, a place that reminds us of tall picture books from childhood. There, you can walk at peace along the streets and in the public parks, without having to wonder whether a ripple will course through the skin of your forearms. We think of our children playing happily in green backyards, where sunflowers and honeysuckle bloom against white fences. But soon a restlessness comes. A town without phantoms seems to us a town without history, a town without shadows. The yards are empty, the streets stretch bleakly away. Back in our town, we wait impatiently for the ripple in our arms; we fear that our phantoms may no longer be there. When, sometimes after many weeks, we encounter one of them at last, in a corner of the yard or at the side of the car wash, where a look is flung at us before the phantom turns away, we think, Now things are as they should be, now we can rest awhile. It's a feeling almost like gratitude.

Explanation #5

Some argue that all towns have phantoms, but that only we are able to see them. This way of thinking is especially attractive to those who cannot understand why our town should have phantoms and other towns none; why our town, in short, should be an exception. An objection to this explanation is that it accomplishes nothing but a shift of attention from the town itself to the people of our town: it's our ability to perceive phantoms that is now the riddle, instead of the phantoms themselves. A second objection, which some find decisive, is that the explanation relies entirely on an assumed world of invisible beings, whose existence can be neither proved nor disproved.

Case Study #5

Every afternoon after lunch, before I return to work in the upstairs study, I like to take a stroll along the familiar sidewalks of my neighborhood. Thoughts rise up in me, take odd turns, vanish like bits of smoke. At the same time I'm wide open to striking impressions — that ladder leaning against the side of a house, with its shadow hard and clean against the white shingles, which project a little, so that the shingle bottoms break the straight shadow-lines into slight zigzags; that brilliant red umbrella lying at an angle in the recycling container on a front porch next to the door; that jogger with shaved head, black nylon shorts, and an orange sweatshirt that reads, in three lines of black capital letters: EAT WELL / KEEP

FIT / DIE ANYWAY. A single blade of grass sticks up from a crack in a driveway. I come to a sprawling old house at the corner, not far from the sidewalk. Its dark red paint could use a little touching up. Under the high front porch, on both sides of the steps, are those crisscross lattice panels, painted white. Through the diamond-shaped openings come pricker branches and the tips of ferns. From the sidewalk I can see the handle of an old hand mower, back there among the dark weeds. I can see something else: a slight movement. I step up to the porch, bend to peer through the lattice: I see three of them, seated on the ground. They turn their heads toward me and look away, begin to rise. In an instant they're gone. My arms are rippling as I return to the sidewalk and continue on my way. They interest me, these creatures who are always vanishing. This time I was able to glimpse a man of about fifty and two younger women. One woman wore her hair up; the other had a sprig of small blue wildflowers in her hair. The man had a long straight nose and a long mouth. They rose slowly but without hesitation and stepped back into the dark. Even as a child I accepted phantoms as part of things, like spiders and rainbows. I saw them in the vacant lot on the other side of the backyard hedge, or behind garages and toolsheds. Once I saw one in the kitchen. I observe them carefully whenever I can; I try to see their faces. I want nothing from them. It's a sunny day in early September. As I continue my walk, I look about me with interest. At the side of a driveway, next to a stucco house, the yellow nozzle of a hose rests on top of a dark green garbage can. Farther back, I can see part of a swing set. A cushion is sitting on the grass beside a three-pronged weeder with a red handle.

The Disbelievers

The disbelievers insist that every encounter is false. When I bend over and peer through the openings in the lattice, I see a slight movement, caused by a chipmunk or mouse in the dark weeds, and instantly my imagination is set in motion: I seem to see a man and two women, a long nose, the rising, the disappearance. The few details are suspiciously precise. How is it that the faces are difficult to remember, while the sprig of wildflowers stands out clearly? Such criticisms, even when delivered with a touch of disdain, never offend me. The reasoning is sound, the intention commendable: to establish the truth, to distinguish the real from the unreal. I try to experience it their way: the movement of a chipmunk behind the sunlit lattice, the dim figures conjured from the dark leaves. It isn't impossible. I exercise my full powers of imagination: I take their side against me. There is nothing there, behind the lattice. It's all an illusion. Excellent! I defeat myself. I abolish myself. I rejoice in such exercise.

You

You who have no phantoms in your town, you who mock or scorn our reports: are you not deluding yourselves? For say you are driving out to the mall, some pleasant afternoon. All of a sudden—it's always sudden—you remember your dead father, sitting in the living room in the house of your childhood. He's reading a newspaper in the armchair next to the lamp table. You can see his frown of concentration, the fold of the paper, the moccasin slipper half hanging from his foot. The steering wheel is warm in the sun. Tomorrow you're going to dinner at a friend's house—you should take a bottle of wine. You see your friend laughing at the table, his wife lifting something from the stove. The shadows of telephone wires lie in long curves on the street. Your mother lies in the nursing home, her eyes always closed. Her photograph on your bookcase: a young woman smiling under a tree. You are lying in bed with a cold, and she's reading to you from a book you know by heart. Now she herself is a child and you read to her while she lies there. Your sister will be coming up for a visit in two weeks. Your daughter playing in the backyard, your wife at the window. Phantoms of memory, phantoms of desire. You pass through a world so thick with phantoms that there is barely enough room for anything else. The sun shines on a hydrant, casting a long shadow.

Explanation #6

One explanation says that we ourselves are phantoms. Arguments drawn from cognitive science claim that our bodies are nothing but artificial constructs of our brains: we are the dream creations of electrically charged neurons. The world itself is a great seeming. One virtue of this explanation is that it accounts for the behavior of our phantoms: they turn from us because they cannot bear to witness our self-delusion.

Forgetfulness

There are times when we forget our phantoms. On summer afternoons, the telephone wires glow in the sun like fire. Shadows of tree branches lie against our white shingles. Children shout in the street. The air is warm, the grass is green, we will never die. Then an uneasiness comes, in the blue air. Between shouts, we hear a silence. It's as though something is about to happen, which we ought to know, if only we could remember.

How Things Are

For most of us, the phantoms are simply there. We don't think about them continually, at times we forget them entirely, but when we encounter them we feel that something momentous has taken place, before we drift back into forgetfulness. Someone once said that our phantoms are like thoughts of death: they are always there, but appear only now and then. It's difficult to know exactly what we feel about our phantoms, but I think it is fair to say that in the moment we see them, before we're seized by a familiar emotion like fear, or anger, or curiosity, we are struck by a sense of strangeness, as if we've suddenly entered a room we have never seen before, a room that nevertheless feels familiar. Then the world shifts back into place and we continue on our way. For though we have our phantoms, our town is like your town: sun shines on the house fronts, we wake in the night with troubled hearts, cars back out of driveways and turn up the street. It's true that a question runs through our town, because of the phantoms, but we don't believe we are the only ones who live with unanswered questions. Most of us would say we're no different from anyone else. When you come to think about us, from time to time, you'll see we really are just like you.

RICARDO NUILA

Dog Bites

FROM *McSweeney's*

WE TALKED ABOUT IT explicitly. There wasn't a brochure he
handed to me in his office ("Do you have any questions?") or a
turn-off-the-TV chat over dinner. It just popped into his mind.

"You might have Syndrome X," he'd say to me, sitting on his
La-Z-Boy, reading his journals, whatever X was that month. Dad
had diagnosed me with Asperger's, a mild case of Rett ("extremely
mild"), Münchausen, lead poisoning, and congenital neurosyphi-
lis, to name a few. There was never any treatment. "Which is all
right," he'd reassure me.

Dad was explicit about everything growing up. I was treated like
an adult from as far back as I remember. For instance, I knew exactly what happened to Mom.

"Your mother works as a nurse in Rwanda. There was a genocide
there and she felt herself morally obligated to help out," he told
me. "To this day she continues her work there."

This when I was in second grade.

"Do you understand?"

"What's a genocide?" I said.

"A genocide is the mass execution of a people based on ethnicity. Race. Like the Holocaust."

"Okay."

Being a doctor, Dad was in the advice business. "I'm a truth
provider" is how he described it—he didn't believe in the
"Hands / touching hands / reaching out" healer mumbo jumbo. It
was a sentiment even more present in his private life, in how I was
raised. As he himself had been kept in the dark, he made it a point
to keep me out.

His mother had censored all the books he read and looked through his journals to make sure no evil contacted his brain. She was Basque. When he was in medical school in San Antonio, one of his classmates placed a flap of cadaver skin inside a notebook (an old joke). Grandmama found it and the two had a fight that ended with Dad moving in with an uncle in Switzerland, where he learned a whole new way of being. He was on Lake Constance, the breeding ground for Calvinism, lying out on a manmade beach amid naked Germans and Frenchmen, the fathers uncircumcised, the mothers sun-damaged, the children shoveling sand into where there shouldn't be sand. Things we consider abominable. But this, Dad decided, was life, the truth, the way. This *shamelessness*—what else was there? He threw off his swimming trunks and in the very cold sea swam with the naked children as if they were a school of dolphins. That same afternoon he met my mother, the two of them standing naked on a sandbar. He told her how his primary goal in life was family, *real* family, no secrets, no shame. They were married, and life (licensing, visas, etc.) brought them back across the pond, me baking in the oven. And so I am *Fabriqué* in *Confoederatio Helvetica*. This I learned when I was six.

Every Saturday morning after baseball, Dad held "Professor Rounds" at IHOP. My questions ("Ask me anything") were addressed first, and then Dad asked *me* questions, about my friends and teachers and the shows I watched on TV (very difficult to talk about childhood without talking about TV). He made "teaching points." It was during Professor Rounds that I learned that my best friend Billy Rod's dad was an alcoholic and that his wife had left him for another man she was second cousins with.

"Do you know what second cousins are?" Dad said.

Dad was inclined toward the mathematical aspect of medicine, which he manifested in his graphs. The man had a graph for everything: number of daily smiles versus life expectancy (upward-sloping), life expectancy versus alcohol consumption (bell-shaped), salary versus happiness (steep slope until the ordinate of *Whatever You Decide Is Right for You,* then flat as the desert). He kept a whiteboard in the trunk of his car and wore only shirts with pockets for the colored markers he kept on his person, tip down ("Gravity, son"). People gathered around when he taught, sometimes to laugh, sometimes to learn, but always they'd interject, *volunteer,* when Dad erased the board with his hand. "No, here," they'd say, and hand him something to wipe with—a spit-tipped napkin, a receipt—*cringing* when he rubbed away the Magic Marker himself, oblivious to their pleas. Because all Dad was thinking about was his next graph, what were his axes, what was his scale.

Dad explained second cousins to me the best way he knew how:

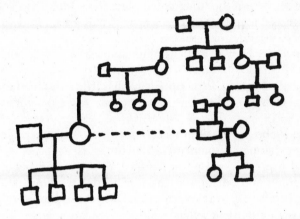

Problems were one thing; how you *represented* them was another. His main example of this was Billy Rod's father (see above), who stopped drinking when his son and I were in fifth grade. Before then, Billy's dad showed up at all the baseball practices but none of the games, always in his long-sleeved shirt with red and white horizontal stripes and white deckboard pants, his hair tucked into a loose ponytail. He yelled "Ricky Rags" whenever I got a hit, which made me feel accomplished, so much so that I doubted the alcoholism business.

"Think about it," Dad said. "What father has time to go to the practices?"

Dad said if you looked at Billy Rod's dad's liver, you'd see one huge scar, and he rubbed the ones on my elbows and knees. He said if he kept it up he'd turn yellow one day and grow breasts. I didn't tell Billy any of this.

When Billy's dad cut his hair and started coming to the games, Dad said he was "cautiously optimistic." And when we were invited to Billy's birthday party up at the lake, Dad said that it was as much a celebration of sobriety as it was of Billy's twelfth birthday.

On the drive to the lake, Dad asked what boys would be there, what their dads did, etc. When Billy's dad came up, Dad expressed the greatest admiration for him. As far as Billy's mom, Dad said she got what she deserved.

"It's like the animal kingdom," he said.

We were speeding down the highway, the two of us, me looking out for cops down the straight, flat road, something I was good at.

"Disgraced members of a pack pick up and leave," Dad said.

"Where do they go?" I said.

"Anywhere. They're eschewed. You know what that means?"

"No."

"Cast off. It's like the mountain gorillas. Have you seen them on channel eight?"

"No."

"The big boss is the silverback. Nature selects him, and the silver-hair genes along his spine are turned on."

I had a pretty good understanding of genes and pedigrees. I could go on and on about them, which I did, for hours at a time. Genes, pedigrees, and baseball stats. Dad listened to every word I had to say about these things.

I said, "Does the silverback's son also become a silverback?"

Right then we slowed down. It wasn't uncommon for Dad to get up to a hundred, meaning that when he stepped off the gas in the presence of "ringers," those refurbished cop cars people buy at auction, you'd feel like you'd been caught looking at a changeup.

But this was no ringer. It was a cop—a sheriff, no less. He was idled perpendicularly in the shadow of an overpass on the median, the red dot of his radar pointed at us the entire way. Dad said the worst thing you could do was brake in these situations (has to do with the Doppler effect, per Dad), and in the moment of truth he didn't, he idled all the way through the speed trap like we were hovercrafting. I turned my head to see if the cop would follow us, but Dad pinned me to the seat.

"Come on, Ricky," he said. "We're supposed to be a team."

That's when it happened. Nothing made Dad suffer more than my syndrome being triggered. I'd stop looking people in the eye and become detached, spacy. If there was something to chew on I'd chew on it, didn't matter if it was my nails or the drawstring from the hood of my sweatshirt. Sometimes I tasted blood, I chewed so much, or if it wasn't blood, something salty. What really got Dad was my silence, how I could go days, weeks, as long as two whole months without a word. Dad was so garrulous he didn't know what to do.

"Come on, Ricky," he said again. He grabbed my thigh. "Did you know that all cops are former criminals? They become cops to legitimize a tendency toward violence."

I didn't budge.

"Come on, Ricky. Tell me how many at bats Candy Maldonado had his rookie season." And when that didn't do it, "Tell me how many hemophiliac great-granddaughters Queen Victoria had." (*Nobody* enjoyed a good trick question like Dad.)

When all else failed, he tried scaring me into talking. "You wanna drive?" He let go of the steering wheel and threw his hands in the air. "Steering wheel's yours. Go for it."

Dad often let me drive home from IHOP, me seated on his lap, his hands on mine. I remember my hands trembling the first time I gripped the steering wheel and thinking it was part of my syndrome, but when Dad's hands came over mine the tremors disappeared and my hand sweat evaporated. I squeezed his wrist when I wanted to brake.

Neither of us grabbed the wheel. We drifted into the right lane ("You sure you want to do this, son?") and then onto the shoulder. He turned off the ignition (I didn't know you could do that) and we rolled to a stop.

Dad couldn't even look at me. He started the car only after I stopped chewing.

For a hundred miles the only words that passed between us were Dad asking, "Can you please pick up my markers?" In throwing up his hands he'd knocked them clear out of his pocket.

We stopped at a scenic view (Dad stopped at *every* scenic view) and I went to the bathroom alone, the markers still in my hand. I didn't have any pockets and there wasn't any place for me to put them, so I stood in the bathroom waiting for I'm not sure what, maybe for the markers to be magically lifted off me, or for the dirty floor to be cleaned so I could set them down. A man dressed like a park ranger said something to me and I left the bathroom still wanting to go, the Magic Markers in my hand.

Sitting on a picnic table, his sunglasses on, the whiteboard on his lap, Dad gave the Professor Rounds of his life. "Gimme those," he said, taking the markers. He drew a Cartesian plane, and when assigning the axes, he paused as if to consider the scale. Then he looked at our surroundings and put the whiteboard down.

"Will you look at that?" He took me on his lap and pointed at the landscape. "Mesas. These are badlands, son."

As soon as I got home I looked it up in the encyclopedia, *badlands.*

Dad put his arm around me. There were three cumulus clouds in the sky.

"Son, doesn't matter if you're a silverback or not. That's just how nature decides."

This got me talking. "Did you eschew Mom?"

"Of course not," he laughed. "What are you, crazy?"

And in truth I did feel a little bit crazy. He laughed hard, as if my question had been unfathomable, and all my odd behaviors, all my silent moments and my not wanting to put the markers on the ground so I could pee, it all seemed crazy. I didn't laugh out loud, but I was sort of laughing on the inside.

Dad explained again how my mother was in Rwanda helping those she felt morally obligated to help. I asked him why he hadn't felt morally obligated himself, and he told me he felt morally obligated to raise me where there wasn't strife, and then he explained to me what strife was. I was talking again, and Dad couldn't be happier. He asked me if I wanted to drive a little.

The last thing I outgrew was the feeling of driving with Dad, and part of the reason was because of our drive down Scenic Drive Road. It only went for half a mile, but it was vacant and it transected a landscape of mesas. We got up to fifty once, our windows down, and as far as I knew the world was perfectly flat.

"Son, we need to get back on the road," Dad said after a while. I went over to shotgun and he adjusted the rearview. I thanked him.

"Son, today I consider myself the luckiest man on the face of the earth. Who said that?"

Dad liked lobbing me easy ones.

"Lou Gehrig."

"Exactly, son. Exactly."

Here's the thing with Billy's gift: Dad and I picked it out together. We called all the different sporting-goods stores in the metro area, and we even called up the equipment manager for the Wichita Aeros. Which begs the question, what in the world were we doing getting Billy Rod a vintage Mark Grace first baseman's glove in the first place?

Despite my dad's efforts, there were things I didn't realize while growing up, like how I invariably gave the most expensive gifts at all the birthday parties. When I mean expensive, I mean *exceedingly* expensive, the most expensive gift by a long shot, more expensive than all the other gifts *combined,* including the parents' gifts. What I mean is two season tickets to the Aeros, a one-week registration at the Huntsville, Alabama, Space Camp, an original Rickey Henderson Oakland A's jersey, to name a few. *Monster* gifts, the kind that made parents go, "Whoa, whoa, whoa! Would you look at that! Thank Ricky and his father!" when opened (and always opened last, I might add, as Dad emceed the presents part of all parties). Gifts that nonsyndromic kids would feel ashamed to give.

The first thing I did when we got to the Rods' was make a bee-line for the bathroom, right past Billy's dad. I could hear Dad ask Mr. Rod, "So how're things going?" and I knew exactly what he meant.

Dad pulled me close to him when I came out of the bathroom. "Ricky," he said. "Aren't you going to say hello to your best friend's father?"

Billy's dad was wearing a polo shirt and some really comfortable-looking but ostentatious plaid shorts. His short hair was wet and slicked back and he had hound-dog rings below his eyes. Something crucial to know about the Rods is that they came from money, which is why Billy's dad made the mistake of marrying a good-looking woman. I think what Dad meant by this was that he married *nothing but* a good-looking woman.

"He doesn't have to," said Billy's dad, messing with my hair. I would've bet a million dollars he was gonna call me "Ricky Rags" that afternoon. "The boys are playing Wiffle ball. Why don't you two gear up?"

Dad always took a long time getting ready for anything, especially baseball (he was third-base coach). Mr. Rod left us inside after waiting some. I waited until I couldn't wait anymore and then I started snooping around. Billy's house was made entirely of wooden boards stacked one on top of the other, a perfect trapezoid (nice pointy roof). In the highest part of the roof, locked in by three beams, was an old Indian-style canoe. It looked as if the whole house had been built *for* the canoe, as if each member of Billy's family had held it high while the workers nailed the boards and the beams together. The canoe featured in many of the Rod family pictures, old pictures of Billy's dad rowing, Billy and his brothers with their paddles on their father's head, etc. In fact, there were photographs everywhere in Billy's house, and not just of the canoe. There were Polaroids of the boys dressed like mariachis, portraits of Billy's grandfather looking away from the camera, even little passport photos of Billy and his brother doing blow-faces. Every room had pictures, and not just one or two: whole collages. In the utility room there was a stack of them like you'd find in the back room of a gallery.

I found no evidence of Billy's mom in any of the photos. I couldn't tell if this was something new, as in since she'd skipped town. Or maybe she was the one *taking* all the pictures, making the collages, gluing the pictures so as to hide herself.

I had to find her. She was somewhere in the house, I was sure, except she wasn't. It was like *Where's Waldo?*, only without Waldo. One of the collages on top of the washer, where Billy's dad stacked the presents, had a picture of a woman wearing a headscarf and sunglasses. I hopped up to take a closer look. The collage was of the Rods at the Renaissance Festival, and in the picture, Billy and his dad are ready to take a bite out of two massive turkey legs they're holding crisscrossed like lovers do with champagne. You can see a Mrs. Rod–like figure in the back right-hand corner, sitting alone on a bench.

And this is what happened: I started thinking about Billy's mom *not* taking those pictures, sitting on a nearby bench wherever her family went, letting her boys be boys. I pictured her sitting quietly, and then I realized that I was sitting quietly in the Rod utility room with nothing but Billy's presents. All the gifts looked nice except mine. The wrapping paper was wrinkled.

Dad came into the utility room. I could tell he'd been knocking for some time.

"Ricky," he said. "What are you doing?"

He had this look of disbelief on his face.

How else can I explain it? I'd opened all of Billy's gifts.

Was it the first time I'd opened a friend's birthday presents? Yes. Was it the first time I'd caused my father shame? Of course not.

Dad pulled me off the washer. He picked up a piece of wrapping paper.

"Ricky, what are you doing?" he said again.

Part of my problem is I don't cry. I've been told it has to do with an inhibitory synesthesia involving the limbic system, but I don't know, it's been a part of me since birth (Apgars of eight and eight, zeroes on grimace). Right then I thought to myself, I should really, *really* be crying. I opened my mouth to see if it would help, but all it did was make me feel thirsty. Imagine that: a kid who hardly talks, with his mouth perfectly agape, having opened all his best friend's gifts at his birthday-slash-dad's-sobriety party.

"I don't understand." That's all Dad could say.

He led me outside and sent me off ("Go ahead, son. I'll take care of this"), and I slipped into the father-son Wiffle ball game like a cat into the attic, no "Let Ricky bat," nothing. Dad didn't arrive until much later. All the dads yelled, "What's up, Doc?" as he skipped down the stairs and took his position along the third-base line. I was on first and Billy's dad was batting, and instead of giving me the sign to run, Dad gave it to the batter. Billy's dad hit one hard down the line, and I ran hard from first to second to third. Mr. Rod was right behind me when Dad waved us in.

Truth is, it should have been an easy inside-the-park home run. Candy Maldonado would've made it. But Billy faked like he had caught the ball and ran toward his dad, yelling, "I got it, I got it." In retrospect, it was a clever move, like the old fake-back-to-the-pitcher-to-get-the-man-leading-off. I don't think anybody on the field believed him, though, and the thing is, a third-base coach should *know* when a fielder's faking. That's his job.

Unfortunately, that wasn't the case. Dad jumped in front of Billy's dad with the hold sign as the big man rounded third. I don't think either of them saw what was coming until the very end, when it was too late.

Billy's dad tried to put on the brakes, but he stumbled, and instead of falling down he elbowed my dad square in the head. He gunned it home right after, and before the real Wiffle ball was relayed in he was standing on home plate beside me, messing with my hair.

"Excellent base running, Tricky Ricky," he said, all winded.

*

I was taking cuts when Mr. Rod approached me an inning and a half later. "Whydontcha check on your old dad," he said. "I don't see where he went."

After catching that elbow, Dad had stumbled down the line like he was drunk. "Doc, you all right? We need to call 911?" said the dads. It took him a while, but he gave them a thumbs-up. The rest of the inning he gave no signs. We probably lost him during the changeover.

I ran toward the Rod house like I was stealing home. As if Billy's presents were still wrapped and ready to go. And maybe they were, by then.

Far away from the action, on the Rod deck, Dad was rocking in a rocking chair. At first I thought he hadn't heard me sprinting up the stairs, he rocked so thoroughly. I sat beside him looking at what he was looking at, the ground, mostly, when out of nowhere he looked over at me and said, "Come on, Ricky," like I'd interrupted him. I didn't know what he meant.

A couple of minutes later he asked, "Son, what are we doing?"

"We're having fun," I said. I thought that's what he wanted to hear. He rocked the rocking chair all the way to the tip and back.

"Son, I have feelings and I remember events, but the feelings don't match the events." He grabbed my hands and placed them on his head. "The brain is in a box, son."

Being my father's son, I knew exactly what this meant. It meant he was bleeding inside his skull. It meant the knock had jarred loose a vessel and that blood was pooling, flooding synapses, compressing neurons, killing thoughts. It meant Dad needed a neuro-surgeon.

To be fair, the man was a hypochondriac, his own worst patient. He wasn't sick often, though when he was he acted like he was in the grips of a deathly illness. "Spinal meningitis," he called it. What were flulike symptoms to normal people was neurosepsis to him. I was his little orderly. I'd hang towels over the windows to exclude the light and draw daily bubble baths for him that when ready he'd eschew, saying they'd "have to wait" to avoid the risk of ascending paralysis and secondary drowning. In case of shock, I was *not* to call an ambulance ("They're a racket, son"). Every time the virus hit (or bacteria, whatever it was), I missed three days of school, though

Dad insisted the wisdom I gained in providing him care superseded whatever I would have read in my textbooks. And that's the point: Dad might have been half jokester, but he was all teacher. Even at his sickest moments, the man *had* to teach.

We set off for the emergency room right then and there, no interrupting Wiffle ball, no informing the dads. I never got the chance to break in Billy's glove, though even with my father bleeding into his brain, I thought about it.

Dad started off steering, but pretty soon he was swerving. He wasn't braking when I squeezed his wrists. What I did was grip the steering wheel through my sweatshirt. I didn't care that my hands were sweaty. At each stop the car jumped and Dad's head rocked forward until his seat belt locked. Then he yawned.

"Stay awake," I urged. His yawns didn't sound tired at all.

"She's a good-looking woman, son."

At first I thought he was talking about Billy's mom, but then I could've sworn he said something about my mom, and then the whole thing sounded like it was about his own mom. He was definitely talking about somebody's mom.

The closest hospital was the Thomas Mantle Memorial Hospital. When we pulled into the ambulance port, my first thought was, The Mick's brother? A couple of ambulance guys, upon seeing Dad stumble from the car, brought out a stretcher and a fluorescent green backboard. They taped down his head and put his neck in a c-collar. One of them parked our car.

We waited in the triage line for what seemed like forever. The ambulance guy went to see about his partner, leaving me alone to push Dad's stretcher. I tried my best to snap him out of his state, doing things I knew he'd do if not for the blood in his brain, like guessing the diagnosis of those who entered the ER ("Kidney stone, Dad"). Useless.

When it was our turn in line, the triage nurse started asking us questions. Instead of answering them in a calm and dignified manner, I went off into syndrome land. The triage nurse would have none of this. She grabbed my shoulders, told me to speak. The words were on my lips; I would have said them, if not for a naked lady who cut the line in front of us.

She wasn't totally naked—she had a towel on—but whenever she raised her arms, I made sure to cover my eyes. She cut right in front of Dad and me. The triage nurse asked, "What happened?" and the lady took off her towel. She had cuts all over her back. Some of them were bleeding. Others looked raw.

"What happened?" I said.

"Dog bites!" she said. She looked at me. "You a dogcatcher?"

The bites may have looked bad, but they weren't enough to get her treated ahead of Dad. The triage nurse asked the lady to take her place in line, but she refused, and stormed out.

When they came to wheel off Dad to CAT scan, I kissed him on a small space on his forehead where there wasn't tape. While I waited, the naked lady made another brief appearance to collect her towel.

As she was leaving, I heard the triage nurse talking with security.

"Those aren't dog bites," she said.

When they called me in to see Dad, I felt something, like an aura. Those dog bites are an omen, I told myself over and over. I couldn't think of the mathematical term — *forecast?* They'd reinforced my certainty that Dad had taken a turn for the worse.

I found Dad sitting in front of a large computer, scrolling with a mouse, silent. I slipped in behind him and watched as he scrolled back and forth through radiographs of his brain. Then he turned around, all surprised.

"Ricky! What are you doing?"

He had that incredulous look on his face. I started chewing.

"They're not dog bites." Of all things, this is what I said.

"What?" He grabbed me in his arms and gave me a bear hug. "Son, that was a close one. Look." He scrolled through images of his brain on the screen. "Look at those gyri, son. Brain wrinkles but no blood. Nothing but an old-fashioned brainshake."

He patted his breast pocket as if he was looking for markers, but he had none.

Dad never accompanied me to another birthday party. Not because he didn't want to — the parties changed venues from roller rinks and lake houses to high school gymnasiums and then to grassy lots in the middle of nowhere. Parents weren't invited. Gift-giving stopped. Around the time Billy and I began to concern ourselves with good-looking women, we lost touch.

I ran into him years later. He confided to me after a keg stand that he missed my father. I told him that I did too. Dad and I had disagreed about my future, and I ended up enlisting in the air force to pay for a private college that in the end wasn't worth the money. I asked Billy if his family still had that canoe. He was headed on a canoe trip that night, in fact, with his brothers and friends. He couldn't believe I remembered.

Would you believe the military forced me to become a doctor? Not forced, but strongly suggested, *incentivized* it. Those with a personal or family history of Syndrome X (whatever it was that month) were encouraged to seek desk jobs, but desk jobs weren't for me, and so I studied medicine. (During the interview process, some air force doc told me, "We can't find anything wrong with you." I have my doubts.) Dad pretended like it was no big thing when I told him. Now we get together once a week and talk late into the evening, always about patients.

My son has something called Raynaud's syndrome. What this means is that his fingers turn dark blue when it's cold. It's more an inconvenience than a danger in a temperate climate like ours, but whenever there's the slightest chill in the air, I make him wear mittens. I buy him a pair every birthday.

Some nights when I'm tucking him in and telling him a story, I take off his gloves and show him his little fingers turning blue. Then I pretend like I'm chewing on them.

"Dog bites, dog bites," I say.

Except the other night the bright guy corrected me.

"They don't look like dog bites."

So I indulged him. "What do dog bites look like, then, son?"

And what did my little professor do? He bit me! Right on the wrist.

No! I told him, little boys don't do that, human bites are dirtier than animal bites. But all he did was laugh like he knew better.

ID

FROM *The New Yorker*

"FOR AN *eiii-dee*," they were saying. "We need to see Lisette Mulvey."

This was unexpected.

In second-period class, at 9:40 A.M., on some damn Monday in some damn winter month she'd lost track of, when even the year — a "new" year — seemed weird to her, like a movie set in a faraway galaxy.

It was one of those school mornings — some older guys had got her high on beer, for a joke. Well, it *was* funny, not just the guys laughing at her but Lisette laughing at herself. Not mean-laughing — she didn't think so — but like they liked her. *"Liz-zette"* — *"Liz-zette"* — was their name for her, high-pitched piping like bats, and they'd run their fingers fast along her arms, her back, like she was scalding hot to the touch.

They picked her up on their way to school. The middle school was close to the high school. Most times, she was with a girlfriend — Keisha or Tanya. They were mature girls for their age — Keisha especially — and not shy like the other middle school girls. They knew how to talk to guys, and guys knew how to talk to them, but it was just talk mostly.

Now this was — math? — damn math class that Lisette hated. It made her feel so stupid. Not that she *was* stupid. It was just that sometimes her thoughts were as snarled as her hair, her eyes leaking tears behind her dark-purple-tinted glasses — *pres-ciption* lenses — so that she couldn't see what the hell the teacher was scribbling on the board, not even the shape of it. Ms. Nowicki would say in her bright hopeful voice, "Who can help me here? Who can tell us what the next step is?" and most of the kids would just sit on their asses, staring. Smirking. Not wanting to be called on. But then Lisette was rarely called on in math class—sometimes she shut her eyes, pretending that she was thinking really hard, and when she opened them there was one of the three or four smart kids in the class at the board, taking the chalk from Nowicki. She tried to watch, and she tried to comprehend. But there was something about the sound of the chalk clicking on the board—not a *black* board, it was green—and the numerals that she was expected to make sense of: she'd begin to feel dizzy.

Her mother, Yvette, had no trouble with numbers. She was a blackjack dealer at the Casino Royale. You had to be smart, and you had to think fast—you had to know what the hell you were doing—to be a blackjack dealer.

Counting cards. This was forbidden. If you caught somebody counting cards you signaled for help. Yvette liked to say that one day soon she would change her name, her hair color, and all that she could about herself, and drive out to Vegas, or to some lesser place, like Reno, and play blackjack in such a way that they'd never catch on—counting cards like no amateur could do.

But if Lisette said, "You're going to take me with you, Momma, okay?" her mother would frown as if Lisette had said something really dumb, and laugh. "Sweetie, I'm just joking. Obviously you don't fuck with these casino guys."

Vegas or Reno wasn't where she'd gone this time. Lisette was certain of that. She hadn't taken enough clothes.

In seventh grade, Lisette had had no trouble with math. She'd had no trouble with any of her school subjects. She'd got mostly B's and her mother had stuck her report card, open like a greeting card, to the refrigerator. All that seemed long ago now.

She was having a hard time sitting still. It was like red ants were crawling inside her clothes, in her armpits and between her legs. Stinging and tickling. Making her itch. Except that she couldn't scratch the way she wanted to—really hard with her fingernails, to draw blood—and there was no point in just touching where her skin itched. That would only make it worse.

The ridge of her nose, where the cartilage and bone had been "rebuilt"—a numb sensation there. And her eye—her left eye, with its tears dripping out. *Liz-zette's crying! Hey—Liz-zette's crying! Why're you crying, Liz-zz-zette?*

They liked her, the older guys. That was why they teased her. Like she was some kind of cute little animal, like—a mascot?

First time she'd seen J.C. (Jimmy Chang—he'd transferred into her class in sixth grade), she'd nudged Keisha, saying, "Ohhhh," like in some MTV video, a moan to signal sex-pain, though she didn't know what that was, exactly. Her mother's favorite music videos were soft rock, retro rock, country and western, disco. Lisette had heard her in the shower, singing-moaning in a way she couldn't decipher—was it angry or happy?

Oh, she hated math class! Hated this place! Sitting at her desk in the row by the windows, at the front of the classroom, made Lisette feel like she was at the edge of a bright-lit room looking in—like she wasn't a part of the class. Nowicki said, "It's to keep you involved, up close like this," so Lisette wouldn't daydream or lose her way, but it had just the opposite effect. Most days Lisette felt like she wasn't there at all.

She swiped at her eyes. Shifted her buttocks, hoping to alleviate the stinging red ants. Nearly fifteen damn minutes she'd been waiting for the teacher to turn her fat back so that she could flip a folded-over note across the aisle to Keisha, for Keisha to flip over to J.C., in the next row. This note wasn't paper but a Kleenex, and on the Kleenex a lipstick kiss—a luscious grape-colored lipstick kiss—for J.C. from Lisette.

She'd felt so dreamy blotting her lips on the Kleenex. A brand-new lipstick, Deep Purple, which her mother knew nothing about, because Lisette, like her girlfriends, wore lipstick only away from home, and it was startling how different they all looked within seconds—how mature and how sexy.

Out of the corner of her eye she was watching J.C.—J.C., stretching his long legs in the aisle, silky black hair falling across his forehead. J.C. wasn't a guy you trifled with. Not J.C. or his "posse." She'd been told. She'd been warned. These were older guys by a year or maybe two. They'd been kept back in school, or had started school later than their classmates. But the beer buzz at the back of Lisette's head made her careless, reckless.

J.C.'s father worked at the Trump Taj Mahal. Where he'd come from, somewhere called Bay-jing, in China, he'd driven a car for some high government official. Or he'd been a bodyguard. J.C. boasted that his father carried a gun. J.C. had held it in his hand. Man, he'd fired it!

A girl had asked J.C. if he'd ever shot anybody and J.C. had shrugged and laughed.

Lisette's mother had moved Lisette and herself to Atlantic City from Edison, New Jersey, when Lisette was nine years old. She'd been separated from Lisette's father, but later Daddy had come to stay with them when he was on leave from the army. Then they were separated again. Now they were divorced.

Lisette liked to name the places where her mother had worked. They had such special names: Trump Taj Mahal, Bally's, Harrah's, the Casino Royale. Except she wasn't certain if Yvette still worked at the Casino Royale—if she was still a blackjack dealer. Could be Yvette was back to being a cocktail waitress.

It made Lisette so damn—fucking—angry! You could ask her mother the most direct question, like "Exactly where the hell are you working now, Momma?" and her mother would find a way to give an answer that made some kind of sense at the time but melted away afterward, like a tissue dipped in water.

J.C.'s father was a security guard at the Taj. That was a fact. J.C. and his friends never approached the Taj but hung out instead at the south end of the Strip, where there were cheap motels, fast-food restaurants, pawnshops, bail-bond shops, and storefront churches, with sprawling parking lots, not parking garages, so they could cruise the lots and side streets after dark and break into parked vehicles if no one was watching. The guys laughed at how easy it was to force open a locked door or a trunk, where people left things like, for instance, a woman's heavy handbag that she didn't want to carry while walking on the boardwalk. Assholes! Some of them were so dumb you almost felt sorry for them.

Lisette was still waiting for Nowicki to be distracted. She was beginning to lose her nerve. Passing a lipstick kiss to J.C. was like saying, "All right, if you want to screw me, fuck me—whatever—hey, here I am."

Except maybe it was just a joke. So many things were jokes—you had to negotiate the more precise meaning later. If there was a later. Lisette wasn't into thinking too seriously about later.

She wiped her eyes with her fingertips, like she wasn't supposed to do since the surgery. *Your fingers are dirty, Lisette. You must not touch your eyes with your dirty fingers. There is the risk of infection.* Oh, God, she hated how both her eyes filled with tears in the cold months and in bright light, like the damn fluorescent light in all the schoolrooms and corridors. So her mother had got permission for Lisette to wear her dark-purple-tinted glasses to school. They made her look cool—like she was in high school, not middle school, sixteen or seventeen, not thirteen.

"Hell, you're not thirteen—are you? You?" one of her mother's man friends would say, eyeing her suspiciously. But, like, why would she want to play some trick about her *age?* He'd been mostly an asshole, this friend of her mother's. Chester—*Chet.* But he'd lent Momma some part of the money she'd needed for Lisette's eye doctor.

This morning Lisette had had to get up by herself. Get her own breakfast—Frosted Wheaties—in front of the TV, and she hated morning TV, cartoons and crap, or, worse yet, "news." She'd slept in her clothes for the third night in a row—black T-shirt, underwear, wool socks—dragged on her jeans, a scuzzy black sweater of her mother's with *TAJ* embossed on the back in turquoise satin. And her boots. Checked the phone messages, but there were none.

Friday night at nine her mother had called. Lisette had seen the caller ID and hadn't picked up. *Fuck you, going away. Why the fuck should I talk to you?* Later, feeling kind of scared, hearing loud voices out in the street, she'd tried to call her mother's cell phone. But the call hadn't gone through. *Fuck you. I hate you anyway. Hate hate hate you!*

Unless Momma brought her back something nice, like when she and Lisette's father went to Fort Lauderdale for their "second honeymoon" and Momma brought back a pink-coral-colored outfit—tunic top, pants. Even with all that had gone wrong in Fort Lauderdale, Momma had remembered to bring Lisette a gift.

Now it happened—and it happened fast.

Nowicki went to the classroom door, where someone was knocking and—*quick!*—with a pounding heart Lisette leaned over to hand the wadded Kleenex note to Keisha, who tossed it onto J.C.'s desk. J.C. blinked at the note like it was some weird beetle that had fallen from the ceiling, and without glancing over at Keisha or at

Lisette, peering at him through her tinted glasses, with a gesture like shrugging his shoulders—J.C. was so *cool*—all he did was shut the Kleenex in his fist and shove it into a pocket of his jeans.

Any other guy, he'd open the note to see what it was. But not Jimmy Chang. J.C. was so accustomed to girls tossing him notes in class, he didn't have much curiosity about what it was that the snarl-haired girl in the dark glasses had sent him—or maybe he already had a good idea what it was. *Kiss-kiss. Kiss-kiss-kiss.* The main thing was that J.C. hadn't just laughed and crumpled it up like trash.

By now Lisette's mouth was dry like cotton. This was the first time she'd passed such a note to J.C.—or to any boy. And the beer buzz that had made her feel so happy and hopeful was rapidly fading.

She'd had half a beer, maybe. Swilling it down outside in the parking lot, where the buses parked and fouled the air with exhaust, but the guys didn't seem to notice, loud-talking and loud-laughing, and she could see the way they looked at her sometimes: Lisette Mulvey was *hot.*

Except she'd spilled beer on her jacket. Beer stains on the dark-green corduroy, which her mother would detect, if she sniffed at them. Whenever she returned home.

This Monday, in January—it *was* January. She'd lost track of the actual date like she'd lost track of the little piece of paper from the eye doctor that her mother had given her, for the drugstore, for the eye drops. This her mother had given her last week, the last time she'd seen her, maybe Thursday morning. Or Wednesday. It was some kind of steroid solution that she needed for her eye after the surgery, but she couldn't find that piece of paper now, not in her jacket or in her backpack or in the kitchen or in her bedroom—not anywhere.

Nowicki was at the door now, turning to look at—who? Lisette? It was like a bad dream, where you're singled out—some stranger, a cop, it looked like, coming to your classroom to ask for *you.*

"Lisette? Can you step out into the hall with us, please?"

Next to Nowicki was a woman in a uniform—had to be Atlantic City PD—Hispanic features and skin color, and dark hair drawn back tight and sleek in a knot. Everybody in the classroom was riveted now, awake and staring, and poor Lisette in her seat was paralyzed, stunned. She tried to stand, biting at her lip. Fuck, her feet were tangled in her backpack straps. There was a roaring in her ears, through which the female cop's voice penetrated, repeating what she'd said and adding, "Personal possessions, please," meaning that Lisette should bring her things with her. She wouldn't be returning to the classroom.

So scared, she belched beer. Sour-vomity-beer taste in her mouth and—oh, Christ!—what if the cop smelled her breath?

In the corridor, a worse roaring in her ears, out of the woman's mouth came bizarre sounds. *Eiii-dee. If you are Lisette Mulvey, come with me.*

Eiii-dee, eiii-dee—like a gull's cry borne on the wind, rising and snatched away, even as you strained desperately to hear it.

Turned out there were two cops who'd come for her.

The Hispanic policewoman introduced herself: Officer Molina. Like Lisette was going to remember this name, let alone use it. The other cop was a man, a little younger than the woman, his skin so acne-scarred you'd be hard put to say if he was white.

Both of them looking at Lisette like—what? Like they felt sorry for her, or were disgusted with her, or—what? She saw the male cop's eyes drop to her tight-fitting jeans with a red rag patch at the knee, then up again to her blank terrified face.

It wouldn't be note-passing in math class that they'd come to arrest her for. Maybe at the Rite Aid the other day—plastic lipstick tubes marked down to sixty-nine cents in a bin. Lisette's fingers had snatched three of them up and into her pocket, without her even knowing what she was doing.

"You are Lisette Mulvey, daughter of Yvette Mulvey, yes?"

Numbly Lisette nodded.

Officer Molina did the talking. Lisette was too frightened to react when the policewoman took hold of her arm at the elbow, not forcibly but firmly, as a female relation might, walking Lisette down the stairs, talking to her in a calm, kindly, matter-of-fact voice that signaled, *You will be all right. This will be all right. Just come with us.*

"How recently did you see your mother, Lisette? Or speak with your mother? Was it today?"

Today? What was today? Lisette couldn't remember.

"Has your mother been away, Lisette? And did she call you?"

Lisette shook her head.

"Your mother isn't away? But she isn't at home, is she?"

Lisette tried to think. What was the right answer? A weird scared smile made her mouth twist in the way that pissed off her mother, who mistook the smile for something else.

Molina said, "When did you last speak with your mother, Lisette?"

Shyly Lisette mumbled that she didn't know.

"But not this morning? Before you went to school?"

"No. Not—this morning." Lisette shook her head, grateful for something to say that was definite.

They were outside, behind the school. A police cruiser was parked in the fire lane. Lisette felt a taste of panic. Was she being arrested, taken to *juvie court?* The boys in J.C.'s posse joked about *juvie court.*

In the cold wet air she felt the last of the beer buzz evaporate. She hated how the cops—both cops—were staring at her, like they'd never seen anything so sad or so pathetic before, like she was some sniveling little mangy dog. They could see the pimply skin at her hairline and every knot in her frizz-hair that she hadn't taken the time to comb or run a brush through, let alone shampoo, for four, five days. She hadn't had a shower either. That long, her mother had been *away.*

Away for the weekend with—who? That had been one of Momma's secrets. Could be a new "friend"—some man she'd met at the casino. There were lots of roving unattached men in Atlantic City. If they won in the casino they needed to celebrate with someone, and if they lost in the casino they needed to be cheered up by someone. Yvette Mulvey was the one! Honey-colored hair, not dirt-colored like Lisette's, in waves to her shoulders, sparkling eyes, a quick soothing laugh that a man wanted to hear—not sharp and ice-picky, driving him up the wall.

Lisette had asked her mother who she was going away for the weekend with and Momma had said, "Nobody you know." But the way she'd smiled—not at Lisette but to herself, an unfathomable look on her face like she was about to step off a diving board into midair—had made Lisette think suddenly, *Daddy?*

She knew that her mother was still in contact with her father. Somehow she knew this, though Momma had not told her. Even after the divorce, which had been a nasty divorce, they'd been in contact. That was because (as Daddy had explained to her) she would always be his daughter. All else might change — like where Daddy lived, and if Daddy and Mommy were married — but not that. Not ever.

So Lisette had persisted in asking her mother, was it Daddy she was going away with? Was it Daddy? Was it? — nagging at Momma until she laughed, saying, "Hell no! No way I'm seeing that asshole again."

Her mother had gone away for the weekend. "I can trust you, Lisette, right?" she'd said, and Lisette had said, "Sure, sure you can."

Alone in the house meant that Lisette could stay up as late as she wanted. And watch any TV channel she wanted. And lie sprawled on the sofa talking on her cell phone as much as she wanted.

It was a short walk to the mini-mall — Kentucky Fried Chicken, Vito's Pizzeria, Taco Bell. Though it was easier just to defrost frozen suppers in the microwave and eat in front of the TV.

The first night, Keisha had come over. The girls had watched a DVD that Keisha brought and eaten what they could find in the refrigerator. "It's cool your mother's gone away. Where's she gone?"

Lisette thought. Possibly her mother had gone to Vegas after all. With her man friend, or whoever. This time of year, depressing cold and wet by the ocean — the smartest place to go would be Vegas.

"She's got lots of friends there, from the casino. She's welcome to go out there anytime. She'd have taken me, except for damn, dumb school."

"So when did you last speak to her?"

The cops were staring at her now, waiting for an answer, as she was guiltily faltering, fumbling. "Could've been, like, just yesterday — or the day before."

Her heart thumped in her chest like a crazed sparrow throwing itself against a window, like the one she'd seen in a parking garage once, trapped up by the ceiling, beating its wings and exhausting itself.

Yvette Mulvey was in trouble with the law — was that it?

The only court Lisette had been in was Ocean County Family Court. There, the judge had awarded custody to Yvette Mulvey and visitation privileges to Duane Mulvey. If something happened to

Yvette Mulvey now, Lisette would be placed in a foster home. It wasn't possible for Lisette to live with her father, who was a sergeant in the U.S. Army, and, last she'd heard, was about to be deployed to Iraq for the third time. *Deployed* was a strange word — a strange sound. *De-ployed.*

Daddy hadn't *meant* to hurt her, she knew. Even Momma believed this, which was why she hadn't called 911. And when the doctor at the ER had asked Lisette how her face had got so bruised, her nose and eye socket broken, she'd said that it was an accident on the stairs — she'd been running, and she'd fallen.

Which was true. She'd been running, and she'd fallen. Daddy shouting behind her, swiping with his fists — not meaning to hit her. But he'd been pissed. And all the things that Daddy had said afterward were what she'd wanted to hear; they'd made her cry, she'd wanted so badly to hear them.

"And your father? How recently did you see your father, Lisette?"

In the cruiser, the male cop drove. Molina sat in the passenger seat, swiveled to face Lisette. Her cherry-red lips were bright in her face, like something sparkly on a billboard that was otherwise weatherworn. Her sleek black hair shone like a seal's coat, her dark eyes shone with a strange unspeakable knowledge. It was an expression that Lisette saw often on the faces of women — usually women older than her mother — when they looked at her not in disapproval but with sudden sympathy, *seeing* her.

Lisette was uneasy with the expression. She'd seen it on Nowicki's face too. Better was the look of disgust, dismay.

Must've been two, three times that Molina explained to Lisette where they were taking her — to the hospital for the ID. But the words hadn't come together in a way that was comprehensible.

Eiii-dee. Eiii-dee.

"We will stay as long you wish. Or not long at all — it's up to you. Maybe it will be over in a minute."

Molina spoke to Lisette in this way, which was meant to soothe but did not make sense. No matter the words, there was a meaning beneath them that Lisette could not grasp. Sometimes adults were uncomfortable with Lisette because they thought she was smirking, but it was just the skin around her left eye, the eye socket that had been shattered and repaired, and the frozen look of that part of her face because some of the nerve muscles were dead. "Such a freak accident," her mother had said. "Told her and told her not to—not to run—on the stairs. You know how kids are!" And half pleading with the surgeon, though she already knew the answer to the question, "Will they heal ever? The broken nerves?"

Not broken but *dead.*

At the hospital they parked at the rear of the building. In a lowered voice Molina conferred with the male cop. Lisette couldn't hear what they were saying. She had no wish to hear. But she wanted to believe that the Hispanic woman was her friend and could be trusted. It was like that with Hispanic women, the mothers of her classmates—mostly they were nice, they were kind. Molina was a kind woman, you could see how she'd be with children and possibly grandchildren. Weird that she was a cop and carried a gun—*packed heat,* it was said.

Lisette's mother knew some cops—she'd gone out with a cop. She'd said that the life of a cop was so fucking boring; once in a while, something happened and happened fast and you could be shot down in that second or two, but mostly it was very, very boring, like dealing blackjack cards to assholes who think they can win against the house. *You never win against the house.*

They were standing just inside the hospital, on the first floor by the elevators. People moved around them, past them, like blurs in the background of a photograph. It seemed urgent now to listen to what Molina was telling her as she gripped Lisette's arm again. Did Molina think that Lisette was going to try to escape? The male cop held himself a little apart, frowning.

What Molina was saying did not seem relevant to the situation, but later Lisette would see that, yes, everything that the policewoman had said was relevant: asking Lisette about Christmas, which was maybe two or three weeks earlier, and New Year's—and what had Lisette and her mother done over the holidays, anything special?

Lisette tried to think. *Holidays* wasn't a word that she or Momma would use. "Just saw some people. Nothing special."

"You didn't see your father?"

"No."

"When was the last time you saw him?"

Lisette tried to think: he'd been gone by the time of the face surgery and the eye surgery. She'd been out of school. Must have been the summer. Like, around July Fourth.

"Not more recently than that?"

Lisette swiped at her eye. Wondering, was this some kind of trick like you saw on TV cop shows?

"On New Year's Eve, did your mother go out?"

Yes. Sure. Momma always went out, New Year's Eve.

"Do you know who she went out with?"

"No."

"He didn't come to the house to pick her up?"

Lisette tried to think. If whoever it was had come to the house, for sure Lisette had hid from him, just like she hid from Momma's women friends, and why? No reason, just wanted to.

Lisette, how big you're getting!

Lisette, taller than your mom, eh?

They took the elevator down. Down to the floor marked "Morgue."

Here the hospital was a different place. The air was cooler and smelled of something like chemicals. There were no visitors. There were very few hospital staff people. A female attendant in white pants, a white shirt, and a cardigan sweater told them that the assistant coroner would be with them soon.

They were seated. Lisette was between the two cops. Feeling weak in the knees, sick—like she'd been arrested, she was in custody, and this was a trick to expose her. Casually—for she'd been talking of something else—Molina began to ask Lisette about a motel on the south edge of the city, the Blue Moon Motel, on Atlantic. Had Lisette heard of the Blue Moon Motel? Lisette said no, she had never heard of the Blue Moon Motel. There were motels all over Atlantic City, some of them sleazy places, and she did not think—as Molina seemed to be saying—that her mother had worked at any of these motels, ever. If Yvette Mulvey had worked at the Blue Moon Motel, she'd have heard of it. She had not. Lisette said that her mother was not a motel maid or a cocktail waitress but a blackjack dealer, and you had to be trained for that.

Lisette said, like she was groping for a light switch, "Is Momma in—some kind of trouble?"

A twisty little knot of rage in her heart against Momma. All this was Momma's fault.

Molina said that they weren't sure. That was what the ID might clear up.

"We need your cooperation, Lisette. We are hoping that you can provide . . . identification."

Weird how back at school she'd heard *eiii-dee*, not ID. It was like static was interfering, to confuse her. Like after she'd fallen on the stairs and hit her face and her head and she hadn't been able to walk without leaning against a wall, she'd been so dizzy, and she'd forgotten things. Some short circuit in her brain.

"Can you identify these? Do these look familiar, Lisette?"

A morgue attendant had brought Molina a box containing items, of which two were a woman's handbag and a woman's wallet. Molina lifted them carefully from the box, with gloved hands.

Lisette stared at the handbag and the wallet. What were these? Were they supposed to belong to her mother? Lisette wasn't sure if she had ever seen them before. She stared at the brown leather handbag with some ornamentation on it, like a brass buckle, and straps, and the black wallet, shabby-looking, like something you'd see on a sidewalk or by a Dumpster and not even bother to pick up to see if there was money inside.

Molina was saying that these "items" had been "retrieved" from a drainage ditch behind the Blue Moon Motel.

Also behind the drainage ditch was a woman's body—a "badly damaged" woman's body, for which they had no identification yet.

Carefully Molina spoke. Her hand lay lightly on Lisette's arm, which had the effect of restraining Lisette from swiping and poking at her left eye, as she'd been doing.

"The purse has been emptied out and the lining is ripped. In the wallet was a New Jersey driver's license issued to Yvette Mulvey, but no credit cards or money, no other ID. There was a slip of paper with a name and a number to be called in case of emergency, but that number has been disconnected. It belonged to a relative of your mother's who lives, or lived, in Edison, New Jersey? Iris Pedersen?"

Lisette shook her head. This was all too much—just too much for her to absorb. She didn't recognize the handbag and she didn't recognize the wallet—she was sure. She resented being asked.

These items were so grungy-looking it was an insult to think that they might belong to her mother.

Close up she saw that Molina's eyes were beautiful and dark-thick-lashed, the way Lisette's mother tried to make hers, with a mascara brush. The skin beneath Molina's eyes was soft and bruised-looking, and on her throat were tiny dark moles. It did not seem right that a woman like Molina, who you could tell was a mother—her body was a mother's body for sure, wide hips and heavy breasts straining at the front of her jacket—could be a cop; it did not seem right that this person was carrying a gun, in a holster attached to a leather belt, and that she could use it, if she wanted to. Anytime she wanted to. Lisette went into a dream thinking that if she struck at Molina, if she kicked, spat, or bit, Molina might *shoot* her.

The male cop you'd expect to have a gun. You'd expect he would use it.

Daddy had showed them his guns, the ones he'd brought back from Iraq. These were not army-issue but personal guns, a pistol with a carved wood handle and a heavier handgun, a revolver. He'd won these in a card game, Daddy said.

Maybe he hadn't brought them from Iraq. Maybe he'd got them at Fort Bragg, where he was stationed.

Lisette was saying that if her mother's driver's license had been in that wallet maybe it was her mother's wallet, but definitely she didn't recognize it.

As for Iris Pedersen—Aunt Iris—that was her mother's aunt, not hers. Aunt Iris was old enough to be Lisette's grandmother and Lisette hadn't seen her in years and did not think that her mother had either. For all they knew, the old lady was dead.

"We tried to contact her and the Edison police tried to contact her. But—"

An ID by someone who knew Yvette Mulvey well was necessary, Molina said, to determine if, in fact, the dead woman was Yvette Mulvey—or another woman of her approximate age. The condition of the body and the injuries to the face made it difficult to judge from the driver's license photo. Or from the photos on file at the casinos where Yvette Mulvey had worked.

Molina went on to tell Lisette that they had tried to locate her father—Duane David Mulvey—to make the ID for them, but he was no longer a resident of Edison, or, so far as they knew, of the State of New Jersey.

Lisette said, "My father's in the U.S. Army. My father is a sergeant in the U.S. Army. He used to be stationed at Fort Bragg but now he's in Iraq," and Molina said, "No, Lisette. I'm afraid that has changed. Your father is no longer a sergeant in the U.S. Army, and he is no longer in Iraq. The army has no record of Duane Mulvey at the present time—he's been AWOL since December twenty-sixth of last year."

Lisette was so surprised she couldn't speak. If Molina hadn't been gripping her arm, she'd have jumped up and run away.

She was shivering. The corduroy jacket wasn't really for winter—this nasty wet cold. Momma hadn't been there that morning, scolding her, "Dress warm! For Christ's sake, it's January."

Another morgue attendant, an Indian-looking man—some kind of doctor—had come to speak in a low voice to the police officers. Quickly, Lisette shut her eyes, not listening. Trying to picture the classroom she'd had to leave—there was Nowicki at the board with her squeaky chalk, and there was J.C. slouched in his desk, hair in his face, and Keisha, who breathed through her mouth when she was excited or scared, and there was Lisette's own desk, empty—though now it was later, it was third period, and J.C. wasn't in Lisette's English class, but there was always the cafeteria. When the bell rang at 11:45 A.M., it would be lunchtime and she'd line up outside the doors, with the smell of greasy food, French fries, macaroni and cheese, chili on buns . . . Lisette's mouth flooded with saliva.

She smiled, seeing the purple-lipstick kiss on the Kleenex, as J.C. would see it when he unfolded it—a surprise!

Her mother didn't want her to wear lipstick, but fuck Momma. All the girls her age did.

Last time she'd seen Momma with Daddy, Daddy had been in his soldier's dress uniform and had looked very handsome. His hair had been cut so short.

Not then but an earlier visit, when Daddy had returned from Iraq for the first time, Lisette's mother had covered his face in purple-lipstick kisses. Lisette had been so young she'd thought that the lipstick kisses were some kind of wound, that her daddy was hurt and bleeding.

The times were confused. There were many times. There were many Daddys—she could not "see" them all.

There was the time Daddy took Momma to Fort Lauderdale. They'd wanted to take Lisette but it hadn't worked out—Lisette had had to be in school at that time of year. She'd gone to stay with her mother's friend Misty, who worked at Bally's. They were planning on ten days in Florida but Lisette's mother had surprised her by returning after just a week, saying that that was it, that was the end, she'd had to call the police when he'd got drunk and beaten her, and in a restaurant he'd knocked over a chair he was so angry—that was it for her, no more.

Yvette had had man friends she'd met in the casinos. Most of them Lisette had never met. Never wished to meet. One of them was a real estate agent in Monmouth County—Lisette could almost remember his first name. It was something unusual, like Upton, Upwell . . .

The Indian man looked very young to be a doctor. Behind his wire-rimmed glasses, his eyes were soft-black, somber. His hair was black, but coarse, not silky-fine like J.C.'s hair.

He was leading the cops and Lisette into a refrigerated room. Molina had a firm hold on Lisette's hand. "We will make it as easy for you as we can, Lisette. All you have to do is squeeze my hand—that will mean yes."

Yes? Yes what? Desperately Lisette was picturing the school cafeteria, the long table in the corner where the coolest guys sat—J.C. and his friends, and sometimes certain girls were invited to sit with them. Today maybe J.C. would call Lisette over to sit with them—*Lisette! Hey Liz-zette!*—because he'd liked the purple-lipstick kiss, and what it promised.

"Take your time, Lisette. I'll be right beside you."

Then—so quick—it was over!

The female body she was meant to ID was not anyone she knew, let alone her mother.

This one had hair that was darker than Yvette's, with brown roots showing, and it was all matted like a cheap wig, and the forehead was so bruised and swollen, and the eyes—you could hardly see the eyes—and the mouth was, like, broken. You couldn't make

sense of the face, almost. It was a face that needed to be straightened out, like with pliers.

"No. Not Momma." Lisette spoke sharply, decisively. Molina was
holding her hand—she was tugging to get free.

This was the *morgue;* this was a *corpse.*

This was not a woman but a *thing*—you could not really believe
that it had ever been a woman.

Only the head and the face were exposed. The rest of the body
was covered by a white sheet but you could see the shape of it,
the size, and it was not Lisette's mother—obviously. Older than
Momma, and something had happened to the body to make it
small—smaller. Some sad, pathetic, broken female, like debris
washed up on the shore.

It was lucky the sheet was drawn up over the chest. The breasts.
And the belly, and the pubic hair—the fat-raddled thighs of a
woman of this age, you would not want to look at. Guys were quick
to laugh, to show their contempt. Any girl or woman who was not
good-looking, who was flat-chested or a little heavy—she had to
walk fast to avoid their eyes.

"This is not Momma. This is no one I know."

Molina was close beside Lisette, instructing her to take her time.
It was very important, Molina was saying, to make an *eiii-dee* of the
woman, to help the police find who had done these terrible things
to her.

Lisette pulled free of Molina. "I told you—this is not Momma! *It
is not!*"

Something hot and acid came up into her mouth—she swallowed it down. She gagged again, and swallowed, and her teeth
chattered like dice being shaken. She wanted to run from this nasty
room, which was cold like a refrigerator but smelled of something
sweet, sickish—like talcum powder and sweat—but Molina de-
tained her.

They were showing her some clothes now, from the box. Dirty,
bloodstained clothes, like rags. And a coat—a coat that resembled
her mother's red suede coat but was filthy and torn. It was not the
stylish coat that Momma had bought a year ago, in the January
sales at the mall.

Lisette said that she'd never seen any of these things before. She
had not. She was breathing funny, like her friend Keisha, who had

asthma, and Molina was holding her hand and saying things to comfort her, bullshit things, telling her to be calm, it was all right. If she did not think that this woman was her mother, it was all right: there were other ways to identify the victim.

Victim. This was a new word. Like *corpse, drainage ditch.*

Molina led her to a restroom. Lisette had to use the toilet, fast. Her insides had turned to liquid fire and had to come out. At the sink she was going to vomit but could not. Washed and washed her hands. In the mirror a face hovered — a girl's face — in purple-tinted glasses, her lips a dark grape color. The scarring around the left eye wasn't so visible if she didn't look closely, and she had no wish to look closely. There had been three surgeries and after each surgery Momma had promised, "You'll be fine! You'll look better than new."

They wanted to take her somewhere — to Family Services. She said that she wanted to go back to school. She said that she had a right to go back to school. She began to cry. She was resentful and agitated and she wanted to go back to school, and so they said, "All right, all right for now, Lisette," and they drove her to school. The bell had just rung for lunch, so she went directly to the cafeteria — not waiting in line but into the cafeteria without a tray and still in her jacket, and, in a roaring sort of haze, she was aware of her girlfriends at a nearby table. There was Keisha, looking concerned, calling, "Lisette, hey — what was it? You okay?" and Lisette said, laughing into the bright buzzing blur, "Sure I'm okay. Hell, why not?"

RICHARD POWERS

To the Measures Fall

FROM *The New Yorker*

FIRST READ-THROUGH: you are biking through the Cotswolds when you come across the thing. Spring of '63. Twenty-one years old, in your junior year abroad at the University of York, after a spring term green with Chaucer, Milton, Byron, and Swinburne. (Remember Swinburne?) Year One of a life newly devoted to words. Your recent change, of course, has crushed your father. He long hoped that you would follow through on that Kennedy-inspired dream of community service. You, who might have become a first-rate social worker. You, who might have done good things for the species, or at least for the old neighborhood. But life will be books for you, from here on. Nothing has ever felt more preordained.

Term's out, and it's time to see every square mile of this island. Bicycle clips, a Blue Guide, a transistor radio, and skin-hugging rain. Villages slip past on valley roads as twisty as the clauses in Henry James. The book turns up in a junk shop in an old Saxon market town whose name you will remember as almost certainly having an *m* in it. Among the rusted baby buggies and ancient radios you find old cooking magazines, books on fly-tying and photography, late-fifties spy novels with cardboard covers worn as soft as felt.

The thing pops out at you: *To the Measures Fall*, by someone named Elton Wentworth. There's nothing else like it in the shop. It's a fat tome with rough-cut pages in a deluxe, tooled binding. The dust jacket has disappeared, but the front matter suggests that you know all about Mr. Wentworth already. Born in 1888, the author of twelve previous books and the winner of awards too numerous to mention.

The first line reads, "A freak snow hit late that year, two weeks after the sand martins returned to the gravel pits near the South Downs." The next few paragraphs sketch out a hard-pressed town, Wotton-on-Wold, much like the one you are in, with the *m* in it. On page 3, the author reveals the date: 1913. On the last page, a village search party finds the body of a young amputee captain who served at the Somme lying at the bottom of said gravel pits. Only seven years have passed, but the lilting opening cadences have darkened into fragments from another world.

The book seems to be a sweeping portrait of rural England before and after the First World War. You check the title page: copyright 1948. Aside from two bold exclamation points at the end of Chapter 1, the pages are unblemished, perhaps unread.

Pencilled into the upper right hand of the inside front is a price: 10/6 d. Exorbitant. You draw seven pounds a week for student expenses. A three-course Chinese dinner on Station Road costs four shillings, and lunch in the canteen is half that. A 12-inch LP runs only a pound, and even a two-minute call to the States is cheaper than Mr. Wentworth's book. Half a guinea for a used novel you've never heard of? Robbery. But something about that opening is too strange for you to resist. Besides, you've just devoted your life to literature. You graze the start of Chapter 2, in which Trevor, a spindly farmer's son with Addison's disease, baffles his parents by insisting on going to university. You need to know how this beginning can reach so macabre an end.

The shop's owner is a beaked old man with a gray hairline like a cowl slipping off his head. It's humiliating to bargain with him, but you're desperate.

How much do you offer the junk-store owner for his used book?

You are, by the way, female. Lots of folks think you shouldn't be out biking alone, even in the Cotswolds. See pages 214 to 223 of Mr. Wentworth's epic.

How much would you have offered for the book had you been male?

*

You buy the book, lug it around on the rest of the bike tour, drag it back up north with you, but somehow fail to read it. When summer ends, and with it your English idyll, you're shocked to discover how many essential novels you've bought and haven't got around to reading.

Now the problem is packing them all into a suitcase that is lighter than forty-four pounds. You could mail them to the States, but they'd cost more to ship than you spent to buy them. You resort to the time-honored system of three piles:

1. Keep for all time.
2. Suspend in Purgatory.
3. Cast forever into the outer darkness.

By the evening before the homeward flight, *To the Measures Fall* is stuck stubbornly in Purgatory, along with Wheelock's *What Is Poetry?*, James Purdy's *Malcolm, The Bull from the Sea,* by Mary Renault, John Braine's bestseller *Life at the Top,* and Updike's *The Centaur,* which has got mixed reviews. *Life at the Top* might be tricky to get hold of in the States. Who knows how long Updike will be read? *Malcolm,* on the other hand, is already on every undergraduate syllabus in the country. Renault, guilty pleasure, is the one you'd really love to have in your carry-on. The further adventures of Theseus and Hippolyta, with sun-drenched temples, earthquakes, and human-god miscegenation: how better to fill eight hours of captive reading? But your bag will hold only four more volumes. **Choose which two books get dumped forever.**

Wentworth makes the cut, if only as a souvenir of that magical cycling tour. Weirdly, browsing through the bookshop in the Oceanic Terminal at Heathrow, you notice a reprint of one of his earlier novels, about coal miners in Wales. It's a Penguin, with that orange spine that's synonymous with great books. There's a jacket blurb from Winston Churchill calling Wentworth "this island's Balzac . . . our much revered, much imitated national asset," and another from Dame Edith Sitwell, DBE, calling him "England's most distinguished living author of the novel of community."

"National asset" makes Wentworth sound like a hulking stone country house given away by pauperized aristocrats for tax deductions. And "most distinguished" feels a bit dated, against a backdrop of Mods, Rockers, the Angry Young Men, and *Beyond the Fringe.*

Still, two immortal literary lions have praised this man to the skies. What an incredible deal, getting that first edition for eight shillings. Clearly the balding junk-shop owner didn't know what he was selling. Far out over the Atlantic, as you approach Greenland, a twinge of conscience hits you. What good is all the cultivation in the world if you use it to cheat ignorant people?

How much *should* you have paid the shopkeeper? Exceed his proposed price, if necessary.

Back in the States, you look up Elton Wentworth. He isn't England's most distinguished living anything. He died right around the time that you realized you'd sooner sell cigarettes from a shoulder tray than go into social work. In addition to sheep in the Cotswolds and coal in Wales, he did Lincolnshire fishermen and three generations of Brummie factory workers. He wasn't England's Balzac; he was the James Michener of the Midlands.

You read the first hundred pages of *To the Measures Fall,* hacking your way through thickets of dialect. The prose can be brutally beautiful. But the semester starts, you fall in love, get deflowered, watch Kennedy die and the Beatles invade, get high to listen to Coltrane, and discover Heller, Ellison, Ferlinghetti, and Bellow—writing that flows across the page in huge bright swaths that you didn't know English could permit. So the First World War was a bad scene. Aren't we over that yet? And what was Wentworth doing, bringing out a book wrapped in Edwardian nostalgia three years after Dachau?

You graduate in the spring and pack up your worldly possessions again, just as the U.S.S. *Maddox* fires on three patrol boats in the Gulf of Tonkin, letting Johnson widen a war in a country that, until recently, was as fictional to you as Wentworth's South Downs.

Does the book go to Goodwill, the Salvation Army, or the twenty-five-cent pile at your graduation lawn sale?

You survive two years of graduate classes, the General Comprehensive Test (flubbing the question on Tobias Smollett), marriage to a Faulkner guy, and a grueling four-hundred-book Special Field Exam on "The Electra Complex in Postwar American Prose," a subject that you begin to hate long before your committee can lob the first question. All the while, there's Biafra, Black Power, the levitation of the Pentagon, My Lai, back-to-back assassinations, the siege of Chicago, street warfare, and city centers burning in an annual summer ritual. Drugs are everywhere, making people see God or murder their families. Books go surreal, psychedelic, and sometimes you wonder whether they're causing the mayhem or just profiting from it.

The dissertation—your baggy monster—becomes a four-year excuse to read everything except those writers you threaten to write about. On a hot June Thursday, early in the new decade, right around the time when five men break into the DNC headquarters in D.C., you find yourself patrolling your own shelves, like a hopeful bidder at an estate sale. It's a shock to come across that deluxe binding, which you distinctly remember throwing out a long time ago. The Cotswolds: cruel joke. Elgarian imperial residue.

You take it down and browse. You stop to fix dinner for your husband, who, an invalid of high modernism, cannot fix it for himself. But you're back at Wentworth until four A.M., when you end up at the bottom of the South Downs gravel pit, 1920, your throat feeling as if you'd been taking swabs at it with a pipe cleaner. You don't know what hurts more: the swirling moral turbulence of the book or the belated discovery that everything you thought about it was wrong. You missed it all: register, mood, irony, ambiguity, subtleties of characterization, narrative arc, even basic plot points. You can't read. It's like finding out, at thirty, that you're adopted.

You're not yet sure that it's great literature. But the thing took you underwater and held you there for the better part of thirteen hours, and two days later you're still winded. Its single, history-slapped village is a whole world, whose heft and weight and strange sinuous tangle of syntax stands for nothing but itself. Its portraits—particularly that of Sarah, the mother of doomed Captain Trevor and the furtive wife of idealism-scarred Francis Beck—seem so clearly ripped from microscopic observation that it's cheating to call them fiction. This story is not your life. It's not your time or place. It's just a scrap of torn diary floating up from a scorched past. What does the thing want from you?

Give the book a final grade:
Fail

Low Pass
Pass
Pass with Honors
Highest Distinction

You make your husband read it. You do the Lysistrata thing until he does. This is a mistake, as he reads it way too fast. "Very well done," he reports, wanting his sugar cube. "Skillful. First-rate social realism. Why haven't more people written about this guy?"

It isn't skillful. It isn't social realism. You read it again, taking a week this time. Now the book gets more troubling. More weirdly allegorical. You can't put your finger on what bothers you. Something to do with hoping against your better judgment. You lie awake on a hot August night wondering how a thing might be good and real and true for a while, then made irrelevant, or worse, by later events.

You've got very close with your thesis adviser. In fact, if you remember right, you're sleeping with him. The two of you are in an actual bed somewhere, in the dark, a luxury you can no longer imagine how you managed. Maybe it's an OPEC, oil-crisis thing: turn off the lights when not in use. The two of you are playing that old favorite: which classic would you never dare admit to anyone but your lover in the dark that you haven't read? You offer *Silas Lapham* and he ups the ante to *Billy Budd* and you try to trump with *The Sound and the Fury*, which he blows out of the water with *Huck Finn*. You ask him if he's ever read any Wentworth. He just snickers, thinking it another game.

You obsess about the thing. You read all the criticism. Most of it damns itself with due diligence: "Trevor Beck and Erikson's Theory of Psychosocial Development"; "Wool, Surplus Value, and Class Unrest in Wentworth's Wotton-on-Wold." No article has an insight strong enough to explain why you should be reading it rather than the book again.

You learn all kinds of things about Elton Wentworth, some of which you wish you hadn't. Blacklisted for pacifist activity under the Defence of the Realm Act. Went to Russia between the wars and came back extolling the enlightened social state. Right up until Munich, a prominent appeaser. But come September 1939, he turned British superpatriot and personal propagandizer for

Churchill, which helps explain the latter's jacket blurb. After the
war, he fought decolonization tooth and nail, in a series of interviews with dozens of natives on three continents who all declared
the British Empire the best thing ever to happen to its colonial subjects. At the age of eighty-one, he was jailed for three months for
participating in violent demonstrations against nuclear weapons.

In short, the author of that autonomous, ungrudging, unjudging
book with no villains and fewer heroes, in which every moral position is plausible but flawed, was himself a hopeless, card-carrying,
repeat-offending true believer.

**Grade Elton Wentworth's public performance. Separate marks
for form, style, and intent.**

In one of the Wentworth biographies, you come across a photograph of a note to Wentworth from Sir Winston himself. The letter's signature vaguely resembles the inked scrawl that you've
never paid attention to, on the inside front cover of your copy,
underneath the penciled price that now fills you with shame. The
signature in the reproduced note reads "Winnie." The drooping,
obscured squiggle in your copy looks more like "Hump-hump
Clunluch."

You are insane, of course. Hallucinating from overresearch.
There is no way on any likely earth that a book belonging to one of
the century's most famous personages could end up in a junk shop
in the Cotswolds. Winston Churchill, Nobel Laureate in Literature,
wasn't about to write his name in his bloody books. *If found, please
return to House of Commons, London.*

You try to erase the penciled price, for a better look. But you suc-
ceed only in smearing the signature. You look up every occurrence
of Churchill's signature on record in the university's library. There
is a similarity. The book gives you nothing else to go on, except the
two bold exclamation points at the end of the first chapter. The
one on the right seems distinctly Churchillian.

You'd take the book to an appraiser, but you get paranoid. This
is exactly the kind of scenario in which the naive get bilked. On
your next trip to the city, you show it to an antiquarian whom
you've bought from many times. He listens to your theory with a
tight, embarrassed smile. He says that even if you did get the signature certified — which could cost considerable blood, toil, tears,

and sweat—the simple signature, without any further marginalia, might not greatly increase the book's value. Given the dicey nature of the scribble, you may not want to pay for appraisal. But he's willing to give you fifty dollars for the copy, for a good customer. Fifty bucks could buy two years of used novels.

Deal or no deal?

You keep the copy, for reasons that reason doesn't understand. But two and a half months later you wipe out on literature altogether. You're out of time in the graduate program, and still no diss. Your husband says no kids until you finish, but you can't finish. The thesis isn't even embarrassing. Psychoanalytic readings reek of . . . six years ago, and this new poststructural stuff gives you hives.

You crash and burn. The house goes to pot. You glue yourself to the Watergate hearings for weeks. The whole mad circus is like a Dickens serial saga. You talk to the screen, cheering and hissing. You even develop a little thing for Sam Ervin.

You get a job adjuncting at a nearby college, intros and surveys. But drumming up enthusiasm for Wharton and Cather is murder. These days, it's all Pynchon and Barthelme, Coover and Gaddis and Gass. The canon goes up in smoke. You realize, belatedly, that you're a co-opted, false-consciousness servant of Empire, a capo of privileged heteronormative white paternalism, but it's too late to retool. Around the fall of Saigon—plagued by those films of people on the embassy rooftop clutching the runners of escaping helicopters—you bail out into law school. It's the only practical choice. And doesn't law, at bottom, involve the same act of eternal verbal negotiation as reading?

The marriage breaks up under the pressure of 1L. Your only recreational reading for the next two years is the *Congressional Record*. You get a good job, with a decent boutique firm, specializing in intellectual property. None of your dozens of bright, well-read colleagues have ever heard of Wotton-on-Wold.

You marry again, this time for real, to a big police-procedural fan in corporate litigation. At the last possible moment, you have kids. Three of them: one reader and two watchers, who get their ABCs from purple and green televised puppets. Nothing will ever light up the cortex faster than cathode rays. Yet, with your reader daughter, the whole awful, gut-wrenching seduction happens all

over again. Urban ducklings, Wild Things, Purple Crayons—it
doesn't matter. Your daughter, glazed-eyed and body-snatched,
chants "Read, Mommy, read," like she's off in Neverland already,
even before the first verb. And you, fallen Wendy, eviscerated by
the eternal recurrence of it all, hear Peter snarl at you for growing
guilty and big and old, while something inside you cries, "Woman,
woman, let go of me."

A few years pass, and still your daughter is reading furiously.
You'll lose her eventually, to the rising flood of film: the swelling
archive of video that offers whole new republics of visual democ-
racy. Who knows how long the page will hold her attention? Do
you rush her into the good stuff while you can? Maybe, if you time
things right, the whole crumbling Edwardian stage set of Wotton-
on-Wold will strike her as some kind of hyper-Narnia.

When should you push Wentworth on Jane?
1. **Never too early.**
2. **Never too late.**
3. **Never gonna happen.**

Your children become the heroes of their own plots, timeworn
narratives in unrecognizable new bindings. The eighties pass while
your energies are spent elsewhere—on building up the college-
tuition war chests, on making partner, on helping companies copyright common English words. You still read for pleasure: all kinds
of things. The hunger remains, but, as with sex, the costumes must
grow ever more elaborate to produce the same transport. You're
caught somewhere between reading for recognition and reading
for estrangement.

Mostly what you read are reviews. Too few hours left to do more
than scan the books that you know you'd love. At least you can read
what the gatekeepers say about this fall's lineup. And, often, imagining a book from its synopsis beats what you do manage to slog
through.

The reviews accumulate faster than you can flip through them.
What you really need is a thumbnail summary of the thumbnail
summaries. A year or so after Grenada or Iran-contra or some such
thing, while blasting through last year's stack of unread literary
weeklies prior to pitching them, you come across the fact that *To
the Measures Fall*, long out of print, is being reissued in an anno-

tated Essential Library edition—part of a general renaissance of
Wentworth, who, the review laments, has been in a twenty-year decline. The reviewer calls *Measures* the "once celebrated, now forgotten British *Magic Mountain.*" He claims that Wentworth's wartime
Midlands still have as much to reveal as any of the marginalized re-
gions of the earth. Can that possibly include Lesotho, Lebanon,
the Punjab?

The retrospective appreciation feels like one of those lifetime-
achievement awards that you get for having the courtesy to stay
dead. The new cover for the Essential Library edition is dazzling;
it makes Wentworth look like the next Alice Walker. You're not
sure what constitutes a decent interval between "much revered
national asset" and "unfairly undervalued." For the reviewer, the
revival proves the one universal truth about literary merit: quality
will surface, in the run of time. The trick is to stop time at just the
right moment.

Who is Elton Wentworth, exactly? Choose one.

**1. The currently most unjustly underrated author of his genera-
tion.**

2. The formerly most justly overrated author of his generation.

**3. The soon-to-be least unjustly rerated author of his genera-
tion.**

New annotated editions flood the market. Does your boat go up?
You break down and pay an appraiser ten times what you would
have, ten years ago, to look at your copy. Churchill's marked-up
volume, it turns out, went for eight hundred pounds at Sotheby's,
just as the new Wentworth renaissance hit. Your copy belonged to a
Cotswold sheep farmer named H. H. Cleanleach. The appraiser offers you ten bucks off his fee.

The boys in Information Processing install a terminal in your
office that fulfills your old dream: rapid access to abstracts of all
the articles that you can no longer find time to read. In between
researching briefs, you follow the boomlet in Wentworth studies.
The reader-response people take him up, then those who study
reputational revision. There's a minor heyday in swarming any author still in the state of pre-post-exhaustion, just before the idea of
single-author studies gives out.

A modernist at New Mexico State proves that *To the Measures Fall* was really written around 1928, suppressed by Wentworth for two decades, then published, despite his objections, in a form he didn't want. A Barnard associate prof proves that half the novel was the work of Wentworth's longtime mistress. A graduate student at Indiana proves that the book is riddled with historical error. Scholars of all ranks show how Wentworth was the product of a thousand horrific cultural blindnesses and Eurocentric brutalities.

Write a brief letter to no one, about what you once thought the book might mean.

The Berlin Wall falls, and the Evil Empire falls with it. The Cold War ends, and for a moment history does too. You stop reading anything that is more than two months old.

You don't exactly remember the nineties. The Gulf, of course. Something about Somalia and Sarajevo. Smoke everywhere. Lots of colored ribbons tied around America's trees. The firm keeps dangling the promise of senior partnership, but it never quite happens.

The 1993 feature film adaptation of *To the Measures Fall* stars Daniel Day-Lewis and Emma Thompson. There's an extended hallucinatory sequence depicting the suicidal "slow walk" at the Somme (filmed in Scotland), graphically matched to a torrid sex scene on the heath outside Wotton-on-Wold (filmed in a Hollywood sound studio). A tie-in paperback edition appears, with a glossy movie-still cover featuring the gorgeous leads.

Rate the film:
1. Worth the price of a movie ticket.
2. Worth videotaping, when it comes on TV.
3. Worth denouncing at a dinner party.
4. Worth a class-action suit by readers everywhere.

On your fifty-fifth birthday—the age at which the terminally ill Sarah Beck must identify her son's body at the foot of the South Downs gravel pit—you join a book group. The kids are grown, the career's on autopilot, the husband is off playing paintball, and it's time to read again. Books are back, in more flavors than ever. Cool books, slick books, innovative remixes, massive doorstops, funny jeux d'esprit, weepy Uighur bildungsromans, caustic family sagas from Kazakhstan. Books in every market niche and biome: avant-après-post-retro. Back too is the long-dead art of communal reading. Okay: maybe a few of your book group members are in it for the finger food. But you'd forgotten what a pleasure it is to discuss out loud—aimless talk about love and lust, responsibility, hope, and pain. Together, over two years, you read the major national selections. Your fellow members bring their old secret freight out of deep storage. You take nine months to work up to your request. You're unsure of your friends. Unsure of your ability to reread. Unsure of just what's in that treacherous book these days.

You read it slowly this time, a chapter a night, over the course of weeks. This time through, the book is no more than a grand, futile gesture of *nevertheless* in the face of human frailty: Francis Beck's refusal to believe that his wife is ill—a feckless cowardice that turns, by insistence, almost heroic; Alice Wright's paralyzing premonition, which she can't act upon without destroying the man who would destroy her; Trevor's premeditated signal to Alice, ready to launch itself from beyond the grave.

Two club members report flinging the book across the room in a rage. Another demands her three days back. Accusations multiply: it's mawkish, it's cerebral, it's meandering, it's manipulative, it's cold and cunning and misanthropic, it's wrecked by redemption. *How are we supposed to care about these characters? I just wanted them all to get a life.*

But a few people in the group don't know what hit them. One friend hated the first fifty pages but wanted fifty more after the end. The quietest man in the group comes back from Wotton-on-Wold wrapped in brittle bewilderment at his own existence.

It's a custom of the group—introduced by the male minority— to assign every book a letter grade. Yours gets a C+.

What percentage of your pleasure has gone out of the book forever? Fractions permitted.

Overnight, the World Wide Web weaves tightly around you. A novelty at first, then invaluable, then life support, then heroin. It's a chance to recapture everything you've ever lost: college friends, out-of-print rarities, quotations that had vanished forever. Your online hours must come from somewhere, and it isn't from your TV viewing. You lose whole days on the roller coaster of real-time eBay auctions. Volumes of Wentworth go off at every price, from triple digits down to a buck ninety-nine. You rescue a few, to give to friends, someday, or whenever.

It thrills you to discover a site where all the shameless, recidivist Wentworth readers in the world gather to post their guilty pleasures. You subscribe to a feed. Six months later, the community spirals into civil war as a thread between sock puppets and anonymous avatars goes up in flames.

You watch the Amazon ratings for *To the Measures Fall* drop steadily, from a high of four and a half stars to a low somewhat below that of a defective woodchipper. The wisdom of crowds means to send Wentworth into a third and final eclipse. You consider logging in at Comfort Suites across the country, creating all kinds of personae to rescue the book for another generation of Wentworth readers, whenever they dare to come out of hiding.

How many aliases do you create to rate the book?

1. Just enough to boost the book back to its rightful rating.

2. Sarah Beck would never create an alias.

Then the new century. Terror and sci-fi become life's dominant genres.

War turns perpetual.

The last print newspapers head toward extinction.

More words get posted in five years than were published in all previous history.

Global warming threatens to flood coasts inhabited by half a billion people.

Most of the planet suffers from drought or tainted water.

Name the book that best captures life as now lived.

Two months before you plan to retire, you learn that you have a massive hilar tumor, nestled up in the stem of your lungs, where nothing can reach it. It's right where Sarah Beck's is, if you're imagining correctly.

Your daughter the reader brings you the book, to keep you company in a state-of-the-art cancer center, in your bed next to a window that looks out onto a brick wall ten feet across a cement courtyard. You read it again. Not the whole book, of course—you couldn't possibly read a whole anything. But you manage a few pages, searching for a creature that recedes in front of your gaze.

This time, the book is about the shifting delusion of shared need, our imprisonment in a medium as traceless as air. It's about a girl who knew nothing at all, taking a bike ride through the Cotswolds one ridiculous spring, mistaking books for life and those roiling hills of metaphor for truth. It's about a little flash, glimpsed for half a paragraph at the bottom of a left-hand page, that fills you with something almost like knowing.

A freak snow hits late that year. You lie in bed, an hour from your next morphine dose, your swollen index finger marking a secret place in the spine-cracked volume, the passage that predicted your life. For a moment you are lucid, and equal to any story.

Score the world on a scale from one to ten. Say what you'd like to see happen, in the sequel.

JESS ROW

The Call of Blood

FROM *Harvard Review*

MORNINGS HE FINDS Mrs. Kang upright in bed, peeling invisible ginger with an invisible knife. She watches her hands with rapt attention, picking up the stalks from a pile at her right and dropping the peeled pieces into a bowl on her lap. A cloud of white hair rises from her scalp, fine as spun sugar. The first time he tries to raise her, putting his hands gently beneath her armpits, she bats them away; the second time she forgets to resist. She weighs eighty-eight pounds on a good day. In the wheelchair she sits up, ramrod-straight, and waves a finger at him. *E na pun no ma!* Her voice like wind in a crevasse. You are a bad boy!

Hyunjee, her daughter, says, No offense, Kevin. But if she knew it was a black man taking care of her, it would finish her off.

Hyunjee has a funny way of smiling, like squinting into the sun. He can tell she finds this thought faintly entertaining.

I'm not *black,* he says. My father was from Jamaica and my mother was from Queens. Irish Queens.

Oh, I know, she says. It's complicated. But it wasn't complicated for her. She was held up three times after Dad died and she was trying to run the place alone. She had nightmares for years afterward. Wouldn't admit it, though. Typical Korean mother.

Hyunjee's hair is already streaked gray on one side, though she can't be much older than forty. She wears it long with a wooden clasp, and loose-cut linen clothes, all in blues and browns and blacks. A jewelry maker—he has her card—who doesn't wear any herself. Divorced, with two little girls who come only once every two weeks or so. She comes every day, with food in a stack of steel boxes.

She was saying something different today, he says. Something like *Dung gum kuei go chora.*

Dung jum kuel go chora. Scratch my back.

Okay. I'll remember that.

You don't have to do *everything* she says, you know.

If she's itchy it means that her skin is too dry, he says. It could be a sign of dermatitis. That's what you're paying me for, to watch out for those things. The hospital nurses won't do it.

He shifts his weight from one leg to the other, trying to relieve the bone-ache in his arches, but nothing helps. These Nikes are two weeks old; he's tried lacing them loose, tight, in between. There's no stepping out of the shadow of this pain.

It's too bad, she says, her back to him, shoveling leftovers into the garbage, filling the room with the smell of sour cabbage and garlic. Until last year her English wasn't bad. She used to watch *Oprah* every day. But after she woke up from the stroke — nothing. What a shame, you know? All that wasted effort.

Not wasted. She used it to survive.

She used to say speaking English made her tongue tired. And it's true! Even I remember that, from when I was first learning. All the correct sounds in Korean are wrong in English. It's absurd, really, if you think about it. Nobody should have to work that hard to ask for a glass of water.

Count yourself lucky, he thinks, that she can speak at all.

He could tell her about the saddest cases, the old women with half-melted faces, their minds wiped clean by a clot smaller than a baby's fingernail. But nurses don't compare. To do so would be to suggest this patient is not the only patient in the universe, their only and every and always, their one sole concern. Doctors, yes. Doctors comfort by comparing, by giving the odds. Nurses never say, *It could be worse.*

His mother, on the other hand, never lost her gift for languages, right up to the end. Fluent in Latin and French by seventeen, thanks to the Carmelite Sisters of Charity, she took up patois with the steely determination of a missionary. His father's parents, so the story went, refused to believe that the woman they'd spoken to on the phone was white until she stepped onto the tarmac in Kingston, shielding herself from the sun with a blue parasol. Years after his father died she stayed on as a part-time community liaison for Catholic Social Services. It wasn't unusual, when he was in high school, to come home and find her at the kitchen table, sorting the bills, the phone clasped between shoulder and chin, her face the color of boiled lobster, saying, *Y'cyaan stay wid dat man, soon as 'im get money 'im gone.*

It embarrassed him, in a small, private way. He himself could understand his Jamaican relatives only barely and could not speak patois at all. Like the taste of ackee and jerk chicken: a foreign thing colored by the guilt of having once been familiar. At fourteen he had refused to go to the family Christmas party in Flatbush, and somehow that single gesture, that flutter of adolescent pique, had poisoned the well. No more presents, not even a birthday card. Tell them, he told his mother finally, years later, tell them I'm not ashamed to be part Jamaican, that's not it, I meant no harm. I was just a kid. She looked at him over the rim of her coffee mug and said, Well, you *meant* no harm. That must be some consolation.

When his mother died, his father's family held a Nine-Nights ceremony after the mass and didn't invite him. He was twenty-one, two weeks off the plane from Saudi Arabia, desperate for a pair of flabby arms and a perfumed shoulder, a mouthful of curry goat. Instead he stumbled home from the Liffey at three A.M. Two days later he was on the graveyard shift at St. Vincent's, picking buckshot from a gangbanger's backside. Like the grunts always said: When you get off the plane, go down on your knees and kiss the ground. Tunnel into it like an earthworm. Don't make any serious decisions for the first six months. He was lucky, having never fired a shot, flipped a switch, thrown a grenade; he could carry on the same work with no interruption, one war zone to another. Like switching saline bags on an IV, a continuous flow of tears.

Sometimes he feels his brain curdling. *Curdling:* exactly the word for it. A snatch of conversation in the elevator, the headlines on Hyunjee's copy of the *Times,* a few bars of a song someone whistles in the bathroom: always it takes him a moment too long to see the point, to put words to the melody. Synapses atrophy, lose their shape, their elasticity, their charge. Why should he be surprised? An hour spent folding towels, testing bathwater, dividing pills into groups for the night nurses: not a single abstract thought. Even the taking of vital signs boils down to a series of small muscle movements: tightening the Velcro, flicking off the old thermometer cup, squeezing the wrist with two fingers, just so. The brain carries the numbers as long as it takes to insert a quarter into a vending machine. The body drones on, he thinks, the autonomous nervous system taking care of itself quite nicely with the cerebral cortex switched off.

Have you been a nurse for a long time? Hyunjee asks, her back turned, watering the row of potted plants on the windowsill.

Since 1989, on and off.

Is that the proper word to use? I'm not up on the terminology.

If there was another term for it, it wouldn't matter. A nurse is a nurse.

You don't seem old enough to have been working in 1989.

I joined the army when I was eighteen. I was a medic in the Gulf War.

Oh.

He can hear her thoughts recalibrating, one assumption leapfrogging backward over another. It's okay, he wants to tell her, no one ever believes it. That certain slackness in the way he moves, as if he was all double-jointed, Renée had said. Hard to imagine him in formation with the helmet and the gun. His mother used to say, What is it about you that always finds the farther corner of the room?

I thought medics were doctors.

Medics are just grunts with a little bit of extra training. The MDs work in the field hospitals, out of sight, way back from the front lines.

She sticks a finger into the soil of each pot before and after watering, frowning, as if the perfect dampness is hard to achieve. A large hydrangea, the color of barely boiled tea, two long trailing ivy plants, a kind of small shrub with tiny, waxy leaves. He's never seen anyone look after plants so intently. What is her house like? he permits himself to wonder. Pristine, presumably. No dust bunnies in the corners. All uniform colors. Lots of wood, no clutter. Elaborate cabinetry. Hidden richness on all sides.

And how long did you stay in the army?

Not long. Discharged in '92.

She's brought him a stack of forms to fill out from the insurance company, a whole Conditions of Care portfolio and six-month review. Most of it she could fill in herself. Not that he would point that out to her in so many words. That's not the way a private nurse keeps clients, especially the guilty ones, the ones who want to feel like they're doing everything they can. Still, he has to grit his teeth now and then, turning a page to see another row of boxes waiting for the near-puncturing tip of his pen. Little black flashes of rage at her helplessness. Unacceptable, he tells himself, inappropriate, ridiculous.

My feet are freezing. She speaks to the window, to no one in particular. The puddles on Second Avenue are fifteen feet across. I always mean to buy a new pair of boots and never get around to it.

I can get you a pair of hospital slippers if you want.

Her laugh is high and piping and uncharacteristically girlish.

Thanks. I'm not *that* desperate.

Some indefinite tension lingers in the air. As if it's a joke and he guessed the punch line by accident too soon. So it is with me, he thinks, never one for chitchat.

I've been meaning to ask you something, she says. And I want you to give me a frank answer. I should have her at home, shouldn't I? I mean, medically speaking, there's nothing keeping her here, right? It's not as if I don't have the space. The girls can bunk up again. You just have to say the word—

You'd have to pay me almost double. Plus a night nurse. Rentals too. Home dialysis equipment, a hospital bed, a wheelchair, plus all the supplies. It would mean turning your house into a miniature clinic. Plus trips back here when she gets an infection or has to have a stent changed.

All that's required? I mean, like, by law or something?

At moments like these her face drains of expression, a strange placidity, the opposite, he thinks, of real calm, of actual relaxation. Without looking back she reaches behind her and touches the old woman's foot, the tender ankle with its close webwork of veins.

It's the standard of care.

Her village in Korea didn't get electricity till the eighties, she says. Her father dug the family well by hand. She grew up eating meat once a week if she was lucky.

Then she's one of the fortunate ones.

I don't know if that's what she'd call it.

Good thing there's no choice in the matter.

These are the kind that just *go,* a resident said to him once, in a low voice, when they were alone in the room. You could turn around and the hematode simplex is dividing and you'd never know. A hundred things depend on her saying *right* and *left.* Fucking Alzheimer's. You might as well be back with the dogfish in Gross Anatomy. She's a regular time bomb, this one. But I don't have to tell you that.

He fixed the resident with a look. Why, he said. Why don't you have to tell me that.

You went to med school. I can tell. Your notes are too detailed.

I guess that's a compliment.

Well, then, you *should* have gone to med school.

He muttered under his breath. *Quae vero inter curandum, aut Etinam Medicinam, minime faciens, in communi hominum vita, vel videro, vel audiero, quae minime in vulgus esseri oportear, ca arcana esse ratus, filebo.*

What's that?

What I may see or hear in the course of the treatment or even outside of the treatment in regard to the life of men, which on no account one must spread abroad, I will keep to myself, holding such things shameful to be spoken about.

Damn.

My sergeant was kind of a sadist. Made us memorize it before we could run an IV.

Seriously, though. Was it the money?

He's a healthy, six-foot-two Indian kid with long, tapering fingers, trying to make himself older with thin gold wire-loop glasses and a rep tie. From one of those leafy midwestern suburbs, Shaker Heights or Grosse Pointe. A certain guilelessness, the product of a vigorous, uncynical, public-school upbringing. Doctor and Doctor Sharma with the matching Mercedes. Work as a nurse in New York long enough, he thinks, and you'll meet everyone: the upwardly mobile, the failing fast, and the stick-it-outs, the in-betweens, too perverse or lazy to be counted.

Yeah. Somehow my fairy godmother never came along.

Well, you never know, right? There's loans. You're still young.

Listen, he says, I *like* nursing. Want to know why? Because it's women's work.

Dr. Sharma draws in his shoulders, protectively, and blinks.

Seriously, he says. Look at her. Nothing to be done, right? Tacrine, donepezil—they ran through that years ago. Vitamin E supplements? And then a whole slew of antidepressants. She was diagnosed as ALZ-likely twenty years ago and ever since it's been a comedy of fucking errors. One doctor coming in after another and trying to fix it. That's not how it works, man. Pay attention to the basic science! Until they find every single one of those triggers in the DNA and figure out how to turn them off, all anyone's going to be able to do is be there day by day, trying to keep those synapses exercised. For nurses, man, that's life. That's medicine.

Look, Sharma says. I get it. It's not just changing bedpans. I just can't see living in New York on a nurse's salary.

You just have to travel light. No kids, no encumbrances. I'm not looking for a condo on the Bowery.

I was thinking more like a three-bedroom in Flushing.

What, he wants to ask, is it Sympathy for Doctors Day? You mean I'm not the only martyr in the building? Well, he says, it's a sad world when a young MD can't make a mortgage payment.

Yeah. Businesslike now, his pride wounded, he knocks Mrs. Kang's chart with two knuckles and lets it clatter back into its holder at the foot of the bed. I should get back to my rounds.

It's not about the body, he's thinking, and not *not* about the body. Her clothes are loose, squared-off, raw silk, unbleached cotton, cashmere. Drapery. They generalize her figure. Only when she squats or reaches or bends low does he become aware of the generosity of her hips, the smooth unfreckled cleft of her breasts. She never arouses him, not in person, not in daydreams. Nothing as obvious as that. *Her smoldering frustration.* Like her scent, not perfume, not soap, but there in the room nonetheless, slightly sweet and damp.

So unlike the clatter and innuendo outside in the corridor. Men can't resist a woman in scrubs, even the ugliest mismatched laundry-room rejects; he certainly never could. That was the one benefit of switching to paramedic in the days after Renée, or, to be honest, *during* and after: the whole parade of them, doe-eyed, fresh RNs, lacy bras and thongs underneath, in spare rooms, in supply closets, in his bed at four A.M. after a shift and an hour slamming beers. It's the oldest feeling in the world, or the second oldest, after just plain lust: survivor's guilt. Like all the stockbrokers shacking up after the towers fell. Terror sex, they called it, but it had nothing to do with terror. You look at pain, you gape at it, and then tear yourself away and eat Froot Loops. Pure instinct. A shift of heart attacks and gunshot wounds and eight-year-old girls with fingers burned off and what else could you possibly want? A candy bar, a shot of Jameson, a bacon double cheeseburger, and your face buried in Nicole Scangarello's pussy in the back seat of her Altima pulled over at a rest stop on the way out to Huntington Beach.

He was never particular in those days. You took what came. Hospitals, again: a great equalizer. Sponsor of thousands of mongrel births. He never understood the guys who swore by Bronx Dominicans or Flatbush Chinese or Staten Island Italians. And the girls: were they aroused by his blackness? Not likely. Not that he ever knew. His body was never so remarkable as to engender much comment. It was a body, it was available, it was alive; that was the coin of the realm. He doesn't miss the sex so much, the messiness of all that grappling, all those unfamiliar shapes beneath the fingers, the odd discoveries, pounding away to get the nut no matter if the sweetness is gone, but he misses the reassurance. And misses being awake so often in the hour of necessity, the hot glare of the streetlights just before dawn.

Hyunjee has his home number. Not just his cell, his business number, which he turns to silent on weekends and the evenings—a substitute for his old answering service—but the old black rotary phone that just rings: no answering machine, no caller ID, no volume control, not even a plug to unhook from the wall. He gave it to her the first day her mother was admitted; it was something about the hapless way she fell into the chair in the waiting room and curled her legs to one side. New Yorkers don't act that way when engaging a service, signing a contract. It unnerved him when he showed her the payment schedule and she barely glanced it over. He flipped over his card and scrawled the number across the back. I'll always be at one of these, he said. Don't worry.

Now he checks his cell messages on a Sunday morning, no less. In case she's too shy to bother him at home. Sweaty, after running, peeling off his shirt and nylon jacket, draping a towel around his shoulders. The way she molds the dirt into little mounds with her fingertips. Her deftness with the metal chopsticks that never click against the side of the bowl. I could use a little pruning. A stupid way to put it. A woman's face creased with quiet anxiety. *Care*, he thinks, I could use someone else's care. I've grown too good at it myself.

Watch yourself, now. As if the world needed a whole new dimension of tired and pathetic. You'd have to wait till after the old woman died, and then what? A phone call two weeks after the funeral? *I thought we might have dinner?*

You can't afford it, he thinks, there comes a point in life when every investment is a loss, every additional effort is a mistake. Do yourself a favor. Do yourself a service. The luxury of not waiting out another six months of heartache. He steps into the plastic stall with its long skid mark of rust running from the faucet to the drain, thinking, Do something about that, if you want to do something. And leaves the water on cold for a moment longer than usual, till his teeth are chattering.

When he walked into the classroom on the first day of Korean 110 the teacher covered her mouth, to cover a laugh, or a grimace of horror, perhaps some new fusion of the two she'd never imagined. He wedged himself into a chair between Katrina Lee and Jenny Park and tried his best to follow her explanation of *hangul*, a jumble of little circles and boxes and stick-figure men.

It's a very difficult language, she said to him afterward. Even for them — she indicated the young Korean American women vanishing through the door, zipping backpacks, flipping open their mobile phones. They grow up hearing it and still it takes them years. What makes you interested in learning it?

I have a Korean girlfriend.

He'd been flipping through the course catalog on the toilet — it came in the mail, unbidden, three times a year — meditating on the question of other possible lives. Introduction to Reiki. Advanced Flavors of the Mediterranean. Systems Analysis and the Diversified Portfolio. The listing for the introductory language classes said, *No previous experience necessary, for the absolute beginner.* He liked that phrase, its wishful absurdity. As if there was any such thing as an absolute beginner.

Then she can teach you, yes?

She's shy. Anyway, she doesn't have enough time. I want to learn it properly, from the ground up. Her parents don't speak English.

She crossed her arms and gave a broad, worldly laugh. That's very well-intentioned of you, she said. But the problem might not be the language barrier.

Am I making you uncomfortable? he was tempted to say. She didn't even bother to disguise the way she moved behind the desk when he came near. Uninhibited fear and discomfort. You could almost respect her for it.

Well, it's my money, he said.

It amazes him now, three months gone, the term nearly finished. Every word he speaks out loud sending ripples of wincing distaste through the room. Teacher Cho has perfected the art of derision by example. *Bol,* she says, flapping her tongue at him to demonstrate the way it should be placed: curled behind the teeth, a little coiled snake. Not *bowl. Bol.* Long after he's gotten it right. *That's you,* Renée used to say, *stubborn as a rock when you've made up your mind.* Meant not entirely as praise. But mostly.

Mul jum kajigo wara, Mrs. Kang says.

I want some water.

Mul jum kajigo wara.

A sentence flowing at him out of a dream. He stands by the window, scrubbing iodine off the toe of his sneaker. He wipes his fingers on a paper towel and inches his neck around until his head rotates half the distance between them.

Cham gam manyo, mul kajoda deureul kayo? he asks.

Mul kajoda.

Her eyes shift in his direction: wet drops of onyx, bright as always, brighter than seeing eyes can ever be. Who does she think is speaking? he wonders. She stretches out a palsied finger, pointing at the bathroom door. A tap. A pump. A well. Eventually the disease squeezes out every memory, he knows that, even the earliest: the bottle, the mother's breast. But right now, who am I to her? Son, father, uncle, nurse, servant?

Mul. He catches himself saying it. The tip of the tongue placed exactly in the middle of the palate. *Mul. Mul.*

And here you thought it would never happen, he thinks. You thought it would never click. All that wasted time.

Kevin—

Hyunjee in the doorway, looking from one face to another.

He's forgotten the daughters: their names, their ages, the particular blur of each face. The taller of the two full-grown, shoulder-high on him, the other some indeterminate late-childhood shape, all bright wholesome fabrics and plastic beads. They're uptown for the weekend with their father, but he's thinking, as they walk up Second Avenue from the Thai restaurant back toward her apartment, that he should have something to say on the general subject of children, why he and Renée never had any, the difficulties of being a single mother—being a child of one—the hardships of the New York City schools. A certain widening of the circle of the conversation. He needs to bring things up to date, to gesture toward the immediate past, the impending future. Amy, Elizabeth, Lisa, Allison? Nondescript, easy names, names indicative of compromise, of shying away from the fashionable, not making things more difficult than they would already be.

Though one could hardly say she's given him much of an opening. Come get a bite with me tomorrow, was all she said. Stanley's got the girls for the weekend. I could use some adult conversation. This whole you-studying-Korean thing—she waved her hand, as if to say, *I don't get it, I don't have to get it.* I mean, she said, it's strange, isn't it, spending so much time together, never actually getting to know each other. Maybe to you it's not. But you don't have to come if you don't want to. Strictly optional.

And now he's lightheaded, pathetic dateless creature, swinging along the sidewalk as if he owns Manhattan, free-associating through the past, a tour of sedimented longings he hasn't unearthed in years.

There's something I meant to ask you about, she says, after they've walked a block in silence. Next week's her birthday. I was wondering if it would be appropriate to celebrate. In the room, I mean.

He wonders if he should be annoyed; business on a date, isn't that one of those basic rules? Instead he opts for generosity, a light laugh. Of course, you should do anything you want. She's not in a coma, you know. Anything she recognizes helps.

It's also her wedding anniversary.

All the better. A tape recording of your father, maybe? Or a piece of his clothing.

And a bottle of soju. She used to drink herself silly and talk to his picture, every year. Stories from her village. I should have used a tape recorder. Is there some rule against getting the patients drunk?

He laughs so loudly passersby look up from their conversations, startled. She doesn't need it, he says. That's the good side of Alzheimer's. You're permanently blotto.

She opens the door, drops her keys in a glass bowl in the hallway, opens the refrigerator, and carries a bottle and two glasses across the living room to the sliding door of the balcony, without looking at him, without asking permission. Shucking her mules absentmindedly halfway across the carpet. A chrome-and-glass coffee table, a pair of black leather couches, an Eames chair, enormous plastic-looking ferns. *His* furniture. Everything you can't afford to replace in a divorce, and the kids want it anyway, no matter how horrible, it's what they've grown into, and the continuity matters.

I'm curious about something, she declares, and I want to be honest about it. No pussyfooting around. I want to know what it was like over there.

It wasn't even a real war. Not like the one they're in now.

That's a poor excuse for an answer.

I'll tell you this much, he says. Sand gets into everything. I had this expensive camera, a Nikon, and it was trashed by the time I left. Sand driven through the seal into the lens. It sticks to your skin. The slightest bit of moisture makes it stick. You get so that it sticks to your dick and keeps you from jerking off.

The wine has a cloying floral bouquet, like sweet perfume; he licks his lips trying to get rid of it. Half my high school signed up, he says. Four tables right outside the main doors starting in April. Like shooting fish in a barrel. They took the kids who graduated two or three years ahead of us, the ones we looked up to, and sent them back as recruiters. It was a goddamned reunion out there every day. Gave them nice watches, good insurance policies, anything they could show off.

So you were manipulated into it.

I was looking for another father. A certain perverted kind of unconditional love. And instead what you get is Daddy slapping you across the face every other minute.

I understand that.

No you don't, he wants to say, quickly, a splash of cold water across the eyes. But says, instead, It wasn't for me. Some really get into the camaraderie aspect, the brotherhood. It feels good to be needed when you're that age. And, you know, it teaches you to get your shit together. Get up and take a shower in the morning, no complaining. It's a *job*. They say it's the best and worst training for the rest of your life.

He chuckles. As long as we're on unpleasant topics—

He's a lawyer. You might have heard his name. Stanley Pollack. Civil rights stuff, mainly, First Amendment issues. Whistleblower cases. Pretty high profile. He's a commentator on WNYC.

Does that bother you?

What, hearing his voice? Come on. We're on the phone two or three times a week anyway. He's a pretty involved father. Or at least he talks a good game. The divorce was amicable in the end, I guess. We used a mediator. No betrayals, no infidelities. Not that I know of, anyway. Just pain. Ordinary, exhausting, unglamorous pain. We married too young; we got tired. You know the one about the wooden peg in the table?

You mean the round peg in the square hole.

No, no. Say you've got a wooden peg stuck in a table and you want to get it out. The only way is to bang in another peg. You're always back where you started, in other words.

So you throw away the table.

Something like that. I was never good at analogies.

And the girls?

The girls are over there having a grand old time. Takeout sushi and movies on cable till three A.M. if they want. He lets them watch *Sex and the City* and they come home talking about cocaine and anal sex. The only rule is they can't leave the apartment. Stan's a paranoid old New Yorker. Still won't walk through Central Park at night.

He'll have a hard time when they get older.

They *are* older. Samantha's having her bat mitzvah in October.

Is that right, he says. Trying to connect the word with a particular age. Is it like confirmation, he wonders, or like a sweet sixteen. Or neither.

I converted before we were married. Not that we ever went to synagogue. But the bat mitzvah's nonnegotiable. His parents are footing the bill.

Underneath her cardigan is a flimsy silk tank top, almost the top of a nightgown. Off comes the sweater, wadded up in her lap. He's surprised by the broadness of her shoulders. Not unlike Renée's, in truth. On a long thin chain she wears a flat gold disk the size of a nickel, polished, catching the light. He reaches and turns it between his fingers. No markings on either side. Like a slug for busting old Coke machines, a penny on the railroad tracks, burned smooth.

That a piece of yours?

She swallows the last of her wine and pours another glass.

We could sit here and ask each other questions all night, she says. We could get to know each other incredibly well in a couple of hours. Is that what you want?

But there is one more story, the one he tells her in the smearing blue light of six-thirty, before his shift begins and he becomes her employee again. Renée's last day in the apartment. He was just home from work, and heard her moving around in the bedroom, talking on the phone, so he'd think it was her mother and would pick up the line in the kitchen. That was their strange habit, these party-line calls, because Shirley loved him—more than her own daughter, Renée always claimed—and would always be clamoring for him to get on the phone. She lived in South Carolina, a good place to raise children, she always reminded them, better than the snowy wastes of Hollis.

It wasn't Shirley, of course. It was a man's voice, grinning at her across the line, making her giggle. Baby, I *know* you want me to get it out! it said. I *know* you can't stand waiting another minute! But I'm gonna *make* you wait! He dropped the receiver into its cradle as if it was white smoking iron and stared straight ahead. A head of cabbage, an ice tray left out on the counter to melt. His own keys, left casually in the bowl next to the door. The simplest objects had a way of betraying you: all the unpredictable meanings they took on. He stared at each one, each thing, making an inventory, before walking out the door.

Only later did he realize he was waiting for her to come out of the bedroom and explain.

They run into each other now, every so often, when he's back visiting a friend in the neighborhood. She held on to the apartment but not the man, Rodney or Rudolph or Randolph, even after she bore him the son he claimed he wanted more than anything, more than a winning lottery ticket or a house in Barbados. A daughter and two sons. Her mother lives across the street now, he's heard. Whenever he sees her he feels as if they're meeting in a garden, a lawn hedged with bright flowers, or a patio with a fountain in the middle. An absolute and unshakeable peace. As if one pain canceled out another.

There's a special place in hell reserved for people like that, Hyunjee says, rolling onto her back and dropping her fingers lightly against his thigh. Betrayal by telephone is in a category all by itself.

I stopped blaming her a long time ago.

Cosmic retribution, though. *That* you can hope for.

No, he says, that's not my life. That's not a way to live.

If it had been me I would've been cured of sex for good.

Maybe I am.

Don't say things like that, she says. I hate repartee. It's boring. Not when I can still feel you inside me. You haven't been cured of anything. Thank god.

All right, then. Have it your way.

I would have wanted those years of my life back. Presumably that's why I'm still alone. My capacity for forgiveness is too low.

Is that a warning?

Immediately he wishes he'd stopped up his mouth, sucked in a wad of cotton, a roll of toilet paper. Even a brick would've done, in a pinch.

It might be, she says. Would you like it to be?

She's beginning to refuse food. When Hyunjee lifts the lid and releases the smell of *kalbi* into the room her eyes pucker in alertness and fear. *My teeth hurt,* she says. *My teeth are falling out.* Though they show no signs of looseness, no dark spots, no obvious cavities. He calls down a request for a dental consult. Forty-eight hours, they tell him. They're all away at a convention at Foxwoods.

Let her get hungry, Hyunjee says. She'll eat when she's hungry.

She isn't a three-year-old. Though, he might say, of course, on most days there isn't that much of a difference.

Well, what, then? IV nutrition?

Not now.

So what? We just let her stay like this?

That's what the expression means, he thinks: *to suck the air out of a room.* They circle each other like wary lions. When she crosses the room to get a new bottle of moisturizer he moves around the far side of the bed, pretending, for the fifth time, to check the catheter bag. The room is stifling; she hasn't unbuttoned her sweater. At every opportunity she backs against a wall with her arms crossed. If he brushed her arm, let alone slid a palm against her waist, what would she do? Swat the offending appendage like a fly? He's tempted to find out. It's been four days, and he hasn't fully regained the use of his lower body; he still suffers from the occasional bolt of pure liquid joy.

The idea is to encourage them to make choices, he says. You know that. Choice is higher-level cognitive function.

It'll all go to waste.

You ought to make less, you know. *You* don't eat it.

She shoots him a nasty look. Fine. *You* try, then. See if she'll listen to you.

He pulls up a stool at the edge of the bed and pries open the lid of the smallest container. Kimchi. He can't eat it, though Hyunjee has offered many times: the smell makes his eyes water, but it's the image that gets him: the bulbous Napa roots, the rubbery leaves leaking bloody juices, like little hearts, scraps of human tissue, packed in a surgical basin.

Mama, he says loudly, and immediately, with no hesitation, she reaches out for the chopsticks, lifts a strand of cabbage out with great delicacy, and guides it to her mouth.

When we moved here, Hyunjee says, in '71, there wasn't a single other Korean family in Kew Gardens. Maybe fifty total in all of

Queens. You couldn't buy a Napa cabbage in the whole borough, let alone the right kind of rice or *kochichang*. My aunt who lived in L.A. sent big boxes of supplies through the mail. When anyone flew back from Korea they would bring a suitcase full of sheets of nori. There was so little that after a while she stopped forcing me to eat it. She cooked for her and Dad and let me boil hot dogs and eat macaroni and cheese. In public she let me speak back to her in English, but at home she insisted on Korean. Thank god. I wanted out of the whole thing, right from the get-go. I was eleven, for Christ's sake.

Mrs. Kang digs out a hunk of rice and lifts it to her lips, her fingers trembling with the effort. As she chews her face takes on a puzzled, faraway look.

Seriously. Try to imagine it. You're a little girl, and someone pushes you down on the asphalt at recess, and you've got a skinned knee and your pants are torn, and you're crying and wishing your mother was there and not wishing your mother was there and wanting to speak Korean and not wanting to speak it. And nobody else knows what the difference is between you and Connie Choy in the seventh grade, nobody knows what a Korean *is*, or cares, aren't those places just all the same anyway? What matters is you're here. Nobody gives a shit about the Japanese invasion or President Rhee or two thousand years of this dynasty and that dynasty. You learn to hate your own inconvenient self. And then before you know it you're in high school and you've forgotten all about it, you're just a *good girl*, a straight-A girl, you have your own little slot, and you ace the APs and the only boys you talk to are the Jewish boys you debate in history and kick the shit out of in calculus. And then one of them asks you to the prom, and you don't say no, you sneak out of the house through the basement window, and that's it, a quick sweaty fuck in the back of a rented limo. After that you're an American teenager for sure. Crying in the bathroom when your period's late.

She puts down the chopsticks as if she's finished, then sticks in her fingers, picks another chunk of cabbage from the bowl, stares at it contemplatively, and tries to touch it to her lips. It winds around her finger, dribbling red juice down onto the knuckle.

All I'm saying is I'm sick of complications. I envy her sometimes. One language. One place. One set of memories. Sick, right? Sometimes I think human beings just weren't meant to live this way.

What way?

Oh, you know. So fucking mixed up. Spring rolls and matzoh balls. Filipinos doing your nails and Koreans doing your laundry and Guatemalans bringing your Chinese food and Hasids handing you pamphlets every time you come out of the subway. There comes a point where it has to stop, doesn't it? The human mind can't contain so many contradictions. I'm not trying to sound like a racist. It isn't racism to love your own kind. Whoever said we had to do penance for all historical sins by living in such an upside-down world? I'm tired of it.

Penance? he thinks. This is penance?

You know what the latest thing is? Samantha had this bright idea of having her bat mitzvah reception at one of the Korean barbecue places on Thirty-second Street. She lives for that stuff. And of course Stan's parents—well, they've been once, they know what it's like. Plates and plates of raw bloody meat. It's not that they're kosher, I'd hardly even call them observant. They might even agree to it. But they'd be humiliated, of course. *Devastated.* So I'm the one who has to drop that particular bomb on her. And of course she pulls out the whole routine: *I thought I could have anything I wanted. Am I supposed to, like, not be Korean, or something?* And all I want to say to her is, Honey, you have no idea where this ends. *I* have no idea where it ends. And I'm tired of trying to explain it to them. You'd like to think they just accept it, because they don't know anything else. But they're not. They're climbing out of their bodies. It *isn't* natural. Like hell they'd ever be allowed to pray at the Wailing Wall.

I thought only men prayed there.

Oh, stop it. Don't quibble. You know what I mean.

She reaches out and holds her mother's chin still while he wipes the juice from her lips. Bright blossoms on each cheek, her ears flushed pink, lurid growths, poisonous mushrooms. Not for the first time he marvels at the vivid effects of pale skin, a taxonomy of stifled feeling.

I'm sorry, she says. I really should stop. I don't know what's taken hold of me. Maybe I'm coming down with something. I'm a little dizzy. *Shit.* She gives him an anxious passing look. He can't help but notice the ripples of skin around her eyes, and how they never seem to move as much as they should, as much as he wants them to. I've screwed everything up now, haven't I?

He manages a dry chuckle, a little flourish of manly detachment.
I know better than to think I know what to expect, he says.

But your situation is completely different. Wouldn't you say? You
belong here. Your parents both spoke English, for Christ's sake.
Irish and Jamaican—that's like the American dream. That makes
sense.

Hyunjee, he says, be careful.

What does that mean?

When you're deciding what makes sense to *you.*

You want to know the worst thing about me? She gives him a
wild-eyed, beseeching look, but it's purely formal, a warning: what
is he supposed to do, run down the hall for a straitjacket, wrap her
mouth shut with gauze tape? They put up that huge new mosque
on Ninety-sixth Street, she says, with the electric zipper sign on the
fence. Twenty-four hours a day it says the same thing: *There is no
God but Allah, and Mohammed is his prophet.* I pass it every time I
drive out to Queens to go grocery shopping. And I always think,
just for a second, I *hate* you. Every single time. I just want to stop
the car and say, Go back to fucking Egypt, if you're so sure. Go back
to Saudi Arabia. Sometimes I'm just so sick of having to be polite.
I'm just so sick of pretending that coexistence is easy or natural.
It's like I'm allergic to New York, but I *am* New York; it's an autoim-
mune thing. Sometimes you have to think, no wonder someone
wanted to drop a bomb on this place and start over. I mean, we're
all sitting around, acting as if it's going to make sense someday, but
it never, never will.

Well, he says, maybe you should go back to Korea and see what
that's like. Leave the kids here. Leave them with what's-his-name.
They'll do what kids always do. Survive. Adjust. *You* go back. If it
means that much to you.

Her hands, beautiful, large, uncreased, unlined hands, don't
know what to do with themselves. While she stares at him, her
mouth puckering into a little triangular divot, as if halted in the
midst of formulating a response, they move up and down her
thighs, rubbing her pants pockets, as if she's not sure if she remembered her keys.

I don't get it, she finally says. Are you obtuse? You haven't been
listening. Is that supposed to be funny?

Her face, once again, frozen in midlook, eyebrows raised, as if surprised by any intensity, any feeling at all, even her own. Expecting to be hurt, he thinks, when *he* ought to be hurt, expecting it all to end badly.

All right, forget it. It was rhetorical.

You don't *rhetorically* tell someone to go back where they came from. I belong here. I paid my dues.

No one's suggesting otherwise.

And I'm not saying I'm a bad person either. I appreciate what you did. It was a very *sweet*—no, a very . . . She waves a hand at the air, pinches the bridge of her nose, as if to let out the pressure of the thought.

It was a gesture, he says. A somewhat disproportionate gesture.

And I would love, believe me, I would love to respond in kind. But a life can only contain so much dissonance, don't you think? I'm just saying I'm *tired*.

No one ever suggested a relationship, he says, keeping his face blank. If that's what you mean. Did we misunderstand each other?

She shrugs and smoothes the sheet around her mother's legs.

Because otherwise we would have to be very careful. Things could get awkward.

Is that a threat?

Of course not. It's an assessment. I'm not going anywhere until you say the word.

Well, then, she says, you don't have anything to worry about.

He's moved his bed to the far end of the room, away from the radiator, from the hot water pipes, underneath the window permanently propped open two inches with an old paperback copy of *The Fountainhead*. Never could sleep in heat of any kind. In the desert, when he was assigned the night shift and had to sleep in the glowing heat of the tent under the midday sun, he tore the liner out of his sleeping bag and soaked it with water out of his own precious supply. Like sleeping covered with wet paper towels. He's thought about moving his bed onto the roof, but not in Red Hook, not with six connected buildings on one block, and kids moving across them at all hours of the night with guns and yayo. On a good winter night the slipstream of cold air from the window keeps him happily underneath a pile of blankets. He's so far away he barely hears the phone ringing on the most distant wall of the kitchen next to the stove. A railroad apartment, a run-to-the-phone apartment. His cell turned off and charging on his bedside table.

It's too late to call, Hyunjee says. What time is it, anyway? Her voice is shaky, her breathing careless. I *knew* it was too late to call.

Hang up, he says. I'll see you tomorrow.

Oh, come on, she says. Don't sulk. I've been rehearsing this apology all night.

He lowers himself into a chair and props his bare feet on the table next to a dirty juice glass. In the sallow wash of the streetlights they look pale and knobby, angular. A starving man's feet. A runner's feet.

Listen, she says, those things I said, which I'm not going to repeat—

I remember them.

I was working something out. I was trying on a different frame of mind, and I'm sorry you had to be there to witness it. Sometimes I have to be the one person in the room who says what everybody else is thinking. Okay, okay, that's too presumptuous. What some people *might* be thinking. We're all so easily insulted these days, you know? Just quivering, waiting for someone to slip up so we can all take offense. It's just as tribal and parochial and dimwitted as the creationists in Kansas. Believe me, I should know. Offensive behavior is sending my kids to college.

Hyunjee, he says, you know what your problem is? You're too good at this game. You know you can talk your way out of anything.

So what, then? What's your solution? You were the one with all the questions the other night.

I'm just saying there are some problems talking can't solve.

Oh, she says. That old conundrum. Language is the sickness and the cure.

No, he's thinking, that's not how I would have put it. And then he has the impulse to say, to fire right back, Love is the sickness and the cure. Shoot me now, he thinks, I've turned into a Hallmark card. And the worst of it is he's never believed any such thing. He would have said it without meaning it, to be clever, or provocative, to try it on for size. That's what you do around these people, he tells himself, you spatter words around like fingerpaint and call that a conversation, you say horrible things and take them back and say, that's a relationship, that's what I always wanted.

Hyunjee, he says, I accept your apology.

And just like that everything's back to normal?

No, he thinks, isn't that the point? Nothing was, nothing *is* ever normal. I'll see you tomorrow, he says, and lifts the heavy receiver away from his ear, holding her protesting voice between thumb and index finger for a moment before dropping it, clattering, onto the cradle.

She's popped an infection, the night nurse said on the phone. *Fever one-oh-two. They think it's the stent. Should I call her?* And he said, Ten minutes ago. Licking the dust of sleep off his lips. You know how she is. Get off and do it right now. Tell her I'm coming. *But it's four-thirty—don't I still get the rest of my shift?* Do it now! he shouts. Do it! And then clear out. Consider your ass fired.

Sorry, he keeps saying to Hyunjee, on the way back from the coffee machine, sorry, sorry. Should never have hired her. Should never have even looked at her twice.

Would you shut up?

Her skin, under the fluorescent lights, is shockingly gray. *Corpse-like.* Raw-lipped, bare-eyed, in red Harvard sweatpants and a hooded sweater. She backs into the wall of the elevator and closes her eyes.

I mean, it looks like they've got it under control, right? The drug's working. I shouldn't bring the girls in to say goodbye, right?

She'll still be here in the morning.

Then go home. I'll stay.

Is that really what you want?

I don't think you should work for me any longer, she says, opening her eyes and staring past him at the wall. I mean, I'll pay you. I'll keep paying you. What, a month's severance, two months, is that fair?

He laughs, the dazed, punch-drunk laugh all nurses have at the end of the graveyard shift. He can't help himself. Hyunjee, he says, you think that'll make it better? A golden handshake?

I made a mistake, okay? Distractedly she undoes the haphazard knot holding her hair in place, and lets it fall across her forehead, the streak of gray curving like a nautilus shell. I needed someone to be objective, she says, flicking the hair back with her thumb. Not that I thought I wasn't a good daughter. Not that I felt guilty. But she deserves more than that, you know? Everybody deserves more than one. It wasn't her fault that they didn't know what endometriosis was back in those days. It's not that she wanted a son. She just wanted a second try. And she was right, goddamn it! Nobody should ever be so fucking alone that they have to hire strangers to be family. I'm sorry. I can't help myself. Here, hold this.

She holds out her coffee cup to him, and zips her sweater up to the neck, and begins to cry, dropping her hands in front of her like a rag doll, and when he embraces her, when he covers her face with his chest, does not raise them, does not wrap them around his waist, but shrinks into him, into herself, like a dried-out stem, he thinks, like a twig, clasping his awkward paws around her with a Styrofoam cup of hot liquid in each, like urine samples, or blood vials, anything vital, anything carrying the body's warmth away.

This is the way to tell the story. When the grandchildren ask, how was it that they met, those two, a Portuguese sailor and an ex-nun from Estonia, or, how did they communicate, if he didn't speak Finnish and she didn't speak Taiwanese, you don't say, he was already drunk when they met in the airport bar. Or, they were locked in the basement accidentally for three hours before the manager let them out. You say, in this case there was no other way. The world is made choice after choice after choice. The body makes logic, not the other way around.

And then they ask, is it fair, is it just, to reduce it to that? Isn't it the height of selfishness, these willy-nilly associations, this refusal to plan, this projecting the future from the momentary bubble of your own ego?

Well, you say, which is it better to be seduced by: the future in the form of a woman with hair the color of streaming silver, or the future in the form of an organizing principle?

Samantha, she says, when he backs open the door in the morning, his arms full of new bedding. Samantha. Pearl. Turn around. I want you to say hi to Kevin.

They turn away from the bed awkwardly, darting looks at one another: *It's just the nurse. It's just the nurse, right?* Hi, the older one says, flipping her bangs back. Tiny bright green eyes. Um, thanks for taking such good care of Grandma.

I'm Pearl, the little one says. Yeah, thanks.

Kevin's coming out to lunch with us. Aren't you?

There's no one to take over. I'd have to make a call.

It's all right. Just an hour.

Aren't you kids supposed to be in school?

In-service. Pearl sucks a lollipop, knocking it against her teeth. Professional development day.

Something is sticking in his throat, a crooked knuckle, a little jagged stone. He can't look at them straight on. Little suns, he thinks, little flames of the future. Their shifting brown limbs, their twitching fingers. Outrageous, the claims they make on us! Outrageous, the way they judge us from thirty years hence!

So, Hyunjee asks, interrupting his reverie. Are you coming or not?

It makes a kind of tableau, he thinks, a frieze, these women's faces, women and soon-to-be women, waiting to see what he'll do next. As if in some obscure way that's what he's always wanted. *The measure of a man.* Behind the girls, Mrs. Kang stirs, wraps her blue fingers around the rail, and pulls her face a few inches up from the pillow.

I never had a son, she says. *Nahantaenen adeul op da!* I don't know who you are.

GEORGE SAUNDERS

Escape from Spiderhead

FROM *The New Yorker*

"DRIP ON?" Abnesti said over the PA.

"What's in it?" I said.

"Hilarious," he said.

"Acknowledge," I said.

Abnesti used his remote. My Mobi-Pak™ whirred. Soon the Interior Garden looked really nice. Everything seemed super-clear.

I said out loud, as I was supposed to, what I was feeling.

"Garden looks nice," I said. "Super-clear."

Abnesti said, "Jeff, how about we pep up those language centers?"

"Sure," I said.

"Drip on?" he said.

"Acknowledge," I said.

He added some Verbaluce™ to the drip, and soon I was feeling the same things but saying them better. The garden still looked nice. It was like the bushes were so tight-seeming and the sun made everything stand out? It was like any moment you expected some Victorians to wander in with their cups of tea. It was as if the garden had become a sort of embodiment of the domestic dreams forever intrinsic to human consciousness. It was as if I could suddenly discern, in this contemporary vignette, the ancient corollary through which Plato and some of his contemporaries might have strolled; to wit, I was sensing the eternal in the ephemeral.

I sat, pleasantly engaged in these thoughts, until the Verbaluce™ began to wane. At which point the garden just looked nice again. It was something about the bushes and whatnot? It made you just want to lay out there and catch rays and think your happy thoughts. If you get what I mean.

Then whatever else was in the drip wore off, and I didn't feel much about the garden one way or the other. My mouth was dry, though, and my gut had that post-Verbaluce™ feel to it.

"What's going to be cool about that one?" Abnesti said. "Is, say a guy has to stay up late guarding a perimeter. Or is at school waiting for his kid and gets bored. But there's some nature nearby? Or say a park ranger has to work a double shift?"

"That will be cool," I said.

"That's ED763," he said. "We're thinking of calling it NatuGlide. Or maybe ErthAdmire."

"Those are both good," I said.

"Thanks for your help, Jeff," he said.

Which was what he always said.

"Only a million years to go," I said.

Which was what I always said.

Then he said, "Exit the Interior Garden now, Jeff, head over to Small Workroom 2."

II

Into Small Workroom 2 they sent this pale tall girl.

"What do you think?" Abnesti said over the PA.

"Me?" I said. "Or her?"

"Both," Abnesti said.

"Pretty good," I said.

"Fine, you know," she said. "Normal."

Abnesti asked us to rate each other more quantifiably, as per pretty, as per sexy.

It appeared we liked each other about average, i.e., no big attraction or revulsion either way.

Abnesti said, "Jeff, drip on?"

"Acknowledge," I said.

"Heather, drip on?" he said.

"Acknowledge," Heather said.

Then we looked at each other like, What happens next?

What happened next was, Heather soon looked super-good. And I could tell she thought the same of me. It came on so sudden we

were like laughing. How could we not have seen it, how cute the
other one was? Luckily there was a couch in the Workroom. It felt
like our drip had, in addition to whatever they were testing, some
ED556 in it, which lowers your shame level to like nil. Because
soon, there on the couch, off we went. It was super-hot between us.
And not merely in a horndog way. Hot, yes, but also just right. Like
if you'd dreamed of a certain girl all your life and all of a sudden
there she was, in your Domain.

"Jeff," Abnesti said. "I'd like your permission to pep up your language centers."

"Go for it," I said, under her now.

"Drip on?" he said.

"Acknowledge," I said.

"Me too?" Heather said.

"You got it," Abnesti said, with a laugh. "Drip on?"

"Acknowledge," she said, all breathless.

Soon, experiencing the benefits of the flowing Verbaluce™ in
our drips, we were not only fucking really well but also talking
pretty great. Like, instead of just saying the sex-type things we had
been saying (such as "wow" and "oh God" and "hell yes" and so
forth), we now began freestyling re our sensations and thoughts,
in elevated diction, with eighty percent increased vocab, our well-
articulated thoughts being recorded for later analysis.

For me, the feeling was, approximately: Astonishment at the
dawning realization that this woman was being created in real time,
directly from my own mind, per my deepest longings. Finally, after all these years (was my thought), I had found the precise arrangement of body/face/mind that personified all that was desir-
able. The taste of her mouth, the look of that halo of blondish hair
spread out around her cherubic yet naughty-looking face (she was
beneath me now, legs way up), even (not to be crude or dishonor
the exalted feelings I was experiencing) the sensations her vagina
was producing along the length of my thrusting penis were precisely those I had always hungered for, though I had never, before
this instant, realized that I so ardently hungered for them.

That is to say: a desire would arise and, concurrently, the satisfaction of that desire would also arise. It was as if (a) I longed for
a certain (heretofore untasted) taste until (b) said longing became nearly unbearable, at which time (c) I found a morsel of food

with that exact taste already in my mouth, perfectly satisfying my longing.

Every utterance, every adjustment of posture bespoke the same thing: we had known each other forever, were soul mates, had met and loved in numerous preceding lifetimes, and would meet and love in many subsequent lifetimes, always with the same transcendently stupefying results.

Then there came a hard-to-describe but very real drifting-off into a number of sequential reveries that might best be described as a type of nonnarrative mind scenery, i.e., a series of vague mental images of places I had never been (a certain pine-packed valley in high white mountains, a chalet-type house in a cul-de-sac, the yard of which was overgrown with wide, stunted Seussian trees), each of which triggered a deep sentimental longing, longings that coalesced into, and were soon reduced to, one central longing, i.e., an intense longing for Heather and Heather alone.

This mind-scenery phenomenon was strongest during our third (!) bout of lovemaking. (Apparently Abnesti had included some Vivistif™ in my drip.)

Afterward, our protestations of love poured forth simultaneously, linguistically complex and metaphorically rich: I daresay we had become poets. We were allowed to lie there, limbs intermingled, for nearly an hour. It was bliss. It was perfection. It was that impossible thing: happiness that does not wilt to reveal the thin shoots of some new desire rising from within it.

We cuddled with a fierceness/focus that rivaled the fierceness/focus with which we had fucked. There was nothing *less* about cuddling vis-à-vis fucking, is what I mean to say. We were all over each other in the super-friendly way of puppies, or spouses meeting for the first time after one of them has undergone a close brush with death. Everything seemed moist, permeable, *sayable*.

Then something in the drip began to wane. I think Abnesti had shut off the Verbaluce™? Also the shame reducer? Basically, everything began to *dwindle*. Suddenly we felt shy. But still loving. We began the process of trying to talk après Verbaluce™: always awkward.

Yet I could see in her eyes that she was still feeling love for me.

And I was definitely still feeling love for her.

Well, why not? We had just fucked three times! Why do you think

they call it "making love"? That was what we had just made three
times: love.

Then Abnesti said, "Drip on?"

We had kind of forgotten he was even there, behind his one-way
mirror.

I said, "Do we have to? We are really liking this right now."

"We're just going to try to get you guys back to baseline," he said.
"We've got more to do today."

"Shit," I said.

"Rats," she said.

"Drip on?" he said.

"Acknowledge," we said.

Soon something began to change. I mean, she was fine. A handsome pale girl. But nothing special. And I could see that she felt
the same re me, i.e., what had all that fuss been about just now?

Why weren't we dressed? We real quick got dressed.

Kind of embarrassing.

Did I love her? Did she love me?

Ha.

No.

Then it was time for her to go. We shook hands.

Out she went.

Lunch came in. On a tray. Spaghetti with chicken chunks.

Man, was I hungry.

I spent all lunchtime thinking. It was weird. I had the memory
of fucking Heather, the memory of having felt the things I'd felt
for her, the memory of having said the things I'd said to her. My
throat was like raw from how much I'd said and how fast I'd felt
compelled to say it. But in terms of feelings? I basically had nada
left.

Just a hot face and some shame re having fucked three times in
front of Abnesti.

III

After lunch in came another girl.

About equally so-so. Dark hair. Average build. Nothing special,
just like, upon first entry, Heather had been nothing special.

"This is Rachel," Abnesti said on the PA. "This is Jeff."

"Hi, Rachel," I said.

"Hi, Jeff," she said.

"Drip on?" Abnesti said.

We Acknowledged.

Something seemed very familiar about the way I now began feeling. Suddenly Rachel looked super-good. Abnesti requested permission to pep up our language centers via Verbaluce™. We Acknowledged. Soon we too were fucking like bunnies. Soon we too were talking like articulate maniacs re our love. Once again certain sensations were arising to meet my concurrently arising desperate hunger for just those sensations. Soon my memory of the perfect taste of Heather's mouth was being overwritten by the current taste of Rachel's mouth, so much more the taste I now desired. I was feeling unprecedented emotions, even though those unprecedented emotions were (I discerned somewhere in my consciousness) exactly the same emotions I had felt earlier, for that now unworthy-seeming vessel Heather. Rachel was, I mean to say, *it*. Her lithe waist, her voice, her hungry mouth/hands/loins—they were all *it*.

I just loved Rachel so much.

Then came the sequential geographic reveries (see above): same pine-packed valley, same chalet-looking house, accompanied by that same longing-for-place transmuting into a longing for (this time) Rachel. While continuing to enact a level of sexual strenuousness that caused what I would describe as a gradually tightening, chest-located, sweetness rubber band to both connect us and compel us onward, we whispered feverishly (precisely, poetically) about how long we felt we had known each other, i.e., forever.

Again the total number of times we made love was three.

Then, like before, came the dwindling. Our talking became less excellent. Words were fewer, our sentences shorter. Still, I loved her. Loved Rachel. Everything about her just seemed *perfect:* her cheek mole, her black hair, the little butt-squirm she did now and then, as if to say, Mmm-mmm, was that ever good.

"Drip on?" Abnesti said. "We are going to try to get you both back to baseline."

"Acknowledge," she said.

"Well, hold on," I said.

"Jeff," Abnesti said, irritated, as if trying to remind me that I was here not by choice but because I had done my crime and was in the process of doing my time.

"Acknowledge," I said. And gave Rachel one last look of love, knowing (as she did not yet know) that this would be the last look of love I would be giving her.

Soon she was merely fine to me, and I merely fine to her. She looked, as had Heather, embarrassed, as in, What was up with that just now? Why did I just go so overboard with Mr. Average here?

Did I love her? Or her me?

No.

When it was time for her to go, we shook hands.

The place where my MobiPak™ was surgically joined to my lower back was sore from all our positional changes. Plus I was way tired. Plus I was feeling so sad. Why sad? Was I not a dude? Had I not just fucked two different girls, for a total of six times, in one day?

Still, honestly, I felt sadder than sad.

I guess I was sad that love was not real? Or not all that real, anyway? I guess I was sad that love could feel so real and the next minute be gone, and all because of something Abnesti was doing.

IV

After Snack Abnesti called me into Control. Control being like the head of a spider. With its various legs being our Workrooms. Sometimes we were called upon to work alongside Abnesti in the head of the spider. Or, as we termed it: the Spiderhead.

"Sit," he said. "Look into Large Workroom 1."

In Large Workroom 1 were Heather and Rachel, side by side.

"Recognize them?" he said.

"Ha," I said.

"Now," Abnesti said. "I'm going to present you with a choice, Jeff. This is what we're playing at here. See this remote? Let's say you can hit *this* button and Rachel gets some Darkenfloxx™. Or you can hit *this* button and Heather gets the Darkenfloxx™. See? You choose."

"They've got Darkenfloxx™ in their MobiPaks™?" I said.

"You've all got Darkenfloxx™ in your MobiPaks™, dummy," Abnesti said affectionately. "Verlaine put it there Wednesday. In anticipation of this very study."

Well, that made me nervous.

Imagine the worst you have ever felt, times ten. That does not even come close to how bad you feel on Darkenfloxx™. The time

it was administered to us in Orientation, briefly, for demo purposes, at one-third the dose now selected on Abnesti's remote? I
have never felt so terrible. All of us were just moaning, heads down,
like, How could we ever have felt life was worth living?

I do not even like to think about that time.

"What's your decision, Jeff?" Abnesti said. "Is Rachel getting the
Darkenfloxx™? Or Heather?"

"I can't say," I said.

"You have to," he said.

"I can't," I said. "It would be like random."

"You feel your decision would be random," he said.

"Yes," I said.

And that was true. I really didn't care. It was like if I put *you* in
the Spiderhead and gave you the choice: which of these two strangers would you like to send into the shadow of the valley of death?

"Ten seconds," Abnesti said. "What we're testing for here is any
residual fondness."

It wasn't that I liked them both. I honestly felt completely neu-
tral toward both. It was exactly as if I had never seen, much less
fucked, either one. (They had really succeeded in taking me back
to baseline, I guess I am saying.)

But, having once been Darkenfloxxed™, I just didn't want to do
that to anyone. Even if I didn't like the person very much, even if I
hated the person, I still wouldn't want to do it.

"Five seconds," Abnesti said.

"I can't decide," I said. "It's random."

"Truly random?" he said. "Okay. I'm giving the Darkenfloxx™
to Heather."

I just sat there.

"No, actually," he said, "I'm giving it to Rachel."

Just sat there.

"Jeff," he said. "You have convinced me. It would, to you, be random. You truly have no preference. I can see that. And therefore I
don't have to do it. See what we just did? With your help? For the
first time? Via the ED289/290 suite? Which is what we've been testing today? You have to admit it: you were in love. Twice. Right?"

"Yes," I said.

"Very much in love," he said. "Twice."

"I said yes," I said.

"But you just now expressed no preference," he said. "Ergo,

no trace of either of those great loves remains. You are totally
cleansed. We brought you high, laid you low, and now here you
sit, the same emotionwise as before our testing even began. That is
powerful. That is killer. We have unlocked a mysterious eternal secret. What a fantastic game-changer! Say someone can't love? Now
he or she can. We can make him. Say someone loves too much?
Or loves someone deemed unsuitable by his or her caregiver? We
can tone that shit right down. Say someone is blue, because of true
love? We step in, or his or her caregiver does: blue no more. No
longer, in terms of emotional controllability, are we ships adrift.
No one is. We see a ship adrift, we climb aboard, install a rudder.
Guide him/her toward love. Or away from it. You say, 'All you need
is love'? Look, here comes ED289/290. Can we stop war? We can
sure as heck slow it down! Suddenly the soldiers on both sides start
fucking. Or, at low dosage, feeling super-fond. Or say we have two
rival dictators in a death grudge. Assuming ED289/290 develops
nicely in pill form, allow me to slip each dictator a mickey. Soon
their tongues are down each other's throats and doves of peace are
pooping on their epaulets. Or, depending on the dosage, they may
just be hugging. And who helped us do that? You did."

All this time, Rachel and Heather had just been sitting there in
Large Workroom 1.

"That's it, gals, thanks," Abnesti said on the PA.

And they left, neither knowing how close they had come to getting Darkenfloxxed™ out their wing-wangs.

Verlaine took them out the back way, i.e., not through the Spiderhead but via the Back Alley. Which is not really an alley, just a
carpeted hallway leading back to our Domain Cluster.

"Think, Jeff," Abnesti said. "Think if you'd had the benefit of
ED289/290 on your fateful night."

Tell the truth, I was getting kind of sick of him always talking
about my fateful night.

I'd been sorry about it right away and had got sorrier about it
ever since, and was now so sorry about it that him rubbing it in my
face did not make me one bit sorrier, it just made me think of him
as being kind of a dick.

"Can I go to bed now?" I said.

"Not yet," Abnesti said. "It is hours to go before you sleep."

Then he sent me into Small Workroom 3, where some dude I
didn't know was sitting.

V

"Rogan," the dude said.

"Jeff," I said.

"What's up?" he said.

"Not much," I said.

We sat tensely for a long time, not talking. Maybe ten minutes passed.

We got some rough customers in here. I noted that Rogan had a tattoo of a rat on his neck, a rat that had just been knifed and was crying. But even through its tears it was knifing a smaller rat, who just looked surprised.

Finally Abnesti came on the PA.

"That's it, guys, thanks," he said.

"What the fuck was that about?" Rogan said.

Good question, Rogan, I thought. Why had we been left just sitting there? In the same manner that Heather and Rachel had been left just sitting there? Then I had a hunch. To test my hunch, I did a sudden lurch into the Spiderhead. Which Abnesti always made a point of not keeping locked, to show how much he trusted and was unafraid of us.

And guess who was in there?

"Hey, Jeff," Heather said.

"Jeff, get out," Abnesti said.

"Heather, did Mr. Abnesti just now make you decide which of us, me or Rogan, to give some Darkenfloxx™ to?" I said.

"Yes," Heather said. She must have been on some VeriTalk™, because she spoke the truth in spite of Abnesti's withering silencing glance.

"Did you recently fuck Rogan, Heather?" I said. "In addition to me? And also fall in love with him, as you did with me?"

"Yes," she said.

"Heather, honestly," Abnesti said. "Put a sock in it."

Heather looked around for a sock, VeriTalk™ making one quite literal.

Back in my Domain, I did the math: Heather had fucked me three times. Heather had probably also fucked Rogan three times, since, in the name of design consistency, Abnesti would have given Rogan and me equal relative doses of Vivistif™.

And yet, speaking of design consistency, there was still one shoe to drop, if I knew Abnesti, always a stickler in terms of data symmetry, which was: wouldn't Abnesti also need Rachel to decide who to Darkenfloxx™, i.e., me or Rogan?

After a short break, my suspicions were confirmed: I found myself again sitting in Small Workroom 3 with Rogan!

Again we sat not talking for a long time. Mostly he picked at the smaller rat and I tried to watch without him seeing.

Then, like before, Abnesti came on the PA and said, "That's it, guys, thanks."

"Let me guess," I said. "Rachel's in there with you."

"Jeff, if you don't stop doing that, I swear," Abnesti said.

"And she just declined to Darkenfloxx™ either me or Rogan?" I said.

"Hi, Jeff!" Rachel said. "Hi, Rogan!"

"Rogan," I said. "Did you by any chance fuck Rachel earlier today?"

"Pretty much," Rogan said.

My mind was like reeling. Rachel had fucked me plus Rogan? Heather had fucked me plus Rogan? And everyone who had fucked anyone had fallen in love with that person, then out of it?

What kind of crazy-ass Project Team was this?

I mean, I had been on some crazy-ass Project Teams in my time, such as one where the drip had something in it that made hearing music exquisite, and hence when some Shostakovich was piped in actual bats seemed to circle my Domain, or the one where my legs became totally numb and yet I found I could still stand fifteen straight hours at a fake cash register, miraculously suddenly able to do extremely hard long-division problems in my mind.

But of all my crazy-ass Project Teams this was by far the most crazy-assed.

I could not help but wonder what tomorrow would bring.

VI

Except today wasn't even over.

I was again called into Small Workroom 3. And was sitting there when this unfamiliar guy came in.

"I'm Keith!" he said, rushing over to shake my hand.

He was a tall southern drink of water, all teeth and wavy hair.

"Jeff," I said.

"Really nice meeting you!" he said.

Then we sat there not talking. Whenever I looked over at Keith, he would gleam his teeth at me and shake his head all wry, as if to say, "Odd job of work, isn't it?"

"Keith," I said. "Do you by any chance know two chicks named Rachel and Heather?"

"I sure as heck do," Keith said. And suddenly his teeth had a leering quality to them.

"Did you by any chance have sex with both Rachel and Heather earlier today, three times each?" I said.

"What are you, man, a dang psychic?" Keith said. "You're blowing my mind, I itmit it!"

"Jeff, you're totally doinking with our experimental design integrity," Abnesti said.

"So either Rachel or Heather is sitting in the Spiderhead right now," I said. "Trying to decide."

"Decide what?" Keith said.

"Which of us to Darkenfloxx™," I said.

"Eek," Keith said. And now his teeth looked scared.

"Don't worry," I said. "She won't do it."

"Who won't?" Keith said.

"Whoever's in there," I said.

"That's it, guys, thanks," Abnesti said.

Then, after a short break, Keith and I were once again brought into Small Workroom 3, where once again we waited as, this time, Heather declined to Darkenfloxx™ either one of us.

Back in my Domain, I constructed a who-had-fucked-whom chart, which went like this:

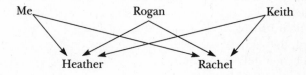

Abnesti came in.

"Despite all your shenanigans," he said, "Rogan and Keith had exactly the same reaction as you did. And as Rachel and Heather did. None of you, at the critical moment, could decide whom to

Darkenfloxx™. Which is super. What does that mean? Why is it super? It means that ED289/290 is the real deal. It can make love, it can take love away. I'm almost inclined to start the naming process."

"Those girls did it nine times each today?" I said.

"Peace4All," he said. "LuvInclyned. You seem pissy. Are you pissy?"

"Well, I feel a little jerked around," I said.

"Do you feel jerked around because you still have feelings of love for one of the girls?" he said. "That would need to be noted. Anger? Possessiveness? Residual sexual longing?"

"No," I said.

"You honestly don't feel miffed that a girl for whom you felt love was then funked by two other guys, and, not only that, she then felt exactly the same quality/quantity of love for those guys as she had felt for you, or, in the case of Rachel, was about to feel for you, at the time that she funked Rogan? I think it was Rogan. She may have funked Keith first. Then you, penultimately. I'm vague on the order of operations. I could look it up. But think deeply on this."

I thought deeply on it.

"Nothing," I said.

"Well, it's a lot to sort through," he said. "Luckily it's night. Our day is done. Anything else you want to talk about? Anything else you're feeling?"

"My penis is sore," I said.

"Well, no surprise there," he said. "Think how those girls must feel. I'll send Verlaine in with some cream."

Soon Verlaine came in with some cream.

"Hi, Verlaine," I said.

"Hi, Jeff," he said. "You want to put this on yourself or want me to do it?"

"I'll do it," I said.

"Cool," he said.

And I could tell he meant it.

"Looks painful," he said.

"It really is," I said.

"Must have felt pretty good at the time, though?" he said.

His words seemed to be saying he was envious, but I could see in his eyes, as they looked at my penis, that he wasn't envious at all.

Then I slept the sleep of the dead.

As they say.

VII

Next morning I was still asleep when Abnesti came on the PA.

"Do you remember yesterday?" he said.

"Yes," I said.

"When I asked which gal you'd like to see on the Darkenfloxx™?" he said. "And you said neither?"

"Yes," I said.

"Well, that was good enough for me," he said. "But apparently not good enough for the Protocol Committee. Not good enough for the Three Horsemen of Anality. Come in here. Let's get started—we're going to need to do a kind of Confirmation Trial. Oh, this is going to stink."

I entered the Spiderhead.

Sitting in Small Workroom 2 was Heather.

"So this time," Abnesti said, "per the Protocol Committee, instead of me asking you which girl to give the Darkenfloxx™ to, which the ProtComm felt was too subjective, we're going to give this girl the Darkenfloxx™ no matter what you say. Then see what you say. Like yesterday, we're going to put you on a drip of—Verlaine? Verlaine? Where are you? Are you there? What is it again? Do you have the project order?"

"Verbaluce™, VeriTalk™, ChatEase™," Verlaine said over the PA.

"Right," Abnesti said. "And did you refresh his MobiPak™? Are his quantities good?"

"I did it," Verlaine said. "I did it while he was sleeping. Plus I already told you I already did it."

"What about her?" Abnesti said. "Did you refresh her MobiPak™? Are her quantities good?"

"You stood right there and watched me, Ray," Verlaine said.

"Jeff, sorry," Abnesti said to me. "We're having a little tension in here today. Not an easy day ahead."

"I don't want you to Darkenfloxx™ Heather," I said.

"Interesting," he said. "Is that because you love her?"

"No," I said. "I don't want you to Darkenfloxx™ anybody."

"I know what you mean," he said. "That is so sweet. Then again: is this Confirmation Trial about what you want? Not so much. What it's about is us recording what you say as you observe Heather getting Darkenfloxxed™. For five minutes. Five-minute trial. Here we go. Drip on?"

I did not say "Acknowledge."

"You should feel flattered," Abnesti said. "Did we choose Rogan? Keith? No. We deemed your level of speaking more commensurate with our data needs."

I did not say "Acknowledge."

"Why so protective of Heather?" Abnesti said. "One would almost think you loved her."

"No," I said.

"Do you even know her story?" he said. "You don't. You legally can't. Does it involve whiskey, gangs, infanticide? I can't say. Can I imply, somewhat peripherally, that her past, violent and sordid, did not exactly include a dog named Lassie and a lot of family talks about the Bible while Grammy sat doing macramé, adjusting her posture because the quaint fireplace was so sizzling? Can I suggest that, if you knew what I know about Heather's past, making Heather briefly sad, nauseous, and/or horrified might not seem like the worst idea in the world? No, I can't."

"All right, all right," I said.

"You know me," he said. "How many kids do I have?"

"Five," I said.

"What are their names?" he said.

"Mick, Todd, Karen, Lisa, Phoebe," I said.

"Am I a monster?" he said. "Do I remember birthdays around here? When a certain individual got athlete's foot on his groin on a Sunday, did a certain other individual drive over to Rexall and pick up a prescription, paying for it with his own personal money?"

That was a nice thing he'd done, but it seemed kind of unprofessional to bring it up now.

"Jeff," Abnesti said. "What do you want me to say here? Do you want me to say that your Fridays are at risk? I can easily say that."

Which was cheap. My Fridays meant a lot to me, and he knew that. Fridays I got to Skype Mom.

"How long do we give you?" Abnesti said.

"Five minutes," I said.

"How about we make it ten?" Abnesti said.

Mom always looked heartsick when our time was up. It had almost killed her when they arrested me. The trial had almost killed her. She'd spent her savings to get me out of real jail and in here. When I was a kid, she had long brown hair, past her waist. During the trial she cut it. Then it went gray. Now it was just a white poof about the size of a cap.

"Drip on?" Abnesti said.

"Acknowledge," I said.

"Okay to pep up your language centers?" he said.

"Fine," I said.

"Heather, hello?" he said.

"Good morning!" Heather said.

"Drip on?" he said.

"Acknowledge," Heather said.

Abnesti used his remote.

The Darkenfloxx™ started flowing. Soon Heather was softly crying. Then was up and pacing. Then jaggedly crying. A little hysterical, even.

"I don't like this," she said, in a quaking voice.

Then she threw up in the trash can.

"Speak, Jeff," Abnesti said to me. "Speak a lot, speak in detail. Let's make something useful of this, shall we?"

Everything in my drip felt Grade A. Suddenly I was waxing poetic. I was waxing poetic re what Heather was doing, and waxing poetic re my feelings about what Heather was doing. Basically, what I was feeling was: Every human is born of man and woman. Every human, at birth, is, or at least has the potential to be, beloved of his/her mother/father. Thus every human is worthy of love. As I watched Heather suffer, a great tenderness suffused my body, a tenderness hard to distinguish from a sort of vast existential nausea; to wit, why are such beautiful beloved vessels made slaves to so much pain? Heather presented as a bundle of pain receptors. Heather's mind was fluid and could be ruined (by pain, by sadness). Why? Why was she made this way? Why so fragile?

Poor child, I was thinking, poor girl. Who loved you? Who loves you?

"Hang in there, Jeff," Abnesti said. "Verlaine! What do you think? Any vestige of romantic love in Jeff's Verbal Commentary?"

"I'd say no," Verlaine said over the PA. "That's all just pretty much basic human feeling right there."

"Excellent," Abnesti said. "Time remaining?"

"Two minutes," Verlaine said.

I found what happened next very hard to watch. Under the influence of the Verbaluce™, the VeriTalk™, and the ChatEase™, I also found it impossible not to narrate.

In each Workroom was a couch, a desk, and a chair, all, by design, impossible to disassemble. Heather now began disassembling her impossible-to-disassemble chair. Her face was a mask of rage. She drove her head into the wall. Like a wrathful prodigy, Heather, beloved of someone, managed, in her great sadness-fueled rage, to disassemble the chair while continuing to drive her head into the wall.

"Jesus," Verlaine said.

"Verlaine, buck up," Abnesti said. "Jeff, stop crying. Contrary to what you might think, there's not much data in crying. Use your words. Don't make this in vain."

I used my words. I spoke volumes, was precise. I described and redescribed what I was feeling as I watched Heather do what she now began doing, intently, almost beautifully, to her face/head with one of the chair legs.

In his defense, Abnesti was not in such great shape himself: breathing hard, cheeks candy-red, as he tapped the screen of his iMac nonstop with a pen, something he did when stressed.

"Time," he finally said, and cut the Darkenfloxx™ off with his remote. "Fuck. Get in there, Verlaine. Hustle it."

Verlaine hustled into Small Workroom 2.

"Talk to me, Sammy," Abnesti said.

Verlaine felt for Heather's pulse, then raised his hands, palms up, so that he looked like Jesus, except shocked instead of beatific, and also he had his glasses up on top of his head.

"Are you *kidding* me?" Abnesti said.

"What now?" Verlaine said. "What do I—"

"Are you fricking *kidding* me?" Abnesti said.

Abnesti burst out of his chair, shoved me out of the way, and flew through the door into Small Workroom 2.

VIII

I returned to my Domain.

At three, Verlaine came on the PA.

"Jeff," he said. "Please return to the Spiderhead."

I returned to the Spiderhead.

"We're sorry you had to see that, Jeff," Abnesti said.

"That was unexpected," Verlaine said.

"Unexpected plus unfortunate," Abnesti said. "And sorry I shoved you."

"Is she dead?" I said.

"Well, she's not the best," Verlaine said.

"Look, Jeff, these things happen," Abnesti said. "This is science. In science we explore the unknown. It was unknown what five minutes on Darkenfloxx™ would do to Heather. Now we know. The other thing we know, per Verlaine's assessment of your commentary, is that you really, for sure, do not harbor any residual romantic feelings for Heather. That's a big deal, Jeff. A beacon of hope at a sad time for all. Even as Heather was, so to speak, going down to the sea in her ship, you remained totally unwavering in terms of continuing to not romantically love her. My guess is ProtComm's going to be like, 'Wow, Utica's really leading the pack in terms of providing some mind-blowing new data on ED289/290.'"

It was quiet in the Spiderhead.

"Verlaine, go out," Abnesti said. "Go do your bit. Make things ready."

Verlaine went out.

"Do you think I liked that?" Abnesti said.

"You didn't seem to," I said.

"Well, I didn't," Abnesti said. "I hated it. I'm a person. I have feelings. Still, personal sadness aside, that was good. You did terrific overall. We all did terrific. Heather especially did terrific. I honor her. Let's just—let's see this thing through, shall we? Let's complete it. Complete the next portion of our Confirmation Trial."

Into Small Workroom 4 came Rachel.

IX

"Are we going to Darkenfloxx™ Rachel now?" I said.

"Think, Jeff," Abnesti said. "How can we know that you love neither Rachel nor Heather if we only have data regarding your reaction to what just now happened to Heather? Use your noggin. You are not a scientist, but Lord knows you work around scientists all day. Drip on?"

I did not say "Acknowledge."

"What's the problem, Jeff?" Abnesti said.

"I don't want to kill Rachel," I said.

"Well, who does?" Abnesti said. "Do I? Do you, Verlaine?"

"No," Verlaine said over the PA.

"Jeff, maybe you're overthinking this," Abnesti said. "Is it possible the Darkenfloxx™ will kill Rachel? Sure. We have the Heather precedent. On the other hand, Rachel may be stronger. She seems a little larger."

"She's actually a little smaller," Verlaine said.

"Well, maybe she's tougher," Abnesti said.

"We're going to weight-adjust her dosage," Verlaine said. "So."

"Thanks, Verlaine," Abnesti said. "Thanks for clearing that up."

"Maybe show him the file," Verlaine said.

Abnesti handed me Rachel's file.

Verlaine came back in.

"Read it and weep," he said.

Per Rachel's file, she had stolen jewelry from her mother, a car from her father, cash from her sister, statues from their church. She'd gone to jail for drugs. After four times in jail for drugs, she'd gone to rehab for drugs, then to rehab for prostitution, then to what they call rehab-refresh, for people who've been in rehab so many times they are basically immune. But she must have been immune to the rehab-refresh too, because after that came her biggie: a triple murder—her dealer, the dealer's sister, the dealer's sister's boyfriend.

Reading that made me feel a little funny that we'd fucked and I'd loved her.

But I still didn't want to kill her.

"Jeff," Abnesti said. "I know you've done a lot of work on this with Mrs. Lacey. On killing and so forth. But this is not you. This is us."

"It's not even us," Verlaine said. "It's science."

"The mandates of science," Abnesti said. "Plus the dictates."

"Sometimes science sucks," Verlaine said.

"On the one hand, Jeff," Abnesti said, "a few minutes of unpleasantness for Heather—"

"Rachel," Verlaine said.

"A few minutes of unpleasantness for Rachel," Abnesti said,

"years of relief for literally tens of thousands of underloving or overloving folks."

"Do the math, Jeff," Verlaine said.

"Being good in small ways is easy," Abnesti said. "Doing the huge good things, that's harder."

"Drip on?" Verlaine said. "Jeff?"

I did not say "Acknowledge."

"Fuck it, enough," Abnesti said. "Verlaine, what's the name of that one? The one where I give him an order and he obeys it?"

"Docilryde™," Verlaine said.

"Is there Docilryde™ in his MobiPak™?" Abnesti said.

"There's Docilryde™ in every MobiPak™," Verlaine said.

"Does he need to say 'Acknowledge'?" Abnesti said.

"Docilryde™'s a Class C, so —" Verlaine said.

"See, that, to me, makes zero sense," Abnesti said. "What good's an obedience drug if we need his permission to use it?"

"We just need a waiver," Verlaine said.

"How long does that shit take?" Abnesti said.

"We fax Albany, they fax us back," Verlaine said.

"Come on, come on, make haste," Abnesti said, and they went out, leaving me alone in the Spiderhead.

X

It was sad. It gave me a sad, defeated feeling to think that soon they'd be back and would Docilryde™ me, and I'd say "Acknowledge," smiling agreeably the way a person smiles on Docilryde™, and then the Darkenfloxx™ would flow, into Rachel, and I would begin describing, in that rapid, robotic way one describes on Verbaluce™/VeriTalk™/ChatEase™, the things Rachel would, at that time, begin doing to herself.

It was like all I had to do to be a killer again was sit there and wait.

Which was a hard pill to swallow, after my work with Mrs. Lacey.

"Violence finished, anger no more," she'd make me say, over and over. Then she'd have me do a Detailed Remembering re my fateful night.

I was nineteen. Mike Appel was seventeen. We were both wasto. All night he'd been giving me grief. He was smaller, younger, less popular. Then we were out front of Frizzy's, rolling around on the ground. He was quick. He was mean. I was losing. I couldn't believe it. I was bigger, older, yet losing? Around us, watching, was basically everybody we knew. Then he had me on my back. Someone laughed. Someone said, "Shit, poor Jeff." Nearby was a brick. I grabbed it, glanced Mike in the head with it. Then was on top of him.

Mike gave. That is, there on his back, scalp bleeding, he gave, by shooting me a certain look, like, Dude, come on, we're not all that serious about this, are we?

We were.

I was.

I don't even know why I did it.

It was like, with the drinking and the being a kid and the nearly losing, I'd been put on a drip called, like, TemperBerst or something.

InstaRaje.

LifeRooner.

"Hey, guys, hello!" Rachel said. "What are we up to today?"

There was her fragile head, her undamaged face, one arm lifting a hand to scratch a cheek, legs bouncing with nerves, peasant skirt bouncing too, clogged feet crossed under the hem.

Soon all that would be just a lump on the floor.

I had to think.

Why were they going to Darkenfloxx™ Rachel? So they could hear me describe it. If I wasn't here to describe it, they wouldn't do it. How could I make it so I wouldn't be here? I could leave. How could I leave? There was only one door out of the Spiderhead, which was autolocked, and on the other side was either Barry or Hans, with that electric wand called the DisciStick™. Could I wait until Abnesti came in, wonk him, try to race past Barry or Hans, make a break for the Main Door?

Any weapons in the Spiderhead? No, just Abnesti's birthday mug, a pair of running shoes, a roll of breath mints, his remote.

His remote?

What a dope. That was supposed to be on his belt at all times. Otherwise one of us might help ourselves to whatever we found, via Inventory Directory, in our MobiPaks™: some Bonviv™, maybe, some BlissTyme™, some SpeedErUp™.

Some Darkenfloxx™.

Jesus. That was one way to leave.

Scary, though.

Just then, in Small Workroom 4, Rachel, I guess thinking the Spiderhead empty, got up and did this happy little shuffle, like she was some cheerful farmer chick who'd just stepped outside to find the hick she was in love with coming up the road with a calf under his arm or whatever.

Why was she dancing? No reason.

Just alive, I guess.

Time was short.

The remote was well labeled.

Good old Verlaine.

I used it, dropped it down the heat vent in case I changed my mind, then stood there like, I can't believe I just did that.

My MobiPak™ whirred.

The Darkenfloxx™ flowed.

Then came the horror: worse than I'd ever imagined. Soon my arm was about a mile down the heat vent. Then I was staggering around the Spiderhead, looking for something, anything. In the end, here's how bad it got: I used a corner of the desk.

What's death like?

You're briefly unlimited.

I sailed right out through the roof.

And hovered above it, looking down. Here was Rogan, checking his neck in the mirror. Here was Keith, squat-thrusting in his underwear. Here was Ned Riley, here was B. Troper, here was Gail Orley, Stefan DeWitt, killers all, all bad, I guess, although, in that instant, I saw it differently. At birth, they'd been charged by God with the responsibility of growing into total fuckups. Had they chosen this? Was it their fault, as they tumbled out of the womb? Had they aspired, covered in placental blood, to grow into harmers, dark forces, life-enders? In that first holy instant of breath/awareness (tiny hands clutching and unclutching), had it been their fondest hope to render (via gun, knife, or brick) some innocent family bereft? No; and yet their crooked destinies had lain dormant within them, seeds awaiting water and light to bring forth the most violent, life-poisoning flowers, said water/light actually being the requisite combination of neurological tendency and environmen-

tal activation that would transform them (transform us!) into
earth's offal, murderers, and foul us with the ultimate, unwashable
transgression.

Wow, I thought, was there some Verbaluce™ in that drip or
what?

But no.

This was all me now.

I got snagged, found myself stuck on a facility gutter, and squatted there like an airy gargoyle. I was there but was also everywhere.
I could see it all: a clump of leaves in the gutter beneath my see-
through foot; Mom, poor Mom, at home in Rochester, scrubbing
the shower, trying to cheer herself via thin hopeful humming; a
deer near the Dumpster, suddenly alert to my spectral presence;
Mike Appel's mom, also in Rochester, a bony, distraught check-
mark occupying a slender strip of Mike's bed; Rachel below in
Small Workroom 4, drawn to the one-way mirror by the sounds of
my death; Abnesti and Verlaine rushing into the Spiderhead; Verlaine kneeling to begin CPR.

Night was falling. Birds were singing. Birds were, it occurred to
me to say, enacting a frantic celebration of day's end. They were
manifesting as the earth's bright-colored nerve endings, the sun's
descent urging them into activity, filling them individually with
life-nectar, the life-nectar then being passed into the world, out of
each beak, in the form of that bird's distinctive song, which was,
in turn, an accident of beak shape, throat shape, breast configura-
tion, brain chemistry: some birds blessed in voice, others cursed;
some squawking, others rapturous.

From somewhere, something kind asked, *Would you like to go
back? It's completely up to you. Your body appears salvageable.*

No, I thought, no, thanks, I've had enough.

My only regret was Mom. I hoped someday, in some better place,
I'd get a chance to explain it to her, and maybe she'd be proud of
me, one last time, after all these years.

From across the woods, as if by common accord, birds left their
trees and darted upward. I joined them, flew among them, they
did not recognize me as something apart from them, and I was
happy, so happy, because for the first time in years, and forever-
more, I had not killed, and never would.

MARK SLOUKA

The Hare's Mask

FROM *Harper's Magazine*

ODD HOW I MISS HIS VOICE, and yet it's his silences I remember now: the deliberateness with which he moved, the way he'd listen, that particular smile, as if, having long ago given up expecting anything from the world, he continually found himself mugged by its beauty. Even as a kid I wanted to protect him, and because he saw the danger in this, he did what he could.

By the time I was five I'd figured out—the way kids usually do, by putting pieces together and working them until they fit—that he'd lost his parents and sister during the war. That they'd been there one morning, like keys on a table, then gone. When I asked he said it had been so long ago that it seemed like another life, that many bad things had happened then, that these were different times, and then he messed up my hair and smiled and said, "None of us are going anywhere, trust me." When we went to the doctor he'd make funny faces and joke around while the doctor put a needle in his arm to show me it didn't hurt. And it came to me that everything he did—the way he'd turn the page of a book, or laugh with me at Krazy Kat, or call us all into the kitchen on Saturday evenings to see the trout he'd caught lying on the counter, their sticky skin flecked with bits of fern—was just the same.

He used to tie his own trout flies. I'd come down late at night when we still lived in the old house, sneaking past the yellow bedroom where my sister slept in her crib, stepping over the creaking mines, and he'd be sitting there at the dining room table with just the one lamp, his hooks and feathers and furs spread out on the wood

around him, and when he saw me he'd sit me on his knee, my
stockinged feet dangling around his calves, and show me things.
"Couldn't sleep?" he'd say. "Look here, I'll show you something
important." And he'd catch the bend of a hook in the long-nosed
vise and let me pick the color of the thread, and I'd watch him
do what he did, his thin, strong fingers winding the waxed strand
back from the eye or stripping the webbing off a small feather or
clipping a fingernail patch of short, downy fur from the cheek of
a hare. He didn't explain and I didn't ask. He'd just work, now
and then humming a few notes of whatever he'd been listening
to—Debussy or Chopin, Mendelssohn or Satie—and it would appear, step by step, the slim, segmented thorax, the gossamer tail,
the tiny, barred wings, and he'd say, "Nice, isn't it?" and then, "Is it
done?" and I'd shake my head, because this was how it always went,
and he'd say, "Okay, now watch," and his fingers would loop and
settle the thread and draw it tight so quickly it seemed like one motion, then clip the loose end close to the eye with the surgical scissors. "Some things you can finish," he'd say.

I don't know how old I was when I was first drawn to their faces on
the mantelpiece—not old. Alone, I'd pull up a chair and stand on
it and look at them: my grandfather, tall, slim, stooped, handsome,
his hair in full retreat at thirty; my grandmother with her sad black
eyes and her uncomfortable smile—almost a wince—somehow
the stronger of the two; my aunt, a child of four, half turned toward her mother as if about to say something . . . My father stood to
the right, an awkward eight-year-old in a high-necked shirt and tie,
a ghost from the future. I'd look at this photograph and imagine
him taking it down when we weren't around, trying to understand
how it was possible that they could be gone all this time and only
him left behind. And from there, for some reason, I'd imagine him
remembering himself as a boy. He'd be standing in the back of a
train at night, the metal of the railing beneath his palms. Behind
him, huddled together under the light as if on a cement raft, he'd
see his family, falling away so quickly that already he had to strain to
make out their features, his father's hat, his mother's hand against
the black coat, his sister's face, small as a fingertip . . . And holding
on to the whitewashed mantelpiece, struggling to draw breath into
my shrinking lungs, I'd quickly put the picture back as though it

were something shameful. Who knows what somber ancestor had passed on to me this talent, this precocious ear for loss? For a while, because of it, I misheard almost everything.

It began with the hare's mask. One of the trout flies my father tied—one of my favorites because of its name—was the Gold Ribbed Hare's Ear, which required, for its bristly little body, a tiny thatch of hare's fur, complete with a few long, dark guard hairs for effect. My father would clip the hair from a palm-sized piece of fall-colored fur, impossibly soft. For some reason, though I knew fox was fox and deer hair was deer hair, I never read the hare's mask as the face of a hare, never saw how the irregular outline spoke the missing eyes, the nose . . . Whatever it was—some kind of optical illusion, some kind of mental block—I just didn't see it, until I did.

I must have overheard my parents talking one night when they thought I was sleeping and made of it what I could, creeping back up to my room with a new and troubling puzzle piece that I would have to place, and would, in my way. I couldn't have known much.

The full story was this. As a young boy growing up on Taborská Street in Brno, Czechoslovakia, my father would have to go out to the rabbit hutch in the evenings to tend the rabbits and, on Fridays, kill one for dinner. It was a common enough chore in those days, but he hated doing it. He'd grow attached, give them names, agonize endlessly. Often he'd cry, pulling on their ears, unable to choose one or, having chosen, to hit it with the stick. Sometimes he'd throw up. Half the time he'd make a mess of it anyway, hitting them too low or too high so they'd start to kick, and he'd drop them on the floor and have to do it again. Still, this is what boys did then, whether they liked it or not.

In September of 1942, when he was nine, a few months after the partisans assassinated Reichsprotektor Reinhard Heydrich in Prague, my father's family hid a man in the rabbit hutch. My grandfather, who had fought with the Legionnaires in Italy in 1917, built a false wall into the back, making a space two meters long and a half meter wide. There was no light. You couldn't stand up. The man—whose name my father never knew, but who may have been Miloš Werfel, who was captured soon afterward and sent to Terezín, where he was killed the following spring—stayed for nine days.

Both had their burdens. My father, who had to go on making his miserable trips to the hutch to keep from attracting the neighbors' attention, now had to slide a food plate through the gap between the false wall and the floorboards, then take the bucket of waste to the compost pile, dump it, clean it out, return it. By the time he was done taking care of the rabbits, the plate would be empty. Werfel, for his part, lying quietly in the dark, broken out in sores, had to endure my father's Hamlet-like performances. To whack or not to whack. There were bigger things than rabbits.

Nine days. What strange, haunted hours those must have been that they spent in each other's company, neither one able to acknowledge the other (my father was under strict orders, and Werfel—if it *was* Werfel—knew better), yet all the time aware of the other's presence, hearing the slow shift of cloth against wood or air escaping the nose, or even, in Werfel's case, glimpsing some splinter of movement through a crack.

Who knows what Werfel thought? Poet, partisan, journalist, Jew—each an indictment, any two worthy of death—he must have known where things stood. Not just with himself, but with the boy who brought him food and took the bucket with his waste. Partisans weren't supposed to have children—this was just one of those things. As for my father, he didn't think about Werfel much. He didn't think how strange it was that a grown man, his suit carefully folded in a rucksack, should be lying in his underwear behind a board in the rabbit hutch. He didn't think about what this meant, or what it could mean. He thought about Jenda and Eliška.

Jenda and Eliška were rabbits, and they were a problem. That September, for whatever reason, my father's Uncle Lada hadn't been able to bring the family any new rabbits, and the hutch was almost empty. Jenda and Eliška were the last. My father, who had been protecting the two of them for months by taking others in their place, thought about little else. With that unerring masochism common to all imaginative children, he'd made them his own. They smelled like fur and alfalfa. They trusted him. Whenever he came in, they'd hop over to him and stand up like rabbits in a fairy tale, hooking their little thick-clawed feet on the wire. They couldn't live without each other. It was impossible. What he had yet to learn was that the impossible is everywhere; that it hems us in at every turn, trigger set, ready to turn when touched.

And so it was. Locked in by habit, my father had to go to the hutch to keep Mrs. Čermáková from asking after his health because the other evening she'd just happened to notice my grandfather going instead, had to go because habit was safety, invisibility, because it held things together, or seemed to; because even in this time of routine outrages against every code and norm—*particularly* in this time—the norm demanded its due. And so off he went, after the inevitable scene, the whispering, the tears, shuffling down the dirt path under the orchard, emerging ten minutes later holding the rabbit in his arms instead of by its feet, disconsolate, weeping, schooled in self-hatred . . . but invisible. The neighbors were used to his antics.

It wasn't enough, something had been tripped; the impossible opened like a bloom. Two days after my father, his eyes blurring and stinging, brought the stick down on the rabbit's back, the hutch felt different; Werfel was gone. Five days later, just before nine o'clock on the morning of October 16, 1942, my father's parents and sister were taken away. He never saw them again. He himself, helping out in a neighbor's garden at the time, escaped. It shouldn't have been possible.

Sixteen years later my father had emigrated to New York, married a woman he met at a dance hall who didn't dance, and moved into an apartment on Sixty-third Road in Queens, a block down from the Waldbaum's. Four years after that, having traded proximity to Waldbaum's for an old house in rural Putnam County, he'd acquired a son, a daughter, and the unlikely hobby of trout fishing. And in 1968, that daughter came to the table, poured some milk on her Cap'n Crunch, and announced that she wanted a rabbit for her sixth birthday.

I'd begun to understand some things by then—I was almost nine. I knew, though he'd never show it, how hard this business with the rabbit would be for him, how much it would remind him of. Though I couldn't say anything in front of him, I did what I could behind the scenes. I offered my sister my gerbils, sang the virtues of guinea pigs, even offered to do her chores. When she dug in, predictably—soon enough it was a rabbit or death—I called her stupid, and when she started to cry, then hit me in the face with a plastic doll, I tried to use that to get the rabbit revoked. It didn't work. She'd been a good girl, my mother said, incredibly. We lived in the country. I had gerbils. It wasn't unreasonable.

That weekend we drove to the pet store in Danbury (I could come too if I behaved myself, my mother said), and after a last attempt to distract us from our mission by showing my sister the hamsters running on their wheels or pawing madly at the glass, I watched as my father leaned over the pen, lifting out one rabbit after the other, getting pine shavings on his lap while she petted their twitching backs or pulled their stupid ears . . . I wanted to hit her. When I took my father's hand at one point he looked down at me and said, "You okay?" and I said, "Sure." My sister picked out an ugly gray one with long ears, and as we were leaving the store I stuck out my foot and she hit herself on one of the metal shelves and my father grabbed me and said, "What's the matter with you, what's gotten into you these days?" and I started to cry.

It got worse. I wouldn't help set up its cage. I wouldn't feed it. I refused to call it by its name. I started calling it Blank for some reason. When my sister asked me something about it, I'd say, "Who? You mean Blank?" and when she started to cry I'd feel bad but I couldn't stop and part of me felt better. When it kept my sister up at night with its thumping and rustling and my parents moved its cage to the living room, I started walking around the other way, through the kitchen. I'd pretend to myself that I couldn't look at it, that something bad would happen if I did, and even watching TV I'd put my hand up as if scratching my forehead, or thinking, so that my eye couldn't slip. Sometimes I'd catch my father looking at me, and once he asked me if I'd like a rabbit of my own. When I said no, he pretended to be surprised.

It was sometime that fall that I had a bad dream and came down the stairs to find him sitting at the table under the lamp, tying his trout flies. He looked up at me over the silly half-glasses that went over his regular glasses that helped him to see. "Well, hello," he said. "Haven't done this in a while."

"I couldn't sleep," I said.

"Bad dream?"

"No," I said. I could hear the rabbit in the dark behind us, thumping around in his cage.

"He can't sleep either," my father said.

"What's that one called?" I said, pointing to the fly he had in the vise.

My dad was looking at me. "This one?" he said. And he told me, then showed me how it was made, clipping four or five blue-gray spears for the tail, then selecting a single strand from a peacock feather for the body. I watched him secure it with a few loops of thread, then start to wind it toward the eye of the hook, the short dark hairs sparking green with every turn through the light . . . And that's when I saw it, not just the thick, familiar chestnut fur of the cheeks and head and neck, but now, for the first time, the missing nose and ears, the symmetrical cavities of the eyes, even the name itself, reaching back to deepest childhood through the medium of my father's voice saying, "Pass me the hare's mask," "Let's take a little bit off the hare's mask."

It was the next day that I took the hare's mask and hid it in my room. When he asked me if I'd seen it I lied, and when he came back upstairs after going through everything in the dining room (as though that piece of fur could have jumped from the table and hidden itself behind his books), I swore I didn't have it and even let myself get indignant over the fact that he wouldn't believe me. Eventually, he left. "For Christ's sake," I heard him saying to my mother downstairs, "it didn't just disappear," and then, "That's not the point and you know it."

I slept with it under my pillow. I'd keep it in my pocket and run my thumb over the thin edge of the eye socket and the soft bristly parts where my father had clipped it short. When no one was home I'd hold it up to the rabbit cage and, appalled at myself, thrilled and shaky, yell, "Look, look, this was you" to the rabbit, who would sometimes hop over and try to nibble at it through the wires. I pushed my nose into it, breathing in that indescribable deep fur smell.

And that's how he found me, holding the hare's mask against my face, crying so hard I didn't hear him come into the room, two days before my ninth birthday. Because he'd understood about dates, and how things that aren't connected can seem to be, and that he'd been nine years old when it happened. And he held me for a long time, petting my hair in that slightly awkward, fatherly way, saying, "It's okay, everything's going to be okay, everything's just fine."

It was some years later that I asked him and he told me how it went that night. How he'd opened the dirt-scraping door to the hutch and entered that too-familiar smell of alfalfa and steel and shit already sick with the knowledge that he couldn't do what he absolutely had to do. How he lit the lamp and watched them hop over to him. How he stood there by the crate, sobbing, pulling first on Jenda's ears, then Eliška's, picking up one, then the other, pushing his nose into their fur, telling them how much he loved them . . . unaware of the time passing, unaware of anything, really—this is how miserable he was—until suddenly a man's voice speaks from behind the wall and says, "You're a good boy. Let me choose." My father laughed—a strange laugh: "And I remember standing there with my hands in the wire and feeling this stillness come over me, and him saying, 'Jenda. Take Jenda, he's the weaker of the two. It's not wrong. Do it quickly.'"

Contributors' Notes

CHIMAMANDA NGOZI ADICHIE was born in Nigeria. She is the author of two novels, *Half of a Yellow Sun*, which was a finalist for the National Book Critics Circle Award, and *Purple Hibiscus*, which won the Commonwealth Writers' Prize. Her short story collection, *The Thing Around Your Neck*, was published in 2009. She is the recipient of a 2008 MacArthur Foundation Fellowship and was named in *The New Yorker*'s "20 Under 40" list of the most important fiction writers under forty years old.

• I am fascinated by Lagos, where I live part of the year. I am fascinated by the humor and resilience, by the increasing sprawl of both gated estates and squalid slums, by the people who drive past me in the always-crawling traffic, and by the overall air of mutability, the sense that anything can change at any time. I have run into old friends who have completely reinvented themselves and become other people in a manner that strikes me as particularly Lagosian. Nigeria's shift from military to democratic rule brought social changes in the last decade but perhaps none as dramatic as the speed with which some young men became wealthy, particularly in Lagos. One such young man is an acquaintance whose life I reimagined in this story.

MEGAN MAYHEW BERGMAN lives on a small farm in Shaftsbury, Vermont, with her veterinarian husband and daughter. Scribner will publish her first collection of stories, *Birds of a Lesser Paradise*, in March 2012. Bergman's work has been nominated for the Pushcart Prize and has appeared in the *New York Times Book Review*, the 2010 *New Stories from the South* anthology, *Ploughshares, One Story, Narrative, Oxford American,* and elsewhere.

• Within six weeks in 2009, my husband graduated from veterinary school, I gave birth to my first child, my beloved mother-in-law passed away, and we put our old, rickety southern house on the market and moved to Vermont. And yes—we had a camel cricket infestation in the basement that did not amuse the realtor.

My husband's parents were both veterinarians. For a few years they fostered an African gray parrot. After my husband's mother died, I couldn't help but think of the bird (relegated to a sanctuary after years of bad behavior) that still held her voice. Thus, the quest to hear her voice began to take imaginary shape.

When I wrote "Housewifely Arts," I was consumed with what it meant to make a home, grieve for a parent, and become a good parent in my own right. I was bewildered by my constant failures, but heartened by the mess of love and good intentions underneath them all.

TOM BISSELL was born in Escanaba, Michigan, in 1974. He is the author of several books, including the story collection *God Lives in St. Petersburg,* which won the Rome Prize, and *Extra Lives: Why Video Games Matter,* which did not. His next book, *Magic Hours: Essays and Adventures,* a collection of his nonfiction, will be published in 2012. Currently he lives in Portland, Oregon, and teaches writing at Portland State University. "A Bridge Under Water" marks his second appearance in *The Best American Short Stories.*

▪ Uncomfortable Fact #1: Two things in "A Bridge Under Water" have an autobiographical tint. I did very nearly get kicked out of a synagogue while living in Rome, for roughly the reasons depicted. I also once went from zero to breakup with someone over whether our theoretical children would be Jewish. Uncomfortable Fact #2: A large part of the reason I wrote this story was to determine why I can sometimes be an insufferable dick. Writing it, I hope, made me somewhat less insufferable and markedly less dickish. The great gift of being a fiction writer—even, in my case, a relatively infrequent one—is the chance it can give you to perceive and thus understand yourself from without while also gaining some measure of sympathy for beliefs and positions you have previously judged to be unacceptable. Imagination, if nothing else, allows the fiction writer to achieve a magnanimity that he or she has been denied by life as it is, lamentably, lived.

Finally, "A Bridge Under Water" was rejected at least fifteen times before Sven Birkerts and William Pierce kindly agreed to publish it in *Agni.* Although I'd like to imagine that its publication within this august volume has moved the editors who spurned it to smack their heads, fire their assistants, and rend their garments, I'm also pretty certain that none of them care. Nor should they care. But the frequency of its rejection seems like a helpful thing to mention, given how many young and apprentice writers tear through *BASS* every year, as I once did, wondering how one's work winds up so enshrined. One answer: Yell into a hole, and pretend as though you're having a conversation. Yell long enough, and suddenly you might be.

JENNIFER EGAN is the author of *The Invisible Circus*, which was released as a feature film by Fine Line in 2001; *Emerald City and Other Stories; Look at Me*, which was nominated for the National Book Award in 2001; and the best-selling *The Keep*. Her most recent book, *A Visit from the Goon Squad*, a national bestseller, won the 2011 National Book Critics Circle Award for Fiction, was a finalist for the Pen/Faulkner Award and the L.A. Times Book Prize, and was longlisted for the UK's Orange Prize. Also a journalist, Egan writes frequently for the *New York Times Magazine*.

▪ "Out of Body" is a section of my new book, *A Visit from the Goon Squad*, which unfolds in thirteen discrete parts that are very different from each other. It was probably the part I had the most trouble writing—initially I tried writing from Sasha's point of view about her time in college, but it was dead on arrival: the single interesting part of it involved her memories of traveling in Asia, and a troubled boy she met there named Leif. So I moved Leif to NYU, where I named him Bobbie and began writing from his point of view about his friendship with Sasha. Second-person narration has interested me for years because of my work as a journalist; people tend to slip into the second person when discussing emotional things, to distance themselves from those emotions. Bobbie spoke in the second person right from the start, but I struggled to see and hear him clearly in his new environment, and the chapter continued to founder. One day, on a crowded New York subway, I spotted a guy with reddish stubble talking to his friend. He was very masculine, and I thought, "I'm not writing about Bobbie, I'm writing about Rob. And there he is." I didn't even look at the guy again, but I held his image in my mind, and when I began writing again, the second-person voice was much more lively and specific. That's when the story began to finally come together; when Leif transformed into Bobbie, bulked up, grew some stubble, and became Rob.

NATHAN ENGLANDER is the author of the story collection *For the Relief of Unbearable Urges* and the novel *The Ministry of Special Cases*. He is currently at work on a play based on his short story "The Twenty-seventh Man."

▪ I will pretty much get on a plane to anywhere in the world if it's to do an event with the Israeli writer Etgar Keret (and yes, the little boy in the story is named after him). So a couple of years back, I flew to Rome to give a talk with Etgar, and—a nice surprise—there in the first row of the audience was an Italian friend of mine. After the talk, we ended up on the roof of her building telling stories for hours. One of those stories was about Etgar's father, and matching uniforms, and the Sinai Campaign. I really never (at least until now) write stories about things overheard, or based on the tales friends tell—it's just not how I work. And I don't think I'd have dared to write this one if not for the confusion caused when you mix American overpoliteness with Israeli straight talk. I wanted to tell Etgar something about the narrative structure of the story. But I didn't want to be rude and talk about a personal account in an inconsiderate way. So I asked, in Hebrew, "Would you mind if I engaged with that story as a story?" And Etgar turned and said, "Sure. Take it." As in, It's yours, go write it. And there I was backpedaling and apologizing and saying, No, no, that wasn't my intent. But Etgar made it clear. He writes about talking fish and fake angels and women that turn into hairy men after dark, and really, this is not the kind of thing he would do. So a year went by, and I was living in Berlin for a few months and thinking about history and the Holocaust and Israel, and that's when I sat down to write "Free Fruit."

ALLEGRA GOODMAN is the author of five novels—*The Cookbook Collector, The Other Side of the Island, Intuition, Paradise Park,* and *Kaaterskill Falls*—and two collections of short stories, *The Family Markowitz* and *Total Immersion.* Her fiction has appeared in *The New Yorker, Commentary,* and *Ploughshares.* Her essays and reviews have appeared in the *New York Times Book Review, New Republic, Boston Globe, Wall Street Journal,* and *American Scholar.* Raised in Honolulu, Goodman studied English and philosophy at Harvard and received a PhD in English literature from Stanford. She is the recipient of a Whiting Writers' Award, the Salon Award for Fiction, and a fellowship from the Radcliffe Institute for Advanced Study. She lives with her family in Cambridge, Massachusetts, where she is writing a new novel.

• Whenever I finish a novel, I write a couple of short stories. It's a chance to play and to experiment. In this case, I'd finished a long, richly layered novel, *The Cookbook Collector,* and I thought, Now for something completely different! "La Vita Nuova" is shorter than most of my stories. The style is spare. Every word counts, and every detail has particular weight. I tried dozens of beginnings before I decided on Amanda and her wedding dress. Once I settled into her point of view, the wry narrative followed. While the story is quite structured, I wrote it without a plan, improvising all the way through the last line. In the weeks I worked on it, I dreamed about it all the time.

EHUD HAVAZELET has written three books, the story collections *What Is It Then Between Us?* and *Like Never Before* and the novel *Bearing the Body.* The latter two were named *New York Times* Notable Books. Other awards in-

clude California and Oregon book awards, the Wallant Award, and fellowships from Stanford University and the Whiting, Guggenheim, and Rocke-
feller foundations. He teaches writing at the University of Oregon and
lives with his family in Corvallis, Oregon.

▪ Stories begin in autobiography, a bit of occasion you investigate for
meaning, consequence. This one began that way, with reaching that age
where women don't look at you anymore the way they once did; with cold
mornings on Riverside Drive thirty years ago; with me trying to show off to
my girlfriend how well I could drive (I couldn't) and rear-ending a lieutenant in the Mineola Police Department on my first road trip after getting
my license.

Another source is Chekhov and his great story "The Lady with the Dog."
I've been fascinated a long time by the moment when Gurov, before taking the acquiescent Anna to bed, pauses for a leisurely-seeming snack. It
seems to me a wonderful example of what Chekhov creates better than
anyone, and what I tried to capture for my own Gurov—a moment where
nothing at all seems to happen and yet everything has changed.

CAITLIN HORROCKS is the author of the story collection *This Is Not Your
City*. Her work appears in *The PEN/O. Henry Prize Stories 2009*, *The Pushcart
Prize XXXV*, *The Atlantic*, *The Paris Review*, *One Story*, and elsewhere. Her
awards include the Plimpton Prize. She lives in Grand Rapids, Michigan,
where she teaches at Grand Valley State University.

▪ I am a good and dedicated sleeper. It's a state I look forward to and
find very difficult to let go of in the mornings, especially dark winter ones.
When I read an article a few years ago about historical sleep patterns,
including alleged winter hibernation, I was immediately intrigued, and
frankly a bit jealous.

"The Sleep" was a pretty direct attempt to imagine what hibernation
might look like in a modern town; once I'd put the Rasmussens to bed, it
looked tempting enough to me that it had to spread. But when most of the
population was participating, the sleep became more complicated. That
arc, of an entire town hibernating, and what might drive them to it, and
whether that sleep was a good or bad thing, was in place from the beginning.

As I worked, I had to solve smaller questions, like how much explanation the reader might need of the logistics of the hibernation (there used
to be a lot more about canned goods) and what triggered Al's initial decision. Jeannie was alive in the earliest drafts, and at first killing her off felt
like a cheap trick. But it soon felt necessary, and it made the sleep more
explicitly an escape, a refusal to engage with certain kinds of pain: her
death, Reggie's return, whether and how the town itself was dying. I began

the story sort of envious of them all, but I think by the end I'd convinced myself to prefer wakefulness.

BRET ANTHONY JOHNSTON holds degrees from Texas A&M Corpus Christi, Miami University, and the Iowa Writers' Workshop. He is the author of *Corpus Christi: Stories* and the editor of *Naming the World and Other Exercises for the Creative Writer*. He's on the core faculty at the Bennington Writing Seminars, and he's the director of creative writing at Harvard University. More information can be found online at www.bretanthonyjohnston.com.

▪ In an ideal world, I would have the composed restraint to lay out, in a pithy and revelatory paragraph, how "Soldier of Fortune" came to be written. I would also position myself as totally unaffected by the story's inclusion in this anthology; I would have you believe I'm jaded to this kind of thing, maybe even a little resentful of having been asked to write such a paragraph because doing so would be a distraction from my Very Important Real Work. I would come off as serious and enigmatic, intimidatingly so. Brooding, too. I would definitely be a brooder. Or I would leave you with the impression that I don't much care for this story — "That old thing? I wrote it in an hour! I had one hand tied behind my back and both eyes closed!" — and you, in turn, would be struck by my aloofness, my authenticity and smarts, so struck that you'd buy multiple copies of my books. (You'd want spares lying around for folks who visited, but you'd also be worried about thieves and fires. You'd keep extra copies of the books at your office and in your car, just in case.) The problem, though, is how embarrassingly excited I am about this news, and how my embarrassing excitement has pretty much wiped from my memory every piece of data relating to this story except, of course, that it's been selected for the anthology. Honestly, right now, I hardly remember writing it. I know I wrote it when I was, to quote Flannery O'Connor, "on vacation" from writing a novel, and I know the whole story came from a chunk of the first line, the chunk about Holly's family having lived across the street from the narrator's for all but two years. I have no clue about the origin of that line; I'd been walking around with the sentence in my head for as long as I could remember. But then, on my vacation from the novel, those missing two years really started to needle me, and because they were so conspicuous in the sentence, I suspected I'd find a story if I went digging around in that pocket of lost time. So I did. Then, once the narrator's friend revealed himself to be an aficionado of camouflage pants, I bid on and won (!) a copy of *Soldier of Fortune* magazine from eBay. The magazine was from 1986, so that became the year the story takes place. And the year got me thinking about Reagan, et al. And somewhere in here I remembered this horrible thing that happened to an elementary school friend's younger brother, an accident involving water and a microwave oven. The name Hensley comes from the skateboarding legend Matt Hensley, although the fact that the name Matt also appears in the story didn't register with me until much later, after the thing was published. There's also an embedded reference to a song by the band Tool in the story. Would it be weird or ill-advised to admit I'm not nearly as convinced about the geology teacher's relationship to Sam as other folks seem to be? If you've never been to a truck stop in Texas, you should know that hats like the one Holly buys Sam for his birthday do exist. I lived, for much of my youth, across the street from a very nice family with a collie and an aboveground pool, and I went to the high school with a mustang for a mascot; I tried to get a joke about the statue's staggering anatomical correctness into that scene, but couldn't make it work. The story was revised upwards of ten or twelve times, and it's severely indebted to Linda B. Swanson-Davies and Susan Burmeister-Brown over at *Glimmer Train*. I'm also deeply indebted to them, and to Heidi Pitlor and Geraldine Brooks, and to eBay seller Guntimes007, for whom I should have obviously left much better feedback.

CLAIRE KEEGAN was raised in Ireland. Her first collection, *Antarctica* (1999), a *Los Angeles Times* Book of the Year, won the Rooney Prize for Irish Literature and the William Trevor Prize. *Walk the Blue Fields* (2007) was published to huge critical acclaim and won the Edge Hill Prize. "Foster" won the Davy Byrnes Award, judged by Richard Ford. The story was abridged for *The New Yorker* and published in its original form by Faber & Faber. Keegan lives in rural Ireland.

▪ The story began with the image of the girl's hand reaching over the water. That stayed in the back of my mind for a long time. And then I started thinking about the well we used at home. People always said that the water from the well made better tea. The well wasn't on our land but down from us in a field called Byrne's Lawn. Remembering how it felt to go down there to fetch water, I made a start. Then I was given a deadline, switched, and finished another story. Winter came and I went for a walk on the strand in Wexford with a friend of mine. There were two lights on the water when we came up across the dunes. By the time we were leaving, he noticed three. I went back to the story in the new year, wrote the walk into the text, and found the character of Kinsella. Maybe I wanted to write about a man who has lost his son. I knew little except that it needed to be written from a child's point of view and, later, that it would have to take place in summer. At no point in the writing of the story did I have clear feelings about where the story was going, much less how it would conclude.

SAM LIPSYTE is the author of the story collection *Venus Drive* and three novels: *The Ask,* a *New York Times* Notable Book for 2010, *The Subject Steve,* and *Home Land,* a *New York Times* Notable Book and winner of the first annual Believer Book Award. His fiction has appeared in *The New Yorker, Harper's Magazine, Open City, The Paris Review, n+1, The Quarterly, Tin House, Noon,* and many other places. A 2008 Guggenheim Fellow, Lipsyte lives in New York and teaches at Columbia University.

▪ This was one of those stories that took twenty years but also happened very quickly. I tried to write a version of it when I was right out of college. It was unbelievably awful. All the fiction I wrote then was awful, but I recall being especially disappointed because I could feel the charge of this piece, hear the rhythms, see the images. I just wasn't ready to transmit. I tried several drafts and showed it to some people, even though I knew already it was dead on the page. The story remained a stern reminder of how much of writing is failure. The percentages don't necessarily improve.

But somehow I got lucky with this one. Two decades later I was sitting at the computer wrestling with a new story, although *wrestling* is probably too macho and romantic a description of what I was doing. What I was doing was more like grooming a corpse for visitors. Eventually I shut off the machine and sat there in disgust. What I usually do in this situation is stand and pace, or distract myself with music or coffee or books, or else just lurk at a window and mutter obscenities. Instead I clicked open a new blank document and, without thinking about it, typed a first sentence. The words were different, but I knew exactly what I had written. My old story had returned to me. I want to say it came rushing out but it was more like a calm, steady stream. I can only think of the long life cycles of certain cicadas, the way they spend most of their seventeen years buried. "The Dungeon Master" just needed to gestate.

REBECCA MAKKAI's debut novel, *The Borrower,* was published in June. This is her fourth consecutive appearance in *The Best American Short Stories,* and her short fiction appears regularly in journals including *Tin House, Ploughshares,* and *New England Review.* She lives north of Chicago with her husband and daughters.

▪ This story was five years in the writing, and it changed more in that time than anything else I've done. (Suffice it to say that at one point it was called "Frost" and was about, among other things, buying babies at the supermarket.) Two elements stayed constant throughout its long and painful genesis, however: the character of poor Peter, who had forgotten how to act, and the sense of aching loss.

When I started the story, I was at that point in my twenties when I realized that the adult world to which I had worked so hard to acclimate myself was in fact changing and disappearing. I felt this transformation around me in Chicago: two local icons, Marshall Fields and the Berghoff, went up in smoke at around the same time (although the Berghoff has since reinvented and reopened), while the Art Institute hid its armor upstairs and put its crown jewel, Marc Chagall's *America Windows,* in storage. And I felt it in those people whose entire lives and personalities changed before my eyes, just when I thought I had them all figured out. (As I write this note in March, I'm saddened that even Drew's NPR is now fighting for its life.) I wanted to write about the metamorphosis of one person—someone around whom the narrator's adult personality had grown like a vine—whose existential crisis would seem, to his friend, like a crumbling of the entire known world.

It should be noted that Rob Spillman of *Tin House* edited this story under the most heroic of circumstances. Shortly after his hand was badly injured when a water-filled light fixture fell on it, I e-mailed him to say (rather hormonally, I fear) that my C-section was scheduled in a week, and if he wanted anything changed, he'd better act fast. Between the two of us—he typing one-handed, I separated from my desk by an enormous belly—we managed to get it done.

And speaking of miracles of artistic collaboration . . . I realize that the event Drew coordinates would be impractical and even financially irresponsible, but nevertheless I hereby challenge the Art Institute of Chicago: make it happen, and I'll be your first volunteer.

ELIZABETH MCCRACKEN is the author of *Here's Your Hat What's Your Hurry* (stories), *The Giant's House* and *Niagara Falls All Over Again* (novels), and *An Exact Replica of a Figment of My Imagination* (memoir). She is at work at another novel and is currently the James A. Michener Chair in Creative Writing at the University of Texas at Austin.

• "Property" happened.

The characters are entirely made up, but the house isn't, and neither is the plot. I'd been living in Europe; I was supposed to come back to the States for a job; someone died; my husband and I delayed our arrival by several months; when we arrived, the house was in a bad state. The picture of Pablo Picasso was of another famous twentieth-century figure, in a field relevant to the actual landlord, but the mess: that's true, from Teddy Grahams to condom wrappers to disgusting bathmat. Nearly a year later, we moved out and went away for the weekend and received a series of phone calls from the landlords, who were genuinely bewildered that we'd thrown out their old spices. Suddenly the insult of the filthy house months back was fresh again, and in a fury I began to write this story.

Not till I got to the end did I realize the truth: Our landlords loved their house. They loved their broken things. They even loved their sticky elderly grocery store spices. It was incomprehensible to them that we did not love these things too. I don't think I would have realized that had I not written the story; even now, I would still be muttering about the salad spinner.

As a younger person I wrote nearly nothing that was particularly autobiographical. This is, I think now, not because I was philosophically opposed to it nor because I lacked material. What I lacked was the ability to work myself into a tizzy about everyday things: my passionate feelings were reserved for things deserving of passion, most of which were enormous and abstract and therefore hard to make into interesting fiction. Though there's a buzz of grief behind this story (as there was everywhere at that moment in my life), what prompted the actual writing of it was a landlord-tenant dispute. Not a love affair, not a death, not a birth. I suppose I'm grateful that the story helped me understand them, but still, I would like to make it clear: my motivation was not connection, but revenge.

STEVEN MILLHAUSER is the author of twelve works of fiction, most recently *We Others: New and Selected Stories* (2011). His stories have appeared in *Harper's Magazine, The New Yorker, Tin House, McSweeney's,* and other publications. He was born in Brooklyn, grew up in Connecticut, and now lives in Saratoga Springs, New York.

▪ For a long while I wanted to write a story about a phantom woman. It never came to fruition, for reasons I can only guess at. One day, unexpectedly, a different kind of phantom story appeared to me and dared me to write it. The story "Phantoms" is the result of that dare.

RICARDO NUILA is an assistant professor at Baylor College of Medicine, where he works as a primary-care doctor, a hospitalist, and an educator. His first published story appeared in the *Indiana Review* and was listed as "notable" in *The Best American Nonrequired Reading 2010.*

▪ After this story was published, some colleagues, friends, my dad, asked me, "The main character's name is Ricky and he's a doctor: is this autobiographical?" The most autobiographical aspect of this story is that I concussed myself while playing Wiffle ball. I had come off a difficult call where I'd spent the night dealing with a septic patient. I got home and drove immediately to my friend's bachelor party and joined in a game of Wiffle ball. I played first base. Someone hit what amounted to a bunt, the pitcher fielded it, tossed it my way, and I caught it, only my head was in the path of the runner. I didn't lose consciousness.

I played one inning disoriented before subbing myself out. My friend came to check on me and I told him we needed to rule out a cerebral hemorrhage. I started to describe the anatomy: Monro-Kellie doctrine, subdural versus epidural hematoma, middle meningeal artery, etc. I had my friend examine my eyes for a blown pupil. This fazed him enough to drive me to a hospital, where a good neurological exam and an unnecessary CAT scan were performed, showing all was well. As I waited in the ER for discharge, a naked lady with scratches on her back came in. She was obviously drunk; it looked like she'd been jumping into a lake and had fallen on the rocks. The triage nurse asked her what happened and she said, "Dog bites," which I doubted very much.

JOYCE CAROL OATES, 2010 recipient of the National Humanities Medal, is the author most recently of *A Widow's Story* and *Give Me Your Heart*. She is a recipient of the National Book Award, the PEN/Malamud Award for Excellence in the Short Story, and the 2010 Ivan Sandrof Award for Lifetime Achievement of the National Book Critics Circle. Since 1978 she has been a member of the American Academy of Arts and Letters and a member of the faculty of Princeton University.

▪ In February 2008 a call came for me late at night: my husband, Raymond Smith, was critically ill and I must come to the hospital at once. But when I arrived, my husband had died just minutes before. I was allowed to stay with him for a while . . . But next morning when friends took me to the funeral home to which his body had been delivered, and the funeral director said that the body had to be "identified," I was suddenly not able to move — I could not bring myself to see my dead husband a second time. There was a kind of collapse in my brain — when I realized what I had done, or had failed to do, we were already leaving the funeral home and it was too late. (My friends had identified my husband in my place.) After that I was haunted by the specter of my husband "unidentified" — "unacknowledged."

Some months later, "ID" was written in a burst of emotion — in its original form it is much longer, and we know much more, perhaps more than we need to know, about the intimacy and the anxiety between the mother and the daughter. The story is one in which a crucial ID is not made — and so the daughter's ID (her identity) will forever be askew. There has been a series of unsolved murders of solitary women in Atlantic City, New Jersey — the ideal setting for such tragedy.

RICHARD POWERS is the author of ten novels. His most recent, *Generosity*, is a finalist for the Arthur C. Clarke Award.

▪ I wrote "To the Measures Fall" as my contribution for a course I taught at Stanford in early 2010. I asked a small group of spectacular students to write a work that in some way blurred the boundaries between fiction and nonfiction. They all put themselves on the line with their creations, so I figured I should as well.

JESS ROW is the author of two collections of short stories, *The Train to Lo Wu* and *Nobody Ever Gets Lost,* in which "The Call of Blood" appears. His fiction has appeared in *The Atlantic, Granta, Conjunctions, Ploughshares,* and many other journals and has been selected for two previous volumes of *The Best American Short Stories* (in 2001 and 2003). He has received a Whiting Writers Award, a PEN/O. Henry Award, and two Pushcart Prizes, and in 2007 he was named a "Best Young American Novelist" by *Granta.* His nonfiction and criticism appear often in the *New York Times Book Review, The New Republic,* and *Threepenny Review.* He teaches at the College of New Jersey and the Vermont College of Fine Arts. His website is jessrow.com.

▪ In his novel *G.,* John Berger writes, "One minute of life is passing by. Paint it as it is." I don't think I've ever written a story as much in that spirit—wanting to capture the multilayered quality, the simultaneity, of everyday experience—as "The Call of Blood." In a sense, you could say it's a story about how New Yorkers returned to daily life after September 11—to the ordinary enervating flux and unhappiness of getting through the day, as a kind of escape from the cataclysmic grief that followed the event itself.

I take it for granted that for most New Yorkers, and indeed for many human beings on the planet today, at least some of our daily unhappiness arises from living in a world of bizarre, uncomfortable juxtapositions—as Hyunjee puts it, "Spring rolls and matzoh balls. Filipinos doing your nails and Koreans doing your laundry and Guatemalans bringing your Chinese food and Hasids handing you pamphlets every time you come out of the subway." People who are multiracial by birth, like Kevin, live with these juxtapositions in the most intense, intimate way, of course, but so do those of us who are part of multiracial, multiethnic families. And so do many others, simply by virtue of being observant and alive. The master narratives of late capitalist culture—that in a global economy a rising tide lifts all boats, or that fundamentalism thrives only in closed societies—haven't fared terribly well in the early twenty-first century, yet no other narratives have replaced them. We're told that diversity is good and exclusion is bad, but we know (whether we want to admit it or not) that those notions are really just a smokescreen for a socioeconomic order that reinforces and exploits ethnic tensions all the way up and down the ladder. It's a kind of dissonance that at times verges on collective schizophrenia.

In her book *The Melancholy of Race,* Anne Anlin Cheng writes that the ideal of ethnic diversity—the metaphor of the salad bowl, of having "a little bit of everything"—is a kind of "pathological euphoria." Hyunjee's attitude could be called the hangover that sets in after pathological euphoria has ceased. Her exhaustion and disgust are misplaced, but very real. And so, to me, is her courage (and Kevin's courage) in taking up a love affair that violates the social order of their world. "What would it mean to reside within inassimilable difference and incommensurability," Cheng asks, "to experience one's ontology as constantly at odds with the available cultural dressing?" Superficially we might say this experience of being "at odds" applies only to members of minority groups, but in the twenty-first century, who is not, to some context, a member of a minority? Who, in the twenty-first century, has not experienced some sense of dispossession, homelessness, alienation, self-estrangement? That's the common bond that unites Kevin and Hyunjee, I think, and in a different world—a better world—could unite all the rest of us.

GEORGE SAUNDERS is the author of three short story collections: *Civil-WarLand in Bad Decline, Pastoralia,* and *In Persuasion Nation.* A 2006 MacArthur Fellow, he teaches in the creative writing program at Syracuse University.

▪ I don't remember much about the origins of "Escape from Spiderhead" except writing the first half-page or so after a long day of working on something else. I was always interested in the idea that who we are seems to have an awful lot to do with just simple chemistry, much as we like to think otherwise. So a flu or, per Dickens, "a bit of undigested beef" changes the world, as will a piece of good news or an hour of prayer.

MARK SLOUKA's books, which have been translated into eighteen languages, include *Lost Lake* (stories), the novels *God's Fool* and *The Visible World,* and two works of nonfiction, *War of the Worlds,* a cultural critique of technological society, and, most recently, *Essays from the Nick of Time.* His stories and essays have appeared in *Granta, Agni,* and *The Paris Review,* among other publications, as well as in *The Best American Essays, The Best American Short Stories,* and *The PEN/O. Henry Prize Stories.* A contributing editor at *Harper's Magazine,* he lives with his family in Brewster, New York.

▪ To write "The Hare's Mask" I had to warm the actual event, knead and stretch it until it became malleable to the imagination. The basic material is historical fact: my father's family sheltered a Jewish refugee in a rabbit hutch during the war; as a boy my father had to kill rabbits for dinner. After that, the picture begins to blur and shape itself to other needs. I'm the trout fisherman, not my father; though there's a picture of my father's family on the mantelpiece, his parents and sister survived the war by some years; I never had a sister *or* a rabbit, while my son, now grown, had both.

Who knows where these things begin, really? I suppose, looking at the picture on the mantel, recalling the old stories, listening to our daughter's rabbit thumping in the dark, I sensed a story about history's losses, time's compensations, and a child's ability to misread the world. To get at it, I had to mix three generations. It was easy enough; in my heart, they were already blurred.

Other Distinguished Stories
of 2010

Editorial Addresses of American and Canadian Magazines Publishing Short Stories

Able Muse Review
467 Saratoga Ave. #602
San Jose, CA 95129
$22, Nina Schyler

Agni Magazine
Boston University Writing Program
Boston University
236 Bay State Road
Boston, MA 02115
$20, Sven Birkerts

Alaska Quarterly Review
University of Alaska, Anchorage
3211 Providence Drive
Anchorage, AK 99508
$18, Ronald Spatz

Alimentum
P.O. Box 776
New York, NY 10163
$18, Paulette Licitra

Alligator Juniper
http://www.prescott.edu/alligator_
juniper/
$15, Melanie Bishop

American Letters and Commentary
Department of English
University of Texas at San Antonio
One UTSA Boulevard
San Antonio, TX 78249
$10, David Ray Vance, Catherine Kasper

American Short Fiction
P.O. Box 301209
Austin, TX 78703
$30, Stacey Swann

Amoskeag
Southern New Hampshire University
2500 N. River Road
Manchester, NH 03106
$7, Michael J. Brien

Anderbo
anderbo.com
Rick Rofihe

Annalemma
annalemma.net
Chris Heavener

Antioch Review
Antioch University
P.O. Box 148

Yellow Springs, OH 45387
$40, Robert S. Fogerty

Apalachee Review
P.O. Box 10469
Tallahassee, FL 32302
$15, Michael Trammell

Apple Valley Review
Queen's Postal Outlet
Box 12
Kingston, Ontario K7L 3R9
Leah Browning

Arroyo
Department of English
California State University, East Bay
25800 Carlos Bee Boulevard
Hayward, CA 94542

Arts & Letters
Campus Box 89
Georgia College and State University
Milledgeville, GA 31061
$15, Martin Lammon

Ascent
English Department
Concordia College
readthebestwriting.com
W. Scott Olsen

At Length
atlengthmag.com
Dan Kois

The Atlantic
600 NH Avenue NW
Washington, DC 20037
$39.95, C. Michael Curtis

Avery
3657 Broadway
1E
New York, NY 10031
Adam Koehler

The Baltimore Review
P.O. Box 36418
Towson, MD 21286
Susan Muaddi Darraj

Bamboo Ridge
P.O. Box 61781
Honolulu, HI 96839
Eric Chock, Darrell H. Y. Lum

Bark
2810 8th Street
Berkeley, CA 94710
$15, Claudia Kawcynska

Barrelhouse
barrelhousemagazine.com
$9, the editors

Bayou
Department of English
University of New Orleans
2000 Lakeshore Drive
New Orleans, LA 70148
$15, Joanna Leake

The Believer
849 Valencia Street
San Francisco, CA 94110
Heidi Julavits

Bellevue Literary Review
Department of Medicine
New York University School of
Medicine
550 First Avenue
New York, NY 10016
$15, Danielle Ofri

Bellingham Review
MS-9053
Western Washington University
Bellingham, WA 98225
$12, Brenda Miller

Bellowing Ark
P.O. Box 55564
Shoreline, WA 98155
$20, Robert Ward

Blackbird
Department of English
Virginia Commonwealth University
P.O. Box 843082
Richmond, VA 23284–3082
Gregory Donovan, Mary Flinn

Black Warrior Review
P.O. Box 862936
Tuscaloosa, AL 35486–0027
$16, Christopher Hellwig

Bloodroot Literary Magazine
P.O. Box 322
Thetford, VT 05075
Do Roberts

Blue Earth Review
Centennial Student Union
Minnesota State University, Mankato
Mankato, MN 56001
$8, Ande Davis

Blue Mesa
Creative Writing Program
University of New Mexico
MSC03–2170
Albuquerque, NM 87131
Samantha Tetangco

Bomb
New Art Publications
80 Hanson Place
Brooklyn, NY 11217
$25, Betsy Sussler

Boston Review
35 Medford Street, Suite 302
Somerville, MA 02143
$25, Joshua Cohen, Deborah Chasman

Boulevard
PMB 325
6614 Clayton Road
Richmond Heights, MO 63117
$20, Richard Burgin

Brain, Child: The Magazine for
Thinking Mothers
P.O. Box 714
Lexington, VA 24450–0714
$22, Jennifer Niesslein, Stephanie Wilkinson

Briar Cliff Review
3303 Rebecca Street
P.O. Box 2100

Sioux City, IA 51104–2100
$10, Tricia Currans-Sheehan

Callaloo
MS 4212
Texas A&M University
College Station, TX 77843-4212
$50, Charles H. Rowell

Calyx
P.O. Box B
Corvallis, OR 97339
$23, the collective

Camera Obscura
obscurajournal.com
M. E. Parker

Canteen
70 Washington Street, Suite 12H
Brooklyn, NY 11201
$35, Stephen Pierson

The Carolina Quarterly
Greenlaw Hall
CB #3520
University of North Carolina
Chapel Hill, NC 27599
$18, the editors

Carpe Articulum
8630 SW Scholls Ferry Road, Suite 177
Beaverton, OR 97008
$59.95, Rand Eastwood

Cerise Press
P.O. Box 241187
Omaha, NE 68124
Karen Rigby

Chautauqua
Department of Creative Writing
University of North Carolina,
Wilmington
601 S. College Road
Wilmington, NC 28403
$14.95, Jill and Philip Gerard

Chicago Review
5801 South Kenwood
University of Chicago

Chicago, IL 60637
$25, V. Joshua Adams

Chicago Quarterly Review
517 Sherman Ave.
Evanston, IL 60202
$17, S. Afzal Haider

Cimarron Review
205 Morrill Hall
Oklahoma State University
Stillwater, OK 74078-4069
$24, E. P. Walkiewicz

Cincinnati Review
Department of English
McMicken Hall, Room 369
P.O. Box 210069
Cincinnati, OH 45221
$15, Brock Clarke

Coe Review
Coe College
Cedar Rapids, IA 52402
Cordon Mennenga

Colorado Review
Department of English
Colorado State University
Fort Collins, CO 80523
$24, Stephanie G'Schwind

Columbia
Columbia University Alumni Center
622 W. 113th Street
MC4521
New York, NY 10025
$50, Michael B. Sharleson

Commentary
165 East 56th Street
New York, NY 10022
$45, Neal Kozody

Confrontation
English Department
C. W. Post College of Long Island
University
Greenvale, NY 11548
$10, Martin Tucker

Conjunctions
21 East 10th Street, Suite 3E
New York, NY 10003
$18, Bradford Morrow

Crab Orchard Review
Department of English
Southern Illinois University at
Carbondale
Carbondale, IL 62901
$20, Carolyn Alessio

Crazyhorse
Department of English
College of Charleston
66 George Street
Charleston, SC 29424
$16, Anthony Varallo

Cream City Review
Department of English
University of Wisconsin, Milwaukee
Box 413
Milwaukee, WI 53201
$22, Jay Johnson

Crucible
Barton Collge
P.O. Box 5000
Wilson, NC 27893
$16, Terrence L. Grimes

Cutbank
Department of English
University of Montana
Missoula, MT 59812
$12, Lauren Hamlin

Daedalus
136 Irving Street, Suite 100
Cambridge, MA 02138
$41, James Miller

Denver Quarterly
University of Denver
Denver, CO 80208
$20, Bin Ramke

Descant
P.O. Box 314
Station P

Toronto, Ontario M5S 2S8
$28, Karen Mulhallen

descant
Department of English
Texas Christian University
TCU Box 297270
Fort Worth, TX 76129
$12, Dave Kuhne

Dogwood
Department of English
Fairfield University
1073 N. Benson Road
Fairfield, CT 06824
Pete Duval

Downstate Story
1825 Maple Ridge
Peoria, IL 61614
$8, Elaine Hopkins

Ecotone
Department of Creative Writing
University of North Carolina,
Wilmington
601 South College Road
Wilmington, NC 28403
$16.95, David Gessner

Electric Literature
electricliterature.com
Andy Hunter, Scott Lindenbaum

Epiphany
www.epiphanyzine.com
$18, Willard Cook

Epoch
251 Goldwin Smith Hall
Cornell University
Ithaca, NY 14853-3201
$11, Michael Koch

Esquire
300 West 57th Street, 21st Floor,
New York, NY 10019
$17.94, fiction editor

Event
Douglas College

P.O. Box 2503
New Westminster, British Columbia
V3L 5B2
$24.95, Rick Maddocks

Fantasy and Science Fiction
P.O. Box 3447
Hoboken, NJ 07030
$39, Gordon Van Gelder

The Farallon Review
1017 L Street
No. 348
Sacramento, CA 95814
$10, the editors

Fiction
Department of English
The City College of New York
Convent Ave. at 138th Street
New York, NY 10031
$38, Mark Jay Mirsky

Fiction Fix
www.fictionfix.net
April E. Bacon

Fiction International
Department of English and
Comparative Literature
5500 Campanile Drive
San Diego State University
San Diego, CA 92182
$18, Harold Jaffe

The Fiddlehead
Campus House
11 Garland Court
UNB P.O. Box 4400
Fredericton, New Brunswick E3B 5A3
$55, Mark Anthony Jarman

Fifth Wednesday
www.fifthwednesdayjournal.org
$20, Vern Miller

Five Points
Georgia State University
P.O. Box 3999
Atlanta, GA 30302
$21, David Bottoms and Megan Sexton

The Florida Review
Department of English
P.O. Box 161346
University of Central Florida
Orlando, FL 32816
$15, Jocelyn Bartkevicius

Flyway
206 Ross Hall
Department of English
Iowa State University
Ames, IA 50011
$24, David DeFina

Fourteen Hills
Department of Creative Writing
San Francisco State University
1600 Halloway Ave.
San Francisco, CA 94132-1722
$15, Amy Glasenapp

Fugue
uidaho.edu/fugue
$18, Craig E. Buchner

Gargoyle
3819 North 13th Street
Arlington, VA 22201
$30, Lucinda Ebersole, Richard Peabody

Georgetown Review
400 E. College Street
Box 227
Georgetown, KY 40324
$5, Steven Carter

Georgia Review
Gilbert Hall
University of Georgia
Athens, GA 30602
$35, Stephen Corey

Gettysburg Review
Gettysburg College
300 N. Washington Street
Gettysburg, PA 17325
$28, Peter Stitt

Ghost Town/The Pacific Review
Department of English
California State University,

San Bernadino
5500 University Parkway
San Bernadino, CA 92407
Gina Hanson

Gigantic
thegiganticmag.com
Ann DeWitt

Glimmer Train Stories
1211 NW Glisan Street, Suite 207
Portland, OR 97209
$36, Susan Burmeister-Brown, Linda Swanson-Davies

Good Housekeeping
300 West 57th Street
New York, NY 10019
Laura Matthews

Grain
Box 67
Saskatoon, Saskatchewan 57K 3K9
$30, Sylvia Legris

Granta
841 Broadway, 4th Floor
New York, NY 10019-3780
$39.95, John Freeman

Grasslands Review
Creative Writing Program
Department of English
Indiana State University
Terre Haute, IN 47809
$8, Brendan Corcoran

Gray's Sporting Journal
P.O. Box 1207
Augusta, GA 30903
$36.95, James R. Rabb

Green Mountains Review
Box A58
Johnson State College
Johnson, VT 05656
$15, Leslie Daniels

Greensboro Review
3302 Hall for Humanities
and Research Administration

University of North Carolina
Greensboro, NC 27402
$14, Jim Clark

Gulf Coast
Department of English
University of Houston
Houston, TX 77204-3012
$16, Nick Flynn

Hanging Loose
231 Wyckoff Street
Brooklyn, NY 11217
$22, group

Harper's Magazine
666 Broadway
New York, NY 10012
$21, Ben Metcalf

Harpur Palate
Department of English
Binghamton University
P.O. Box 6000
Binghamton, NY 13902
$16, Barrett Bowlin

Harvard Review
Lamont Library
Harvard University
Cambridge, MA 02138
$20, Christina Thompson

Hawaii Review
Department of English
University of Hawaii at Manoa
P.O. Box 11674
Honolulu, HI 96828
$20, Stephanie Mizushima

Hayden's Ferry Review
Box 875002
Arizona State University
Tempe, AZ 85287
$14, Cameron Fielder

High Desert Journal
P.O. Box 7647
Bend, OR 97708
$16, Elizabeth Quinn

Hobart
P.O. Box 11658
Ann Arbor, MI 48106
$18, Aaron Burch

Hotel Amerika
Columbia College
English Department
600 S. Michigan Avenue
Chicago, IL 60657
$18, David Lazar

Hudson Review
684 Park Avenue
New York, NY 10065
$62, Paula Deitz

Hunger Mountain
www.hungermountain.org
$12, Anne de Marcken

Idaho Review
Boise State University
1910 University Drive
Boise, ID 83725
$10, Mitch Wieland

Image
Center for Religious Humanism
3307 Third Avenue West
Seattle, WA 98119
$39.95, Gregory Wolfe

Indiana Review
Ballantine Hall 465
1020 East Kirkwood Avenue
Bloomington, IN 47405-7103
$17, Catalina Bartlett

Inkwell
Manhattanville College
2900 Purchase Street
Purchase, NY 10577
$10, Todd Bowes

Iowa Review
Department of English
University of Iowa
308 EPB
Iowa City, IA 52242
$25, Russell Scott Valentino

Iron Horse Literary Review
Department of English
Texas Tech University
Box 43091
Lubbock, TX 79409-3091
$5, Leslie Jill Patterson

Isotope
Utah State University
3200 Old Main Hill
Logan, UT 84322
$15, the editors

Italian Americana
University of Rhode Island
Providence Campus
80 Washington Street
Providence, RI 02903
$20, Carol Bonomo Albright

Jabberwock Review
Department of English
Drawer E
Mississippi State University
Mississippi State, MS 39762
$15, Michael P. Kardos

Jewish Currents
45 East 33rd Street
New York, NY 10016-5335
$25, editorial board

The Journal
The Ohio State University
Department of English
164 W. 17th Ave.
Columbus, OH 43210
$15, Kathy Fagon

Joyland
joylandmagazine.com
Emily Schultz

Juked
110 Westridge Drive
Tallahassee, FL 32304
$10, J. W. Wang

Kenyon Review
www.kenyonreview.org
$30, the editors

Lady Churchill's Rosebud Wristlet
Small Beer Press
150 Pleasant Street
Easthampton, MA 01027
$20, Kelly Link

Lake Effect
Penn State Erie
4951 College Drive
Erie, PA 16563-1501
$6, George Looney

Lalitamba
110 W. 86th Street, Suite 5D
New York, NY 10024
Florence Homolka

The Literary Review
Fairleigh Dickinson University
285 Madison Avenue
Madison, NJ 07940
$24, Minna Proctor

The Los Angeles Review
redhen.org/losangelesreview
Kate Gale

Louisiana Literature
SLU-10792
Southeastern Louisiana University
Hammond, LA 70402
$12, Jack B. Bedell

Louisville Review
Spalding University
851 South Fourth Street
Louisville, KY 40203
$14, Sena Jeter Naslund

Lumina
Sarah Lawrence College
Slonim House
One Mead Way
Bronxville, NY 10708
Lillian Ho

Madison Review
University of Wisconsin
Department of English
H. C. White Hall
600 North Park Street

Madison, WI 53706
$25, *Elzbieta Beck*

Make
www.makemag.com
Tom Mundt

Mānoa
English Department
University of Hawaii
Honolulu, HI 96822
$22, *Frank Stewart*

Massachusetts Review
South College
University of Massachusetts
Amherst, MA 01003
$27, *Ellen Dore Watson*

McSweeney's
826 Valencia Street
San Francisco, CA 94110
$55, *Dave Eggers*

Meridian
Department of English
P.O. Box 400145
University of Virginia
Charlottesville, VA 22904-4145
$12, *Jazzy Danziger*

Michigan Quarterly Review
3574 Rackham Building
915 East Washington Street
University of Michigan
Ann Arbor, MI 48109
$25, *Johnathan Freedman*

Mid-American Review
Department of English
Bowling Green State University
Bowling Green, OH 43403
$12, *Michael Czyzniejewski*

Minnesota Review
Department of English
Carnegie Mellon University
Pittsburgh, PA 15213
$30, *Jeffrey Williams*

Minnetonka Review
P.O. Box 386
Spring Park, MN 55384
$17, *Troy Ehlers*

Mississippi Review
University of Southern Mississippi
118 College Drive, #5144
Hattiesburg, MS 39406-5144
$15, *Frederick Barthelme*

Missouri Review
357 McReynolds Hall
University of Missouri
Columbia, MO 65211
$24, *Speer Morgan*

Montana Quarterly
2820 W. College Street
Bozeman, MT 59771
Megan Ault Regnerus

Mythium
1428 North Forbes Road
Lexington, KY 40511
$15, *Ronald Davis*

n+1
68 Jay Street, #405
Brooklyn, NY 11201
$30, *Keith Gessen, Mark Greif*

Narrative
narrativemagazine.com
the editors

The Nashville Review
331 Benson Hall
Vanderbilt University
Nashville, TN 37203
Matthew Maker

Natural Bridge
Department of English
University of Missouri, St. Louis
St. Louis, MO 63121
$10, *Mark Troy*

New England Review
Middlebury College

Middlebury, VT 05753
$30, *Stephen Donadio*

New Letters
University of Missouri
5100 Rockhill Road
Kansas City, MO 64110
$22, *Robert Stewart*

New Millennium Writings
www.newmillenniumwritings.com
$12, *Don Williams*

New Ohio Review
English Department
360 Ellis Hall
Ohio University
Athens, OH 45701
$20, *John Bullock*

New Orphic Review
706 Mill Street
Nelson, British Columbia V1L 4S5
$30, *Ernest Hekkanen*

New Quarterly
Saint Jerome's University
290 Westmount Road
N. Waterloo, Ontario N2L 3G3
$36, *Kim Jernigan*

The New Yorker
4 Times Square
New York, NY 10036
$46, *Deborah Treisman*

Nimrod International Journal
Arts and Humanities Council of Tulsa
600 South College Avenue
Tulsa, OK 74104
$17.50, *Francine Ringold*

Ninth Letter
Department of English
University of Illinois
608 South Wright Street
Urbana, IL 61801
$21.95, *Jodee Rubins*

Noon
1324 Lexington Avenue

PMB 298
New York, NY 10128
$12, *Diane Williams*

The Normal School
5245 North Backer Ave.
M/S PB 98
California State University
Fresno, CA 93470
$5, *Sophie Beck*

North American Review
University of Northern Iowa
1222 West 27th Street
Cedar Falls, IA 50614
$22, *Grant Tracey*

North Atlantic Review
15 Arbutus Lane
Stony Brook, NY 11790
$10, *editorial board*

North Carolina Literary Review
Department of English
555 English
East Carolina University
Greenville, NC 27858-4353
$25, *Margaret Bauer*

North Dakota Quarterly
University of North Dakota
Merrifield Hall, Room 110
276 Centennial Drive, Stop 27209
Grand Forks, ND 58202
$25, *Robert Lewis*

Northern New England Review
Humanities Department
Franklin Pierce University
Rindge, NH 03461
$5, *Edie Clark*

Northwest Review
5243 University of Oregon
Eugene, OR 97403
$20, *Ehud Havazelet*

Notre Dame Review
840 Flanner Hall
Department of English
University of Notre Dame

Notre Dame, IN 46556
$15, John Matthias, William O'Rourke

Noun vs. Verb
Burning River
169 S. Main Street, #4
Rittman, OH 44270
Chris Bowen

One Story
232 Third Street, #A111
Brooklyn, NY 11215
$21, Maribeth Batcha, Hannah Tinti

On Spec
P.O. Box 4727
Edmonton, Alberta T6E 5G6
$24, Diane L. Walton

Open City
270 Lafayette Street, Suite 1412
New York, NY 10012
$30, Thomas Beller, Joanna Yas

Orion
187 Main Street
Great Barrington, MA 01230
$35, the editors

Our Stories
www.ourstories.com
Alexis E. Santi

Oxford American
201 Donaghey Avenue, Main 107
Conway, AR 72035
$24.95, Marc Smirnoff

Pak N Treger
National Yiddish Book Center
Harry and Jeanette Weinberg Bldg.
1021 West Street
Amherst, MA 01002
$36, Aaron Lansky

Pank
Department of the Humanities
Michigan Tech
14000 Townsend Drive
Houghton, MI 49931
$15, the editors

Paris Review
62 White Street
New York, NY 10013
$34, Lorin Stein

Pearl
3030 East Second Street
Long Beach, CA 90803
$21, Joan Jobe Smith

PEN America
PEN America Center
588 Broadway, Suite 303
New York, NY 10012
$10, M. Mark

Phoebe
MSN 2C5
George Mason University
4400 University Drive
Fairax, VA 22030
$12, Emily Viggiano

The Pinch
Department of English
University of Memphis
Memphis, TN 38152
$24, Kristen Iverson

Playboy
730 Fifth Ave.
New York, NY 10019
Amy Grace Lloyd

Pleiades
Department of English and
Philosophy
University of Central Missouri
Warrensburg, MO 64093
$16, Kevin Prufer

Ploughshares
Emerson College
120 Boylston Street
Boston, MA 02116
$30, Ladette Randolph

PoemMemoirStory
HB 217
1530 Third Avenue South

Birmingham, AL 35294
$7, *Kerry Madden*

Post Road
postroadmag.com
$18, *Rebecca Boyd*

Potomac Review
Montgomery College
51 Mannakee Street
Rockville, MD 20850
$20, *Julie Wakeman-Linn*

Prairie Fire
423-100 Arthur Street
Winnipeg, Manitoba R3B 1H3
$30, *Andris Taskans*

Prairie Schooner
201 Andrews Hall
University of Nebraska
Lincoln, NE 68588-0334
$28, *Hilda Raz*

Prism International
Department of Creative Writing
University of British Columbia
Buchanan E-462
Vancouver, British Columbia V6T 121
$28, *Rachel Knudsen*

A Public Space
323 Dean Street
Brooklyn, NY 11217
$36, *Brigid Hughes*

Puerto del Sol
MSC 3E
New Mexico State University
P.O. Box 30001
Las Cruces, NM 88003
$20, *Evan Lavender-Smith*

Realms of Fantasy
P.O. Box 243
Blacksburg, VA 24063
$19.99, *editors*

Redivider
Emerson College
120 Boylston Street

Boston, MA 02116
$10, *Matt Salesses*

Red Rock Review
English Department, J2A
Community College of Southern
Nevada
3200 East Cheyenne Avenue
North Las Vegas, NV 89030
$9.50, *Richard Logsdon*

Reed
One Washington Square
San Jose, CA 95192
Nick Taylor

River Oak Review
Elmhurst College
190 Prospect Avenue
Box 2633
Elmhurst, IL 60126
$12, *Ron Wiginton*

River Styx
3547 Olive Street, Suite 107
St. Louis, MO 63103-1014
$20, *Richard Newman*

The Roanoke Review
221 College Lane
Salem, VA 24153
$5, *Mary Crockett Hill*

Room Magazine
P.O. Box 46160
Station D
Vancouver, British Columbia V6J 5G5
$10, *Clélie Rich*

Rosebud
N3310 Asje Road
Cambridge, WI 53523
$20, *Roderick Clark*

Ruminate
140 N. Roosevelt Ave.
Ft. Collins, CO 80521
$28, *Brianna Van Dyke*

Salamander
Suffolk University

English Department
41 Temple Street
Boston, MA 02114
$23, Jennifer Barber

Salmagundi
Skidmore College
Saratoga Springs, NY 12866
$20, Robert Boyers

Salt Hill
salthilljournal.com
$20, Kayla Blatchley

Santa Clara Review
Santa Clara University
500 El Camino Road, Box 3212
Santa Clara, CA 95053
$16, Nick Sanchez

Santa Monica Review
1900 Pico Boulevard
Santa Monica, CA 90405
$12, Andrew Tonkovich

Sewanee Review
735 University Ave.
Sewanee, TN 37383
$48, George Core

Shenandoah
Mattingly House
2 Lee Avenue
Washington and Lee University
Lexington, VA 24450-2116
$25, R. T. Smith, Lynn Leech

Short Story America
shortstoryamerica.com
Tim Johnston

Slake
P.O. Box 385
2658 Griffith Park Boulevard
Los Angeles, CA 90039
$60, Joe Donnelly

Slow Trains
P.O. Box 100145
Denver, CO 8025
Susannah Indigo

Sonora Review
Department of English
University of Arizona
Tucson, AZ 85721
$16, Astrid Duffy

South Dakota Review
University of South Dakota
414 E. Clark Street
Vermilion, SD 57069
$30, Brian Bedard

The Southeast Review
Department of English
Florida State University
Tallahassee, FL 32306
$15, Katie Cortese

Southern Humanities Review
9088 Haley Center
Auburn University
Auburn, AL 36849
$15, Dan R. Latimer

Southern Indiana Review
College of Liberal Arts
University of Southern Indiana
8600 University Boulevard
Evansville, IN 47712
$20, Ron Mitchell

Southern Review
Old President's House
Louisiana State University
Baton Rouge, LA 70803
$40, Jeanne M. Leiby

Southwest Review
Southern Methodist University
P.O. Box 750374
Dallas, TX 75275
$24, Willard Spiegelman

Strangeland
strangeland.org
Tim Parsa

Subtropics
Department of English
University of Florida
P.O. Box 112075

Gainesville, FL 32611-2075
$26, David Leavitt

The Sun
107 North Roberson Street
Chapel Hill, NC 27516
$36, Sy Safransky

Sycamore Review
Department of English
500 Oval Drive
Purdue University
West Lafayette, IN 47907
$14, Anthony Cook

Tampa Review
The University of Tampa
401 W. Kennedy Boulevard
Tampa, FL 33606
$22, Richard Mathews

Think
P.O. Box 454
Downingtown, PA 19335
$20, Christine Yorick

Third Coast
Department of English
Western Michigan University
Kalamazoo, MI 49008
$16, Laura Donnelly

Threepenny Review
2163 Vine Street
Berkeley, CA 94709
$25, Wendy Lesser

Timber Creek Review
8969 UNCG Station
Greensboro, NC 27413
$17, John Freiermuth

Tin House
P.O. Box 10500
Portland, OR 97296-0500
$24.95, Rob Spillman

TriQuarterly
629 Noyes Street
Evanston, IL 60208
$24, Susan Firestone Hahn

Upstreet
P.O. Box 105
Richmond, MA 01254
$10, Vivian Dorsel

Vermont Literary Review
Department of English
Castleton State College
Castleton, VT 05735
Flo Keyes

Virginia Quarterly Review
One West Range
P.O. Box 400223
Charlottesville, VA 22903
$32, Ted Genoways

War, Literature, and the Arts
Department of English and Fine Arts
2354 Fairchild Drive, Suite 6D45
USAF Academy, CO 80840-6242
$10, Donald Anderson

Water-Stone Review
Graduate School of Liberal Studies
Hamline University, MS-A1730
1536 Hewitt Ave.
St. Paul, MN 55104
$32, the editors

Weber Studies
Weber State University
1405 University Circle
Ogden, UT 84408-1214
$20, Michael Wutz

West Branch
Bucknell Hall
Bucknell University
Lewisburg, PA 17837
$10, Paula Closson Buck

Western Humanities Review
University of Utah
255 South Central Campus Drive
Room 3500
Salt Lake City, UT 84112
$18, Barry Weller

Willow Springs
Eastern Washington University

501 N. Riverpoint Boulevard
Spokane, WA 99201
$18, Samuel Ligon

Witness
Black Mountain Institute
University of Nevada
Las Vegas, NV 89154
$10, the editors

Yale Review
P.O. Box 208243
New Haven, CT 06520-8243
$34, J. D. McClatchy

Zoetrope
The Sentinel Building
916 Kearney Street

San Francisco, CA 94133
$24, Michael Ray

Zone 3
APSU
Box 4565
Clarksville, TN 37044
$10, Amy Wright

Zyzzyva
P.O. Box 590069
San Francisco, CA 94159
$44, Howard Junker